Praise for *After Hours on Milagro Street*

"Sparks fly and tempers flare in the p............ ....to-lovers romance that launches a sizz........... ....re."

....iew

"A romance with both heat and heart."

...oklist

"Sensual, scorching, and steeped in luminous, glimmering prose, *After Hours on Milagro Street* is proof that Angelina Lopez is the new queen of small-town romance—and of our hearts!"

—Sierra Simone, *USA TODAY* bestselling author of *A Merry Little Meet Cute*

"Lust, animosity and forced proximity make for a potent cocktail in this emotional enemies-to-lovers romance... Lopez excels at penning strong women who know exactly what they want."

—*Washington Post*

"Highly recommend to anyone looking for a change-up from lighthearted romcoms but not willing to go full-blown angst, anyone who appreciates an alpha heroine, and anyone who loves a big family, ghosts, and page scorching sex."

—Elizabeth Everett, author of *A Perfect Equation*

"Lopez combines her signature steamy approach with a romance steeped in questions of gentrification, family, and what home really means."

—*Entertainment Weekly*

"Engaging writing and a complex, layered plot that pulls readers into Jeremiah and Alex's developing relationship... Lopez's likeable protagonists, with immediate chemistry and connection, shine in this steamy novel (the first in a planned series)."

—*Library Journal*, starred review

"Everything I want in a contemporary romance: instant chemistry between the leads, a boisterous and loyal family, angsty pasts, passion, social justice, and so much more!"

—Danielle Jackson, author of *The Accidental Pinup*

Also available from
Angelina M. Lopez and Carina Press

Milagro Street Series

After Hours on Milagro Street

The Filthy Rich Series

Lush Money
Hate Crush
Serving Sin

Full Moon Over Freedom

Angelina M. Lopez

HARLEQUIN

Recycling programs
for this product may
not exist in your area.

ISBN-13: 978-1-335-63993-6

Full Moon Over Freedom

Copyright © 2023 by Angelina M. Lopez

For questions and comments about the quality of this book, please contact us
at CustomerService@Harlequin.com.

Harlequin Enterprises ULC
22 Adelaide St. West, 41st Floor
Toronto, Ontario M5H 4E3, Canada
www.Harlequin.com

Printed in U.S.A.

To Paige and Wendy.
Your friendship made me a better mom, writer and woman.
I'm so lucky to have you in my life.

CHAPTER 1

As the ominous clouds of a summer storm gathered on the horizon, Juliana "Gillian" Armstead-Bancroft—former valedictorian, queen of the Neewollah festival, summa cum laude graduate of an almost-Ivy, and once-perfect wife on the arm of Thomas Bancroft of the Maryland Bancrofts—flew over the potholes on County Road 85 in her best friend's huge, flamed-red Ford Fairlane convertible.

The woman known in Freedom, Kansas, as the "Pride of the East Side" dug her demure French-manicured nails into the red-leather-wrapped steering wheel as she shoved the pedal to the metal. The big American classic car bucked and roared beneath her sensible suede loafer. The rain-soaked wind raced through and ravaged her perfectly straightened hair.

Maybe I should just embrace being bad, she'd whined into her margarita during her first night back in town while she floated in her best friend's pool. It'd taken three margaritas to say such a thing, even to Cynthia Madsen, who'd known her since grade school. Having known her since grade school, Cynthia had laughed so hard she'd fallen off her float. Gasping and clinging to the side, she'd ticked off Gillian's options for being bad:

Tattoos. Biker bars. Streaking. Skinny-dipping. Join a cult. Break a heart.

Gigolos. So many gigolos.

That wasn't what Gillian had meant by *being bad*. She'd meant being bad like being a failure. Like being cursed instead of blessed. Like being incompetent at successfully steering the course of her life and, instead, crashing it into her two innocent children.

Right now, with those two innocent children safely tucked away on a weeklong Disney World trip with Gillian's parents, Cynthia's version of bad was as good as any. Head pounding but resolute, Gillian had pointed to the Fairlane this morning as the car she wanted to borrow while she waited for her Lexus SUV to arrive from D.C. Cynthia, owner of Freedom's only remaining manufacturing facility, had an entire garage of classic cars collected by her father and grandfather and didn't bat an eye.

Now, Gillian urged the Fairlane faster as she rocketed past rusted barbed-wire fencing and bullet-holed speed limit signs. She wasn't worried about traffic. County Road 85 connected Freedom's ten thousand souls with the next town over only if those souls were too young, drunk, or horny to use the old highway or the new gleaming interstate that barely acknowledged either town. The pitted two-lane road was prone to flooding thanks to its long stretch beside the Viridescent River, which marked Freedom's eastern border. State and county officials had thrown up their hands at trying to keep the two apart, just like parents had given up trying to keep teenagers out of Old 85's abandoned fields and foreclosed farmhouses.

People—non-horny, non-young people—also avoided Old 85 because it was haunted. Whether it was the ghost car, the Jersey devil, the victims of the first serial-killing family on record (Freedom kept that quiet in its history books), or the ghostly wails of La Llorona on the riverbank, Old 85 had enough terrors on it to maintain its empty, angry disrepair.

This haunted failure of a road on the eastern edge of her dying hometown was the perfect place for the Pride of the East Side to get good at being bad.

Gillian gripped the steering wheel tight against the punishing wind as she raced toward the molten-gray edge of the storm. Her weightless ring finger felt like it could flap up and rip off. When she signed her divorce papers a month ago, she told Thomas she'd lost her wedding ring set.

Selling a 2.12-carat emerald-cut Tiffany engagement ring she'd worn for ten years had to be one way a good mom went bad.

She could also stuff her face with chocolate. She'd denied her lifelong sweet tooth for a decade, even tossing away the packages of chicles her grandmother slipped into her palm when she visited, but now it was roaring back with a vengeance.

If there was anyone who was going to have a bad-for-you candy bar lying around, it was Cynthia Madsen.

Gillian unhooked her lap belt and leaned over to push the chrome button of the glove box. She glanced at the endless lane of straight and empty before she looked inside, praying for a giant Snickers. She saw registration and insurance papers, a gold tube of lipstick, a strip of condoms…

She reared back, then felt ridiculous. Of course Cynthia would have condoms in the glove box.

Finding condoms in a single woman's take-no-prisoners muscle car wasn't the same as finding them on the floor of her husband's Mercedes when she was taking it into the shop. There was no reason her stomach should turn over queasily now. She wouldn't have to take this strip of condoms into her home and then throw them away several hours and one massive blowup later, wondering how she once again became the bad guy.

A good mom noted this reaction and the associated negative emotions so she could discuss it later with the therapist she'd responsibly started seeing a year ago right after she'd asked for the divorce. A bad mom stepped on the gas.

She slammed the glove box closed, swearing to buy one of everything in the candy aisle when she passed a convenience store.

She glanced at the road.

Her bullet of a car was aimed for a man walking on the shoulder.

Gillian stomped the brake.

The tires screamed and skittered as she double-fisted the wheel. The back end fishtailed, dark clouds and tall weeds blurring in the windshield, and she spun the wheel to correct it, fought to keep control of this one thing when she'd lost control of everything else. The ravine down to the river yawned wide in front of her. *Padre Nuestro, que estás en el cielo,* a blessing as lifesaving as her removed seat belt, rolled through her brain before she remembered that God wasn't listening anymore.

She would sail into the river, sink under the Viridescent, and finally join La Llorona like the beautiful and terrifying fantasma had always wailed for her to. That was a better end than hurting one more innocent.

Everything stopped with a hard lurch.

The Fairlane grumbled its irritation. It had miraculously landed parallel to the road and on the opposite gravel shoulder. Rubber stung the air. Still clutching the steering wheel at two and ten, Gillian dropped her head between her arms as far-off thunder gave a warning.

"Hey, sweetheart." His low voice, next to her door, sounded like the soft side of those storm clouds. "You okay?"

What a thing for him to ask when she'd almost killed him. With her tangled hair protecting her face like blinders, she convinced her cramped fingers off the steering wheel to turn off the car. "I'm fine," she said, breathing to calm her galloping heart. "Thank you for asking."

His gentle laugh surprised her. "Darlin', you look like you're anything but fine."

Sweetheart? Darling? This was some smooth-talking redneck she'd almost obliterated. Her middle sister, Alex, would've told this guy to go fuck himself before she'd gotten married and become so nauseatingly happy. Gillian, having molded herself into the picture of dignity and self-possession, was an anomaly in her emotionally volatile family. She would apologize and suggest that this sweet, simple hick hurry himself along before he was drowned in the oncoming storm.

Gillian lifted her head and let the protective covering of her hair slide away. "I am so…"

Sorry got lost in the warm, rain-choked air as she saw him through her sunglasses. Dark eyes fringed in thick lashes stared, astonished, back. Black hair, thick and shiny, was finger-combed out of his face the way it'd never been before. His mouth dropped open in surprise. Those full and soft and so well-known lips were a perfect complement to his strong, defined nose, high, sharp cheekbones, and the hollows beneath that pointed back to his mouth like neon, good-time signs.

"Nicky?"

It couldn't be. The last time she'd seen Nicky Mendoza was on this road thirteen years ago, when she'd hugged and kissed him goodbye, already focused on the three-hour drive to Kansas City and the flight back to Boston to begin her sophomore year in college. Had he been here all this time?

"Nicky, is that you?" He had an afternoon scruff he hadn't been able to grow the last time she'd seen him and slight rays around the corners of his eyes. She reached up like he wasn't essentially a stranger on a deserted road and brushed her thumb over the familiar teardrop scar beneath his right eye. His hand covered hers as he stared back in disbelief. His hard, hot touch was shocking. He turned his head and smelled her wrist.

The tiny movement made her clench between her legs. He

used to do that, inhale her, down her sternum, behind her knee, in the bend of her thigh.

Peaches, he would sigh against her skin.

He pulled off her sunglasses with the same instinctive right to touch, tossed them to the seat, then gathered her face in calloused hands that smelled like leather and turpentine. She couldn't believe he smelled the same.

Without the filter of her sunglasses, gazing at Nicky Mendoza was like trying to stare into the sun. He looked like a fallen angel. He looked like a heaven-sent fantasy against a threatening sky.

His thumb brushed the tip of her nose.

She'd had cosmetic work to slim her wide bridge since the last time she'd seen him, and her eyes had been a contact lens-assisted green since the moment her income had merged with Thomas's. She'd believed, when she'd made the changes, that they were decisions she'd made on her own. For herself.

She tried to pull out of his hands.

"Wait," he said through his teeth, his hands firming on her jaw. "Just...let me look at you. I can't believe..." His forehead clenched like she'd hurt him. "You're too beautiful to be real, hechicera."

He used to call her that—*sorceress*—when he showed her things she'd asked him to show her, taught her things she'd asked him to teach. Nicky Mendoza, who she'd known and trusted since the fifth grade, had been a practical solution to the problem of her virginity when she came home the summer after her freshman year.

Nicky stroked a thumb down her neck, making her suck in a breath. "Are you really here?" he asked, searching her eyes. He was the one who'd discovered how sensitive her neck was. "Or did I trip over one of your spells?"

He still thought she was that girl he'd known. He still thought she was powerful. He didn't know that, even if she'd thought to make this impossible meeting happen, she was stripped of her ability to do so.

A bang of thunder knocked sense into her. Dark clouds churned over their heads.

"Oh my God, Nicky," she said, yanking out of his embrace. "Get in the car."

A bolt of lightning seared the sky.

He strode around the front of the Fairlane and she got to process the whole reality of him. He was still lean, about the same five-ten he'd reached in high school, but his shoulders were broader. He was half brown-Mexican and half white-American like she was, but darker, and dressed head to toe in dusty black: lace-up boots, jeans, and a T-shirt. His strong, striated forearms with leather ties around one wrist were magnificent.

Gillian turned on the car and pulled the lever for the convertible soft top, glad to have tasks to distract her from the astonishing sight of an all-grown-up Nicky opening the passenger door and getting in the car with her. If she'd had any doubt that this was her friend, the black, paint-splattered backpack he set at his feet erased it.

Rain began to patter against the roof as they each latched it on their sides. They sat back in the cloud-darkened daylight and marveled at each other.

"What are you doing out here?" Gillian finally exclaimed.

He was just as stunned as she was. "My Jeep broke down," he said, flinging a hand at the windshield, sending his thick black hair sliding onto his forehead. The last time she'd seen him, he'd worn his hair long and face shadowing. "It just died. I couldn't find anything wrong with it."

"Then call a tow truck! Don't go walking down Old 85."

Nicky knew better than anyone the dangers near the river.

The reality of what had almost happened caught up with her. "Nicky, I almost..." She put her hand to her chest. Her breath stuck like taffy.

"Hey, you didn't." He pulled her hand away then intertwined their fingers. "Take a breath."

His touch felt so familiar, he could've been holding her hand yesterday. His command seemed to open up her airways. She inhaled deeply, breathing in the smell of him: road dust, good leather, an iron tinge. He was viscerally real and here.

He let go of her. "There's still no goddamn signal out here," he said, shoving his hair back. "I can get a signal in the middle of Joshua Tree but still I can't get a signal on Old 85."

"You've been to Joshua Tree?"

Her surprise was as loud as the rain plastering the windshield. He smiled. When he'd been a seductive rebel, that teasing smile had weakened knees and spread thighs.

"Yeah," he said. "I was doing a piece out there."

It was getting stuffy with the top up. Gillian flipped on the AC and got a whoosh of heat. "A piece?"

"Uh-huh," he said. "I paint for a living."

She picked up her expensive sunglasses and put them in their case. "Really?"

He nodded, still giving her that shit-eating smile as he shifted so his back was partly against the door.

"Do you still live in Freedom?" she asked.

"No. San Francisco."

She stiffened her jaw against it dropping open.

"By way of Manhattan," he continued. His smile had grown into a full-fledged smirk. "I moved to New York after a couple of years of art school in Denver."

It was like he could see the bubbles of shock and disbelief over her head.

The Nicky she'd been with that long-ago summer had made his living molding aftermarket fenders and grilles at the factory Cynthia later inherited, Liberty Manufacturing, and had little ambition besides keeping his baby brother out of juvie. When he'd said he hadn't been able to find anything wrong with his Jeep, she'd assumed he was a mechanic. A muscle-shirted, gleaming-with-sweat, grease-on-his-high-cheekbone mechanic.

Thirteen years ago, he'd said he'd never leave Freedom. He'd said he couldn't leave. The members of her large Mexican-American family, who had made Freedom home since the early 1900s, wondered why anyone would want to.

The AC was finally starting to cool down. Rain clattered fast and hard against the windows. She needed to put the car in Drive and get going before this June thunderstorm really let loose.

"I'm so happy for you," she said. "A...friend of mine is a visual artist." She actually was an ex-investment client, but Gillian didn't want to talk about herself. "She paints pieces for the Pottery Barn catalog when gallery sales are slow. I can put you in contact with her, if you'd like."

"Sure," he said.

Of the 256 people in their graduating class, Gillian—with her full ride to Brandeis and exclusive D.C. address and expensive vacations to far-flung destinations—had always believed she'd put the greatest distance between herself and Freedom. But Nicky had blazed his own way out with less support, fewer resources, and no trust-fund husband.

She looked down as she rubbed her hands over her thighs and saw the streaks she'd left on her white linen pants. It was a reminder that while she was looking at him, he was looking back. They were both thirty-two now, but while he looked like the fantasy hitchhiker you pick up in your dreams, she couldn't imagine the state of her white, cowl-necked, sleeveless tank. Who wore all white when they went speeding down a country road in a classic convertible? Pampered East Coast moms trying to outrun their bad decisions, that's who. She could feel the tangled mess of her hair around her face.

She must look pathetic. But the way he stroked her neck and

called her hechicera hadn't made her feel pathetic. Thirteen years ago, she'd asked Nicky to relieve her of the burden of her virginity in part because he'd had so many satisfied customers. Nicky had been a world-class lover for a small-town guy.

"We looked for you at the ten-year reunion," she said as a throb of lightning lit up the darkening outdoors.

"We?"

She shifted to also lean back against her door. "Me and Cynthia."

His smile kicked up. "You two are back together? That's trouble."

The first day of school in the fifth grade, when Nicky had been the shy new boy everyone whispered about, Gillian and Cynthia had lured him onto the playground. From that day on, they played together most recesses and Nicky, trailed by his little brother, Lucas, would walk Gillian home from school. They'd all wandered apart in high school, and Gillian and Cynthia hadn't connected again until the ten-year reunion four years ago.

"I guess that explains this car," he said, grinning.

Gillian gave a huff of a laugh. She knew how ridiculous she looked, a stay-at-home mom in its stripper-red interior. It was actually getting harder to see in the gloom. The strength of the rain against the soft top was making her think they'd stay here and wait this storm out.

She searched around the steering column until she could pull the lever that turned on the headlights. A yellow glow from the instrument panel filled the inside of the car as the engine rumbled.

Nicky, who watched her with the corner of his plush bottom lip caught in his teeth, looked like an erotic fantasy against the red leather.

"When are you heading back to San Francisco?" she asked.

"Tomorrow."

"If I hadn't almost hit you, I would've flown right past you," she said, shaking her head.

Good women didn't pick up hot hitchhikers. But bad ones…

What were the chances they'd fly from opposite coasts to land in Freedom at the same moment? What were the odds that they'd meet again on Old 85? And who could have forecast that her emotional turmoil would provide him safe harbor from a storm?

Who would've imagined that, once again alone in a classic car on this road with this friend she'd trusted to teach her everything, she'd be newly divorced and he'd be…

She glanced at his left hand. No ring.

Nicky could help her feel better. Nicky could help her feel good. She wanted to be bad.

The careful orchestration of a million chance events might have given her the opportunity to be downright naughty.

CHAPTER 2

Gillian licked thin, soft, wide lips as her peachy scent wrapped tentacles around Nicky in Cynthia Madsen's pleasure cruiser. He couldn't believe she was here.

"You in town visiting?" he asked, crossing his arms over his chest and stuffing his hands under his biceps to prevent himself from grabbing her again.

He couldn't believe she was real.

"Yes," she said, her new moss green eyes dragging over his forearms before aiming out the window. Raindrops were bashing the glass and leaving little dripping shadows over the classy white top that showed off her toned arms and the white pants she'd curled up on the seat. Her makeup was smudged beneath her eyes, her honey-streaked dark hair was a mass of snarls, her nose had dirt on the new narrow tip, and her glossy nails were tapping against her thumb.

His girl looked like a Sèvres porcelain plate, a plate once licked by kings, teetering on the edge of a table.

"Where are you living?" he asked. He needed to turn this normal. The afternoon storm had wrapped around the car and it didn't look like they'd be taking off soon. "What are you doing now?" He needed to open a window and let the rain wash away the magic that his hechicera said she had no part in.

If I hadn't almost hit you, I would've flown right past you.

If he'd just skipped his urge to drive Old 85 one last time, he could have avoided all of this. He'd done almost everything in Freedom he was here to do: he'd cleaned out the last apartment he'd rented for his brother, settled Lucas's debts around town, and buried Lucas's ashes underneath a tree with a nice view of the property. Even when he completed his last task and convinced William to sell the farmhouse and move with him to San Francisco, he still wanted his brother to have a nice view. After fucking up in so many ways, he could at least do that for Lucas.

But his desire to revisit his memories of the time he'd spent with this girl on this road meant that he was now stuck in a car with a woman he'd never wanted to see again.

She was still tapping her fingers to her thumb, a habit of nervous counting she'd had since they were kids, and he wanted to twine his hand around hers to make her stop. He wasn't going to fucking touch her.

"I'm…uh… I was living in D.C," she said.

Of course. Gillian had East Coast written all over her. But she was nervous, and he hadn't seen his girl nervous since she'd said *I have a favor to ask you* thirteen years ago.

Like an idiot, he'd said *Sure. Anything you need.*

"My…my children and I—I've got two kids—" His girl was a mom. "We're staying with my parents for the summer. I'm… uh… I'm divorced."

Fuck.

"Girl, I'm sorry." He wasn't just sorry for himself, stuck in this big front seat with her in the dark of a storm. He was so, so sorry for her. He knew his hechicera. The failure of a marriage was not part of her plans for world domination.

She gave him a tiny, nerve-wracked, dangerous smile. "Do you want to help me celebrate?"

Lightning cracked right up his spine.

"I mean…" She swallowed and shrugged and raised her chin to show off her neck. Her priceless fucking neck.

Once, when she'd been sitting in a lilac dress in William's borrowed GTO, he'd tipped her head back and done nothing but kiss and lick and nibble and suck her wildly sensitive neck until the slow slide of two fingers under her skirt and into her soaking panties had made her come, sobbing and shaking, all over his palm. He'd used his wet hand to get himself off and made her watch. He'd been a creative little shit back then.

"Doesn't this feel familiar?" she asked, her voice full of tremors but her reasoning it out like a math problem. "We're in a big classic car on the side of Old 85 and no one knows we're together." She tried to smile. "I'd love another lesson, Nicky."

She reached out to touch his knee in slow-mo surrealness. He snatched up her wrist with thumb and middle finger before she could make contact and tried to ignore how soft her skin was.

"Girl," he said as a boom of thunder rattled the car's frame. "What's going on?"

Nothing about this was familiar. Sure, thirteen years ago, they used the nooks and crannies of Old 85 to take the long, meandering journey to the loss of Gillian's virginity in the back of the GTO. Sure, because of Gillian's insistence, no one had known he was touching her. Loving her.

But he'd known Gillian Armstead since the first day of fifth grade, watched her in high school when she didn't know he was looking. When she'd asked him to teach her about sex, to teach her about pleasure and not tell anyone else because sex was all she wanted from him, she'd done it in her clear, cutting, matter-of-fact way. She'd never tried to seduce him. When Gillian Armstead didn't come straight at a problem, the world was revolving backward.

Inside the car, it was as still as a held breath. She let him manacle her wrist, trap her, as she made some decision with the lifting of her sharp chin. "Can you keep a secret, Nicky?"

He'd always kept her secrets. He nodded once.

"I'm back in Freedom because…because I don't have anywhere else to go." He could feel her delicate bones. "I'm thirty-two years old and my only option is to move in with my parents for the summer." Her mossy eyes went bigger like she couldn't believe the words coming out of her mouth.

"Gillian…" He wrapped his whole hand around her wrist and rubbed his thumb over her warm pulse.

"I'm broke." She shuffled closer on the bench seat and he lowered their hands to his knee, keeping hold of her. "D.C. requires you to be separated for six months before they grant a divorce and all that time I couldn't—I couldn't find a job." She was as shocked as he was. "I'm a financial planner with a master's degree and I'm broke." She gave a sharp high laugh that pinged around the inside of the car. "Doctor, heal thyself, am I right?"

Her pulse rocketed against his thumb. He didn't want to ask, didn't want to know, but he had to. "Is your ex providing—"

She shook her head once, fast and hard, her hair dragging across the edge of collarbone he could see peeking out of her top. "I won't do what the prenup demands to get alimony and child support. I thought I'd find a job and wouldn't need his money."

With the back of her hand resting against his dusty jeans, he let go of her wrist and wrapped his fingers around her palm. She instantly squeezed back. "He's not helping at all?"

She leaned closer like she was afraid of being overheard. "I was so stupid. I signed the divorce papers a month ago without getting any of that ironed out. My lawyer was so angry he quit." Her voice dropped to a whisper. Her eyes were huge. "But last week, Thomas offered to let us stay in our home in

Georgetown and put in a good word for me with a financial group his law firm represents. In return he wants me to…" She swallowed and looked out the window into the blackness.

He didn't want to know. He wanted less to care. "To?"

She looked like she was counting raindrops. "Sign over my portion of the bar. I own Loretta's now with my sisters. Did you know that?"

He didn't. When Nicky and Lucas had walked Gillian home after school and spent their summers running around the east side with her and her cousins, they'd sometimes stop by the bar to eat apple slices and drink glasses of milk that her grandmother would serve them. His family was just a party of three: him, his always-working mom, and his always-sad little brother. He'd been amazed by all the boisterous, hugging Mexican-Americans Gillian called kin flowing in and out of Loretta's. She'd already been focused on a life beyond Freedom and hadn't wanted anything to do with her family's bar.

"It's my fault that I thought of the money as *ours* instead of *his* money when I offered to buy it," she murmured.

"Are you going to sign over—"

"He doesn't want it," she said, sharply. "It's just his way of…" She moved her mouth like there was a nasty taste in it. "I've hired a new attorney who specializes in renegotiating divorce agreements. But she's expensive."

Her fingers gripped his hand hard enough to hurt. "You can't tell anyone about this."

"I won't." He wasn't the asshole she'd chosen.

"No, of course. You're leaving for San Francisco."

Ah.

He got it now. He was her confessional. He was the locked box where she could admit that her master plan had gone tits up. Then he would fly himself a thousand miles away. He'd seen her shock that he'd broken free of Freedom. She knew as little about him as he'd actively avoided about her, and she expected even less. He wanted to hate her. He wanted to yank out of her hold and disappear into the rain.

She leaned close and trapped him with her desperate stare. "I've failed in every way I can," she whispered. "I've lost my magic."

He wasn't going anywhere.

"I've tried limpias, hechizos, baños. I've even called on Santa Muerte. No one's listening. He's not responding."

When she'd first seen Nicky react to the monster no one else could see when they were kids, she'd told him what few knew about her: her mother was training her in the sacred arts of a bruja. She'd made a little red felt pouch that reeked of garlic to ward off his cadejo—that's what she called the snarling black dog that would appear and make him cry—and it had worked better than the doctor's pills that had only made him sleepy.

Now she thought her God had forsaken her.

Her hand turned over in his hold and gripped his knee. "I was afraid, when everything began to fall apart, that I was cursed." She awkwardly reached around the steering wheel with her free hand and turned the car off. They were dumped into sudden darkness, with no AC roar to muffle the violence of the storm.

Her hand began to slide up his thigh. "But the truth is, Nicky, I'm not cursed." She was a longed-for voice in the black. She was a dreamed-about thumb dragging over the seam that ran up the inside of his jeans. "I *am* the curse. I'm destroying everything I touch."

Her touch, absent for thirteen years, was traveling up his thigh like a stroke. "I've always tried to be so good." God. *Good*. "I tried to do everything right. But what has being good gotten me?" She'd never doubted she could get everything she wanted. He'd never doubted it, either. "I think, to break my curse, I need to be bad."

Every muscle in his body went stiff at the bolt of lust.

He heard her shift against the seat, smelled the summer-bright scent of her sway in the dark, felt the unreal presence of her displace the air as she moved closer and her knuckles knocked blindly against his sternum. Her fingers, those precise and busy fingers whose shape and width he'd know anywhere, slid up his chest and gripped his shoulders. Her thumbs stroked the skin under his jaw.

Like his cadejo's hot breath, he could feel the warmth of her lips as she leaned close to his ear.

"C'mon, Nicky," she whispered. Lucas had screamed at Gillian for unintentionally changing his name from Nick to Nicky. It'd been one of the few times his brother had ever spoken directly to her.

He felt her nuzzle into his hair as her tangles brushed his cheek. "Don't you want to help me be bad?"

He'd been her sex teacher and first lover and, fuck, he'd done his job well. She was using all those lessons, teasing, tempting, giving in while staying just out of reach, using her words to tell him what she wanted. How could any man have had her in his arms and bed and life and let her go?

She kissed his cheekbone. The touch of those soft sweet lips rang his bell like a punch. He saw stars as she rubbed over his scruff. She traced her lips down the hollow beneath his cheekbone and he ground his molars together. He could feel her breath at the corner of his mouth.

"Nicky?" Nerves sparked in her voice. "Don't..." She swallowed. "Don't you want to help me break my curse?"

He could have withstood this taunting fantasy of her because that's what this had to be, here in the dark with his eyes closed and his dick hard. But that doubt in her voice made her, this, very real. He didn't know a Gillian who doubted herself. That confident girl who'd approached him at a bonfire on the side of this road and asked him to teach her was not the woman who was in the car with him now. She was truly here asking him, once again, to help her.

He heard her shift as she began to pull back. "Fuck," he cursed, making her jump as he grabbed her waist and arm. He'd never wanted this again. He'd missed her like crazy. With a harsh exhale, he dragged her into his lap and made her straddle him.

"Don't you fucking kiss me," he growled, right against her mouth.

She moaned because she remembered. He hadn't let them kiss the first time they'd been together, the first time he'd put his fingers between her thighs and shown her what he could do with them.

He'd been so angry when she'd asked him to meet her by the hay bales out of sight of the bonfire, the first time she'd talked to him in five years, and sent his hopes soaring by saying *I want to be with you* and *I haven't been with anyone else* then shot them out of the air with her *you can still be with other girls this summer. Sex teacher,* she'd said. *Virginity is a construct, but why should my first time be with a boy fumbling around in the dark? Why shouldn't I learn from the best?*

He'd taught her. He'd taught her to use her words because he'd wanted to hear her beg. He'd taught her to spread her thighs and tell him where she liked it best. He'd refused to kiss her mouth that first time, no matter how sweetly she moaned for it.

She'd stiffened when she'd heard a couple bumping off the hay bales toward them, but he discovered that his girl who thought she was so good liked a little risk. She told him they had to leave and he told her she better come first and she'd whimpered and gotten wetter and come so hard she'd left teeth imprints in the palm he put over her mouth.

He'd slung her over his shoulder and ran her off into the moonlight, solidifying his place as her dirty little secret.

Now he ran his hand down her bare arm, fondled the soft, smooth reality of her, while he buried his hand in her hair and tilted her head back. He bit her neck, made her gasp into the humid air of the car. Her hands smoothed down his biceps, her nails digging into the muscles as she held on. He licked at her pulse, inhaled where she was real and alive, then took her breast into his hand. She was a small, tight handful with always, always, always the hardest fucking nipples. They were never that sensitive but Jesus Christ, now when he pinched one, she gyrated on his lap.

Heat sizzled around them like lightning in the car.

"This is a bad fucking idea," he growled against her peach-decadent skin, sucking on the little bit of collarbone he could get to in her shirt.

"That's the whole point," she panted.

Angrier, he fondled the tip of her earlobe the way he was going to lick her clit, planning on punishing her for hours, and ran his thumbs up the inside of her legs. She widened her thighs, eager and gasping.

"Yeah," he groaned. She wanted lessons and he'd show her what missing class for thirteen years looked like.

Her hands ran down his chest like she loved it, fingers clawing out over his stomach like she worshipped each muscle. She latched onto the obvious pole of his dick in his jeans.

"There's condoms in the glove box," she breathed against his open, panting mouth. Then she squeezed, too hard.

He grunted in pain.

Oh fuck. Fuck.

They were back here again. On Old 85. In a classic car. With her wanting him to use those condoms then go away.

For her, he'd always ignored how bad this was going to hurt.

"Gillian." He grabbed both of her elbows. "Gillian." He forced out the words his brain and body were resisting. "I can't, I'm sorry."

"What?" She had every right for that high-pitched surprise; his dick throbbed in her hands. "Why?" The tremor in her voice almost had him reaching for the glove box. "I know I'm out of practice but if you just give me a chance to—"

Everything in him howled. How could she be out of practice? What manner of asshole had she been married to? Everything in him wanted to make it better.

But he couldn't.

"I'm engaged," he said.

Without the AC on, the air in the Fairlane had become thick and goopy. His words hung in it as her eyes slowly widened. He realized he could see that green hazel again; light was creeping back into the car. The plains storm was rumbling away, taking its violence with it.

Her hands were still gripping his **hard** penis as she straddled his thighs.

"Oh my God," she breathed, jerking her hands off him and scrambling back to the seat.

He'd helped his poor, cursed hechicera verify one thing.

Her God was no longer paying attention.

CHAPTER 3

Two weeks later, Gillian sat at the large oval kitchen table she'd grown up eating at and worked to calmly finish her yogurt cup while she stared at her laptop screen, reminding herself to process the terrifying lack of response emails to the many jobs she'd applied for as merely information, data, instead of proof that her six years devoted to raising her children were the ballast that sank her master's degree, excellent references, and the ninety-hour-weeks she once worked.

When she'd told Thomas that she wanted a divorce a year ago, she'd assumed that finding a financial-sector job in D.C. or another good-sized city would be the easy part. Instead, she wasn't even making it past the first-stage filter. The emails from colleagues who responded enthusiastically when they thought she was still connected to the wealthy and influential Bancroft family had petered out, and the initially thrilled recruiters had stopped responding.

She realized she was counting—*twenty-three*—and that the bottom of her yogurt cup was scraped clean.

She carefully put the cup down and clicked out of her emails, revealing the bank account screen that had sent her looking for positive news on the job front in the first place.

She thought she'd planned so perfectly. But plane tickets to Kansas, storage-unit fees for the few pieces of furniture and household items Gillian had claimed from her elegant George- town row house, her and her son's virtual therapy, and gro- cery store trips so her parents weren't *entirely* supporting her were outpacing the careful nest egg she'd created cashing out her 401(k) and selling her designer clothes, handbags, jewelry, and engagement ring. Her new attorney's fight for some small amount of child support and alimony was proving more gru- eling than she'd budgeted for.

All those years ago, she'd barely read the prenuptial agree- ment before she signed it. So naive. When her brain had stopped shying away from the concept of a divorce and she'd finally re- viewed it, she'd been horrified by its terms. Thomas had made it clear in their first-and-only meeting with a mediator that he expected her to live up to every one of them if she ever wanted to see one red cent.

She'd been so blindly confident she wouldn't need his money, holding her hands over her eyes to avoid the obvious. When she discovered near the end of their separation that Thomas had been monitoring her, she'd panicked. She just wanted out. She'd signed the divorce papers, certain a job offer was just around the corner.

A week before she and her children were forced out of their Georgetown home, out of options except to move in with her parents, Thomas believed he was being magnanimous when he made his offer that ignored the prenup during their final family dinner.

We both only want what's fair, he'd said. *There's no reason to de- file a decade of mutual respect by haggling over pennies.* As his chil- dren sat to his right and left at the opulent table, he offered to let her maintain residence in the home they'd been born in. He would continue to handle the mortgage; she would be responsible for everything else. He also said he would recommend her to a financial firm that, under any other circumstances, Gillian would have loved to have worked for.

All she had to do was sign over her majority ownership of the bar her grandparents started, her sister had built her dreams around, and her large family relied on as a second home.

She hadn't said a word through the rest of the excruciating twenty-five-minute meal, and she'd allowed him to kiss her cheek before he left. His offer was nothing but another way for him to prove that he still blocked the exit to the maze she'd determinedly walked into. But when her declining bank account and empty inbox made her startle awake in her childhood bedroom, the long dark hours were filled with thoughts of her D.C. home and a good job and the pride she was working to retain and a bar she never visited. She didn't even like alcohol.

When she heard the glass doors into the living room slide open, she snapped the laptop closed then quickly swiped beneath her glasses.

"Have you seen Naomi?" her father, Tucker Armstead, asked as he poked his head inside. The slim, diminutive man was usually very neat and tucked in. Right now, there were spears of grass sticking out of his thick blond hair. "I can't find her."

He stepped over the threshold, lugging a giggling thirty-two-pound weight wrapped around his shin.

"Dad," Gillian admonished as she pressed her hand to her burbling stomach. "I asked you to keep an eye on her."

He brushed down his thick blond moustache with his fingers; he kept a little comb in his front pocket to keep that pride and joy well groomed. "I think she turned invisible," he whispered. "Naomi, are you in here?"

"No," Naomi answered, leaning back and giggling, the ends of her tawny hair dragging along the shag carpet. She'd been a towhead with bright blue eyes when she was born. Weary from fourteen hours of labor, Gillian had joked that they needed to put her back in to bake longer.

Thomas hadn't thought it was funny.

Naomi's hair was now a grass-strewn dark blond or light brown, depending on the light, with green-gold eyes that Gillian's contacts aspired to. She was all four-year-old bird bones and knees, shed of the pooch Gillian had loved. Her baby girl now looked so fragile.

Tucker turned to his six-year-old grandson, who was following him inside. "Have you seen your sister?" he asked Ben.

Ben shook his head hard, that shy grin of delight on his face, but didn't say anything.

Gillian swallowed the knee-jerk reaction to ask him to use his words. His therapist had provided creative ways to get Ben to talk more often, but right now she couldn't access them. It was her anxiety she'd be appeasing, not his growth. Ben, who had Gillian's dark hair and eyes and was built like a miniature cement truck, at least looked a little grass-stained and sweaty too.

Her *New York Times*-best-selling author-father had researched how to positively interact with autistic children when he learned they'd be coming to live with them for the summer. Gillian had given her parents some helpful hints—let Ben take his time to warm up to situations, don't try to put words in his mouth, avoid impatience and manage your frustration, sit on the floor with him if he begins to get upset until he's able to self-regulate—but she deeply appreciated how natural her father was with her son. It was a big change from the decent-but-distracted "go out and play" dad who'd stayed home with Gillian and her sisters while pursuing a writing career.

Ben crossed the room to lean against her and Gillian rubbed his back as she murmured into his fragrant buzz cut. He was definitely going to need a bath tonight. "Are you having fun?"

He nodded.

"Do you want a snack?"

He nodded again.

"What do you want?"

Ben gave a little uncomfortable huff. "Orange," he said, leaning his forehead into her neck. "In the water."

"Two bowls of Goldfish, coming right up."

She pulled him close and squeezed. All she wanted was for him to know that he was just right, just the way he was, and that he could claim his space and declare what he needed in it.

The kids' first week away with their dad was planned for the beginning of August.

Gillian's mother came into the kitchen carrying a laundry basket. "I'll get their snack if you're busy."

Gillian glared at the clothes piled so high her five-foot-one mother could barely see over them. "Mom, I told you I can take care of our laundry."

Mary Armstead shook her head as she kept walking toward the newly built laundry room behind the kitchen, her gorgeous black hair without a strand of gray shimmering down her back. "Oh, mija, it's fine." She'd worked as a bank teller until she'd started slinging beers at Loretta's ten years ago. Now, an overloaded basket of laundry was nothing for the fifty-seven-year-old woman.

But Ben was sensitive to certain fabric softeners and Gillian knew that the kids' shared room, her middle sister's old room, had been a clothes-strung mess and, to be honest, Gillian had to make sure her clothes were washed on the correct setting because it was going to be a while until she could go clothes shopping and...

"Mom." She turned around and watched Mary separate clothes through the doorway. "I said I'll take care of it."

Her mother smiled at her with her patient, sweet, irritating smile. "Juliana, if you want to help me, I'm not stopping you."

It's fine and *I'm not stopping you* were such common and, frankly, triggering statements from her mom that Gillian turned back around to see her dad at the snack cabinet, a four-year-old still clinging to his shin, smiling wistfully at Mary as she sprayed fabric cleaner on a pair of jeans.

At the end of that summer thirteen years ago, her mother had kicked Tucker out. Gillian had been so afraid for him, so terrified she would lose him to the alcoholism he struggled with, that she'd offered to come home, offered to have him move in with her in Boston. Her father had refused and, eventually, found his way to AA and dedicated himself to his dream of becoming a fiction writer. Now he was the healthy, successful man in front of her who'd conquered his addiction so dramatically that he helped out at the bar just to be close to her mother and sister.

Mary had invited him to move back in a year ago but had relegated him to her baby sister Sissy's old room under the stairs.

They'd both stepped away from their jobs this summer—Tucker was between books and Mary was taking a break from the bar—to be with the kids while Gillian job searched. Her bad situation would've been hopeless without her parents. But biting her tongue about what she thought of this reunion was proving to be more difficult than she thought.

Her phone started moaning "Ooh baby, baby, get up on this," and Gillian scrambled to answer it. Cynthia had gotten her hands on her phone while Gillian had been snoring in a deck chair.

"Hey," she said, getting up from the oval table and walking on flip-flops into the front room as Naomi and Ben settled in with their afternoon snack.

"Get your ass down to the train station," Cynthia blared out of the phone.

Gillian jerked it from her ear. "What? No, I'm busy, I'm—"

"Revising your résumé for the eighty-eighth time?"

It would be the seventeenth. "No, I—"

"There's somebody here I need you to talk to."

"I don't have time to—"

"Trust me, you'll love him," Cynthia bulldozed over her. "*The American Art Review* called him a leading force behind the New Bravery. They're a group of classically trained painters redefining public art."

"Are you reading that verbatim?"

"Straight from Wikipedia." Cynthia lowered her voice. "I need you. I'm not sure I can afford him."

"Afford him for what?"

"We want him to paint a mural inside the Freedom Historical Museum."

After a lifetime of keeping herself above the fray of the poorer east side vs. wealthier west side squabbles just like her dad and grandfather before her, Cynthia had firmly planted herself with the east-siders after a developer and the sitting mayor had tried to destroy the neighborhood for profit. Now she was as passionate about the museum that would highlight the unique story of the Mexican-Americans on the east side as the rest of Gillian's family.

The restored train station, the future home of the Freedom Historical Museum, was right across Milagro Street from the bar Gillian partly owned, hadn't visited, and didn't want to be anywhere near.

Cynthia was whispering now. "If I can get him onboard, we'll have a bigger mural than what he painted in the plaza of the Transamerica Pyramid."

At the mention of the landmark building in San Francisco, Gillian was truly impressed. "That's great but I really can't." She put a hand to her hair only to realize she'd pulled it back in a messy ponytail. She was in shorts and flip-flops, she wore no makeup, and she had a coffee stain on the bottom of her oversized white linen shirt. "I would impress no one."

"You've got panache and smarts," Cynthia said. "You don't

make money sound dirty like I do. You've got to come soon or he's going to leave. Please…"

Even though Cynthia knew as few details as her family about the fall of her marriage and fruitless job search, she'd been there for her over the last painful year when Gillian's D.C. friends acted like divorce was something they might catch. For the last two weeks, Cynthia had offered up her pool and twenty horse-dotted acres as a playground for Gillian's kids since Gillian was avoiding the public park and pool. There, it would've been too easy to run into a member of her mammoth Mexican-American family, a former classmate who'd elected her senior class president, or someone who'd read her essay in the paper for the Chamber of Commerce scholarship. "Divorce and ruination" was the only response to why the Pride of the East Side was back in town.

She refused to be stuck in Freedom for the summer—*please, just the summer*—with people mirroring her failure back at her. The only person who knew the whole, embarrassing story had at least gone away. Gillian couldn't imagine a scene more humiliating than what had happened in that storm-covered car two weeks ago, but at least Cynthia was helping her avoid any interactions that could equal it.

Now, she was asking Gillian to flex her D.C.-socialite muscle for this one little thing. Cynthia still believed Gillian could accomplish something of value.

She caught a glimpse of her parents in the kitchen. Her dad sat at the table with the kids, his chin in his hands as he watched her mom empty the dishwasher. His fascination with his on-and-off-again wife of thirty-four years was obvious and intense. Gillian remembered walking in on a similar scene in high school. Her father had been swaying gently back and forth like his chair was on rockers. Her mother had been washing dishes like nothing was wrong.

"Fine," she said. It was early afternoon and the bar would

be quiet. It was unlikely the people she was working hardest to avoid would even be at Loretta's to see her sneaking into the train station.

She was right. They weren't at Loretta's.

When she shoved open the station's squealing door, she saw that they were here, standing in a cluster with Cynthia on the other side of the large sunlit space.

With them was the one person she hadn't worried about seeing at all. He was supposed to have gotten on a plane and taken her secrets and humiliation and ridiculous efforts to break her curse with him to the other side of the country.

But he was here. Nicky Mendoza, the one person who knew all her secrets, was standing with the people she was working the hardest to keep her secrets from.

CHAPTER 4

As her beautiful best friend walked across the restored black-and-white Arabesque tile floor toward her on kitten heels, Gillian fought back the recitation of Padre Nuestro like swallowing her gorge. There was no reason to pray to an empty room.

Memories of that afternoon flashed through her brain like horror-movie images she tried to close her eyes against. *I'd love another lesson,* she'd told him. *I don't have anywhere else to go. I'm destroying everything I touch. Don't you want to help me be bad?* She saw his horrified expression when she mentioned the condoms. She heard the sound he'd made when she mangled his penis.

Don't you want to help me break my curse?

Her only comfort had been the confidence that he'd left town before he shared the downfall of Gillian Armstead with anyone who would care. Now, he stood chatting and giving her grandmother his gorgeous, good-time grin.

What had he told her? Gillian stress-counted Cynthia's last seven steps.

"Recognize him?" Cynthia asked as she grabbed her and hugged her, pulling Gillian into her cloud of decadent ginger perfume and shining auburn hair and abundant freckles that decorated even the shell of her lovely ear. Cynthia never diminished her assets and right now she was wearing a floaty flowery shirt that showcased a canyon of cleavage and tight cropped jeans. It was easy to get distracted by how gorgeous she was and miss the evil in her emerald eyes.

"Of course," Gillian said stiffly. "Why didn't you—" *Warn me.* "—tell me Nicky was here?"

Cynthia put her hands on her hourglass hips. "That's it? Why didn't I tell you? Excuse me for trying to end the streak of your bad mood with a surprise. I didn't know you were going for the record." She leaned in. "I mean, that view alone has gotta cheer you up. He was hot in high school but now..."

Cynthia bit her glossy bottom lip and made a throaty whimper that Gillian could have gone an eon without hearing.

"What's he doing here?" she muttered through a forced smile. Nicky laughing with her striking sister and brother-in-law made quite the tableau against the bare, white, two-story-tall wall. The only pieces of furniture in the large central space were restored train benches shoved into one corner. A gleaming balcony of intricately carved wood, original to the building, bisected the wall two-thirds of the way up and ringed the train station where large windows let in bright sunlight.

What were they all doing here?

Cynthia shook her head. "Bein' grumpy dulls your brain," she said. "Don't you remember? Half of his drawings were of you. *He's* the artist."

Gillian cleared the tremor out of her throat.

"Our boy's done good," Cynthia said, a huge grin spreading across her face. "The governor requested a piece for her office, but he said she'd have to change her stance on abortion rights before he'd consider it." She wrapped long glamorous nails around Gillian's arm. "C'mon."

Gillian fell back on her heels as Cynthia dragged her across the room, soul shriveling at the realization that the last time she'd seen this acclaimed artist, she'd offered to introduce him to someone who could get him Pottery Barn work.

Nicky's maturation from the small-town bad boy she'd asked to teach her about sex to this gorgeous, accomplished man felt like a physical blow. He was wearing black again—black T-shirt, black jeans, black boots—with a buttery, pale-tan leather jacket that fit his wide shoulders and sleek torso like a glove. He shoved his thick hair back from his eyes and it settled off his forehead in blue-black, finger-combed perfection.

Her hair had been one huge snarl and mascara had ringed her eyes the last time she'd seen him. Now she was in glasses, no makeup, a frizzy ponytail, and a coffee-stained shirt.

Her humiliation was complete and well deserved. She'd had no right to underestimate him; the first time she'd seen Nicky across the lunchroom all those years ago, it was her first time seeing a real-life hero. In the car, she hadn't asked about Nicky's life, his career, or his love. He'd never talked much about himself, but if she'd shown the mildest curiosity, she would have known he wasn't hers for the taking.

She clung to the mirage of calm as they reached the other side of the room.

"Granmo," she said, bending down to kiss the toffee-colored cheek of her seventy-eight-year-old grandmother. Her skin felt as fine as a butterfly's wing.

"Juliana." Loretta Torres gave a regal nod, smiling beneath her salt-and-pepper cloud of curls. "It's good to see you out of the house."

Her grandmother had founded Loretta's forty years ago with Gillian's long-departed Granpo Salvador. After a scary, hip-breaking fall last year, Loretta had sold the bar and building it was housed in to Gillian and her sisters. She was still there most days, handing out her no-nonsense advice, her smile that soothed babies and summoned unexpected tears in grown-ups, and a welcome that made everyone who walked in the door, Mexican-descent or not, feel like family.

Her grandmother lived next door to her parents, and in the two weeks since Gillian had moved back into her childhood home, she hadn't *entirely* avoided her. Gillian had run over for irregular five-minute visits then used the excuses of her kids to weasel away and her job search to skip the large, mandatory Sunday dinners.

"I'm sorry I haven't been over more," Gillian said. "I've been so busy and—"

"No te preocupas, Juliana," Loretta quickly shushed, rubbing her arm. Being the oldest granddaughter and her Granmo's favorite sometimes placed a heavy burden of expectation. "I know it's tiring to walk the forty steps next door."

Gillian ignored her sister's bad-tempered snort as she turned to the man of the hour and tried to pretend surprise.

"Hey, Nicky," she said as he took her held-out hand. "It's lovely to see you again."

The left side of his mouth ticked up like this was all some big joke they shared, the teardrop scar beneath his eye dimpling. "It's been a long time," he said. Then he gathered up her oversized linen shirt to touch her hip and brushed his lips over her cheek. It was a kiss no different from what she'd given her Granmo, but it left her feeling openhand smacked.

She dropped his hand and stepped out of his orbit. "You're contemplating painting a mural here?"

"I've already agreed to it."

Gillian glared at Cynthia.

"Surprise," her best friend said, shaking jazz hands.

"William's health took a turn while I was visiting," he said.

Gillian hadn't asked about William Baldassaro, the curmudgeonly man who'd been a stand-in father ever since he'd shot the wild dog attacking Nicky and his brother on the banks of the Viridescent. That horrifying incident was all the parents had talked about that summer, had brought rare news crews to town, and was the reason for the scars on Nicky's face and shoulder. She also hadn't asked about his brother, Lucas.

"I figured I could do something productive while I keep an eye on him," Nicky said.

"It's an incredible stroke of luck," beamed her hulking, academic brother-in-law, his brawny arm in a tweed jacket wrapped around his wife's tattooed shoulder. "Having a full-wall mural by a Freedom native and a sought-after Mexican-American artist is the perfect synthesis of everything we're trying to capture. It'll be a magnificent boon to the museum, Milagro Street, and the entire town."

Although Dr. Jeremiah Post had grown up in a family with blood even bluer than Thomas's, the history professor and head of the Freedom Historical Society hadn't gotten the memo about East Coast reserve. He fit right in with the nakedly emotional Torres family. Jeremiah, her sister, and their cousin Joe Torres had been the principal forces spearheading a historical museum in the train station that would highlight Freedom's eclectic past and the Mexican-American community that had once filled Milagro Street.

"Good to see you, Gillian," he said without a trace of sarcasm. He and Alex lived no farther than her grandmother, right across the street from her childhood home, but Gillian *had* been avoiding them.

Alejandra "Alex" Torres-Post, the tattooed and pompadoured celebrity bartender responsible for Loretta's transformation from a struggling dive bar to the only thriving business on Milagro Street, glared through her perfectly painted cat's-eye at Gillian. Good. Gillian had been ignoring her middle sister's calls and texts for a couple of months.

"Ali," she said stiffly. Her voluptuous sister, all but melted against her husband's He-Man side, glowered back.

"So how long will the mural take?" Gillian asked Nicky.

"A couple of months. I'll be here through the summer."

Her pulse shot through the roof. "What?" she barked.

Cynthia gave an embarrassed laugh. "Gillian, don't scare him away. He's painting the mural for free but you keep actin' like that, he may start charging."

"I mean...uh...won't anyone miss you at home?" Why was he taking on a project that would plant him here for months? What woman would let him out of her sight that long?

Nicky bit the corner of his lip. He was picking up what she was putting down. "My fiancée and I both travel for work," he finally said. "We're used to the long-distance thing."

"¿Qué, mijo?" Loretta asked at the same moment Alex said, "You're engaged?"

He hadn't told them?

A slow, satisfied smile grew over his face that made Cynthia give a delighted huff. "To my manager, Virginia Ramos." Gillian's stomach twisted with guilt and jealousy. "We've known each other a long time. She'd take a bullet for me."

Nicky was no longer shy but he still was apparently very private. His fiancée would probably put a bullet in Gillian for what she'd done to him on Old 85.

"That's wonderful, mijo," Loretta said, beaming. The many hours he'd spent eating milk and apples at the bar gave her latitude to call him that. "Are we going to meet her?"

He grinned devilishly, those new lines striking out from his eyes. "Maybe."

Great. Nicky would be working closely with her brother-in-law, best friend, sister, and the many members of her family who were actively involved with the museum while he painted right across the street from Loretta's for the rest of the summer. His jet-setting and adoring fiancée might stop by at any time to receive the quality lovemaking Nicky had tutored Gillian in.

If she thought she was going to steer clear of the bar before, she was going to avoid it like the plague now.

"Congratulations, Nicky," she said. "I need to get going—"

Jeremiah put up a big hand. "Gillian, I've got a proposition I think you'll be excited about. We'd like to offer you a part-time job working for the historical society."

"What?" She shot a look at Nicky. Had he told them she was broke? "Why?"

Nicky pursed his lips together.

"Nick's mural has given us an opportunity to apply for a unique grant," Jeremiah said. "If we win it, the size of the award would allow us to invest in Milagro Street in a way that could get it back on its feet."

Gillian swallowed her scoff. Her grandmother liked to wax rhapsodic about Milagro Street's heyday, when there'd been a Mexican tienda and bakery and community center and a Spanish-speaking newspaper and even a prosperous hotel on the street. But that had been before Gillian was born. She'd only known it as three blocks with a few struggling businesses in the buildings that weren't boarded up.

Newly renovated, Loretta's gleamed like a jewel in the rough at the corner of Milagro Street and Penn. A tiny portion of that was due to Gillian's (Thomas's) investment. But the bulk was thanks to Alex's sweat and determination.

"The application requires historical research, analysis of current economic trends, and budget projections," Jeremiah continued. "The few of us qualified don't have the time and those with the time don't have the qualifications." He smiled charmingly. "You've got both."

She lifted her chin with the last dregs of her pride. "Thank you, Jeremiah, but my job search is going so well we probably won't be here for long. I don't need a part-time—"

Alex smacked her husband's chest with a meaty *thwack*. "I told you."

Alex loved the bar like a child, the east side like a favorite dream, and used to regularly talk, email, and text about what the three Armstead sisters could achieve here together. Their baby sister, Sissy, was part owner as well.

"Remember, mija," her grandmother said, looking at her solemnly through her silver-rimmed glasses. "It was just a year ago they were trying to take control of my building and the whole east side." Alex and Jeremiah's joint effort had prevented the mayor and a development company from demolishing the neighborhood. "Putting businesses back in these buildings would stop that from happening again."

Cynthia shook her arm like a chew toy. "You get to do research. Analysis. Budget projections. Don't tell me that doesn't get your heart pumpin'." Cynthia leaned into her Kansas drawl when she wanted her way. "The application deadline is at the end of the summer and you'll still have plenty of time to job hunt. We'll make it worth your while."

Cynthia named a wage for the summer's labor that made Gillian dig her thumb into her palm to hide her surprise.

Among her many worries was the growing concern that she wouldn't be able to afford to move when she did get a job offer. The grant position would put her back in the black. Her family would never know how low she'd considered crawling.

Nicky watched her steadily. Rather, he watched her hands, where her fingers were tapping her thumb. *145, 146, 147* scrolled through her brain.

She pressed her hand against her thigh.

It'd been so ridiculous to assume Nicky had narced on her. Three weeks ago, she'd lived in one of the toniest zip codes in the country. Now she slept in her childhood bedroom. It wasn't a huge leap to assume Gillian could use the money. There was no end to the number of things she needed to apologize to him for.

Jeremiah pointed at the one-story wing at the north end of the building. "You can use my office." A restored oak wall with large glass panels allowed anyone in the office to look out on the station. "The files you'll need are in there."

Work in the same building as Nicky all summer? She didn't think so.

"You'll need to get measurements and photographs of Milagro Street interiors, and since Nick plans to incorporate the buildings into his designs, he'll accompany you. It'll be safer for you both to enter those abandoned buildings together."

Gillian's acceptance stuck in her throat. What a blow to Nicky, to offer such a gift to his hometown only to be punished for his generosity. "Does that work for you?" she asked, meeting his dark eyes.

Cynthia slung her arms over both their shoulders. "Course it does," she said, jiggling them both. "The gang's all back together. Just think of all the trouble we're going to get up to."

Nicky grinned like everything was dandy. "The Pride of the East Side has never gotten into trouble," he drawled. "You think we can inspire her to be bad?"

Loretta and Jeremiah laughed. Alex gave an audible sound of disgust. Gillian smiled and took what she deserved.

Nicky was a good man. By teasing her with what she'd asked of him that day, he was trying to let her know that he wasn't upset. Working with his former lover, who was now unemployed, broke, and cursed, wasn't going to be a problem for him.

He was barely going to notice her at all.

CHAPTER 5

Nicky was accustomed to living alone.

He was as used to it as William, who'd been a declared bachelor ever since his wife left him after their son died drunk in a car accident. That'd been before Nicky was born.

Nicky and William were so set in their ways that, after he'd made his surprise announcement that he would be sticking around for the summer, he assumed he'd be sleeping most nights in the barn. They'd renovated the two-story Victorian farmhouse on the property he'd bought for William a few years ago, and Nicky had built himself an artist's studio and bedroom in the barn's former hayloft. It'd been his transparent excuse to give William a tinkerer's workshop on the main level, with grease-and-oil-resistant PVC flooring, multiple workbenches, and heavy-duty gray armoires stocked with task-specific tools so William would have a comfortable space for the dozens of projects he always had going. Right now, the man was working on hybrid iris bulbs, a cross-ventilation cooling system he swore would cool the barn as well as air-conditioning, and a flat-tax plan.

But Nicky hadn't been sleeping in the loft bedroom he'd built above his studio. He'd been waking up in the guest bedroom in the house, drinking his morning coffee on the porch with William as they watched the fog burn off the field, and dissecting the world's problems in twin, ugly recliners after supper when William wasn't yelling at *Jeopardy*. Nicky preferred his isolation, but he never liked eating out alone or grimacing through his own cooking. Now, before meals, he got to razz William for his muttered "Ow" every time he used a lancet to prick his finger to check his blood sugar level. After an adulthood of diabetes, William still had the tender fingertips of a toddler.

Still, two weeks of surprisingly enjoyable cohabitation with a grumpy eighty-year-old shouldn't have made him go deaf to the man's *bump-shuffle-shuffle* on the stairs as Nicky hung up from telling Virginia Ramos what he'd done.

"You what?" William barked behind Nicky, making him jump and smear charcoal across his draft.

Shit.

"Boy, tell me my hearing's futzing out along with my heart. You did not do something as toweringly stupid as what you just said you did."

Nicky glanced over his shoulder to see William's pale, wide face poking out of the stained pinewood floor, his eyes squinting behind his heavy, black-framed glasses.

Walking up into the loft was like climbing into heaven's tree house. Double-glazed skylights poured in sunlight and blue sky every five feet along an angled ceiling that followed the roof's pitch. An enormous picture window where the hay door used to be looked out over their ten acres and let in more light.

There was nowhere for Nicky to hide.

He put down his pencil before he wrecked his Milagro Street study and turned on his stool with his most distracting smile. "What're you doing out here? You need me to hold your hand while you test your sugar?" He'd dropped off William's medications and a small plain hamburger from Johnny's on the kitchen counter but hadn't checked in like he normally did.

William just shot him a disgusted glance. He had a round face, thick glasses, and a few precious strands of blond-gray hair he shellacked over his skull every morning. He focused on planting his cane on the main floor and taking the last steps through the opening.

Nicky hated how cautious those steps were. He could feel his smile evaporating as William sat his squat bulk on a nearby stool then rubbed his chest. "You okay?"

William held up an irritated arthritic finger and kept rubbing his chest. Nicky was one second from calling 911. He'd learned with his brother that quick action was the difference between a spritz of Narcan up the nose versus days in the hospital watching staff repeatedly bring his brother back to life. But William wasn't an addict; he was an octogenarian with two heart attacks, a fifty-year bout of diabetes, a quadruple bypass, and a shunt that's ten-year life span had expired two years ago under his belt. He appreciated Nicky's interventions about as much as Lucas did.

Nicky should've just stopped in and flashed his smile instead of leaving without a word. Others always paid for his mistakes.

William finally straightened. "Worry about yourself," he said, stomping his cane between his thick-soled shoes. "What the hell are you thinking?"

Nicky crossed his arms and dropped his smile. "If I wanted you to hear what I had to tell Virginia, I wouldn't have hidden up here to say it. What's done is done. She said she expected a ring with a huge rock. The word she used was *ginormous*."

"Good for her." Virginia had charmed William just like she charmed the pants off everyone.

His manager's shamelessness about taking advantage of a situation was why she was the best in the business. Nicky had met her when she slipped a business card into his pocket in an alleyway near Central Park while one cop had been handcuffing him and the other one was carrying away a dishwashing paycheck's worth of spray paint.

William shifted on the stool. "So this is all about Gillian Armstead?"

They did not talk about this. After that summer thirteen years ago, they did not talk about Gillian Armstead-*Bancroft*. After William's chest pain and quick ER diagnosis of heartburn had given Nicky an excuse to stay in town for the summer, neither of them mentioned the delicious takeout Nicky kept bringing home from Loretta's. And although William hung out with her gossipy tíos who drank coffee at Loretta's every morning, and therefore had surely heard that Gillian was back, he'd never said a single word.

Ripping off the Band-Aid might wrap this conversation up. "I'm going to have to work with her this summer."

"Uh-huh," William said, without sympathy.

Stilted and uncomfortable, Nicky filled in the details: Gillian would be working a few yards from him and he was supposed to turn his back on her and paint a mural. Gillian would be taking pictures and measurements of the deteriorating buildings along Milagro Street, and Nicky was supposed to go into all those dark, empty, no-one-could-see-them rooms with her.

"So you got what you came for," William said.

Nicky gave a sharp, bitter laugh. "Hardly."

"What? Your plan was to sniff her hair for the summer then watch her leave with your heart again?"

"Christ," Nicky said, truly horrified. "I could've gone my whole life without hearing you sound like a rom-com."

"How you think I feel?" William barked back.

Embarrassed for them both, Nicky stood, his stool wheeling out from under him to bang into his drawing table, and stretched his back. He could've gone a couple of rounds with his punching bag hanging in the corner. He strode over to the large window and pressed his forehead against its brain-boiling heat.

He'd told himself he'd earned this after years of denial, not even peeking at the internet for glimpses of her, told himself he could just hang out at Loretta's and enjoy the occasional conversation with her after he apologized for letting things in the car go as far as they did and assuring her it was all his fault. He'd convinced himself that they could settle into casual, friendly chats while he inhaled the world's most decadent peach cobbler scent of her and recorded every twitch of her new-but-the-same face and double-checked that everything was going to turn out okay for his perfect hechicera and drowned himself in the miserable sensation of his happy place feeling that nothing but his art and the presence of Gillian fucking Armstead had ever given him.

He hadn't meant to get wrangled into painting the mural, but how could he say no?

When he'd discovered the job they were going to offer Gillian, he'd smiled through his cold sweat. He knew info they didn't about what she was doing here for the summer, but they weren't going to learn it from him. He figured he could count on her to decline; she already had a lot on her plate. But he'd underestimated how broke she was. Was his brilliant, gifted, gorgeous hechicera really cursed?

He'd visited a curandera in Topeka and a woman who honored Santa Muerte in El Paso and a holy man who'd lived in a cave in the hills outside Guanajuato to try to manage his own problems. He wholeheartedly believed in curses.

His poor girl needed money and, to get it, she was stuck with him.

"You wanted to spend time with her." William had never dismissed what Nicky felt for Gillian; William married his grade school sweetheart. Look how well that had turned out. "Now you can."

"Not like this," Nicky said.

"Why not 'this'? Why not spend some quality time getting to know her as an adult?"

"Because."

"Because. Why?" William stuffed the words with years of frustration.

Nicky wasn't going to get into this argument with him again.

The fact that William Baldassaro had saved his life made the man think he had some claim to its quality and care. William had lived only a couple of blocks from their run-down apartment complex on Freedom's east side; when he realized how stretched thin the mom he'd met weeping in the emergency room was, he'd quietly stepped in to fill in some of the cracks. Becky Mendoza, who cobbled together cashier jobs at the Dollar General and a gas station and occasional waitressing gigs at the Waffle House, was glad for the help, glad they had someone reliable to toss a ball with, tutor them at math, and show up at school events. William was so different than her ex-husband and the men she dated.

Nicky never blamed his mom for the poverty and casual neglect. His father, Raymundo Mendoza, had driven away in his ice-blue tractor trailer with everything except the girl he'd knocked up in high school, two boys, and a crate of classic rock tapes. Becky had done the best she could with what had been dumped on her. He was glad, after he'd left town and Lucas had landed himself in juvie until he turned eighteen, that she'd washed her hands of the both of them and taken herself to Florida for a new husband and a new life.

So it was William who showed up for Nicky's first small gallery opening at the Art Institute of Denver, then came for the larger, more glamorous openings where Nicky always introduced the intelligent, accomplished, sensual women who graced his arm as friends. It was William who joined him for two-man birthday celebrations or Christmases in San Francisco, Chicago, Miami, Paris, Mexico City, wherever he was working, and always pointed out the happy families strolling past restaurant windows.

It was William who finally tracked Nicky down at the Whistler estate nine months ago where Nicky had been "painting" between losing himself between the client's gorgeous thighs and medicating himself with top-shelf mezcal to ignore the yellow eyes and sharp teeth shining from the corners.

It was William who told him about his brother.

With the warmth against his face feeling too much like hot, fetid breath, he shoved off the glass.

"What I told Gillian about Virginia is done," he said. "Let it go."

"It's the damn stupidest thing I've ever heard," William said. "Lucas wouldn't want—"

"Stop."

William didn't know what Lucas would want. After the attack, Lucas had pushed away William's effort to be a positive influence with as much passion as Nicky had clung to it. The only thing Lucas had wanted was Nicky's attention, company, and guarantee that this big brother would keep him safe.

Nicky stared at William, the man who was a father to him in every way but blood, and begged with everything but words that he drop it.

William aimed those Coke-bottle glasses at the floor. "Talking to you is like talking to a brick wall."

Nicky knew that his bullshit was a lot to manage. He couldn't let it become so weighty that William refused to move to San Francisco with him at the end of the summer. He still hadn't brought the move up.

William leaned on his cane to stand. "My burger's probably cold."

"Whose fault is that?"

William made his careful way down the stairs, and Nicky

tracked the *thump-shuffle* of his descent. Nicky had tried to spot him once. Once.

When he made it safely to the bottom, Nicky leaned back against the glass.

"Faking an engagement," William yelled up. "I feel like I'm in an Austen novel." William's movements were soundless over the rubber tiles that were better on his knees. "I hate Austen."

"I know you're more of a Brontë girl," Nicky yelled back.

William gave a colorful reply.

Virginia Ramos had done crazier things than agreeing to be his fake fiancée for a couple of months. She was the reason Nick Mendoza was a brand as well as a name, was the reason an unplanned, overnight spray paint mural from Nicky could stop a community center from getting demolished instead of getting him arrested. She was the reason Nicky could buy farm properties for his pseudo-dad and long, luxurious, ultimately worthless rehab stays for his brother. Virginia was a dear friend, a casual lover with a warm bed in every port, and a fucking mercenary with a law degree.

In that car, Virginia had been his last desperate flail.

Nicky had been in love with Gillian Armstead since the instant she'd waved at him on the first day of fifth grade, striking him with his happy place feeling that never relented in her presence, no matter how bad she sometimes made him feel. When she'd asked him to touch her, to love her, that summer she'd come home from Boston, he'd thought all of his dreams were coming true until she'd made clear what she really wanted from him: An arrangement. His experience.

His silence. He'd gone along with it for three months and it nearly destroyed him.

He refused be convenient for her again. That's what he'd told himself. That was the healthy, self-care prerogative various therapists beat him over the head with. The boy who'd had no self-preservation had to take a reluctant stab at it as a man.

The effort would have been more convincing if he'd left when he said he was going to.

Don't you want to help me be bad?

It was like pounding a nail through his hand. Because he did. Good Lord, he did.

He could fake virtue, say he was trying to help his friend, claim he was acting as an ear and a supportive shoulder to the exhausted mommy who wasn't letting anyone else help her. But he wanted her. Regardless of the way she'd dismissed him when they were lovers and read him wrong now—he caught that look on her face when she thought he'd told her secrets— he still wanted her in a base and dirty way.

For more than a decade, he'd ignored that the best lover of his life still roamed the planet. When she'd landed in his lap, his first instinct was to get her off just like he'd gotten her off the first time: quick and hard and mean. He'd howled out the word *engaged* to protect him from her. To protect her from him. Then he'd ruined it by staying in Freedom. Now, he'd leashed them together and put them on a path that was too familiar: Wandering an abandoned road with plentiful dark corners to touch in secret.

Nicky couldn't touch her. He had a debt. And this summer was going to make him pay and pay and pay.

CHAPTER 6

Gillian forcibly shoved her ex's disturbing morning phone call out of her mind the following Monday as she drove over Milagro Street's cracked pavement to begin her first day of work.

She wanted all of her focus on the owner of the old-school forest-green Jeep Wrangler that she parked beside.

She flipped down the mirror and checked her reflection. The keratin treatment she'd gotten five months ago was on its last legs, so she'd had to wake up early to straighten her hair. She ran a hand down it, soothed by its bedsheet smoothness. Her makeup was on point and she'd put together an outfit that displayed the woman she'd cultivated over the last thirteen years: cream silk shell, beige cashmere cardigan, and black, wide-legged summer slacks.

For the few minutes it would be necessary for her to be in the train station to gather what she needed, she was determined to show Nicky that she was someone other than that needy, chaotic, curse-babbling woman out on Old 85.

Her new boss had come by to go over the details of the grant while his wife had determinedly avoided the house and played in the backyard with the kids. Jeremiah had explained that the

National Endowment for the Arts' Unearthed Treasure grant provided substantial funds for improving the community near a significant piece of art, like Nicky's mural. The eye-popping size of the grant was what made the application so massive. It required thorough research of the neighborhood's history, people, and infrastructure, then a comprehensive plan explaining how the grant would be invested to benefit the neighborhood's future.

Gillian could do this job. The dense terminology she'd seen as she'd explored the NEA's grant website—"modular budget," "training subaward budget," "de minimis rate"—and the multitude of worksheets were actually comforting in their familiarity. She just doubted it would make any difference.

The restored portico that shaded the entrance to the train station gleamed with new brick, but the groves of dandelions shoving through the crumbling sidewalk along Milagro Street seemed to be what paved the future.

Thomas's upgraded offer in this morning's phone call whispered through her brain. They were dangerous thoughts to have so close to Loretta's. She glanced across the street to make sure the bar's parking lot was empty before she reapplied her gloss.

At last, Nicky would see the Pride of the East Side all grown up. With dignity and composure, she would apologize for her behavior, offer to apologize to his fiancée as well if necessary, and promise to keep their interactions to a minimum. She could work on her laptop from anywhere. She didn't need to punish them with daily interactions.

With her classic Givenchy bag on her shoulder—it was black, as big as a briefcase, and the only one she'd kept—she stepped out into the stifling ninety-two-degree morning. She walked toward the propped-open doors of the future Freedom Historical Museum showcasing every inch of her hard-earned East Coast sophistication.

Stepping through the doors was like plummeting into hell.

Thick heat instantly engulfed her. Two waist-high industrial fans roared on each side of the open central space. Sunlight singed her eyes.

The sight of Nicky, without a shirt, burned her to ash.

He stood half-naked and hip cocked on the other side of the room, his brown, sculpted back to her as he held a tablet. He was looking up at the two-story wall that was going to be his canvas.

She licked her newly painted bottom lip as she gazed at his gleaming, sweat-sheened back. The long indent of his spine disappeared into low-slung cargoes. Right above the belt line, she could see the stripe of his black boxer briefs. Above those, above his firm ass, she could see two perfect dimples.

She'd once licked into those dimples, making him shiver where he was stretched out on the GTO's massive back seat. She'd explored his whole back, torturing him with licks and bites and sucks, and then made him turn over and opened up his jeans and…

Nicky turned around. Sunlight sparkled off the damp muscles of his chest and abs. He put his body to good use and it showed. The width of his shoulders and the depth of the hip cuts arrowing down into his paint-splattered pants were new; those four ragged but parallel scars over the hard cap of his right shoulder weren't.

Nicky hadn't attended student government meetings or been in her honors and AP classes in high school, so it'd been on some mysterious day when she'd turned a corner in the hallway and spied a long-haired boy in black with a mouth that promised corruption flash a smile at a girl. She'd walked into a bank of lockers a minute later when she realized that the boy was Nicky. The metamorphosis of her shy, devoted friend into that beautiful bad boy with a dirty grin had been as fascinating as it had been shocking. When she'd heard girls laughing and cawing in the locker room about Nicky's "talents," she'd had to give herself a peppermint-steeped limpia to cleanse her thoughts. She'd been in the middle of midterms and had had no time for the crush trying to take root.

She'd never had time for a crush on a boy from Freedom.

Now, with Nicky just standing there and staring sightlessly back, the fans batting the black hair he held back from his face with a red bandanna, there seemed to be no limit to how gorgeous he could get.

She knew he wasn't showing off. When they'd been children, when seeing his skinny naked chest and tender scars had been normal for two little brown kids running around all summer getting browner, he'd needed a minute to yank his brain out of his creative space whenever he'd been drawing. He'd called it his "happy place" and she understood why he didn't want to leave it.

She watched him come back online as that lush, appreciative smile he shot at everyone spread across his face. "You bring your bikini?" he called, louder than the fans as he grabbed his T-shirt off a stool. "Guy said we're going to be swimming in this for two weeks instead of just one."

He pulled his T-shirt over his head as he walked toward her like he hadn't thrown a thunderbolt into her eyes. Like he hadn't turned her into a pillar of salt.

"What guy?" she cried above the roar. "What's going on?"

"Cynthia didn't text you?"

Cynthia. Cynthia had probably snickered and tucked away her phone the instant Nicky took off his shirt.

"The AC guy, Jeremiah, and Cynthia were here when I showed up," he said, close enough to talk without shouting. "A part on the new system is bad."

Thick flicks of hair poked out of the faded red bandanna. On anyone else, it would have looked ridiculous. On Nicky, it looked like a thorny crown on top of his Jesus-wept face. "He thought he could find a replacement in a week, but Jeremiah just called and said it looks like it'll be two."

Frustration finally shook her out of her lusty daze. Parked near the back wall was his always-present backpack, a standing draft table already scattered with supplies, and a huge jug of water. "You can't work in this for two weeks!"

His grin quirked up on one side. "You worried about me, girl?"

She crossed her arms to cover the flutter in her stomach. "I was already planning to grab the research I need and work out of my parents' house." She raised an eyebrow at him. "But if you die of heat stroke, I'm going to be out of a job."

A huge drop of sweat meandered past her eyebrow and down her face. She swiped at it. Her $300 cardigan was beginning to stick to her skin. She yanked it off and draped it over her bag, tucked her hair behind her ear and felt it starting to curl and kink in the damp heat.

She raised her chin. "Before I go..." She wiped at the sweat beading on her chest. "I want to apologize."

"For?"

"I'm sorry I was...inappropriate with you." How long did he have? "The information I shared with you was...excessive and unnecessary." She grabbed at her silk shell to air it out. "My behavior..."

He bit the corner of his lip. Was he laughing at her?

"I don't know why you think this is funny because I most certainly do not." He glistened like the Skinemax version of a painter while Gillian melted into a puddle of preppy, sexually frustrated mommy goo. "I almost hit you then I dumped my personal problems on you and then I..."

The starch seeped out of her as she listed her sins.

"I'm so sorry I forced myself on you," she said, surrendering any right to pride. "I want you to know, I want your fiancée to know—" He stiffened and that was right, that was good, she'd fondled what didn't belong to her in that car. "—that while we may be forced to work together occasionally this summer, *nothing* like that will happen again. I will never presume again that because we were friends and then..." Was she babbling? "And then, for a short time, more than friends..." She was definitely babbling. "That there is still some emotional or—or physical component that I can just—"

"Hey." He stepped close. "You were having a bad day, girl." He'd always had a way of looking at her like he could see her insides. "You were having a bad day after a string of them. You weren't the only one making poor choices in that car. Ease up on yourself."

He'd kissed and touched, too, perhaps caught in the nostalgia as she demanded his kisses and touches. Now, he was trying to make her feel better. So *Don't tell me what to do* shouldn't have been her knee-jerk response. *Don't tell me how to think, don't tell me how I should perceive.*

"Easing up really isn't my style," she said sharply.

But rather than going red-faced and explosive at her cutting reply, rather than turning his back on her and giving her a silent treatment that could last an excruciating number of days, Nicky looked at her through dark lashes, creasing his teardrop scar as he narrowed his eyes.

"I thought changing up your style was the whole point," he said. "Shrugging off moral lapses is the way a good girl gets bad and breaks her curse." He *tsked* and shook his head. "You *are* gonna need my help this summer."

I'm the curse, she'd said in the middle of the storm. *Don't you want to help break it?*

None of this was funny and yet all of it was ridiculous. She stepped closer and poked him in his hard sternum. "Stop teasing me about that."

He grabbed her finger. "Who's teasing? You know I take curses seriously. You still think you're dealing with one?"

She thought of her ex-husband's morning phone call. "Most definitely," she found herself saying.

She caught the concerned crook of his eyebrows before she dropped her eyes to the lettering on his faded black concert T-shirt. "I tried a baño the other morning to see if it would help." She'd stood naked in her parents' tub and dumped the bucket of smelly ingredients diluted in cold spring water over her head, then stood uncomfortably while she air-dried. The powerful concoction had once been her most effective for washing away bad luck.

"And?" Her sweaty finger in his sweaty grip should've been gross, but it wasn't.

"Nothing. I just reeked of vinegar and garlic all day." She glanced into his eyes. "I can't believe I'm talking about this with you."

"We know more about each other than most long-lost friends do."

They'd been a few months into the fifth grade when she saw him launch himself backward with a startled cry then crawl away from something no one else on the playground could see. His mother picked up both boys from school that day; poor Lucas had been cornered in the bathroom and gotten a black eye. When Nicky came back a week later, she told him about her visits from La Llorona and gave him a warding amuleto filled with rue, garlic, and a medal of St. Benedict, proud to use her baby bruja skills to protect the boy who worked so hard to protect his brother.

Her mom had learned brujería from her Tía Josie, and her Tía Josie had learned it from her Big Grandmo's cousin, and the cousin had brought it from her tiny village of Abosolo, Mexico. The sacred arts Gillian practiced had been augmented by every bruja who handed it down, a mix of Mexican paganism, Spanish Catholicism, and American self-determination. Not many in the vicinity of Freedom, Kansas, believed, but the ones who did knew how to find her and her mother.

They also knew to remain circumspect. As she'd explained to Nicky when they were young, Salem wasn't the only place that had witnessed unjust torments against women.

"Did your husband know about your magic?" Nicky asked.

"Why?"

He shrugged. His hold on one finger had become the light entwining of two. The fan blew his smell of high-end leather right at her. "Seems he wouldn't pull the shit he's tried if he knew."

Nicky's confidence that she was a force to be reckoned with shamed her as much as it fed her.

Her magic was similar to the meditation and focused intentions others started their day with. Hers just included a novena candle, holy water, and, up until a few months ago, a seventy-five percent success rate. She'd used her sacred arts to bolster her confidence before a business meeting, ward her home from the jealousy of the two white women who lived on either side of her, or heal her children when they'd woken up with a fever. But even when she'd loved Thomas—foolishly, she had loved him—she'd found excuses to avoid telling him.

Nicky had always known.

"With or without magic, I still have to answer the phone if the father of my children calls to hassle me on a Monday morning," she grumbled.

"What did he say?"

She clicked her tongue and looked away. She hadn't meant to—

He squeezed her hand. All of their fingers were locked together. "Fess up, girl."

Nicky had so many better things to do than listen to her whine about her divorce. She remembered how proud, how confident she'd been when she'd walked up to him at a bonfire to proposition him.

"Instead of the house and the job, he's offered to provide some alimony and child support," she said woodenly. "Not a lot."

Not what the prenup stipulated. But the ghost of her East Coast dreams whispered that anything was better than nothing. During their six-month separation, Thomas had hacked her email, hired a private investigator, and installed a bug to monitor her phone calls. She *hated* that the ghost still had a voice.

"What's he get in return?" Nicky asked.

"What he asked for before. My portion of the bar."

All I want is what is fair, Thomas had said. *How would you feel if you weren't consulted on an investment of that magnitude?* She had consulted him. He'd told her to do what she wanted. It was her therapist who'd pointed out that Thomas would keep himself out of decisions that he could criticize her for later. *Now I would like some control of that investment. It's a fair trade. Especially since I allowed you to take my children halfway across the country. I'm looking forward to a long visit with them.*

Gillian had pressed her lips against her teeth to keep from responding.

In their last month in the house, she'd called Thomas to let him know she'd be taking the children to live with her family in Kansas while she looked for work. He'd seen his children once since he'd moved out. He'd sounded bored when he agreed. It'd been a three-minute phone call.

She hated to be reminded of the impending week, the first of many, her children would have to spend with their negligent father. But she had to stand firm in the faith that her financial issues would be resolved soon, that she would find a job and her attorney would find a way to get Thomas's contribution. She was so tired of Thomas jingling her family's bar like a bag of chips she could cash in.

"I wish I could get him to stop bringing Loretta's up," she said.

Nicky's touch was strong and comforting. "If you wanted

to just pay him back the money, you've got a best friend and a brother-in-law who would help."

Jeremiah was a trust fund baby, too, but so, so different than Thomas. She couldn't imagine going to him or Cynthia for a loan, much less admitting to her family what the man she'd married was demanding. She couldn't bear the looks on their faces when they understood how wildly she'd let her life fly out of her hands.

Nicky knew it all.

"It won't be necessary to involve them," she said, letting go of the handhold she'd never intended. "I'm going to figure everything out. Everything will be fine. My family will never have to hear about this. But thank you. You're handling all of..." She fluttered a hand over herself. "All of this with a lot more patience and kindness than could be expected."

She stepped back from him. "I hope your fiancée—" *Virginia, her name was Virginia* "—Virginia is handling it as well?"

"I explained," he said evenly. "She understood."

"Good," she said, half relieved and half not understanding at all. She would have hacked off the hands of anyone who'd touched him if he'd been hers.

Things had veered wildly from the benign, in-control professionalism she'd planned on promising him. "I'm going to grab the research and go," she said, turning toward the office. She could at least offer him her absence. "You should think about getting out of here, too."

"Yeah, about that..."

He followed her as she walked to the administrator's office in the station's one-story north wing. There was a matching south wing for ticket sales. The office was dark through the large interior windows inset into the gleaming wood wall that separated the wing from the middle space.

She opened the door and flipped on the lights. Her plan to grab a couple of boxes and retreat to her parents' house to fill in the blanks about Milagro Street died on the vine. Blue plastic tubs of records were stacked floor to ceiling along three walls. Jeremiah had said that the community had "inundated" them with historical records and documents about Milagro Street. Much of it still needed to be organized, which would be part of her job.

Gillian buried her hand in her damp and frizzy hair. "Would you mind aiming a fan this way?" she asked, full of defeat.

"Not at all," Nicky said. "I'm used to working in the heat. I'll push them both closer and just take off my shirt."

She'd truly stepped into hell.

CHAPTER 7

By day four of struggling to keep his eyes away from Gillian Armstead-Bancroft taking off her clothes, Nicky had had it. He knocked on the frame of her open door right after she arrived, his T-shirt back on and his backpack over it.

"Let's get out of here," he said.

She sat on the black-and-white tile reading from a file open on top of a blue tub, already holding her hair twisted off her neck. The two oscillating desk fans played with the tendrils on the side of her face, but didn't blow away the sweat he could see gleaming in the hollow of her throat.

"Get out of here?" she asked, blinking at him with her new eyes.

Gillian's latest metamorphosis into a thin-nosed woman with green eyes was no different than her previous transformation from a little girl always in pink to a slim teenager with a long neck and small breasts and wide eyes that looked at everything, including Nicky, as a challenge she could conquer. Gillian's beauty was baked in deep. She dressed it up different depending on her goals.

For the last three days, the grown-up Gillian had strolled

into his work site looking like the accountant other accountants hired for bachelor parties. She'd sit on the tile in her light sweaters and precisely styled hair and perfectly glossed wide mouth and pull up a blue bin to start going through it. Then, in the unforgiving heat inside the depot, she would shuck her cardigan. She would wiggle it off her shoulders then slip it down her slim tanned arms. While he was trying to concentrate on pictorial theme and color palette and the light at different times of day, she would raise her arms, display the curve of her waist or the press of her breasts, and twist up her hair. Sometimes she would bend over to roll up the cuffs of her pants. She would kick off her loafers. The tender pads of her bare feet would get dusty and dark as she walked around her office.

The Freedom train station was turning them into kids again, forcing him shirtless, her barefoot, and making them swim in the same steamy air.

He couldn't take it another day. He'd stayed to take sips of her. Now he needed a drink. He needed to quench his thirst before he came clean about his fake engagement and showed her the value of getting naked in the train station.

"Yeah, we'll check out one of the buildings on Milagro Street," he said as he leaned against the doorframe. "It can't be any hotter than it is in here."

She let go of her hair and raked her fingers through it. She closed the folder and held it up. "Start with the Elkhart Hotel?"

As she searched through a desk drawer for the keys of the untenanted buildings Jeremiah had secured for her, Nicky closed his eyes and took a quick breath, inhaling her peach-sun-tea scent that the fans were blowing in his direction.

He had his eyes opened and his grin reattached by the time she turned back to face him.

The sun was white-hot when they stepped out from under the shade of the brick portico. The barren emptiness of Milagro Street made it like a ghost town; Nicky wouldn't have been surprised to see a tumbleweed roll by.

Loretta's cheery beer garden across the street with its railroad-tie planter boxes of red-and-white gardenias, red boxcar bar, and closed umbrellas in the middle of café tables looked totally out of place.

Gillian must have seen what he saw. "Trying to resuscitate this street is like pushing a boulder uphill," she said, slipping on her oversized glasses and fluffing back her hair that was starting to kink in the June humidity.

"What've you learned so far?" he asked as they started walking the three blocks toward the once-famed Elkhart Hotel. He planned to incorporate elements of the street's history into the mural. More importantly, he wanted to hear her voice.

"Well, I've learned that when the M.K. & T. ran their train line through here, people thought the oil boom was going to explode Freedom's population to one hundred thousand. Can you imagine? They thought they'd need this second city center on the east side of town."

Nicky had visited a lot of weird places but Freedom, Kansas, with the oil millionaires who once lived here and the moldering early-twentieth-century mansions proving it was true, the monkey from its zoo shot into space, and the Pulitzer Prize-winning playwright who once roamed its streets, was one of the weirdest. Now, as they passed the second-busiest business on the strip, Nicky gave a nod and a wink to the bored check-cashing employee sitting inside behind a barred window. He returned an appreciative smile.

"This area turned out to be most popular with the traqueros, the Mexican immigrants who settled here to work on the railroad. The white business owners gave up on their fine buildings..." She motioned to the boarded-up windows of the Main Street-style buildings they were passing. "...and Mexican business owners moved in and named it Milagro Street."

They passed a run-down mini-mart that everyone knew was a rip-off, but was the only spot on the east side to grab milk if you didn't or couldn't drive. When Nicky's mom couldn't afford to fix their car, they'd shopped here.

"Milagro Street was the center of a thriving Mexican-American community for a couple of generations," Gillian said, looking both ways on the empty cross street before she stepped off the sidewalk. She was wearing an oversized cotton shirt, cropped linen pants, and slim leather loafers. Dust billowed up around her trim ankles. "Loretta talks about how much fun she had running around on Milagro Street. She attended dances at the community center and met friends at the hotel's coffee shop and shopped for her mom at the tienda. But my sisters and I only remember it like..." She pointed to the narrow lot they were passing. Behind the safety fencing with Torres Construction signs on it was the rubble of a demolished building.

Nicky had searched for and found his brother in a couple of these abandoned buildings.

"The train station was called the loveliest north of Texas when it was built, but it closed twenty years ago, and Granmo made the tíos set up rat traps in the station so no colonies eyed Loretta's." Gillian's sharp chin led the way as they walked. "Alex acts like reviving Milagro Street is just an east side vs. west side problem, but my sister and her hubby have bigger problems than the Hughs."

Sitting at the bar at Loretta's, waiting for a glimpse of Gillian, he'd learned that Alex and Jeremiah had stopped two powerful members of the town-founding Hugh clan from bulldozing the whole east side. The developer had gone to jail but longtime mayor Bernie Hugh Mayfield had squirmed away clean.

"Freedom's got a rapidly declining population, a struggling manufacturing base, few employment opportunities to maintain a middle class, and an assimilated Mexican-American community that's forgotten Milagro Street."

Gillian had always been good at measuring what something lacked. "Isn't that your problem, too?" he asked. She was a majority owner of the street's main business, a business she hadn't even glanced at when they passed it.

Her oversized sunglasses aimed his irritated expression right back at him. "I... Yes. My life would be easier if I could start drawing on a return on my investment."

They'd reached the Elkhart Hotel at the end of Milagro Street. It was still a beauty, three stories of deep-red brick with a white elaborate cornice around the top and white, rough-stone lintels over every window. A long plywood barricade protected its entrance and windows.

She shrugged as they stepped into the shade under the metal awning. "Maybe I *should* just sell the bar."

Fuck. She hadn't asked Nicky to stick around town and lie to her, then judge her. She didn't deserve his still-percolating resentment that she'd dismissed him. "That was out of line," he said. "I'm sorry—"

"You obviously believe in the possibility of Milagro Street's resurgence," she said, as she took off her sunglasses and carefully folded them up. "You've dedicated a whole summer to painting a mural here instead of spending it in *San Francisco* with your *fiancée*. You deserve canonization."

She gave him a soft smile full of apology. He was a super-sized piece of shit.

Nicky didn't want to be in Freedom any more than she did. He'd been on his way to the farmhouse to tell William he wanted him to come live with him in San Francisco when his Jeep had stalled on Old 85. The repair shop hadn't been able to find anything wrong with it.

He'd offer to buy William a place on the coast. He'd personally pack and swaddle every project William was working on. This tiny town was stuffed with too many haunting memories.

"Being here is no big deal," he said as he looked over the boarded-up entrance. "I'm used to traveling for work. How're we supposed to get in?"

"Around back." She put her sunglasses back in their case. "Still, staying here for the summer is still quite the commitment. How's William doing? It's a good thing you were in town when he had his health scare."

That heartburn Nicky had lied about to explain why he'd stayed. "He's fine. Around back, you said?"

He headed that way.

"And your mom?"

He stepped back out into the burning sun. "Florida."

The rest of their walk down the sidewalk was in silence.

At the corner of the building, she marched past him and stopped at a heavy rear door.

"Look, I realize I'm not the person you want to spend your summer with," she said, her back to him as she rooted around inside her bag. "But..." She pulled out the key. "...I know next to nothing about you except..." He heard the key click against the lock. "...a blurb Cynthia read on your Wikipedia page." He heard the key jiggle. "While you know...*dammit!*" She pulled the key out and held it up to look at the tab hanging off of it. "...*deeply* personal stuff about me." She lowered the key and inserted it again. "So, if you could just throw me a bone here and..." He heard her strain to turn it. "...share a little with the class so I don't feel like some self-involved, pitiable, desperate...who's upchucked her pathetic life over the first hot guy willing to listen..."

He wanted to lay his hand between the wings of her shoulder blades. He wanted to press his thumbs into the tense muscles.

He stepped up and casually hip-checked her. "Lemme try."

The key didn't budge when he wiggled it. "You're sure this is the right key?"

"It's marked for the hotel," she said, frustrated. "My sister probably walked in when Jeremiah was labeling these. I want to get a spray bottle to separate those two sometimes."

Her frustration wasn't just for the key or her sister or the hot sun beating down on their heads. "I'm going to have to go back and—"

He eyed the standard commercial lock. "I can get us in here." He slid off one strap of his backpack, pulled it to his front, and opened the front compartment to pull out a small canvas case.

Gillian made a sound of disbelief when he unzipped it. "Are those to pick locks?"

"Yep," he said, locating the serrated tension tool that worked best.

Her hand suddenly fell on top of his. When he looked at her, her eyes were headlight wide. "Why do you have lock-picking tools?"

Nicky knocked his hair out of his face. "There are a lot of blank walls hidden behind locked gates: sewers, access tunnels, walkways." Her green eyes were impossibly focused. "Picking locks gives me more canvas."

"But we can't just—" she whispered and her hand clenched over his.

He'd forgotten how much of a rule stickler his will-you-give-me-sex-lessons hechicera thought she was. He turned his hand over and squeezed hers. "C'mon. A little harmless B&E. This might be the next step in breaking your curse." He ran his thumb across the sensitive center of her palm. "You already called me hot. What other way can I help you be bad today?"

"You're—I told you—" She yanked her hand out of his grip, a rosy flush on her wide cheekbones. "Fine."

Flirting with Gillian Armstead had never been a hardship, even when he'd been doing it to cover up all the more-than-flirting feelings he had. A good tease, a sexually soaked threat, had been a sure way to break Gillian out of her head and into the ecstasy of her body. Now it was a way to give her a little harmless pleasure when she was in pain.

He squatted down in front of the lock. Lock picking had also been handy for breaking into whatever shitty motel room, drug dealer's pad, or crap-ass apartment he needed to drag his brother out of.

"My biological dad is from Topeka." He looked up at her. "Did you know that?"

She nodded. The end of her petite nose was getting a little red, but she looked at him in that serious, consuming way like she could have stood in the burning sunlight all day listening to him.

He focused on the lock, inserted the right pick, and started to manipulate the pins.

"Jeremiah said there was a neighborhood started by traqueros in Topeka, too. But when we moved here, I'd never hung out with many Mexicans. When people started writing about me, they called me an upcoming Latinx artist. I just thought of myself as an artist." He shoved up one tumbler at a time. "But it made me think about what they say here in Freedom: 'If you're brown and in town, you're family.' It made me think about the feeling I had when I hung out with you and your cousins or when I worked with Mexican families when I was doing a series of installations in border towns. I have this shared something with other Latinos, even if I have to do the work to figure out what that something is."

The last pin slid into place and he felt give on the tension tool. He turned it and felt the always-gratifying release of the lock. He stood, turned the knob, and held the door open for her. "The railroad workers might be my forefathers just like they're yours. I decided to paint this mural to honor them and show what they achieved."

The ghosts of Milagro Street weren't why he'd decided to stay for the summer. But they were why he'd agreed to do more than hang out at Loretta's and stalk Gillian during it.

She peered into the dark beyond the door. "Crap. I should've brought a—"

He grabbed the Maglite out of his backpack and handed it to her.

"Thanks." She clicked on the light and stepped inside. He followed her in and let the door slam behind him, shutting them into a darkness that was easily fifteen degrees cooler than it was outside.

Gillian shined her light on tarnished brass doorway plaques marking "kitchen," "laundry," "storage," and "offices" but kept walking. "I overheard a coworker who wanted my position call me a rich white Mexican," she whispered. "I was incensed for days, thinking about how hard I'd worked for the privilege of him seeing me, being jealous of me, sneering at me. But I stood on the shoulders of a lot of hardworking Mexicans to get there. We're not entirely self-made. You've absorbed that lesson better than I have."

She suddenly turned around to face him and he realized he'd been following her too close. He was right on top of her, her cheekbones and chin and long neck lightly illuminated by the flashlight she kept lowered. In the temperature drop provided by century-old brick, she smelled like a peach pie cooling on a windowsill. She met his eyes. "You've become the person I always thought I'd be."

The dark beyond their flashlight was too dense. Her eyes were too focused, too intense, too serious about making sure he believed her. The hall was too narrow. It would take two steps to shove her up against a wall.

He tilted the flashlight aimed at his belly up into her face, making her wince. "You don't have to whisper," he said.

She turned around and swept the light over the dark hall-way. "They say the hotel is haunted."

"What building in town isn't?" he said.

The flashlight glinted off a porthole window at the end of the hall, and he followed her as she hurried to it, glad to push through the swinging door and into the hotel lobby, glad to take a breath, even if it was a stale-air-and-mold breath, free of Gillian's admiration. Her admiring him didn't help his cause.

The turn-of-the-century elegance of the lobby was a welcome distraction. "Holy shit," he said as he looked around. Art deco transom windows above the boarded-up revolving door let in natural, diffused light.

"The Elkhart Hotel was built to show off all the new money pouring into Freedom," Gillian said, as they moved farther into the space. "FDR stayed here before he was FDR. So did a vice president and movie stars."

The lobby had high ceilings decorated in elaborate plaster rosettes and plaster ivy as delicate as wedding cake frosting winding down thick ionic pillars. There was a mammoth marble-topped desk for check-in. The floor was made up of various marbles fitted into intricate Grecian designs.

Gillian slid cross-legged down onto it and immediately began pulling out a folder, a tablet, and a measuring tape from her bag. Nicky moved closer to the boarded-up windows where he could get a wide view of the lobby, the entrance to the fine dining room, and—most specifically—a view of her sitting hunched over her folder in the middle of all that decadence.

He pulled his sketch pad and pencils out of his backpack, chose a few pencils from their case and stuck the extras in his pocket, and, still standing, began to draw.

"It says that when downtown hotels became less popular because people wanted to stay in motels near the highway, the Elkhart Hotel was able to stay viable longer because of the thriving Mexican community," she said, her hair around her cheeks.

She always hunched over her work that way. "But once the last oil-and-gas venture in town closed up shop in the eighties and the railroad stopped running passenger service through Freedom, the hotel had to close."

"Do you know anything about the people who worked here?" he asked, feeling that warm comfort surround him as the pencil shushed across the page.

She flipped through a few pages. "There's a lot of praise for the first general manager and his wife, Hester. They were here during its heyday." She kept reading. "Or...wait...his wife's name was Cariña." She flipped through more pages. "Actually I'm seeing both names but Hester's more."

"Maybe Cariña was his first wife and Hester was the second?" Nicky suggested.

"Yeah..." Gillian continued to look over the documents. "I read that a Cariña de la Cruz ran a successful lavandería out of the Day Building on Milagro Street. I wonder if it's the same woman."

"Pictures?"

She quickly rifled through the folder. "Not in here."

"Show me any that you find," he said. "I'm including real people in the mural. I'll listen to any stories you've got." *You can sit in my lap,* he thought as he etched out the floor medallion near her shoe. *You can whisper them into my ear.*

"If it's the same Cariña, I'm curious about the lady who went from washwoman to running a fancy hotel," she mused.

He ran his pencil over her slim, crossed legs, her careless spine, the tips of sweaty curls sitting on her neck. This was fucking perfect. He'd wanted to spend time with her and he'd wanted her to talk to him and now they could spend hours together, talking about others' stories and bypassing their own as he committed her to his sketch pad. He would avoid dark hallways and mind-blowing declarations.

He could help her. He could lend an ear and a shoulder and help her be just bad enough to break her curse. At the end of the summer, he'd wave goodbye as she once again set out for world domination.

Until then, he would indulge his thirst.

That's why he'd never gotten impatient with his brother. He knew how bad addiction could hurt.

CHAPTER 8

After work on Tuesday, Gillian had just wrapped a towel around herself from her early evening shower when her mother pushed open the bathroom door without knocking. That'd been a common occurrence growing up since there'd only been one bathroom for the five of them, a special kind of hell. But now there was a gleaming new half bath on the first floor courtesy of her father's best-selling fiction series.

Mary Armstead didn't have to use the bathroom. Instead, she informed Gillian that she, Tucker, and the children would be leaving soon to eat dinner at Loretta's.

Her mom's irritating, placating smile was clear: If Gillian wanted to spend time with her children after a day at work, she would come as well. If she wanted to cook for herself after a day of moving boxes and rifling through papers and racing Nicky down the stairs of a second-story Milagro Street building after the pile of rags he pushed aside unleashed a family of mice, then the kitchen was hers. But her mother was done making Gillian's efforts to stay hidden easy.

Tonight, Gillian had wanted to rinse off, take in the good TLC of her children's company, then get started on her third round of nudging former colleagues. Her inbox still remained depressingly empty. She needed to find a job and a town and a school, most likely a private one since she doubted a public school could meet Ben's needs. To afford a private school, she would need Thomas's child support. The reality of that pressure was as daunting as the kids' impending trip to visit their father. She'd received an email from Thomas's assistant to begin planning the logistics of the trip.

Thomas was using a bar he'd never stepped a foot in to make her squirm. What would he do when he had control of the two small children he knew were her life?

Her family didn't know the kind of pressure she was under because she hadn't told them. No one knew except her attorney, her therapist, and Nicky. Nicky. Nicky, whose company for the last few workdays was as pleasurable as it was awful. He was as mouthwatering as Valrhona chocolate with his shirt off and as comforting as a nap on a picnic blanket when they were wandering around together. He was someone else's. When he drew, it felt like he was watching only her.

But she couldn't really expect to hide from everyone but Nicky all summer. Perhaps she'd reached a tipping point where her absence was drawing *more* attention. It was Tuesday, which was quiet at the bar, and the early hour her parents liked to eat would mean that it would be even quieter. There would be no reason for Alex to be there.

"I'll be ready in twenty minutes," she said through gritted teeth.

Twenty minutes didn't give her enough time to straighten, so she parted her wet hair into a low ponytail, threw on a cute black Lacoste polo dress with a beige cashmere cardigan and slid on black Tieks with their signature teal bottoms. The pearl earrings she usually wore with this were replaced with silver balls.

It was as good as it was going to get for the Pride of the East Side's first night out.

As she led the kids into Loretta's, Ben flinched at the cow-bells clanging above the door and Naomi had to swing the saloon doors back and forth and her dad murmured something that made her mom blush. She said an ineffective prayer to the unobtrusive San Judas Tadeo medal Mary had nailed into the doorframe when she saw her handsome, grinning first cousin, Joe Torres, hustling toward her. San Judas was the patron saint of lost causes.

"I was close to calling Tía Mary a liar for saying you were back in town," Joe said, hugging her, wearing that infamous grin that had made him everyone's favorite since he'd popped out of the womb. "You beating back job recruiters with a stick, Juliana?"

He followed their group to one of the new booths that lined the outskirt of the bar.

"It's been busy," Gillian demurred as she scooted in next to Ben, and Naomi crawled over Tucker to sit between the grand-parents. Gillian pulled the sugar packets out of her daughter's reach.

Joe's smile softened as he looked down on her, his elbow on the top of the bench, looking fit in a Torres Construction polo and jeans. "How's it going really?"

Joe was two years older than Gillian, the oldest cousin from Gillian's generation, and had always looked out for all of them. With this dark cropped curls, great body, successful construction company, and caretaking instinct, he could have had his pick of lovers and locales.

He swore he'd be buried in Freedom.

"Great." She smiled extra wide to prove it. "We'll be out of town before you know it."

"Sure." Joe was like a Geiger counter for bullshit. He leaned closer. "Sorry about your divorce," he said quietly while her family chattered. "I know the deepest spot at Big Lake, and I've got chains and concrete in my truck. Nod twice if you want me to use 'em."

Gillian faked a laugh then looked around for the waitress. "That won't be necessary."

"Uh-huh."

When she looked up at him, he nodded at her hands.

She had a neat stack of sugar packets on the table and the number eighteen wavering in her brain. Without her consent or knowledge, she'd been counting.

At last, the waitress hustled up behind him. She was Black, in her mid-twenties, with close-cropped hair. She must have been one of the new hires Alex had sworn they'd needed once the renovations were complete.

"I'm so sorry if you were waiting on me," she said as she set waters on their table. "I wasn't sure you needed me."

"Why wouldn't we need our server?" Gillian asked as she shoved the sugar packets in her purse.

The young woman blinked as she handed Gillian a menu. "I—I'm sorry. Alex and Sissy just grab what they need from behind the bar and put their own orders in." She straightened her slim shoulders and stuck out her hand. "My name is Dahlia, I really like this job, and I promise I'll take real good care of y'all."

She, Gillian Armstead-Bancroft, was Dahlia's boss. This young woman thought she'd been reprimanded for inattentive service by one of the owners. Gillian pressed her lips together, shook her hand, and swore to leave all the cash in her purse as a tip.

As Dahlia walked off with their orders, Gillian heard the cowbells clang.

"A little birdie told me my niece and nephew were here!"

Gillian shot a glare at Joe. He shook his head. When she looked at her parents, her dad tilted his head at Mary, who smiled beatifically.

Alex came charging toward the table wearing a black off-the-shoulder Mexican-styled dress that made her strong shoulders, massive breasts, and round hips look incredible. Her short black hair was shorn on the side and styled into high waves, and huge gold hoops dangled above her summer-tanned skin.

Naomi got an "oomph" out of her grandfather as she clambered over him and leaped into her aunt's outstretched arms.

Jeremiah, who was, as always, right behind Alex, stepped around them and squatted near Gillian's side of the booth, making his height less ceiling-brushing. "Hey, Ben," he said, smile lines shooting out from behind his tortoiseshell glasses.

Ben poked Gillian's arm. She scooted out of the booth then watched her son clamber out, place his hand on his uncle's shoulder, then look out Loretta's front window as they began a quiet conversation of great importance.

After a beat, Jeremiah looped his arm lightly around Ben's waist.

Thomas always claimed he "forgot" when he refused to approach Ben at his level during heightened situations. Then, later, he would bemoan the unfairness of not having one child he could "relate" to. That's who she would be abandoning her children to in August.

She blinked hard and felt Joe's eyes on her.

With Naomi perched on her hip, Alex began to spin, her dress whirling out around her. Naomi whooped deliriously, drawing grins from the few other diners.

Gillian's wild child of a middle sister had chosen so much better than she had.

"Alejandra sure was excited about y'all bein' back," Joe murmured.

"We're not back," Gillian said under her breath. "It's just for the summer."

Alex stalled out then stumbled a step or two before she sat

on one of the heavy wooden stools near the bar, her grin from ear to ear. Naomi bounced on her hip and hooted, "Again!"

"There's more work like that grant writing if we've got someone willing to stick around to do it," he said. Joe and their Tía Ofelia, who were both on the board of the Freedom Historical Society, were the ones who'd turned the society's eyes to the unique Mexican-American history in town.

She shot him a look. "I love you," she whispered. "But stop."

As the oldest cousins, they'd always been close, even though they had different views about their hometown. They both worked hard, dictated their paths, and felt the heavy weight of letting people down.

She glanced at Alex and had an excuse to step away.

"What are you doing?" she asked, striding quickly to the bar.

Alex was showing Naomi the buttons on the soda gun then shooting them into a glass. "It's good for her to know how the gun works," Alex said without looking up. Naomi wasn't paying any attention as she traced the bright flowers tattooed on her aunt's arm. "She might work here one day."

Gillian scoffed. "No, she won't."

Alex's eyes shot up and seared Gillian.

Gillian didn't know when her Granmo decided that the Armstead girls would inherit Loretta's, but she'd grown up knowing that she and her sisters would be responsible for the bar. When she was young and thought her Granmo was immortal, the responsibility of it had seemed diaphanous. From her Georgetown address, it had seemed no more important than a nuisance she'd one day have to deal with like her acquaintances dealt with their parents' second estates or racehorses.

When Alex called to suggest that they take over the bar after their grandmother's life-threatening fall, it'd been at the end of a week of Thomas's unending criticism. Gillian had planned the romantic trip to Vermont, so Thomas blamed her for the slush when their travel agent had promised peak skiing. That vacation had died the death of a thousand snide cuts, and Gillian had agreed quickly to being the largest investor in Loretta's.

Alex put Naomi down without taking her glare off Gillian. Her daughter ran to the table where Dahlia was delivering their drinks.

"I'm not here to fight with you," Gillian said.

"Then why are you here?"

"Mom—"

"Of course," Alex huffed.

Mary, in a soft blue denim shirt with a ruffle outlining the bib, walked over and handed Gillian her diet soda.

Alex rolled her eyes.

"What?" Gillian asked.

"Of course, you, as a *bar owner*, would order a pop."

Gillian bristled. "I'm being respectful, in front of Dad." Gillian disliked beer, tolerated wine, and only enjoyed the kind of cocktails that Alex made fun of. But she *hated* that her father's reunion with the daughter who'd rejected him and the wife who'd kicked him out now meant that he, as a recovering alcoholic, had to spend time in a bar. She'd mentioned it to them, out of her dad's hearing, more than once.

"Dad's fine," Alex growled.

"I know he is," Gillian hissed back.

"Girls," Mary said.

Gillian dropped her eyes to the restored floorboards. Coming home made her act like a girl who'd never left.

"Alejandra," Mary said gently. "Why don't you show your sister the renovations?"

"Why? She's not interested in the commitment she made here."

Nicky would be so proud of how dedicated she was to breaking her curse. She was a bad sister, horrible bar owner, broke financial planner, failed bruja, distant daughter, and the kind of mother who only left bartending as a viable career option for her children.

Maybe a tour would get her mother and sister off her back. "I'm sorry, Ali." She plastered on a teasing smile. "Look, I'm here. Let me see what you wasted my money on."

Thomas's money. She smiled bigger into Alex's threatening glare.

The bulk of Gillian's (Thomas's) investment had been used to dig Loretta's out of the financial hole it'd been in, make the bar square with the IRS, and set their grandmother up with a nest egg that Gillian was overseeing. Some had been used for the renovations, but most of those funds had come from the sale of a few cases of Prohibition-era bootleg whisky that Alex and Jeremiah had discovered last year. The age, quality, and rarity of the whisky had made it as big a discovery in the liquor world as Jimmy Hoffa's tomb.

Alex put both hard-working hands on her hips and blew a black curl out of her eyes. "Fine." It was an indication of how much her sister had changed since falling in love with Jeremiah. She'd once been the master of digging in her heels; she'd ignored their father for thirteen years.

"It's been so long since you've been in here, Juli, I doubt you'll remember what it looked like," Alex began with a put-upon sigh. "But maybe you'll notice that we hung on to what people loved about Loretta's."

Gillian ignored the sarcasm as Alex talked about restoring the knock-off Tiffany lamps on the bar, the carved dining chairs their grandparents had purchased in Mexico, the stained-glass windows, and the massive four-sided mahogany bar made from the building's original apothecary counters. The bar's large carved medallion honoring town founder and apothecary owner Wayland Hugh, who they discovered last year was a far-off grandfather, now shined with new lacquer.

Talking about the bar, Alex forgot she was pissed at Gillian. "Beneath the surface, everything's brand-new." The entire building had gotten new plumbing and wiring. There was a new sound system to complement the refurbished stage in the back left corner. The pyramid island in the center of the mahogany bar had been rebuilt to include more storage.

Gillian glanced at her mother. Alex didn't seem to realize that Mary had included elements on the island that made it a functioning altar and sacred space. Among the liquor bottles and stacked jelly-jar glasses and community notices and family pictures on the ofrenda were purposely placed white candles with a cross to summon the presence of God, cut limes sitting in a small plate of salt and cloves to draw up bad energy, and a small San Judas statue meant to draw customers and ward off thieves.

Mary, with her black hair pulled over her shoulder, just smiled placidly. The fact that Loretta's had had an in-house bruja for years but still had been down-and-out made Gillian wonder if Mary's magic was as ineffective as her own.

Alex took them back through the hallway to show Gillian the updated bathrooms then, with a showgirl's flourish, she shoved open the swinging doors to the kitchen. "Ta-daaaaa!"

Gillian was relieved to see the gleaming-new state of everything. She'd been worried about getting sued.

"I had to strong-arm Cici into helping me design it," Alex said above the roar as their head weekday chef, Barbara, worked the grill. "But this is pretty much her dream kitchen so when she gets done trying out for that reality show I told her that—"

"Cici's trying out for a reality show?" Gillian asked as she leaned over to kiss Barbara's cheek. Her mother's childhood friend could always be counted on to keep a level head when faced with the histrionics of the Torres family.

Barbara snorted. "Where've you been?"

Gillian untied Barbara's apron strings then followed Alex and their mother out of the kitchen.

Their sister Cecilia—Sissy or Cici, as Alex and Gillian called her—was one of the most sought-after sous chefs in Kansas City. She'd developed a new menu at Loretta's to replace the subpar food their grandmother had stubbornly served for years. Why Loretta didn't serve her stellar cooking at her eponymous bar was the biggest family mystery. Although Sissy regularly came to Freedom to update the menu with Mexican/diner fusion classics and train the cooking staff, Alex still hoped to permanently lure their baby sister to Freedom to take over the kitchen.

Alex gave Gillian a look over her bare, gleaming shoulder. "Glad to know you talk to her as little as you talk to me," she deadpanned. "Yeah, she's trying out for the next season of *Yes, Chef*."

Gillian's baby sister was drop-dead gorgeous, but her favorite makeup was none, her favorite clothes were scrubs, and her favorite conversation style was quiet. She couldn't imagine Sissy wanting to be on the popular *Yes, Chef* show, where talented (as well as loudmouthed, bold, and extravagant) sous chefs competed for the opportunity to win their own restaurant.

She hadn't wondered once about Sissy since she'd gotten back. Thankfully, as they walked out one of the two garage-door-size openings in the north wall, she had Loretta's biggest transformation to distract her from the reality that she was the worst big sister in the world.

The new beer garden occupied half of Loretta's parking lot. Alex and Joe, whose construction firm had done the renovations, had designed it to honor the traqueros that their family descended from. A bright red boxcar like the ones that had served as homes for the earliest Mexican immigrants had been turned into the outside bar. Railroad ties had been used to create walls, flower boxes, and benches. The outside bar stayed closed on Mondays and Tuesdays because of the lighter crowds, Alex explained, but it wasn't hard to imagine what it would look like with the globe lights lit, closed patio umbrellas unfurled, and outdoor fans spinning.

Alex had successfully transformed their run-down family bar into an eye-catching establishment that would rival the hippest spots Gillian had been to in D.C., Seattle, or Manhattan. Gillian breathed through her suffocating jealousy to say that to her beaming sister.

Alex, like Joe, had never wanted to leave Freedom. She'd been forced to when she'd gotten into one scrape too many when she was sixteen; that scrape and Alex's relentless anger after had broken their family. It'd been a long, hard road back for Alex to open her heart and reclaim what she'd wanted: the bar, their family, this community, and a new love.

Her sister deserved everything she'd worked so hard for.

When they headed back inside, Jeremiah and Joe were eating with her dad and the kids.

Alex nodded at Dahlia and motioned to a booth a few tables away. "We're still talking, so bring our food here," she said. "I'll go get drinks."

Her exquisite vintage wedding ring, which was wide banded with amethyst drops and emerald leaves, clinked along with her other thick silver rings against Gillian's empty glass. "Juli, you want a lime in your Diet Coke?" she asked, her cheeks curled up into happy balls.

Gillian just nodded.

As she slid into the booth with her mom, she caught a whiff of the rosemary, vinegar, and lemon recently sprayed on the table.

"You went a little heavy with the rosemary in that limpia," she said, looking down at the tail end of her manicure. Few knew that Loretta's unique just-cleaned smell was a result of the blessed ingredients Mary included in the cleaning solutions. Rosemary was an antidote to anxiety and depression, but too much of it could make someone sidestep the difficult steps of a necessary journey. "Does Ali ever notice?"

"She doesn't need to," Mary said quietly, linking her fingers on the table. Her mother wore the tiny wedding ring that she'd never taken off. "If I see one of my daughters in distress, I'm going to do what I can to help."

Gillian glanced at her sister chatting animatedly with a customer at the bar. "I know she's upset that I'm not more involved with Loretta's but..."

"I didn't increase the rosemary for her."

Gillian met her mother's dark, patient gaze.

Gillian had been incredibly proud when, as a little girl, she realized her mother was teaching her something she wasn't teaching her sisters. Those skills had seemed to sanctify her place as the oldest and the most responsible. They'd grown less important when she saw how little her mother could actually accomplish with her magic.

Now, not being able to access her brujería left Gillian floundering in a way that surprised even her. "Do you sense anything about me?" she forced herself to ask.

"Like what?"

"Like a mal de ojo," she whispered. "Or any other curse."

Instead of clarifying for Gillian whether she was cursed or not, her mother asked, "Have you prayed?"

It was like asking her if she'd performed the simplest addition. "Of course."

"Have you been sincere in your words?"

Gillian was the best prayer out there. Gillian had received a $500 scholarship and a plaque for CYO Youth of the Year. She was the most sincere goddamn supplicant there was. She glared at her mother.

"Then maybe you're demanding instead of asking. Or perhaps you're praying to the wrong power."

Her mother had just dismissed God's heart-flattening, daunting silence as a misdial. Her mother's motto was: "All shall be well, and all manner of things shall be well." When sometimes it just wasn't.

Her sister came back with three drinks and slid into the booth on their mom's side as Dahlia deposited their plates.

"I haven't even shown you the coolest stuff yet," Alex said like there'd been no break in conversation.

Jeremiah spoke up. "We can move to a bigger table if we all want to sit together," he called. Their five-minute allotment of apart time must have been over.

Alex laid her tattooed arm over the back of the booth to smile at him. "We're still chatting. You good?"

Jeremiah grinned and winked. "Only for as long as you want me to be."

Gillian, Joe, Dahlia, and the few patrons of the bar gave various groans of disgust and delight.

"Dad, do the kids need anything?" Gillian asked. *Please let the kids need something.*

"We've got it under control," Tucker called back. Ketchup was plentiful on Naomi's face and the side of his pale plaid shirt. "Mary, you left your tea. Do you want me to bring it?"

Mary twisted around as well. "Alejandra got me a new one. Thank you, though."

As her sister and mother turned back to face her, they had matching smiles on their faces. With their dark eyes, thick black hair, and generous bra sizes, they'd always looked a lot alike. Gillian was a little taller and built leaner like Tucker, her hair more of a dark brown and coarser. She'd always needed to curl it or straighten it. She'd never felt her brown eyes had the same sparkle theirs had. Since they used the same rose-scented hand lotion, they even smelled alike. They'd manifested similarly happy lives with good men who adored them.

She picked up her jelly-jar glass and took a long, eye-watering drink.

Alex shook Cholula over her beer-battered catfish tacos, the many bangles on her wrist jangling. "The private event space upstairs turned out beautiful," she said, taking a bite. They'd transformed the two former tenant rooms and a storage closet on the second floor into one large space. "But what's really cool is what we did back here." She jabbed her thumb at the wall. "I can't wait for you to see it."

Last year, Alex and Jeremiah had discovered a secret room hiding in the Hugh Building, the home of Loretta's for forty years. To their shock, upstanding town founder Wayland Hugh had been a bootlegger. The evidence of his illegal enterprise was in the hidden room behind the side wall, accessed by a secret staircase that ran along the back wall.

In their research, they learned that Wayland had taught his oldest son, Edward Hugh, the art of bootlegging, then rejected him when that son fell in love with Mexican Rosalinda Padilla. Rosalinda and Edward used their bootlegging enterprise to fund the establishment of Mexican businesses on Milagro Street. It was the Prohibition-era whisky of these two, the Armstead sisters' great-great-great-grandparents, that Alex and Jeremiah had discovered. To tell their story here in the Hugh Building was one of Alex's deepest passions.

If Gillian actually did throw up her hands and sign the bar over to Thomas, decide financial stability for her children had to be the priority, she knew her spite-filled ex would upend all her family's efforts.

"That hidden room is what's gonna put Loretta's on the map," Alex said. "But I need your help."

Gillian blinked. "*My* help?"

Alex put her taco down. This was serious. "Now that the renovations are complete, we need to relaunch Loretta's," she said. "Between the improvements, the cocktail menu, the event calendar, and the food, we've got all the pieces to become a real destination. Our story, the whisky, and what we've done with that room is the catnip. That's what's gonna get foodies blogging about us and travel writers coming for a story. They eat here and then they go to the museum, they see Nick's mural, they see the improvements you're helping bring to Milagro Street…"

The bite of catfish Gillian had eaten with her fork flipped queasily in her stomach.

Alex beamed. "Who knows what kind of difference we can make? We can cement Milagro Street so no one ever threatens to mow down the east side again." People had started calling Alex what they used to call Loretta: the mayor of Milagro Street. Of course, they only said it out of Loretta's hearing.

"You need to help me come up with a big event to reveal the back room." Her sister's perfectly groomed eyebrows were jumping. "Something to get people excited. You've organized galas, you know how to budget and how to talk to the kind of people who can put a new restaurant on the map. In fact…" Alex pulled her phone out of a pocket in her dress and opened up a notes app. "I can tell you some ideas I've been playing with then you can start putting together preliminary numbers and we can—"

Once, a year-and-change ago, Gillian had exchanged texts with her sisters every day for a couple of weeks, fueled by the idea of getting her spreadsheets to work overcoming Loretta's losses. Now, Gillian wiped her mouth, put her napkin over her barely touched plate, and straightened into perfect posture.

"I can't," she said, cutting her sister off.

Alex blinked at her. "What?"

"I can't help you." She swallowed and raised her chin. "I have two children. I'm looking for work. I'm completing the grant application. My summer is full."

"But…" Alex stared openmouthed at her. "You're here. Loretta's is yours, too. You're not going to help me?"

"I'm sorry, Alex." After she put the kids to bed, she would buy a bucket of ice cream and bury it in chocolate sauce. "But I have to focus on my priorities."

"Un-fucking-believable," Alex whispered, aware of the high

voices a few booths over. She stood and threw her napkin on the table. "You want to be done here? Fine. Now that the renovations are finished, it shouldn't be too long before I can buy you out."

Gillian kept her face still. How long was too long? Alex's wealthy husband was sitting right there.

Her sister buying her out ASAP would solve a lot of problems. The money wasn't enough to make up for the years she lost in the labor market raising children, but for a time it would help to fill the gap between her own theoretical income and what Thomas would have provided. Or she could do as Nicky suggested and offer the money to Thomas in lieu of signing over the bar. Handing over a lump sum like that to ensure his alimony and child support would appease his ego, wouldn't it? Even the diminished amount of alimony and child support he was offering until her children turned eighteen would eventually be worth more than the investment and be the generational wealth her kids deserved after being born to such a shitty father.

Alex throwing the money at her would prevent Gillian from asking for it on her knees. Her sister would never have to know what Gillian had contemplated. The damage she was imposing on their relationship could be repaired. They'd fixed their relationship once before.

Before Gillian could say anything, Alex went to the other booth, whispered in Jeremiah's ear, leaned across him to kiss her niece and nephew, then stomped up the stairwell that led to her office.

It was good she hadn't needed a response. For some strange reason, it was choked off in Gillian's throat.

CHAPTER 9

Nicky sat under a large oak tree that had survived the demolition of the former community center on Milagro Street and, behind the cover of his Ray-Bans, sketched Gillian as she finished off her chocolate pudding. His long hair had been a better prop for staring at her when he didn't want her to see.

"I know I've disappointed her," Gillian said as she scraped out the bottom of the cup. "But I wish they'd all stop acting like I have a ton of free time."

His only stab at erotic art was when he created a lithograph series of indigenous pre-Colombian people making love, but he could make a fortune sketching what Gillian's wide mouth was doing to that spoon.

"My family behaves like I'm still some pampered D.C. socialite mom."

He scoffed even as the reminder that she was a mommy made him flip to a new page.

"What?" she asked.

The knobby bark of the tree dug into his back as he sketched the outlines of the pale brick building across the street that they planned to explore after lunch. "Nothin'," he said, knocking his hair out of his face as he focused on the "Day Building" written in sand-colored bricks near the roofline. The building used to house the lavandería of Cariña de la Cruz, the maybe-wife of Charles Bowling, the manager of the Elkhart Hotel. "I just doubt you were ever pampered."

Not the way he would do it.

She put the cup and the plastic spoon he adored back into the brown paper bag. "Don't mention that to the cleaning lady, manicurist, and speech pathologist who came by my house every week," she said as she carefully folded down the top. She reused her lunch sacks.

He shoved tease into his voice. "No nanny?"

They'd talked about this and that since they'd started exploring Milagro Street, both of them walking a tightrope of conversation about movies and books and uncomplicated bits of their pasts that didn't plunge them into shit they wanted to avoid. She'd asked about his journey from Denver art-school student to Manhattan street artist to bougie San Franciscan and he'd told her; it'd been fun to tell her as long as she never asked what had sent him from Freedom to Denver in the first place. She talked about working for one of D.C.'s top financial firms and getting shoved in front of all the financial press because she was a young woman of color. She didn't tell the reporters that she was the *only* woman of color working at the firm, and the firm didn't interfere when she spoke into the microphones about the value of teaching financial literacy to marginalized communities.

He wanted to call up every firm who'd received her résumé and demand to know what the fuck was wrong with them.

Gillian put the lunch sack back in her big purse. "No nanny. Thomas was embarrassed I refused to hire one." She pushed up her large sunglasses so they held back her now-wavy hair and crossed her arms over her knees. She was in linen pants and a boat-neck top with three-quarter sleeves, a queen sitting on a broken parking berm. "My six-year-old, Ben, is autistic." She looked at him. "Did I tell you that?"

He slid off his sunglasses, meeting her intent green gaze as he shook his head. It seemed important that he meet her eyes.

Her chin notched up. "My ex-husband wasn't great with him. He wasn't great with either of them."

"I'm sorry," he said. Gillian and her kids deserved so much better than what they'd gotten. She hadn't talked about the man in days, which had allowed Nicky to avoid any talk about his "fiancée." But now there was something very specific she was saying.

He hung his sunglasses in the neck of his faded gray concert T-shirt. "William and I've talked about whether it would have helped if we'd gotten counseling for Lucas early on. I think the drugs were partly self-medication." He wanted to pull her close and breathe comfort and acceptance into her skin. "I'm not comparing the two. But it sounds like you got help for your son early. His good mom is gonna help him overcome what an asshole his dad is."

The way those wide, hazelly-green eyes looked at him...she turned her face away.

He focused on his sketch pad and began filling in the Day Building's intricate brickwork as he gripped his pencil tight. *I'll take care of you,* he swallowed down into the depths of him. *All I've ever wanted is to take care of you.*

"How's Lucas doing now?" she asked.

The brickwork looked like teeth. "Not getting into trouble."

"Is he still in town?"

He nodded. The farmhouse technically was in a non-incorporated segment of Freedom. "Tell me more about your kids."

In the oppressive high-noon heat and humidity, all he could hear was the shushing of his pencil on the page.

"They like snacks," she finally said. "And bugs. Naomi believes she's a butterfly, and Ben can spend an hour observing an ant drag a crumb to its nest. He likes watching out for his whirlwind of a sister. He calls her 'baby' and it just about kills me." She audibly exhaled. "He's high-functioning and I'm grateful that I was able to get quality care for him early. But he'll start school this fall and the best therapies aren't cheap so I need to get my act together *now* and find a job and start locating services for him and decide what I'm willing to do to pay for them and—"

She cut herself off and he put the pencil down before he tore through the paper.

"One of the reasons your family thinks you're a pampered D.C. socialite," he said as he closed the sketch pad and dropped it into his backpack, "is because you've been so good at convincing them." He zipped up his backpack and stood. "Maybe you need to let them know how shitty you actually are at the role." He put his hand out to her as she looked up at him.

I need to decide what I'm willing to do to pay for them.

Thirteen years ago, she'd been the one with endless choices when he only had one. Now their roles were reversed, and he hated it. Nicky wanted to pull her into his lap. He wanted to pleasure her into mindlessness here in the leafy shadows, then carry her to his Jeep, take her up to his loft, and love her until she passed out into the decade-worth of sleep she needed to catch up on. Then he wanted to write her a huge fucking check.

But what she might accept from her sister, what she didn't want to ask of her brother-in-law or best friend, she certainly wouldn't take from Nicky. She didn't want him to take care of her now any more than she'd wanted it then. Back then, he'd altered his path when he couldn't have more from her. Altered Lucas's, too.

When she put her hand in his, he pulled her to her feet and purposefully held her too close. "The sooner we lift that curse off you, the sooner you can make that son of a bitch pay," he said, letting his eyes roam her face before he zeroed in on her mouth. "Wonder what else we can do to help you be bad?"

She shoved at his chest like she would've when they were innocent. "You're a menace."

"I'm heaven sent," he said. He turned away and pretended to search the ground for anything forgotten as he adjusted his pants.

He trailed behind her as they crossed the street.

The Day Building's boarded-up display window was under a big, attractive brick arch. When Gillian turned the key in the lock of the entry door, it turned without the usual squeal. The building had been shuttered later than most on the street. When they walked into the dark, cool interior, they could still see signs of the discount shoe store Nicky had shopped at before he left for Denver. Metal display cases with slanted shelves were pushed into a corner. Gillian ran her flashlight over the room's high ceiling and exposed brick; there didn't look to be any obvious leaks and the mortar was in decent shape. As part of the proposal, she had to guesstimate how much work a building would need to be move-in ready, and her cousin Joe had come by one sweaty afternoon to give them both tips on what to look for. They'd assess the state of the fuse box and plumbing later, but Nicky gave a sniff and didn't smell any mold or hints of a rodent infestation.

His skin crawled when he thought of all those fucking mice.

Gillian settled cross-legged on the industrial tile. No matter how nice her clothes, she never hesitated to plop down wherever to pull out her folder and curl over what she was reading, reminding him painfully of that little girl he'd worshipped.

Nicky walked over to where some stray sunlight poked through the plywood and took out his sketch pad.

They'd settled into a routine.

The blue tubs in her office were filled with a hodge-podge of old newspaper clippings, family journals, East Side Community Center newsletters, several failed applications to get Milagro Street on the National Register of Historic Places, city government memoranda, train depot employment rosters, and pamphlets for long-gone Milagro Street businesses and organizations. She'd sorted most of them into piles according to building. It was during their explorations that she finally got a chance to read them.

She'd read out loud and Nicky would draw the rooms and the people and the stories. His mural draft proposal was almost complete. His proposal wouldn't show Gillian Armstead-Bancroft taking center stage in every drawing.

Gillian opened the folder in her lap and scanned the top piece of paper with her flashlight.

The Day Building, she read, was built to house a laundromat called Sunny Day Laundry. Laundering was a pain in the ass at the turn of the century so middle- and upper-class families and businesses—like the glamorous Elkhart Hotel—relied on professional laundries. When white business owners moved out and Mexican business owners moved in, a man named Hector de la Cruz took over the business and renamed it De La Cruz Lavandería.

Gillian flipped through photocopied articles from the Spanish-language newspaper that had been printed on Milagro Street, *La Palabra Verdadera*.

He saw her eyes sharpen in the reflected glow of the flashlight. "This article is about Cariña," she said. "She was honored by the Sociedad de Mexicana Señoras y Señoritas. They were the organization that distributed loans so Mexicans could start businesses. It says her customers were 'the crème de la crème of Freedom's best families and businesses.'"

In their pitch for Nicky to paint the mural, Alex, Jeremiah, and Cynthia (over really convincing tequila) had explained how the Armstead girls' long-ago grandmother Rosalinda Padilla had used bootlegging money to provide the microloans through the Sociedad.

Gillian kept reading as Nicky drew a crown of soap bubbles sitting on her wavy, highlighted hair. "Cariña was only twenty-one and unmarried when she took over the lavandería after her father's death."

"Is there a picture?"

She looked through the rest of the documents in the file folder, then shook her head. She closed the folder, put it back in her bag, and pulled out a thick book.

"Nooooooo," Nicky groaned.

She shrugged. "I doubt Cariña is in here but I might as well check."

Jeremiah had given her the book, *The History of Palomino County/By Its Own People, Published 1920*, with a lot of trigger warnings. It was written with fawning, overblown exaggeration anytime a white, land-owning man scratched his ass and with extreme dickishness toward everyone else. But it gave kernels of information about the people and places in the early days of Freedom that she could follow up in better sources.

They'd already gritted their teeth through it a few times.

Gillian ran her finger down the index page. "She's in here," she said. "It says, 'see Bowling Baby.'" She turned to the correct page and read. "The case of Freedom's 'Bowling Baby' riveted the attention of Americans from sea-to-shining-sea as this salacious family farce initiated by a devious Mexican woman played out in daily newspapers for months," she began.

She met Nicky's eyes with a troubled wrinkle between her eyebrows, then kept reading.

"Bowling Bank, the sterling financial institution funding the busy pumpjacks of southeast Kansas, was established by Latham Bowling and his two sons, Charles and Harold. Charles, the eldest, a bachelor, skippered the Elkhart Hotel's staff and facilities to its world-famous status. However, even the mightiest oaks can be felled by Eve's glance. Charles would come to rue the day he captured the attention of adventuress Cariña de la Cruz, who soon lured him into unholy matrimony."

The long passage read like a tabloid piece. Accusing her of fraud, "bewitchment," and being a "laundress with unclean tendencies," Charles took Cariña to court to divorce her by claiming that she'd faked the birth of their son. He said Cariña had feigned a pregnancy then claimed an infant from a local wayward woman's home in an effort to win the $5,000 prize Latham had offered for the first grandson. Charles even produced a woman who said she was the child's birth mother.

"The fraud was too transparent to impose long on the wisdom of the court," Gillian read. "Lady Justice prevailed when Charles Bowling was granted the relief of a divorce, successfully disowned the brat, and returned it to its rightful mother."

Gillian's finger stalled on the page. She looked up at Nicky but wasn't really looking at him. He stopped drawing.

She closed the book, put it facedown on the tile, then pushed it away with the toe of her loafer.

Suddenly, her head whipped up. She peered down the dark hall that led to the back rooms. She aimed the flashlight toward the hall, then scanned over the room's dark corners, the whites of her eyes growing.

"What's wrong?" he said, already snatching up his backpack and shoving his pad inside. His backpack was his go bag, his one item on a deserted island, and the thing he'd be clutching when he died.

She stared up at him, confusion twisting her face, as she slowly raised her free hand. She pressed it hard against her ear.

She started to pant.

With a start like a gun had gone off near her head, she dropped the flashlight and covered her other ear, still staring at him. "You don't hear her, do you?" she called, too loud, her eyes wide and filling with tears.

He was moving before he realized it. In an instant, he was sliding on his knees to land in front of her. There was only one *her* she could be referring to.

He shoved back his hair. "You hear her, that's all that matters." He put his hands on her knees and squeezed. He was here for her. "I got you."

He'd seen the white, misty shroud of La Llorona only once, when they were in the seventh grade and camping by the Viridescent with some of her cousins. Everyone else had gone screaming home. Gillian, biting her lip in terror, had kept roasting her marshmallow by the fire. So Nicky had stayed. So had her cousin Joe.

He'd again heard the fantasma's wailing cries when they'd been making out against the side of an empty barn across Old 85 from the river. He'd put his hands against the boards and kept kissing her, covering as much of her as he could and tasting her tears. Another time, in his back seat and parked on the shoulder, he hadn't heard her but Gillian had. She'd been on top but he flipped them over and rode her until she screamed.

He'd asked her why she went anywhere near the Viridescent. She loved to fish. She'd said she refused to let what they were afraid of make them afraid.

Nicky had his own river-born terror to manage.

Gillian clamped her hands harder over her ears.

"Breathe," he said, looking into her panicked green gaze and showing her how. "What's she saying?"

Gillian took a quavering inhale. "What she always says," she gasped. "Mi niño. Mi corazon. Mi vida." She startled and grimaced again, her hands pressing so hard against her ears he was afraid she would bruise them.

A helpless sob, as powerless as he felt, escaped her. "I hate this place," she cried, the tears in her eyes finally overflowing to run down her face.

Oh, fuck this.

"Come here," he said, scooping her up and pulling her onto his lap. She stiffened, but he wasn't going to leave her alone to this so he cradled her against him and sheltered all he could of her and, like she just needed a fucking break, she wilted against him and folded her arms around his head and buried her face against his neck.

"Nothing bad is going to happen to you while I'm here," he murmured defiantly against her ear. She pressed her face against his throat and started to weep. "I'm not going to let anything happen to you."

She pulled up her knees so her thighs bracketed him; she was trying to get as close as she could get. "I don't even have my magic to protect them," she sobbed against his skin. He could feel the heat of her tears and the grimace of her teeth.

People believed La Llorona was looking for children to replace the ones she'd killed. The legend was that she'd drowned them when she was spurned by her lover, and in her grief and regret, threw herself in the river. La Llorona haunted many waterways that Mexicans lived near, but for Gillian, who'd been plagued by the woman's cries her whole life, the specter was more than a folktale. Gillian now had the children La Llorona seemed to so desperately want.

"My girl, hechicera, I'll help you protect them," he vowed. In the shelter of her arms, he nuzzled her wet cheek, then kissed it as her body hitched and shuddered against him. "We'll get your magic back, baby, I promise."

Her tears were going to wash them away.

He used both hands to pull her face from his neck and sipped at the tears running down her cheek as she clung to him. He kissed the corner of her eye. He wiped under her nose with his thumb then pushed back her curls to kiss her forehead, so hot and flushed. When she pressed that big brain against his lips, he wove kisses over her tender skin and bone.

She wiped her own nose and sniffed as he pressed soft kisses to her poor, battered ear then licked into the shell.

He bit the hinge of her jaw and lightly planted his tongue just behind it to see… She shivered against him. Yes, she was still sensitive there.

He rearranged her so she straddled his lap and slid his hands down her biceps, caressing warm slim muscle and bone through the cotton top, then held her steady as he sucked up tears along her chin and caught them before they escaped. Tears were powerful magic. He couldn't let them fall into the wrong hands.

Licking the salty wetness at the corner of her mouth was like going from satin to silk. She sucked in a quick breath; the fiery essence of her terror and frustration went off like pop rocks in his mouth.

Don't you fucking kiss me, he'd told her at the beginning of the summer. Now he was begging permission. He was asking to kiss her just like he'd asked thirteen years ago after he'd made her come without once touching her dreamed-about lips.

I shouldn't have done that, he'd told her in the shade of an empty grain silo, his long hair in his face to hide how sorry he was. How desperate. *Lesson one: Don't let guys skip steps with you. You deserve good and slow.* Then he'd knocked his hair away and leaned forward to kiss her exactly like he'd fantasized: good and slow. It'd been so much better than any daydream. He never imagined he could make her gasp and moan and melt like cotton candy from his kiss. When she'd reached for the snap of her shorts, he'd gripped her hand hard.

Who's in charge here? he said, low and mean.

You, she stammered.

Right. He'd given her his dirty smile while he'd been on the verge of coming in his pants. *Then let's just kiss for a while.*

What she hadn't realized then, hadn't realized until he did nothing more than kiss her forever against that silo, turning his head and tasting and memorizing it like chiseling it into marble and encouraging her to taste back, was that when he said *a while*, he meant days. His cruelty of no kisses became the camouflaged torture of way too many, days and days of kisses, drawn-out pleasure so she couldn't get tired of him too quickly, kisses that fogged up the GTO and had her dripping on a blanket in the shade, kisses that worshipfully traveled from her lips to her tongue to her face to her ears to her shoulders and then her neck, good fucking Christ, her neck, which he showed her was her Achilles' heel, exposed to everyone, any man could walk up to her and see it, touch it, stroke it, lick it, bite it, suck it, he whispered into her ear, but Nicky was the one who was going to take the most advantage, he'd promised her, swearing the dirtiest threats as he'd held her wrists behind her back as she straddled him and he'd kissed and pulsed up and she'd keened and ground down and then she'd come.

So had he.

That hadn't hurried him along. He'd just started carrying a clean pair of boxers in his backpack.

That girl wasn't the woman she was now. And he couldn't be that angry boy, not with everything she'd lost. This time, she'd asked nothing of him, but he wanted to give her the only thing he could—a moment's healing from everything that hurt her.

He held her precious head in his hand and softly rubbed his lips over hers, sucking up the tears that marred them. "I'll protect you," he swore as he licked at her closed mouth. "I won't let anything hurt you." Her sweet tongue gently reached out to meet his.

He slid his free arm around her waist, anchored her against him, and pushed into her wetness and taste, with none of the teasing he'd taunted her with as kids. After thirteen long and lonely years, he worshipped again at the altar of his hechicera's wide, wonderful mouth.

Gillian Armstead was a full-grown woman now and she pressed hard against his chest. She squeezed his hips with strong thighs, wrapped demanding arms around his neck, let him know with her sultry, guileless sounds how good he was for her, how pleased she was. The pleasure he wondered if he'd exaggerated in thirteen years of fantasies hadn't been fantasized. He curved his hand under her tidy linen-covered ass and rubbed two long fingers against her seam, felt how damp she was through the pants and knew she could feel him hard. She gave her generous, gorgeous moan.

He slid his tongue across hers, savoring the wet, visceral feel of being inside her again, and she remembered to open her mouth wider so he could fuck it. He massaged her soft, damp pussy with two fingers, this missed, soft place of her that he'd been the first to touch, while he fucked her mouth, took her in two places, and she bucked and rode and he'd taught her so well and she had him on her fucking leash.

He refused to think of all the blissed-out men who'd benefited from his teachings. If the wider world knew she was single, he imagined he'd be standing in a line of Ivy League lovers desperate to get their hands back on Gillian Armstead.

He plunged his tongue in deep to claim her and thrummed his fingertips just right. His hechicera came apart gloriously and sobbingly, her warm wet cunt riding the ridge of his cock.

He groaned and grabbed her and shoved up, coming in his jeans.

"Thank you," she moaned into his mouth. "Thank you for making her stop."

Minutes later, after their hips slowed and their kisses waned, she wasn't thanking him.

Their walk back to their separate cars was long and awful and silent.

CHAPTER 10

Confident that she was the most wretched example of a human being that ever existed, Gillian accepted Cynthia's invite to Riverview Park the next afternoon, planning to use her children's distraction at the playground as an opportunity to reveal the horrible thing she'd done with Nicky.

But since meeting them for Tropical Snos then ambling over to this bench in the shade, Cynthia had cooed over Gillian's belted Brooks Brothers summer dress, praised her nose-to-the-grindstone work ethic about finding a job over spending time with friends and family, and amped up her smile when Gillian didn't know about an event Alex was planning at Loretta's on the Fourth of July.

Like any good Catholic girl, Gillian had been looking forward to confession, condemnation, and penance. Now, along with her inescapable guilt, she had a stomach-churning sense that Cynthia was buttering her up. For what, she had no idea.

She bumped Cynthia's shoulder. "Would you stop. They're fine."

Cynthia kept her elegant, freckled fingers over her eyes. "I'm not lookin' 'til those babies come down."

Gillian's kids climbed the steep, ladder-like steps to the top of the two-story-tall metal structure holding the railings like she'd asked. At the top, Naomi called, "Mama, look how high!" waving wildly while her long braid swayed behind her.

Cynthia whimpered.

"You *are* high!" Gillian confirmed, waving back. Four slides of varying humps and slickness descended off both sides of the long, guard-railed platform and a fifth curlicue slide hung off the opposite end.

Ben calmly stood close to his sister. "Going fast!" he said.

"Like lightning," she called back.

This vast playground that they'd played on as kids was the only thing Freedom had to offer that Gillian had never been able to top. With equipment like its two-story slides, massive swings that let you fly when you jumped, and a real fire truck with a two-story fire pole behind it, Riverview Park was the daring amusement park of modern-day playgrounds. Thanks to the largesse of billionaire Roxanne Medina, who'd grown up in Freedom and still contributed to its welfare and upkeep, the playground had been shined up, updated, and expanded with equipment that met all kids' wants and abilities.

Gillian couldn't cover her eyes like Cynthia could. She'd created most of what she was afraid of for her children with her eyes wide open.

She bumped her best friend's shoulder again, this time gently. "Remember when I dared you to a race on the slides then beat you by riding down on a piece of cardboard?" Talking about the way-back-when eased the terrible sense that Cynthia was maneuvering her now.

Cynthia lifted her hands like two flaps. "I remember you launching off the end so fast you just about sprained your ankle."

"I did?"

"Yes," Cynthia said, smacking her thighs. She wore a turquoise jumper and woven platform sandals. "God forbid you don't win at something. Nicky piggybacked you home."

Cynthia breathed in relief when both kids survived their ride down the slides and ran off toward the monkey bars. "How's Nicky doin' anyway? I'd sure like to enjoy *that* sight out of my office window every day." Cynthia's toothy grin, her flick of her auburn hair, the blink of her long lashes—there was just something off and ingratiating.

The mention of Nicky made Gillian's guilt roil like food poisoning. She couldn't believe she'd led him into cheating on his fiancée. She couldn't believe she'd done to Virginia Ramos what Thomas had invited so many women to do to her. She could blame a fraction of what happened on the fact that Virginia remained a vague concept—Nicky never talked about her, never seemed to interact with her during the day. There were no check-in phone calls or secret smiles as Nicky replied to a text.

Guilt over the faceless woman she'd wronged kept her awake last night as much as the concern that La Llorona was showing up blocks from the river. Gillian had only been four or five the first time she'd heard the fantasma. They'd been driving home late from a tía's on County Road 85 and Gillian had been pretending to drowse, hoping her dad would carry her inside, when she'd first heard the wailing through the open window. She'd covered her ears and squeezed her eyes tight. She didn't want to accidentally lure the woman to steal Gillian's tiny baby sisters out of their car seats. Her parents had continued chatting like they didn't hear anything.

Others talked about seeing her ghostly robes or hearing her hair-raising cries once. But Gillian had heard her wails and spied La Llorona's tragic, beautiful face dozens of times.

Nicky had always been her confidant because he was also haunted by what happened to him on the river. Even though he'd been able to pry the huge wild dog that had attacked them off his brother, Lucas's hand was left severely scarred. Gillian had only known Lucas as a timid and easily terrified kid who followed Nicky as close as a shadow and shied from everyone else. Nicky believed his brother had turned to drugs so young as a way to deal with the attack. By the time Gillian came home for that long-ago summer, Lucas's drug addiction had become what his brother struggled to save him from.

Nicky was an innate caretaker. A good, good man. He wasn't responsible for the crush that was growing more oppressive with every day she spent with him. He'd been trying to protect and comfort her, just like she'd begged him to when La Llorona appeared when they were lovers, and it had all gotten wildly out of hand.

On his hand.

The memory of that pleasure had also kept her awake last night, turned on and sick with guilt over it as she remembered the confidence of his fingers between her legs, the crooning tenderness of his words, the demanding hunger of his kiss, and the allure of her favorite sex act, beckoning his orgasm out of him with her own demand. She needed to apologize. Again. Unable to face it this morning, she'd gone to work at the break of dawn, grabbed the stack of papers she'd planned to tackle that day, and worked from home. She'd figure out what to say to him by Monday. Or maybe she'd take Thomas up on his offer, sign over the bar, and light a match to her ties to Freedom.

Cynthia pointed a long nail, pulling her out of her fatalistic thoughts. "They want us to push them on the merry-go-round."

Gillian looked across the playground to see Naomi calling to them as she stood on the multicolored metal. There were a few other children playing and adults looking for shade on this Friday afternoon. A short, round Latina woman looked straight at her from shadows of the wooden pirate-ship play structure.

Cynthia helped Gillian gather the snacks and water bottles

then they started toward the kids. She flashed that nervy smile again. "I wanted to ask you about somethin'."

Gillian didn't think that she'd ever seen Cynthia nervous in her life.

"I'd like to buy your portion of Loretta's."

Gillian swallowed instead of speaking.

"It's a pretty great idea when you think about it," Cynthia said, quickly, her smile sparkling. "You won't be burdened with Loretta's anymore and you'll have more money to help you get settled wherever you land."

This was Alex's solution. Cynthia could buy her portion of the bar now instead of Alex buying it some mythical when. Alex had access to Jeremiah's trust fund, but when her sister hadn't hated her, she'd said that they planned to minimize their dependence on it to guarantee they, the children they hoped to have, and the bar were self-sustaining.

Gillian could give Cynthia's money to Thomas. She could get the alimony and child support he'd promised. Gillian would no longer be a part of Loretta's.

They reached the merry-go-round and Cynthia pushed it while Ben sat in the middle and Naomi stayed standing next to him, calling for "Faster!" before she'd barely spun an inch.

"And don't you worry, Alex and I already talked about it: I'll sell to her the instant she can buy me out." Her daughter whirled past her, laughing. "The bar will always stay in y'alls hands. It solves the problems for everyone."

Gillian imagined that this was what it felt like to be sitting at the opposite end of the large conference table in Cynthia's manufacturing plant. As girls, they used to hide in the wood-and-gilt-edged credenza while her father had meetings and served smelly brown liquid in heavy cut-crystal glasses. Cynthia's style probably involved less alcohol and more compliments for clothing brands she detested.

Gillian looked up and saw the short woman pull back farther into the shadows of the play structure.

The plan would give Gillian cash she desperately needed. It wouldn't cure her problems, but it would give her options. The family would be free of a nebulous threat they didn't know existed. She wouldn't have to disclose the harsh reality of her situation.

Like going through pictures in a shoebox, Gillian saw the beer garden and the boxcar and the new kitchen and the secret ofrenda and her sister's glowing face when she thought Gillian was going to get more involved. It was like going through the pictures before tossing the box in a fire.

It solves the problems for everyone. The problem of Gillian.

She let the metal bars of the merry-go-round bat at her hands twice, slowing it before she stopped it.

"Noooooo," Naomi moaned.

Her son was holding on to a bar and leaning back to look up at the turquoise-blue sky. "Ben, you doing okay?"

"Yes," he said without looking away from the sun.

Gillian took over the ride, giving the bar a shove. "What problem does this solve for you? Why're you so invested in Milagro Street?"

Cynthia gathered her thick auburn hair at her nape and shook it down her back. The blonde and strawberry in it caught the sunlight. "Civic duty," she drawled.

Gillian snorted.

Cynthia's grandfather, who'd founded Liberty Manufacturing, had always been a dependable employer, but he'd only done the bare minimum to keep up appearances with the city council and various organizations, wanting to stay clear of the east-versus-west-side politics. It's why he'd built his ranch miles outside of town when he arrived from Kentucky in the fifties. Cynthia's father had followed his lead, and so had Cynthia until she'd helped to defeat the mayor's plan to take over the east side.

Gillian pushed the bar again and focused on her whooping daughter. "I don't like this sense that I'm being manipulated."

"Manipulated?" Cynthia kept her shocked voice low. "I would never—what're you talking about? I'm trying to get everyone a fair deal."

Yes. It was a fair deal. Just. It's what Gillian deserved.

She began to slow the merry-go-round, keeping her eyes on the different-colored bars sailing by.

Her best friend stepped close to her side. "If I've done something to make you distrust me, I'm sorry. I'm just trying to help you before you screw everything up."

Too late, Gillian thought.

The merry-go-round finished its last rotation. Naomi staggered on the platform then flopped to sit next to her brother. "Baby," he said tonelessly as he put his arm around her.

Cynthia kneeled up onto the metal and gave both kids a kiss on their sweaty heads.

Then she stood where Gillian had no choice but to see her angry, frustrated expression. "It's up to you," she said, no drawl in sight. "I'll talk to you later."

Gillian watched her best friend turn and stride away. Her meeting with her therapist this week was going to be a doozy.

She glanced at the woman still lurking on the edge of the playground. "Do you want to play on the pirate ship before we leave?" she asked her kids.

The two exhausted and queasy muffin cakes were instantly up and bolting across the grass. She followed them at an easy stroll.

"Hello," she called as Ben and Naomi clambered onto the rope netting and began to climb to the bird's nest. She joined the woman in the shade of the tall structure. "How are you?"

"Buena, señora, thank you for asking," the woman responded, lowering her eyes. The heavy-set Afro-Latina woman was maybe ten years older than Gillian, with soft glossy curls cut in a cute, short cut. The woman pulled a Ziploc bag out of her large purse. "I hope you like conchas," she said, holding the bag out to Gillian. "These ones have strawberry filling."

The appearance of the round sweet breads with a crust of red sugar paste was the best thing that had happened to Gillian all day. They also verified what Gillian thought the woman was there for. "I love conchas," she said. "Would you like a blessing?"

Strangers seeking their brujería skills always came with an offering. Over the years, Gillian had received still-steaming croquetas, a bottle of orange Fresca, a gorgeous shell-pink blusa embroidered with turquoise flowers, and a half-full box of what were apparently premium Cuban cigars, according to her thrilled tíos. *Would you like a blessing* was a benign way to greet them in case they were merely generous strangers.

The woman wilted in relief. "Yes, thank you, gracias a Dios," she murmured, hands clasping together and tears popping into her eyes.

You'll have to talk to my mother was on the tip of Gillian's tongue when the woman said, "I need to protect my money from my ex-husband."

Unbidden, Gillian thought of the other woman she'd learned about recently with a crappy ex. When she couldn't sleep last night, she'd reread what she'd learned about Cariña de la Cruz. She'd been a successful business owner by performing the back-breaking and skin-burning labor of washing clothes by hand with lye and harsh soaps. Cariña sounded exactly like the kind of independent, pioneering businesswoman that her grandmother Rosalinda, an independent pioneer, would have wanted on Milagro Street.

And yet they called Cariña an "adventuress." Had she gotten tired of the hard work? Had she traded in her independence for a marriage to Charles Bowling, a rich white man from a good family, and hoped to make herself richer through fraud? How long had Cariña claimed the baby before he was taken away?

Gillian unzipped the bag and offered a concha to the woman. When she shook her head, Gillian began to nibble on it. "Tell me what's going on."

Over the next ten minutes, Yesenia Lozano told her about moving to Freedom two years ago away from her family in Kansas City to escape her lazy and manipulative ex-husband, the pan dulces she'd been selling out of her apartment, and the surprising windfall she'd gotten when her tía died and included Yesenia as beneficiary of the sale of her home in an exploding market. With the money, Yesenia wanted to open a panadería where she could sell her conchas, pan, tres leches, and Mexican wedding cakes, and invite her twenty-year-old daughter and a few cousins to help her run it. But her ex-husband had found out about the inheritance. With his access to her social security number and birthdate, he'd already ruined her credit once.

When her friend working at Tropical Sno texted her about the local bruja heading to the park with her kids, Yesenia had decided to try to get the protection that identity theft counselors and her bank couldn't provide.

As Yesenia wiped tears from her face, Gillian gave herself a moment by searching through her purse with her free hand for a Kleenex. Her other hand held another moist, flavorful concha. The filling was made with fresh strawberries, vanilla, and a hint of mint. Her brain was working too fast for her to speak, like an old processor whirring to life.

Yesenia was the rare Latina recipient of inherited wealth. Only five percent of Latinos inherited money compared with twenty-six percent of non-Latino whites who received it. That number was one small part of why the median fortune of Latino households was nine percent of white households, $14,000 vs. $160,000.

And while women usually managed the household assets,

the system wasn't set up to empower women to become financially literate. Too many women in Yesenia's situation—divorced, undereducated about the financial system, and afraid of being taken advantage of—didn't receive good guidance to help them avoid poor financial decisions and reap the benefits of economic windfalls.

Gillian had done her own "financial planning" in the midst of discovering that Thomas had been spying on her while they were separated. She was certain he'd wanted her to discover it. She'd signed a divorce agreement that provided her nothing and now she was forced to consider selling her own inheritance, her family's bar.

Gillian could help Yesenia.

She pressed the tissue into the woman's hand. "I'll connect you with my mother. She can work a Santo Miguel novena to protect your dollars." As Yesenia gave a soft sob of relief, Gillian squeezed her hand. "But I can help make your money so powerful that your ex can never touch it."

Not all of Gillian's magic had abandoned her.

CHAPTER 11

"But I *like* Freedom."

The sharp voice of the woman in Gillian's office traveled across the train station to where Nicky was doing color corrections on his iPad at his standing desk, putting the final touches on his proposal for the mural. The Freedom Historical Society had been wholehearted fans of his concept so far and he'd be able to send the sketch to Jeremiah by the end of the day as long as he kept his attention off the meeting he didn't know anything about and hadn't been invited to listen in on.

He wondered if Gillian kept her door open because it got stifling in her office. The air-conditioning was fixed but the contractor was still stopping by to tinker with the flow and venting in the hundred-year-old building. Nicky couldn't ask her.

Since he'd touched her five days ago, they'd barely spoken at all.

Now he could hear Gillian trying to pacify the woman she'd called Yesenia. "With a business loan, you'll have options," she said. "You can start a panadería someplace with customers who have a higher median income and education level. You don't want to get stuck here when you have the opportunity for a better—"

"I have friends here," Yesenia said defensively. "Father Juan said he'd order my pan for the dinner after the Spanish Mass on Wednesdays y mi amiga at the nursing home is going to order from me, too. Maybe they're not *educated*, señora." Nicky heard her voice quaver as she naysayed a bruja. "Pero ellos son mi gente."

He wanted to leave and give them privacy. He wanted to go into the office and support Gillian. He could explain to the baker Gillian had put together the investment plan for why she thought anyplace was better than Freedom, with its ghosts that popped up out of nowhere and bars that could be hung like a hatchet over your head and ex-lovers who pulled you into their lap and fondled you when they were supposed to be engaged.

When they'd finally been face-to-face after an uncomfortably long weekend, Gillian had said *I'm so sorry* and *my fault* and *I hope you and Virginia are okay* and, worst of all, *thank you*. As if she needed to thank him for lying to her and forcing her into this summer-long struggle where he made it impossible to touch her then touched her the first chance he got.

He heard a chair scrape the tile floor. "Muchísimas gracias, señora, but I'm just gonna rent a space as soon as possible and try to get the money spent before my ex-husband messes with it. Please thank Señora Armstead for me for the amulet and the protection novenas. I haven't seen that lazy cabrón yet so—"

"Wait...wait," Gillian urged. "I'm sorry. Lo siento. Perdoname."

"Señora, you don't need to—"

"Yes. I do." She sighed heavily. "And don't worry. You haven't offended me. I don't have access to my sacred arts right now, but even if I did, I would never use them against you."

He heard Yesenia's relieved breath.

"I have complicated feelings about Freedom, but I shouldn't project those feelings onto you," Gillian said. "I won't bring up moving again. That's off the table. That will leave us more of the inheritance to invest in higher-risk, higher-reward options to balance—"

"Señora, thank you for all of your ideas but this is not for me." Nicky glanced over his shoulder.

The woman with short, soft curls around her cheeks and a round face shook her head regretfully as she pressed her hands against the cover of a bound report in her lap. She looked a few years older than Gillian. "I just have my GED; I don't know how to do a business plan."

"And I have a master's degree and I don't know how to make arroz con leche," Gillian said, leaning forward from where she sat on the edge of her desk. Her pale yellow dress that buttoned from hem to cleavage was open to reveal one tanned, gleaming knee. "I can help you."

"Investing is for rich white people," Yesenia grumbled.

"How do you think those white people got rich? They or someone in their line started just like you, with very little." Gillian sat back so she could use her hands. "Why shouldn't you be the first one in your line who makes your money make money, who starts providing a little extra for your daughter and her children? You deserve it as much as they do."

Nicky turned back around and tried to focus on his work.

"It's okay for the unknown to feel scary," Gillian continued. "There are risks when you're holding a pile of money. That's why you diversify. You put a little here, and a little there, and a little way over there. Think about it like…dough. You take your big ball of masa, separate it into three bowls, and set them out in three different places. One of them is going to rise the most."

Yesenia gave that *tsk* he was used to hearing from the Mexican-American women in his life, that sound of *you think you're so clever* and *damn, that was clever,* and *I get it even though I don't want you to get on your high horse about being clever.*

"Learning to invest is just like learning to bake," Gillian said, energized. "You start simple, you learn the basics, you understand more as you do it, and you get better at it. How did you learn to bake?"

"My abuela had a tall bucket." The affection was clear in Yesenia's voice. "She'd turn it upside down and have me stand on it when she was making tortillas. She'd let me add the water, teach me how to knead, show me how to squeeze off just the right-size dough balls..."

"My baby sister used to make tortillas with my Granmo," Gillian said. "I had no patience for it."

Yesenia chuckled. "When I first started rolling them out, mine looked like Texas."

"Mine too," Gillian said. "In fact..."

Nicky knew exactly what story she was going to tell. He felt like he was sitting in that office staring in awe at both of them. He felt like he was inside her head.

"My friend out there, we've known each other since we were kids," Gillian said.

Nicky began to make useless movements with his stylus.

"One time we were at my Granmo's house and she asked if we would help her roll out tortillas. I'm the oldest granddaughter and she was hoping I'd take up the tortilla mantle. And I'm like... I used to be perfect at everything I did. But my tortillas... when my Granmo saw how they were shaping up, it was the first time in my life she laughed at me. She didn't mean to; she couldn't help it. And his tortillas—" Nicky could feel the arrow of her finger pointing at his back. "That jerk's tortillas were perfectly round every single time."

Yesenia had a lovely rich laugh.

"I could have killed him."

As the women laughed together, Nicky stared down at his iPad and rubbed his tongue across his teeth to rein back the surge of feeling.

His fake engagement was supposed to be the boundary keeping them apart. But he kept moving the line. He kept inching closer, telling himself he could help her "this much," that he could make sure she was okay, that he could listen to her, then talk to her, then touch her under the guise of comfort. Seduce her under the cover of breaking her curse.

His perfect girl had always had a kink about breaking the rules. Had she gotten off so hard in the Day Building because they shouldn't have been together at all? Right now, he was wrestling with a boundary-smashing urge to tell her that he'd lied. He wasn't engaged. She'd done nothing wrong. She could be pissed at him.

Then, maybe, she'd want to sign up to be his.

The last time he had this urge to break open his rib cage and show her that her name was branded on his heart, Nicky had made a decision that had landed his baby brother in a pit of addiction that all of Nicky's fortune and fame and lock-picking skills couldn't pull him out of. Lucas had never escaped and the cadejo had hounded Nicky for his betrayal. The cadejo hadn't appeared to him in the months since his brother's death and the absence of the heaving, snarling, dripping-fanged black dog felt like an even bigger condemnation of what Nicky had done. Every moment of quiet ticked off a second of trauma-free peace his brother hadn't enjoyed since he was seven.

Even if Gillian finally saw him as more than a temporary solution to an immediate problem, a bad boy to help this good girl, Nicky would still owe his brother. He had an unending debt to pay.

He gripped the desk like an anchor.

When their laughter died down, Gillian said, "I can be your abuela of investing; I can teach you how to be good at that, too."

"Can I think about it?" Yesenia said quietly.

"Of course." Gillian sounded entirely unfazed. She'd saved this meeting all by herself. She hadn't needed his rescue.

"This is a big decision," she continued. "Read over the proposal I put together, take your time. Or..." She huffed uncomfortably. "Take a week or two. I'm only going to be here until the end of the summer. I'll still manage the accounts and meet with you after I move but this will be easier if we take the initial steps while I'm in town."

The train station's door screeched open. Nicky turned to see a big man filling the sunny portal. He only knew one guy with shoulders that wide.

"Nick, come to lunch," the professor called.

He no longer had an excuse to eavesdrop on Gillian's conversation. "Sure," he said, grabbing his backpack. As he turned around, Alex and Cynthia followed Jeremiah inside then all three headed to her office.

"We're getting Gillian, too."

Nicky stood there, trapped. This was the first invite to a group lunch.

He trudged toward Gillian's door. It was going to be up to her big brain to come up with the lie that allowed her to avoid spending time with him.

"Yesenia?" he heard Alex say as he reached the doorway. "What're you doing here?"

During his two weeks waiting for a glimpse of Gillian, Alex had greeted most people walking into Loretta's with a first-name yell and a hug if it was all she had time for, and a longer conversation at the bar or their booth when things were slow. Alex was always recommending this person talk to that person, connecting someone who had a worry or a need with the person who could allay it or provide it.

Yesenia stood and hugged Alex. "Your sister is helping me come up with a plan for my bakery."

"Your bakery?" Alex asked. She looked at Gillian like her older sister was helping Yesenia start a meth lab. "What bakery?"

Yesenia launched into her plans to transform her at-home

baked-goods business into a storefront panadería with her aunt's inheritance.

Cynthia introduced herself and said, "Well, that's so cool. Gillian, you're just making friends and gettin' involved in the community." She nodded at Alex. "That's really awesome, right?"

Cynthia's stunning, Botticelli face held a desperation that probably only Nicky recognized. As another lonely kid without much family, he, too, wanted nothing but Hallmark endings for the Torres clan. The hope on Jeremiah's face said it all: this lunch was some plan concocted to get big and middle sister on the same page or, at least, reading the same book. They still had no idea why she was keeping herself distant from all of them.

I'm not cursed. I am the curse.

"A panadería would be great on Milagro Street," Alex said, peering at Gillian. "There used to be one here when Loretta was young." She gave her sister a small smile. "Granmo would love to have pan dulce in walking distance again."

As Yesenia started to reply, panic filled Gillian's eyes.

"Oh, I wasn't—" Yesenia began and then stopped. She laughed uncomfortably. "Milagro Street is great but..." She motioned to the street.

No one in the room had to be outside to see the empty lots, shuttered buildings, and absolute lack of a pulse except at the corner of Milagro and Penn. "I'd probably find a little spot off Main Street. Where there would be more foot traffic."

Alex looked at her, confused. "But there *will* be more foot traffic." Her defined eyebrows scrunched deeper. "Didn't Juli tell you?"

Cynthia glanced at Jeremiah. Their lunch plan was going to hell before they'd even decided where they were eating.

"Tell me what?" Yesenia said, innocent to all the looks bouncing around the room.

Alex slowly turned toward her sister.

"There are lots of changes coming to Milagro Street," she said tightly to Yesenia while she glared at Gillian. "Come by the bar and let me buy you dinner. I'll tell you all about it. Regardless where you end up, you've got Loretta's as a customer."

Yesenia thanked her and Gillian then hurried out. Nicky wouldn't want to get caught between the mayor of Milagro Street and the local bruja, either.

The slam of the train station door echoed through the building.

"I cannot fucking believe you," Alex said, her hands clenched into fists. Her ripped-collar T-shirt slumped down her bright shoulder. "You're working on a grant to bring businesses to Milagro Street and you didn't tell a potential business owner about it."

Her eyes fell on the desk and flared even angrier. She snatched up the proposal Yesenia had left. "You put together a fucking *binder*?" She slammed it back down. "Her opening the bakery here never occurred to you, did it?"

Alex's voice was thick with angry tears.

"I…" Gillian looked helplessly at her sister. Alex didn't know about Thomas's offer, La Llorona, or Nicky's forced attentions. How could she explain why she thought Milagro Street was the last place anyone would want to be?

She wilted as she gave up trying. "No, it didn't occur to me. I'm so sor—"

Alex cut her off. "I don't want to hear it."

Nicky wanted to stand up for her. He wanted to tell Alex to back off and give his woman some space. But he had no right.

"Why did you invest in Loretta's?" Alex said angrily, swiping at her eye, smearing her black liner. "Why are you here for the summer? How in the fuck did you let Mr. Blond-and-Perfect walk away with his balls and all the money?"

Jeremiah put his hands on his wife's shoulders. "Sweetheart. That's enough."

Alex's face crumbled for a second before she got control of it. Nicky looked away. He wasn't lover or family. He had no right to be here.

Alex sniffed angrily. "After the fireworks tomorrow night, I'm opening the speakeasy for an after-party," she said, voice determined and trembling. "Sissy's drivin' down from Kansas City and I've got contacts coming in from Tulsa and Lawrence. Nick, you're still planning on attending?"

"Of course." He nodded.

She was already glaring at Gillian. "You don't have a choice. You better fucking be there. Because if you're not, don't worry about ever stepping under that cowbell again. Cynthia's ready to write you a check for your portion of Loretta's. Then you can be shed of us."

The betrayal on Gillian's face hurt. "But, Ali, I'm not sure I want to—"

"I'm not going to let you keep hurting me like this, Gillian."

Nicky had never heard her call her sister anything but "Juli." His woman looked devastated.

Alex turned on a heel and walked out of the office. Jeremiah followed her without a word.

Cynthia began, "I'm sorry I—"

Gillian cut her off. "Not now. I'll call you later."

Cynthia turned as well, blinking hard.

When the train station door thudded for the final time, they were once again alone.

Nicky looked down at the black-and-white tile. He was trapped in chains he'd wrapped around himself and locked.

He managed to choke out: "It's not as simple as they think it is, Gillian."

"Everything she said was correct." Her voice sounded like it came from the ocean floor. His girl really thought everything was her fault. She truly believed she was a curse.

He had no right to help her.

He couldn't stand it, and he couldn't stay in here and not touch her, and he couldn't touch her. He turned and walked out of the office.

"Nothing is what they think it is," he said before he crossed the threshold.

CHAPTER 12

Gillian was a morning person who usually followed her kids' bedtime with her own. Nicky had pointed out when they were kids how hard her brain cranked, and she needed to be in bed with a book by 9 p.m. if she wanted to power down in time to be asleep by 10:30.

So even on a normal weekday night, she would have been exhausted by the time she followed a stream of people into Loretta's. But this hadn't been a normal weekday. The day had started with a bang as her dad supervised the kids in the backyard as they waved sparklers, threw bang snaps ("Not at anyone!"), and *ewwwwwwww*'d as enflamed black-snake pellets erupted in turd-like projections. They'd gone to the lake to swim and grill hamburgers instead of attending the family gathering at Tía Elena's. Then, after a day of baking in the sun, they'd stretched out on a blanket in Riverview Park to watch Freedom's fireworks. Ben was asleep in Gillian's lap in five minutes. Naomi had shrieked and laughed and described every sparkle, her arm wrapped around her grandfather's neck and clinging for dear life.

Now her dirty children were passed out in bed and her parents had showered and followed them and Gillian was showered and freshly dressed and makeup'd and so tired she could cry.

She didn't see her sister when she entered the crowded bar, but all she had to do was summon Alex's furious, dejected face to get a jolt as good as her grandmother's bad coffee.

I'm not going to let you keep hurting me like this, Gillian.

Tonight was Gillian's last hurrah at Loretta's.

Thomas had called this morning with an offer more tempting than all the others combined. He wasn't offering a house or a job or the money Gillian desperately needed. He was offering to limit his time with their children.

Just four weekend visits a year, he'd said. *It's really all my schedule will allow.* All she had to do was sign over the bar. *It's such a small thing,* he'd almost crooned.

It was no decision at all. She hoped Cynthia's money would suffice. She had to imagine that receiving that fortune while knowing it would put Gillian back at a financial square one would satisfy Thomas's need to see her squirm. Her only remaining hope was that her attorney could still find a creative way to squeeze some child support out of him. She would sell it all, struggle with it all, if it meant Thomas would have less time to make her children feel the way he made her feel.

Tonight, she would help out where she could and try to enjoy what Alex had accomplished. Tomorrow, she would tell Cynthia yes. At the end of the summer, when she and the children were settled, she would begin the work to repair her relationship with her sister.

She looked around and took in the fact that this place she'd known her whole life was genuinely transformed. Loretta and Salvador had set the tone early that Loretta's was a family place until 8 p.m. when children became verboten. Now she could see how Alex had turned up the volume on the bar as a pleasurable spot for adults. Her updating of the lighting lit the interior strategically and softly, highlighting the ofrenda island, the stage and the stained-glass windows behind it, the darts and pinball machines in the corner, while keeping the new booths and other nooks moody. A couple in a corner booth were already grinning at each other in anticipation. The colored-glass lamps on the bar and the carved chairs were pulled together by the new plaster of paris masks and tin and silver crosses along one wall, creating a sexy, adventurous atmosphere.

Out the opened-up north wall, lights twinkled in the beer garden and the crowd ordering drinks at the boxcar bar looked two deep. Young people from town dressed in their hipster best bopped along to just-loud-enough music that a bespectacled DJ was spinning on stage. The crowd was a good size, big for a Wednesday night when people still had to work tomorrow but far from raucous. Most importantly, it was populated with people she didn't recognize.

"Thank Christ you made it." Gillian turned to see Cynthia eyeing her outfit. "You look sexy as hell."

Surprised, Gillian fussed with the light rust scarf she'd wound around her neck. She'd pulled a drapey soft-rose romper she'd never worn out of her closet. The scarf helped cover some of the flesh and cleavage revealed by the strappy top. She wore gold sandals and dangly gold earrings and she'd left her hair in a ponytail, but had pulled out the front a bit, put in a little leave-in conditioner, and let it curl. It made a comma at her cheek just like Nicky's hair sometimes did.

She'd painted her lips a glistening brown, darker and slicker than what she usually wore but she'd figured... "Do I really look okay?" she whispered.

"Like a million bucks," Cynthia said, grinning. She was wearing a blue keyhole top that displayed her breasts so perfectly Gillian wanted to take a picture and frame it. "Your sister's gonna be thrilled."

Yes. Exactly. She wanted to be of use, if only this one last time. The way she was dressed had nothing to do with the fact that, somewhere in the crowd, Nicky was here, too.

"Okay, here's the setup," Cynthia said. "Your sister has asked the influencers and press to wear the milagros hanging on red ribbons; that's how you'll be able to identify them. Alex is already serving in the speakeasy. Not everyone's gonna get to go; only so many people can be in there at once because of fire codes. But we're making our way through everyone she invited. Now if you can hang out with Nicky and introduce him to those people waiting out here then we can—"

"What?" Gillian stepped back. "Why do I need to introduce Nicky?"

Cynthia goggled at her. "Because it's awkward for him to have to walk up to and say, 'Hi, I'm the famous artist these folks are pinning their hopes on,'" she said. "We want Nicky to have a chance to tell the guests what he's doing and why. You just talk him up a little then let him charm the pants off everyone with his whole I'm-deep-but-can-show-you-one-helluva-good-time vibe."

"Can't someone else do it?" She'd imagined him glimpsing her through the crowd. She hadn't imagined forcing her company on him all evening. "Why me?"

Cynthia's auburn brows furrowed. "Because the rest of us are busy, you know how to network, and you're a *majority owner*."

Not for long.

"How hard can it be to hang out with a guy you've already been hanging out with for weeks?"

Gillian lowered her eyes.

"What's going on with you and Nicky?"

Gillian crossed her arms. "Nothing."

Bar chatter filled the silence between them.

"For the life of me Gillian, I do not get you." Cynthia's words were soft and wrapped in steel. "You are the smartest woman I know, but you cannot seem to comprehend the simplest concept of why you're here. If you refuse to lend a hand, then your sister is done with you. Maybe that doesn't mean much to you anymore, and if that's the case, then…then I just wished you'd stayed ignoring me instead of befriending me again at the reunion."

Ignoring her? She'd never ignored—

Cynthia exhaled a big resolute breath. "If nothing's going on with Nicky, then you won't have a hard time introducing him around. Make sure you tell them that this is just a preview before we relaunch the bar and speakeasy in an event that hasn't been figured out yet because your sister's being forced to arrange it all by herself. Now excuse me. I've got work to do."

Cynthia turned her back on her and stalked off. Gillian counted the number of steps it took for her to disappear into the crowd.

She'd never ignored Cynthia. They'd had different priorities in high school. Gillian prioritized top grades and résumé-building extracurricular activities; Cynthia prioritized a good time. But that wild party girl in high school was not who Cynthia was now. She'd be an excellent co-owner of Loretta's.

This would be Gillian's last time to contribute to the bar she owned and the dream she'd helped her sister birth.

Gillian scanned the crowd. There he was, sitting at the bar. She'd know that lustrous head of black hair anywhere. She swallowed her last bit of pride and started toward him, weaving through people, planning to make it clear that she'd been *assigned* to hang out with him. She wasn't trying to force herself on an engaged man. Again.

She scooched onto the heavy wooden stool next to Nicky before she could chicken out. "They've asked me to introduce you to the people Alex invited," Gillian said immediately.

"Hey." Nicky gave her that trademark heart-racing smile that said *Everything is cool, everything is fine.* "I heard."

For the very first time, the memory that the young rebel

Nicky had sometimes hid behind his sexy smile just like he'd hidden behind his hair bobbed to the surface. Anticipating the end of her struggle with Thomas must have freed up brain cells.

Nicky had given her *so many* sexy smiles this summer. "Is this okay?" she asked him.

His smile faltered. "Of course."

He wore a shoulder-defining black blazer over a dark V-neck T-shirt, and the colored lamp struck blues and reds in his hair. His skillful fingers were linked around a jelly jar of something amber over ice. Like a heart attack right there at the bar, she remembered the feel of those fingers pressing up between her legs.

A flash of red ribbon on the wrist of a man taking a seat on the opposite side of Nicky caught her eye.

"Hi," she said, leaning on the bar to get his attention. "I'm Gillian Armstead-Bancroft, one of the...um..."

"You're one of the sisters!" he said, black eyebrows popping up behind his silver-rimmed glasses. He was handsome with spiky black hair and a clipped accent. "One of the Armstead girls."

That's how Alex had identified them on Loretta's website and it was still one of Gillian's first identifiers. Long before she became the Pride of the East Side.

"Do you know Nick Mendoza?" she introduced. "He's a nationally renowned artist painting a mural across the street."

"Wow," the guy said, with no hesitancy to lift his phone and take a selfie of the two of them while he shook Nicky's hand. "I just thought I was going to finally meet the best bitch in bartending."

Her sister had embraced the title so there was no reason it should make Gillian flinch.

As Dahlia paused in front of them, he asked, "Can I buy you two a drink?"

"That's my line," Gillian said, smiling. It was unfortunate that she didn't have an order that reflected Alex's cocktail prowess on the tip of her tongue as Dahlia looked at her expectantly.

She covered by lifting off her stool to whisper to the influencer, "My sister accuses me of being a girl-drink drunk."

"Get her a rum and Dr. Pepper, light on the rum, a little grenadine, tall glass, and extra cherries," Nicky said.

The man chuckled. "You must like sweet."

Gillian grimaced. "I'm sure Alex would like me to order off the cocktail—"

"This woman likes extra," Nicky said, pointing his thumb with a charming smile. "And she's earned it."

"That's what I love about this part of the country," the man said, grinning. "Everyone knows everyone to their bones."

She met Nicky's dark gaze and it shouldn't have made her melt a little. She'd remembered that he sometimes used his smile to cover his innate broodiness. He knew that she liked sweets. And extra. The tall drink Dahlia sat down was cold and syrupy and perfect.

Leandro Aquino had moved five years ago from Manila to Tulsa with his oil-and-gas job prepared to hate it, he told them after moaning about the perfection of his cocktail. He'd been surprised by Tulsa's renewed downtown and its burgeoning food, drink, and art scene. Exploration became blogging became YouTubing and he'd been able to quit his job a year ago. He'd never secured a seat at the exclusive speakeasy where Alex had worked in Chicago and was thrilled to have a chance to meet her now.

As he spoke, Gillian nodded encouragingly and studied the milagro on his wrist. The quarter-sized tin charm was of a leg to bless the safe passage of the travelers who'd journeyed to Loretta's. The red ribbon deflected negative intentions and sanctified the hand of creators making videos and writing reviews about their night. Alex probably didn't even remember that the suggestion about how to identify the guests had come from their mother.

"Nick grew up right here in Freedom and is one of the premier public-art creators in the country," she told Leandro. "His work has been commissioned for well-known spaces in San Francisco, Denver, Boston, New York. But some of his most popular pieces are the ones that just *mysteriously* show up overnight." She elbowed Nicky conspiratorially while she smiled at Leandro. "One of his pieces along an interior playground wall in El Paso helped preserve a well-loved neighborhood park the day before it was to be bulldozed by the city. Another in Minneapolis across the street from a decades-old coffee shop drew enough customers to close the nearby coffee chain trying to drive them out."

She caught Nicky biting the corner of his lip as he watched her perform. He put back on that smile as he turned to Leandro. "In Freedom, I'm hoping to..."

Nicky laid out why the mural was meaningful and what he planned for it. He drew out Leandro's thoughts about the impact art can have on a community and how a meaningful aesthetic had added to the influencer's memories of good drinks and great meals. Nicky's charm was strategic, but he was inherently a good and responsive listener. He paid attention to Leandro like he planned on painting him.

Seeing him be both commercially cunning and kind was not easing her crush.

"Please get another drink on me," she told Leandro, standing and nudging Nicky to do the same. "We're going to circulate but we hope to see you inside the speakeasy."

Periodically, the noise in the bar rose when the wall panel between the last booth and the stage swung open to reveal people coming through a heavy velvet curtain. What was beyond that curtain and how they'd gotten into the secret room was a mystery the exiters were keeping. Leandro was practically vibrating for his turn.

Gillian focused on finding people with red ribbons hanging around their wrists or necks, giving Nicky a warm introduction, then stepping back to allow him to captivate them. She worked hard to look engaged without giving away how captivated she was as they performed their song and dance.

She'd done this a billion times with Thomas. If she'd ever tried to catch his eyes to signal how successful they were in their joint bullshit or give a quick smirk while some D.C. blowhard went on and on about a house in the Vineyard or a child's travel soccer team, Thomas had never played along. Measuring up and impressing others was serious business. She didn't try to catch Nicky's eyes, but there did seem to be some shared understanding that the job they were doing was both important and silly, with the way he layered his credentials just a tad too thick when a couple of influencers from Kansas City affected boredom, or the way she made outlandish statements when someone believed quizzing Nicky on his art history knowledge proved their IQ.

They were both trying to keep their faces straight after she'd said, "Don't you know anything painted before Groening doesn't count?" She felt a touch on her shoulder.

It was Gina, one of her cousins and a longtime bartender. "Alex is ready for you and Nick," she said, giving Gillian a quick hug hello with a clipboard in hand.

As they followed Gina to the stairs, Nicky murmured, "Did you mean *Matt* Groening?"

"Yes." She kept her eyes forward.

"You've just rearranged that guy's whole worldview. There's going to be a think piece about how *The Simpsons* finally ignited art that mattered and it's going to be all your fault."

She bit her lip against grinning.

Gina led them upstairs. Alex had improved this staircase with better lighting and sturdy handrails after their grandmother's fall. Leandro and a few other guests were following eagerly behind.

"How old's this building?" Leandro asked, marveling at the stained-glass windows.

Gillian gave them a little history of the town founder who'd built the Hugh Building and who would come to despise the Mexican residents and business owners who surrounded it. "Alex actually found out last year that we're related to Wayland Hugh," she said as they topped the stairs. "So that's complicated."

A young woman with a nose ring said, "I heard the building was haunted."

"I will neither confirm nor deny," Gillian said. She pointed at the milagros hanging off red ribbons on each hallway door. "I *will* say that these milagros used to change regularly, and all of us assumed it was one of us doing it."

When Gina opened the door into the private event space that had once been tenant rooms, Gillian marveled along with the group at the rich blue velvet covering the walls, heavy trestle tables of dark wood, and brass bar carts in the corners stocked with cut crystal and alcohol. She hadn't been up here since the renovation. The room's decor turned up the fun of downstairs and underlined it with a sexy opulence.

"Alex wanted guests to start thinking about the roaring twenties," Gina told the group. "It'll prepare you for what you're gonna see next."

In the far back of the room, she opened an unassuming storage closet painted to match the velvet's blue. She paused as the guests took in the empty shelves. Then she tapped a button at the bottom with her toe. It popped forward on the right side and Gina opened the portal to reveal a low-lit staircase descending into the bowels of the building. Gillian couldn't help but feel the same thrill as the guests *oohed* and *aahed*.

Alex had been ten when she discovered this secret their mother and grandmother already knew. She'd come home insisting Sissy and Gillian join her on this adventure. Gillian had always tried to steer her middle sister clear of her most dare-devil ideas, but even she couldn't resist the allure of a secret staircase. They'd snuck away and when they'd been exploring the dark, creaky, web-strewn stairs looking for treasure and booby traps (Alex breaking into cackling laughter every time she said it), they swore a pact to take this secret to their graves. Her mother and grandmother later told them that they could hear them whispering, shrieking, giggling, and shushing each other behind the false wall the whole time.

Sissy had cried while Gillian gathered all of her courage to pick a spider out of her hair and Alex swung the flashlight like a light saber to beat back any other insects that dared to touch their baby sister.

The original bare brick of the narrow stairwell was now covered with an imprinted plaster. Black iron sconces lit the way. As they descended, Gillian found herself sharing with their guests the great secret that would have sunk the aspirations of their town-founding, racist, multi-times-over grandfather: He'd also been a bootlegger who'd made his hooch right here in his eponymous building. This staircase had provided a quick exit through a hidden panel behind the kitchen should authorities come knocking.

The guests' faces in the soft light of the sconces were as delighted as her kids' when she read *The Christmas Story*. At the landing that once led to the kitchen, a false wall had been built. The staircase turned back, and they all trooped down to their destination, anticipation growing with every step.

At the bottom, Gina gave a complicated knock on a wide short door with a black iron ring. Alex had set the stage masterfully. Gillian glanced at Nicky and found him looking back with a grin as excited as her own. He'd spent a lot of time in this building, too.

What was revealed when the door opened made Gillian gasp as tears popped into her eyes.

She'd seen the blueprints and had signed off on the renovations. It'd been before she'd asked for a divorce, but not before she had an inkling that she should want one. She'd already been less involved and emotionally invested than her sister had liked.

No blueprints could match what Alex had accomplished.

The original space under the stairs had been utilitarian, long, narrow, and empty except for a few old barrels, parts of a still, and other distilling equipment when Alex and Jeremiah had discovered it last year. It still felt like a space that time forgot, with the original brick of the exterior wall and aged heavy wood beams across the underside of the stairs, moving up to the tall ceiling. But several crystal-and-copper chandeliers dripped from those beams, creating a sparkle that touched every surface of the low-lit speakeasy. Seats with emerald-velvet backs surrounded small, vintage bistro tables. On the long interior wall with the door that led back into Loretta's, a mosaic of hammered-silver mirrors made the narrow space infinitely large, a crystal ball of sparkling light and fascinated people. Across from the mirrors, against the exterior brick wall, was the bar, a magnificent work of hammered bronze with a marble top. Behind it was a massive painting of a beautiful and regal woman. She had roses in her pin-curled hair, pearls around her neck, a rolled deed to the Hugh Building in her hand, and the buildings of Milagro Street as they would have looked in their heyday stretching behind her.

"Rosalinda's" was painted in a large arching scroll over the top of the portrait.

Alex had named the speakeasy in Loretta's after their great-great-grandmother, Rosalinda Padilla, who'd helped to establish Milagro Street and haunted the Hugh Building until she could put the controlling document for it and all of the east side safely in Alex's hands.

Like a pull in her guts, Gillian turned to see Alex watching her, tears thick in her eyes. Gillian put her fingers over her mouth to hide her trembling lip, but she nodded hard as a tear escaped. *It's beautiful. You did it.* Another tear got away. *Look what you did. Look how you've honored her. I'm so amazed by you.*

This was what Alex had been so impatient to share with her big sister.

Alex quickly looked up into the rafters, blinking hard to prevent her tears from smearing her expertly applied cat-eye liner. She had guests to serve.

"C'mon over, folks," she hollered. She was wearing a siren-red shirtdress with a wide black belt, her hair was glossy and high, and she'd even drawn a little beauty mark beside her slick, red mouth. Gillian knew her brother-in-law; she'd bet a million dollars Alex had to fix her makeup and hair more than once before Jeremiah had let her go.

"Let me tell you what we're servin'," Alex said. She gave a detailed explanation of three cocktails that went entirely over Gillian's head but had the guests humming in appreciation. "But what you probably made the trip to Freedom for..."

She thumped her hands on the marble bar top in a drum-roll. "For tonight's guests only, in a one-time opportunity, we are offering twenty-dollar shots of Poor Eddie's Treasure, the Prohibition-era whisky made by our grandparents and stored in pristine conditions until it was discovered last year."

Gillian was as captivated as the guests in this crescendo moment Alex had expertly created. This was her sister's magic. Gillian had her numbers and Nicky had his backpack and her sister had this, her cocktail shaker and her appreciation for giving people joy.

The guests all ordered the underpriced shots—of course they did, to taste this rare aged whisky was why many of them had come—but they ordered cocktails as well, and as her sister began mixing drinks, dark, gorgeous eyes flashing as she chatted with guests, her lush smile brilliant, they all stayed close to the bar.

Her sister was the snapping blaze they all wanted to warm themselves beside.

Leandro turned to Gillian, eyes wide, his upper lip wet with the whisky he'd just sipped. No one was shooting this whisky.

"I'm used to finding diamonds in the rough, but this is like finding a whole treasure chest," he said, awe in his voice as he swirled the snifter glass with its narrow mouth and wider bowl. He took another tiny taste then closed his eyes in ecstasy. "I don't care if I have to sell my house to buy this regularly. When will you be opening up the speakeasy? I want to get my reservation in yesterday."

Her grin was making her cheeks ache. "We'll probably be opening it near the end of the summer, about the same time the mural is finished. We'll make sure you're on the mailing list."

Was there a mailing list? She could help her sister set up a mailing list.

The possibilities roared through her stronger than any drink. This was a last-minute event purposefully kept small. But what could be achieved if more time, planning, expertise, and sister power went into a launch? What could happen if all of Rosalinda's potential was harnessed and directed? How much impact could Loretta's have?

Their little family bar had already been responsible for inspiring a museum across the street and drawing a world-class artist.

The profit margin for most family restaurants was razor thin and keeping track of the numbers—how many customers fed, the most popular item ordered, the most profitable drinks and dishes—was one way to mitigate that. On one sleepless night, Gillian had discovered a perpetual inventory software that would allow them to track what was going in and out in real time. And while her mom protected the bar with an ofrenda and limpias, Gillian wondered where else they could work in their magic to heal and ease guests. Could they print their menus on paper pulp infused with lemon balm that would bring good luck and open roads? Could they create a lunch special for office workers on Wednesday, which was ruled by Mercury, that would focus the energies of the ambitious planet on their diners? Could they—

She remembered like a slap. She'd lost her magic. She was cursed.

And to limit Thomas's spirit-flattening influence on her children, she'd have to give up her involvement with the bar. She'd have to sell the right to work alongside her sister developing mailing lists and inventory tracking and menus. She'd have to sacrifice the inheritance that her grandmothers—Loretta and Rosalinda—had left for her.

But her children would be safe.

She looked up at the awe-inspiring portrait. Had Rosalinda known Cariña de la Cruz? Had she tried to help the young Mexicana? Or had she, too, believed she was an "adventuress"? Women like Yesenia, who left their homes, their families, their husbands, to find something better for themselves, would have been called adventuresses back then, too.

Gillian stepped away from the bar. Nicky, she was relieved to see, had been drawn into a conversation with a guest. Alex saw her and mouthed, "Thank you" as she shook a copper cocktail shaker near her ear.

She nodded but turned away quickly before Alex could see the new tears.

"Hey." Nicky's voice was low and smooth and as familiar as her heartbeat.

She turned back to say goodbye. He held up a fluted glass with bubbles rising to the surface and a raspberry bobbing at the bottom. "I asked your sister to make this. There's hardly any alcohol in it."

His thoughtfulness was a punch when she had no defenses left. How could any woman stand to go without him for a day, much less weeks?

He motioned to an empty table.

Resigned to the sweet misery, she made her way toward it and steeled herself to have one last drink in this terrifyingly sexy room with this engaged, beloved man.

CHAPTER 13

Gillian perched on the velvet seat and took a sip of the rosy, effervescent cocktail to stall having to look at him.

The drink was sweet and tart and refreshing. "Thank you," she murmured into her glass.

"Did you and Alex arrange that tour ahead of time?" he asked.

She could focus on his hands and avoid mooning over him. His long, artist's fingers loosely held the top of his tulip-shaped whisky glass. The light-shimmering caramel in the glass matched the color of his skin. She'd never admired a man's hands before.

She shook her head. "No. I didn't even know she wanted me to introduce you around when I showed up." Finally, she met his eyes. "That was her idea."

She wanted to be very clear. She wouldn't make him betray the woman he loved again.

His dark eyes flashed to her shoulder and when she looked, she saw her scarf had slipped and the rose strap of her romper was about to slide off. She fixed it and rearranged her scarf. When she looked at Nicky again, he was staring into his glass.

"You're a better owner of Loretta's than you think," he said.

She gave an embarrassed laugh. "Don't let my sister or Cynthia hear you say that. What Alex has done here is incredible; it has nothing to do with me."

"You're a better friend to me than I deserve," he went on as if he hadn't heard her. "I didn't know you knew that stuff about my career."

Revealing the facts that she'd gathered about Nicky by finally typing his name into a browser might have given away more information than she'd intended. She'd felt like the teenager she'd secreted away, the girl who would open her yearbook to pine, when she'd pulled her computer onto her lap in the middle of the night. She'd stayed away from anything written in the last year—she didn't need a face to put to his fiancée's name—but had been captivated by the man he'd fashioned himself into. Reading about how he used his talent and fame and lock-picking skills to make the world a better place was as enthralling as tracing her finger over his lips in his yearbook photo.

"You could've said some choice things that didn't present me so well tonight," Nicky said, eyes still on his glass. "I'm sorry if the job they gave you put you in an uncomfortable position." His jaw was rigid. That smile of his was nowhere in sight.

"I'm not uncomfortable," she said.

Without looking at her, his mouth twisted into a smirk that called bullshit. He reminded her too much of that boy who would hide.

"I mean… I am. But only because I'm sorry I made *you* uncomfortable."

She put her hand across the table to touch his thumb. He looked up at her under the shadow of his heavy lashes.

"I'm…so ashamed," she stammered. The tiny half inch of skin she was touching was hot and silky-hard. "Because of what I've done to you."

His eyes narrowed as he raised his head. "Done to me?"

She drew her hand back, realizing she'd been touching him,

again, without his invitation. "I keep—" She dropped her voice to a whisper. "—*forcing* you into compromising situations. I keep making you do...stuff...you don't want to do because—"

"You're really laying that on yourself, too? You're blaming yourself for what I did?"

He leaned closer. They were separated by the table and their observers. But the stiletto-sharp way he looked at her made them the only two people in this dark, sparkling room.

He tilted up his chin and made sure she watched his mouth. "How was me working you until you came on my fingers your fault?"

Her breath escaped her as her thighs clenched.

Alex slapped her hand on the marble, making the table wobble.

"You two are the Wonder Twins," she praised, eyes wide and smile wider. "I've already got people emailing for an invite to Rosalinda's opening when the mural is unveiled. Did you two plant that idea?"

She'd mentioned to Leandro that they'd probably launch the speakeasy about the same time the mural was done. She could see how guests had linked the two. It was actually a great idea, one she would comment on once she had spit back in her mouth.

Nicky hadn't looked away. He still wasn't smiling.

Alex went on, oblivious. "Y'all take your drinks across the street. Cynthia and I are going to send some guests over so you can show off the train station and Nicky can talk about the mural."

Gillian was grabbed and hugged ferociously by her sister. Alex let her go and took her voluptuous, crackling body back to her dreams coming true.

Never once had Alex *asked* if Gillian and Nicky wanted to go to the train station.

Nicky stood and headed toward the curtained exit. She followed him without saying a word. They skirted the excited roar of Loretta's and took their gallows walk across the lighted street. Nicky unlocked the door then held it open for her, eyes down. When he closed it shut behind them, the clamor of the beer garden went quiet.

Gillian had counted 253 steps to get into the building and every step had made it harder to draw a full breath.

"Why are you blaming yourself?"

She'd left a desk lamp on in her office and moonlight streamed in through the train station's balcony windows. It caught Nicky raw and unfiltered—sharp-eyed, bitten lips, tense body—even with his urbane clothes and good haircut. He still wasn't smiling.

"Because I'm to blame," Gillian said, confused and aroused. She hated being both around him. "You're *engaged*." Her voice rang out as she backed up into the vast space, empty except for the refurbished train benches pushed into corners. She couldn't believe he was making her spell this out. "You didn't want to kiss me in the car and I grabbed you and you didn't want to touch me in the Day Building but I freaked out—"

"Of course you freaked out," he said, belligerent as he stalked her into the room. "La Llorona was there. She wasn't supposed to show up away from the river."

She stopped short. He said it like the mechanics of a ghost's presence was something everyone understood.

While she'd never trusted Thomas enough to tell him about her sacred arts, a bit of intuition that she should have listened to before she married the man, she had once, tucked up against him naked in bed, told him about the beautiful, ghostly woman who'd appeared to her growing up. Thomas had laughed, then hugged and kissed and cuddled her after he said *oh, you're serious*, then spent the next hour and the next day precisely slicing and undermining her, saying without saying that she should *never* mention ghosts again.

"I just…" She tucked the curl of hair she'd left out behind her ear then immediately wished she still had it for cover. She started counting the tile. "I was afraid you thought I was making her appearance up. To get you to kiss me again."

Even though she trusted Nicky, even though Nicky was one of a handful of people who knew her history with La Llorona, she still worried that he thought she'd been manipulating him. Her good hard cry in the arms of a man who'd always made her feel safe had been as pleasurable as the orgasm.

His shadow fell on her as he stepped closer. The guests expecting that charming couple from the bar could walk in any second.

"Gillian," he said. Soft and demanding.

She raised her eyes. She'd never seen anyone look so sad and angry at the same time.

"Is that what he did, hechicera? Did he make you believe you wouldn't be believed?"

Nicky's eyes showed a difficult truth: it was going to take more than a year of therapy to undo the damage her husband had wreaked.

She burst out a laugh as she splayed her arms wide. "He sure did." Nicky's eyes narrowed, creasing that scar on his cheek. She'd rather be shunned than pitied. "You're stuck this summer with someone who chose a man who lacks basic empathy for others. I chose a guy I'm afraid to leave my children alone with. Picture-perfect me chose worse than everyone." She smiled wide although nothing was funny. "Alex chose better. My mom chose better." Nicky was the one person she'd let it all hang out with and she certainly was lifting her skirt now. "And you, with your perfect fiancée—"

"She's not perfect—"

"Whatever." Gillian waved away with her hand. "I chose someone who constantly talks about justice, about what's fair, who believes he's earned the right to taunt me with the thing

I fear most: that he'll make our children doubt themselves like he's made me. This morning he offered to limit his visitation. And you know what? I'm going to take him up on his offer."

Nicky's brow furrowed. "You're going to sign over the bar?"

"I'm going to sell it. To Cynthia. Give him his blood money." She met Nicky's eyes and told him the worst thing she'd ever done. "I chose someone who is emotionally abusive and then tied two innocent people to him for the rest of their lives."

No wonder La Llorona haunted her.

"Tell your family what he's doing," Nicky demanded, the muscles jumping in his moonlit jaw. "Tell them everything. Tell them everything you've told me. They love you, they respect you. If they had all the information, they'd support you."

She realized what he was saying: he wanted her to stop telling *him*. Of course he did. Because he'd decided to paint a neighborhood-invigorating mural didn't mean he'd signed up to refurbish the Pride of the East Side.

"Right. Good idea." Humiliated, she started to move past him, her sandals slapping on the tile.

He grabbed her elbow and swung her to face him. "Where are you going?"

For the first time in her life, she shrank from his touch. "If you could just handle talking to whoever comes over. I'm sorry I've been dumping on you for weeks. You have your perfect fiancée and you don't have to worry about—"

"Why do you keep calling her perfect?"

Anger flip-flopped with her shame. She glared at him. "Because she is, isn't she? A perfect manager who's perfectly beautiful and perfectly in control and perfectly willing to let you sweat shirtless in the hinterlands with some poor, pathetic, divorced mommy who could never be a threat to—"

He grabbed her by her other arm and raised her up on her toes. "Are you jealous?" he breathed, searching her eyes.

He stripped her to her skeleton. Why pretend she had any

pride left? "Of course I am," she said, beyond exhausted. "Of all of your girls. I've always been jealous."

He looked at her with the kind of shock saved for natural disasters. How horrifying for him to realize what he'd been working beside all summer long.

His hands were still manacled around her bare arms.

His upper lip twitched. "Virginia and I sleep together because it's convenient," he said through gritted teeth. "We like each other, we respect each other, we even love each other."

The words ground out of him like glass. His eyes were black and furious.

"As friends," he growled. "Only as friends."

She stared back, stunned.

"When we're together, it's because we're lonely. Not because we miss each other."

She finally made a choked sound of reaction, jerking in his hold. This was so wrong. "Why would you agree to that?" she spat, wanting to punch him with both fists. "How could you waste yourself that way?" She wanted to knock some sense into him. If there'd ever been anyone who deserved *the one* it was Nicky. "Why would you commit yourself to someone you don't lo—"

He pulled her close until their bodies brushed. "I've never missed anyone the way I miss you."

The breath of his words hit her lips like a lightning strike. The heat of his eyes, the promise of his body, the impossibility of what he'd said bolted through her and seared her to the spot.

"What?" The gasp came out of a different woman than who she'd been seconds earlier.

He leaned down so his mouth hovered over hers. "Did he take care of you?"

They'd firmly established that Thomas hadn't taken care of her heart, their family, or their marriage. That wasn't what Nicky was asking.

How dare he ask her that when he'd committed himself to something soulless.

"Not once," she declared, furious, meeting his dark, penetrating eyes.

He answered her anger by feathering his thumb across her bicep as he stared into her, the touch as soft and as light as a breeze, but it felt like it would leave a burn as bright as her sister's tattoos. Her unbound nipples were hard in the soft cotton of her romper—she couldn't wear a bra with it and didn't need to—and she wondered if he could feel them through her soft cotton and his sleek blazer. She could feel his heat. The scent of him filled her head. She could taste him on the molecules in the air.

He leaned closer and brought that succulent mouth close to her ear, dominating all her senses. "Are you telling me," he breathed, low and tempting, "that, until I touched you, you haven't been taken care of in ten years?"

"Thirteen," she snapped, giving her words teeth. "Just two lovers, Nicky. And only one has made me come."

He made a sound like she'd bit him. That light touch on her arm became a massage into the muscle, his fingers dancing like he wanted to grab and didn't dare.

"Let me," he murmured, his lips nuzzling against her temple. "One time. When I can take my time. We've both missed... this. We need it. This one last time then never again."

He said he missed "her" but he'd meant this. The way they were together.

She missed it, too. She was trembling. "But your fian—"

"Don't." His fingers spasmed on her arm before he relaxed them. "Let me take care of you."

The punch of that promise, the temptation of it, had her weeping between her legs. She wanted to be taken care of.

He slid that full, familiar bottom lip up to that spot just below her ear, a spot that only Nicky had discovered, as his hands went to her waist, his fingertips touching her body through the drapey cotton like she was a porcelain vase. "Consider what powerful magic this is," he said against that tingling spot. "There is no better way to be bad. Give me this one time to take care of you and let's break your curse."

One time.

She'd built her life around a moral and righteous structure to be "good," and while she'd wondered at the true value of the charity galas and parent association presidencies, she had felt true gladness when she'd been able to make another person's life easier. With her powers, she'd been able to lighten a mother's mourning heart or drive away an ex-lover's evil intentions. With Thomas's money, she'd taken the burden of the bar off her grandmother's shoulders and had given her sister the ability to steer her own ship.

But what, ultimately, had being "good" ever done for her?

She'd tried to implement Nicky's teachings with Thomas and be a good advocate for herself in bed. After their first pheromone-soaked six months, Thomas had told her that whenever she suggested he kiss her here or touch her there or move a little in that direction, he felt "emasculated." Maintaining the diamond-shine on his masculinity was more important than satisfying his girlfriend. And she'd become his wife anyway.

After years of masking the bitterness of her life with too much sweet, she'd finally accepted that her life needed the astringent limpia of a divorce. She'd gone into therapy and she'd forged forward on a difficult path and she'd refused Thomas's "charity." What had God, the entity she was being good for, have to say about it?

Nothing. God had stopped talking to her.

Maybe her mom, for once, was right. Maybe she needed someone better to pray to.

She tilted her head and met his eyes. "Okay, Nicky. One ti—"

She didn't get out the full promise of *just this one time* before he yanked her up on her toes and took her mouth, turned his head and sank into her like she was a cup and he had been dying. His tongue was fierce and deep, licking into her taste like he could trap and keep it, and his demand had her opening her mouth and curling her toes and jabbing her trimmed nails into her palms.

He sucked on her bottom lip then bit her chin. "Did he know about your neck?"

She wrenched her head away, already panting. "You can't talk about him, I won't talk about her."

That he belonged to someone else shouldn't have added to the guilty heat. He was unrepentant as he shoved her backward, held her up to keep her from stumbling, held her close as he tasted her, her mouth, her hairline, her jaw, her cheek, her shoulder, then pushed her down on a restored train bench. He looked down at her, splayed there, stunned and gasping, and she'd never seen his cadejo but now she'd seen a starving black-eyed wolf. He sat and surrounded her, snatching her up into his arms, shoving his left arm under her neck as his right hand tilted her head back.

"Are you sure?" she gasped out to the century-old medallions on the far-off ceiling as his lips descended on her neck, both a good girl's last flail and a warning to herself. Was she certain this unsatisfied stay-at-home mom could take on Nicky Mendoza?

"I want to," he groaned into the sensitive skin. "I want to, I want to, I want to. I don't ever get what I want."

Nicky was never petulant or sulky. Never demanding. The fact that she could make him all three shouldn't have made her so wet.

He purred to her neck like it had autonomy. "Baby, have you been ignored?" He licked his tongue into the thinnest skin between her clavicles where her blood and breath were closest to the surface.

He bit and kissed and sucked, running his teeth down the arch, impatiently tilting her jaw when she didn't give him access fast enough, feathering his tongue over the skin like...oh God, like... She squirmed against the hard bench, squeezing her thighs together and wanting him to separate them, to put two fingers inside her while he did this like that one time...oh God, that one time... He returned to her mouth, consuming her deep and wet without restraint or apology, and it was an unwelcome verification that her memories of how good they'd been together that summer weren't just a figment of a decade-long sexual frustration.

He let go of her mouth with a hard suck and leaned over her to meet her eyes.

While she was desperate, undone, gobsmacked, he smiled that greedy, thrilled, unapologetic smile she used to only see when they were like this. "Feel good?"

"You know it does," she moaned, lifting her head for more sugar.

He moved his head just out of reach. Her desperation made his grin grow. "Too good to touch me?"

That's when she realized she'd just been lying there. Between his body and the bench, her mouth had been his for the taking while her arms were leaded down with pleasure.

She remembered in Cynthia's car when she'd groped him and hurt him. But he said he missed her. Or this. He'd missed this. And he was teasing her, not mocking her.

Still panting, she slowly licked her top lip and let him watch her do it. "I like it when you take control." His grin dropped away and the perfect bones of his face made his expression brutal. "Your fault, not mine. You taught me how to do this."

"Hechicera," he growled, a threat and a compliment as he slid his hand down her arm and dragged her hand between their bodies to cup his cock.

Her eyelids went heavy as she touched it—thick, hard, a tip

that fit in the meat of her palm, long enough to make her fingers stretch to engulf him—before he was at her mouth again. She shifted toward him and hooked her arm around his neck, locked him into their kiss as she fondled him and celebrated feeling him in her hand again.

He'd taught her how to do this. He'd taught her what he liked. With her hand, her hair, her mouth, her pussy, her breath, her feet, her nipples, her squeezed-together thighs, the cleft of her ass—there wasn't an inch on her body that hadn't stroked his penis. Their arrangement was supposed to have been like teacher and pupil, but at the end of the day, Nicky had been a nineteen-year-old boy. Experienced, empathetic, and sexually mature, but still a nineteen-year-old boy and many of their instructions had been more like an older puppy teaching a younger puppy, both of them rolling around and trying crazy stuff and asking *do you like* and *how about* and *what if I* and sometimes getting it so weird that they had to grab onto each other, laughing until they cried, then start from scratch.

Only the feel of the strap of her romper dragging down her arm could have stopped her from stroking that dear old friend.

She let go to snatch the cotton against her. "Someone could walk in," she said, gasping into his hair, loving this leather-paint smell of him.

"They won't," he growled as he licked her sternum. "I locked the door behind us."

She let go of the cotton to force his chin up to see his face. The stubble on his jaw, the softness of his hair brushing the back of her hand, all the textures of Nicky that she'd missed. She met his black eyes.

He nuzzled those silky lips into her palm. "I don't care what your sister wants. I'm not making you smile when you're upset."

Nicky would have had more chances to shine. But if anyone had tried that door, they'd walked away disappointed. Nicky had chosen to disappoint them to take care of her.

There would be hell to pay tomorrow. But tonight… They had tonight. They had this one last time.

She looked into his eyes.

Hungry wolf. He smiled slowly and he might as well have licked a fang. "You going to let me get you naked?" he drawled.

Nicky had made her teach him what she liked. She liked the temptation and the tease. She liked instruction and command. She liked taking risks.

He leaned forward and nipped at her mouth. "You're gonna let me get you naked."

Shivering with sensation, she shifted on the hard bench to face him and give herself up to him fully.

When he dragged the straps down her arms, he did it slow, watching like he didn't want to miss an inch of skin he revealed. He sucked on his full bottom lip when he saw her tight brown nipples, and she gave a helpless whine and arched her back toward him even though they'd discovered together her breasts weren't very sensitive. Breastfeeding hadn't changed that, although it had changed her: she now had white, seemingly permanent stretch marks on the undersides of her small breasts. She wondered if he noticed. As he moved to his knees on the tile, continuing to slowly peel the romper off of her, he didn't look at her body like the changes motherhood had caused were a problem. In fact, when she lifted her hips so he could get the romper over her butt, he kissed and ran his tongue over the stretch marks between her belly button and the bronze-lace edge of her panties.

Her teeth were hurting her lip. She refused to cry.

He tossed her romper aside then stripped off his blazer, muscular shoulders moving, as his eyes traveled over her body, naked except for high-cut panties and gold sandals.

He was looking into her eyes when he spread her knees.

She was nearly vibrating with how bad this was and how bad she wanted it. They'd made their devil's deal and, who knew, maybe it was enough to break her curse. Maybe there was something good to come out of how selfish she was being and how much damage she was going to wreak.

He ran his nose up the top of her shining thigh. "You still smell like peaches," he murmured against her skin.

The first time he'd done this to her, kneeling in the dirt beside the car, was the first time he told her he loved her smell and he'd hunted all over her for the varieties of it—along the tender skin of her wrist, in her belly button, inside her thigh. She'd nearly died when he'd run his nose over her underwear and said he loved the peach smell there most of all.

"Are you sure you want to do this?" she hummed, smiling heavy-eyed, echoing what she'd asked him that first time.

If you want this and the guy you're with doesn't want to do it, you put your panties on and leave, he'd said, his lush boy mouth hovering above her pale pink panties. *Or come find me. 'Cause I like doing it. A lot. Now watch.* He'd always demanded that she watch and meet his eyes when she was returning the favor.

His answering hungry smile now from between her splayed thighs said he remembered.

She reached out and rubbed her thumb over his plush bottom lip. "But what about the taste?"

She'd asked him that first time if it tasted weird and he'd buried his tongue in her, then lunged up to feed the taste into her mouth. It'd been so dirty and so exciting that her first orgasm had come when he'd gotten back down between her legs and just looked at her poor, quivering clitoris.

The way he looked at her now as he licked her thumb made her release her breath in a long, shaky exhale. "You know me, hechicera," he said. "I fucking drown in it." He tilted his head and let her see his tongue as it touched the bronze silk. He tapped. Rubbed in a little. Tapped and rubbed in a touch harder.

She caught the front of his hair. "Don't tease," she whined.

He smiled without moving his mouth away. "You've gotten bossy."

She shoved up against his mouth, and he laughed as he pulled her panties down her legs.

His laugh rippled away to stillness as he pulled one of her thighs over his lean shoulder. He spread her other thigh wide, looked down at her, then up at her face. She saw his lip tremble before he pressed them together.

"Are you sure you want to do this?" she whispered again, so quiet the sound couldn't move beyond them. The three orgasms he'd given that astonished, overwhelmed girl that long-ago night—he would have made it four if she hadn't kicked him away—had made her wonder if she was falling in love.

"More than anything," he said, as solemn as Mass.

There wasn't a drop of laughter in either of them.

He kept his eyes on hers when he gently spread her apart with his fingers and slowly licked in with a gentleness that was a polar opposite of his hungry, dominating kiss. When he tapped her glistening, pearly clit, her hips twisted involuntarily.

He huffed against her. "Still sensitive?"

She nodded.

"Okay," he whispered, panting a little. "Was it like this?" Still looking at her, he licked softer, wetter, just below her clit, in little paint strokes, then around it, gently circling his head.

Oh God. She nodded again.

He put his full lips over that soft flesh and lightly sucked, his tongue fondling.

She uselessly scratched her nails along the wood of the bench and arched her hips toward him. He remembered exactly how to do it. "Your lips," she groaned.

"Calm down," he growled back.

But if he could hold this back, good luck to him, and she hadn't even realized her eyes were closed as his tongue moved stronger, faster, and when she opened her heavy lids and saw her hips rolling against his beautiful face, his fingers were dug into her thighs and his mouth was rising to a snarl.

"I'm going to fuck you with my fingers," he growled against her wetness, his lips shining with her. He'd entwined sex and talking for her and Thomas's demand for silence had left her impotent. "I'm going to touch you inside."

When those two fingers pushed into her, two, yes, always two, her thighs started to shake on his shoulders. She pushed her hands on the bench behind her and shoved up against his mouth. Her face drew up in anguish. She looked down at him, his flashing fingers, his gorgeous avid mouth. She wanted to grab his hair and hold him to her. She wanted to topple him to the tile and ride.

She was lucky he was muffling her cries with fingers in her mouth to substitute for sucking him when they heard the key grinding in the train station door. He grabbed their clothes then hitched her up and ran them into her office, closing the door and locking it just as the train station door squealed open. He dropped them below the office's glass windows.

"...don't know where they went," Cynthia said. Gillian could hear the murmurs of others. "I can tell y'all a little about this but Nicky's the expert."

Someone said something about "scarf."

Gillian heard Cynthia's heels against the tile. "Yeah, that's hers. She was here." The last thing Gillian had been keeping track of was her scarf.

"Yeah, not sure what her plans are." Cynthia was obviously annoyed. "But don't worry. Loretta's is in good hands."

The dismissiveness when Gillian was forced to make a decision she didn't want to make should have made her furious. She should have been enraged.

But right now, she couldn't be anything but consumed by Nicky because the instant he dropped her naked on top of his blazer, he shoved her thigh back with one hand, covered her mouth with the other, and went to work on her pussy like he was being paid. He tongue-fucked and sucked her like he'd been starving as the voices outside the office became the background of *might get caught*. Her swallowed shrieks clicked in her throat and he had to lean all his weight against her as she came explosively in his mouth.

When Cynthia led the group out, Gillian let him sneak her to his Jeep because she was useless. They drove the three blocks to her home in silence. He said nothing when she got out of the car.

She made it inside before she gave in to quiet overwhelmed sobs.

CHAPTER 14

After another sleepless night, Gillian dragged herself out of bed prepared to tell Cynthia and Alex that she was ready to sell.

She would contact her attorney and have her put together a contract laying out the terms: the money in exchange for limiting visitation to four weekends a year. She wasn't sending him a penny until he signed and notarized. Then she would let Jeremiah know that she had to quit the grant-writing job. Someone else could step in to finish it by the deadline. She'd done all the necessary research, her notes were meticulous, and she'd provide her outline as well as the spreadsheets she'd already color-coded. Someone else just needed to write and analyze and estimate…

When she'd gone back to college after that summer thirteen years ago, she'd wondered if some of the moves she'd made trying to get her family back together had actually broken it further apart. If Milagro Street didn't receive the cash infusion that it would be a contender for with a completed grant, that would be her fault, too.

Perhaps she'd been a curse for much longer than she'd realized.

She couldn't go back to the train station. She couldn't work with Nicky. Even if she decided to finish the grant from home, the job would keep her tethered to the building and the seductive temptation that lurked behind its portico. She'd wanted to be bad and now she felt awful but she knew, given the opportunity, she'd go to him again. She'd always been jealous. He'd always missed her (or missed the way they were together).

She had two babies depending on her to resist diving headfirst into this mess. She wasn't this person. Neither was Nicky.

She couldn't keep going to the train station and seeing what she couldn't have, inside its walls and just across the street. Ignoring Loretta's had been her one defense against this: wanting to claim what she had to give up.

She'd made up her mind about selling the bar so it made no sense when, drinking coffee in her pj's past lunchtime while she let her kids watch limitless TV and ignored the worried looks from her parents, she received a text from Alex and got instantly, ignitingly angry. **Could you come by the bar later?** her sister wrote. **Cynthia and I want to chat.**

She was going to give them what they wanted. They didn't have to shove.

She texted back a time then threw on the first thing she could find in her tiny closet and stomped out the door in flip-flops.

It was then that she remembered she'd left her car on a side street. Loretta's lot had been filled when she'd shown up last night.

Nicky had driven her home.

The July sun wasn't responsible for the shock of heat that burned her.

She walked to Loretta's. She marched through three blocks of the east side, past well-kept postage-stamp yards with plastic flowers in planters, past homes that had resorted to tarps over portions of their roofs, past tire swings and half-hanging porch swings and just-completed new homes with her cousin's name on the signs in the front yards. Her thin, black rubber sandals smacked against new pavement that became cracked sidewalk that then became the original brick the whole town had been paved in that sometimes devolved to grass. The dominating heat of this time of day kept people inside and the streets still. Only the buzzing grasshoppers in over-tall grass watched Gillian Armstead-Bancroft flip-flop furiously by.

Nicky's Jeep was parked outside the train station. By the time the cowbells at Loretta's announced her sweaty arrival, all Gillian could see was red. She stomped up the fourteen steps to her sister's office.

With the door open, Alex was standing behind the huge wooden desk that once belonged to their grandmother in a collarless T-shirt with rolled-up sleeves, black jeans, and Doc Martens, chatting with Cynthia, who lounged in a chair in a blue belted dress, her sapphire pump bobbing on a toe.

"Hey," Alex said, smiling. "You left your hair curly. It looks—"

Gillian slammed the door behind her.

Her natural texture and Kansas humidity had officially broken her hair free of its keratin bond and it curled and frizzed in her face. She was wearing old cutoffs she'd found in the back of her closet and an oversized man's white shirt that must have belonged to her dad.

If there was a scarlet A to be worn declaring how far she'd fallen from that woman who was good and blessed and worthy, she was wearing it.

The smile on her sister's face faded to confusion. "Juli, what's wrong?"

"You wanted to chat," she said, crossing her arms over the shirt she'd tied at her hips and tapping her flip-flop against the refurbished floorboards. "Let's chat. I imagine I'm in trouble because I didn't play tour guide at the train station last night?"

She glared at Cynthia. "I wouldn't worry about it. Regardless of my involvement, Loretta's is going to be in great hands."

Cynthia's eyes narrowed. "That's right." Only Cynthia could recline in a hard, wooden chair. "It'll be fine."

Alex's decorative eyelashes fanned wide. "Juli, that's not what—"

"I'm not here so you can pressure me to hand over the bar?"

"No," Alex declared as Cynthia drawled, "Maybe."

Alex looked at her, exasperated.

"What?" Cynthia said, shoving upright as she wiggled her foot into her shoe. "All we've done is ask her to get involved." She looked squarely at Gillian. "I've been trying to watch out for you and make sure you don't ruin..." She raised both freckled hands into the air. "...everything. I've been proddin' your *ass* so you don't alienate everyone who loves you. You know how many people would kill to have a family like yours?"

Cynthia's mother had left them when she was a baby and her father, an only child like Cynthia, had passed away when she was in college. All she had left were several hundred employees who desperately needed her to keep them employed.

"How I manage *my* relationships with *my* family is *my* business," Gillian said, her voice rising. She was backed into a corner and felt no charity when everyone was yanking at the thing slipping from her fingers. "Whether or not I decide to sell *my* portion of *my* bar is up to *me!*"

It wasn't. But God, it felt good to shout.

"Why do you even want it?" Alex demanded, wading into the fight with her face twisted up. "You've been here a month and this is the third time you've stepped into this business you own." She jabbed toward the wall. "While you've been across the street *every day.*"

Gillian had never considered how her proximity might have scratched at her sister.

"That's just what she does," Cynthia accused, raising her

chin. "When she saw me in the halls in high school, she'd look right through me."

Gillian had launched first strike and it was as gloriously apocalyptic as she'd wanted it to be. They were saying things they couldn't take back. But Cynthia's words pinged off the little bit of hind brain begging her to take shelter. *I just wish you'd stayed ignoring me instead of befriending me,* Cynthia said last night.

"What are you *talking* about?" Gillian asked.

"You," Cynthia shot back. "Your MO. You dropped me like bad news when we went to high school. Then you pick me back up when you needed a friend at the reunion. You Marie Kondo whoever's not bringing you joy."

"We just stopped hanging out in high school," Gillian said, truly mystified. "We were in different classes, had different activities. I had to work my ass off to get a scholarship."

Cynthia scoffed. "Right. And I was smoking in the bathroom and knew my daddy would pay for wherever I wanted to go. I *still* needed my best friend."

Gillian's impulse was to feel guilty. She was trying to unlearn impulses imposed on her for the last ten years. "You can guilt-trip me all you want," she said, straightening her shoulders. "I'm making decisions based on what is best for my family, for me and Ben and Naomi. I won't be manipulated by you or anyone." She was shaking her head, and her hair was batting at her cheeks. "Never, ever, ever again." She was still sweaty from her walk. "You have no idea what I've been through."

"How could she?" Alex cried. "How could I? You won't talk to me. You won't talk to any of us." Real anguish twisted her face. "I was so *worried* about you. I still am but you…you make me so angry. You showed up this summer and I thought… I thought you'd come over to my house and we'd curl up on the couch and talk about what an asshole your ex-husband is. I still got the Häagen-Dazs in the freezer. Then I thought we'd…"

Her sister's lip was trembling as she raised her hand and held Loretta's and all they'd promised each other in her palm.

She fisted her hand, dropped it back to the desk with a thud, and pressed her full lips determinedly together with tears in her eyes. "But you haven't mentioned that asshole's name once. And somehow, I became the bad guy. This business we bought together is the place you avoid. I wouldn't even be here if it wasn't for you."

Alex had had her bags packed ready to return to Chicago, ready to turn her back on Loretta's and Jeremiah and the whole future that made for a very happy present, when Gillian and their family had descended on the bar to beg Alex not to leave.

A fat tear ran down her sister's face. "I don't understand," she said, defeated, swiping at it angrily.

It was a well-established fact that both Alex and Gillian crumbled at the sight of their baby sister Sissy's limpid, violet-eyed tears, and Sissy used it to her advantage without guile. Gillian's secret was that the tears of her fearless middle sister were ten times worse. Alex was the bravest person she knew.

"Well... I'm divorced because of you," Gillian muttered despite herself.

"What?" Alex asked sharply.

Gillian began to count the nails in the century-old wood floor. "I decided to divorce him the same day you decided to stay and fight the developers."

Alex had chosen to stay and fight—for the bar, the neighborhood, and Jeremiah's love, even though she'd hurt him terribly.

"You were so successful in Chicago," she said. Her sister had been featured in *Esquire* magazine. "But you decided to stay here, risk it all, and just leap into the unknown. I've never been that brave. I've never jumped when the odds of success were against me." The nails were a dull gray. "But I knew, at that moment, I couldn't stay on the path I was on. I couldn't keep pretending my life was perfect."

She wrapped her arms around herself.

"Your life wasn't perfect, Juli?" Alex asked.

Gillian shook her head. She swallowed around a boulder in her throat. "I…my marriage was…"

Tell your family, Nicky had urged last night. *Tell them everything.*

Once this was out, she couldn't take it back. Her ability to control her narrative and what her family thought about her would be lost. They'd know what she'd done, the choices she'd made, the thorny crown she'd jammed on her head to coronate the Pride of the East Side.

Who truly was she angry with?

"Thomas was a bad person," she rushed out through bared teeth. She described her ex the way a child would describe someone creeping in the dark. "I chose a bad man. He cheated on me. A lot." Strangely, that was one of the easier details to admit. "He bullied me." Her fingers tapped her elbow as she counted. "He'd get red-faced angry and scream or he'd give me the cold shoulder for days but the worst was when he'd talk and talk and talk about what was fair, creating this equation that didn't add up, and I'd try to follow it, I'm a very smart person, but up became down and down became up and…"

There was a sound in the room and it was Cynthia's shuddery breath.

"… And it was so demoralizing because…" The words pouring out of her felt violent and gross. "Because I always thought I was a very smart person."

She heard rushed steps then smelled sweet ginger then felt fingers brush the hand at her elbow. Still looking down, still clutching herself, she gripped those fingers tightly.

"What's worse is I probably would have stayed longer if not…" She fought to hold this in. This was *definitely* the worst thing she'd ever had to say out loud. She hadn't even had the courage to tell her therapist this.

"He wanted me to get pregnant again. He wanted a son

in his image." She laughed and she could hear how strange it sounded. "That's literally what he said: *A son in his image.* He said he couldn't 'relate' to Ben and Naomi, a son who was autistic and daughter who was...female." She forced herself to stand there for her sister and best friend to see. "He treated them like they were failed versions of a product he wanted to continue iterating. He treated me like if he could reshape me, I'd finally give him the child he deserved and make him happy. He asked me that all the time: *Didn't I want him to be happy?*"

She heard her bighearted sister come rushing around the desk.

But she let go of Cynthia's hand and stepped back. She had to finish this. "I signed a prenup that allows Thomas to say where I live, where I work, who I date, all kinds of control under the pretense of preserving the Bancroft name. I thought I could support us without his money but..." Now she looked at them. "I can't find a job. I can't even make it past the first round."

She'd made both these beautiful women she loved cry.

"All summer, he's offered things I want. Now he's offering to limit how often he sees the kids." She swallowed hard and met her little sister's soul-deep eyes. "All I have to do is sign my portion of the bar over to him. He says it's what's fair."

Alex's eyes went universe-wide.

"That motherfucker," Cynthia growled.

"I was *never* going to do it, Ali," Gillian said, putting her hands over her heart. She felt her tears drip onto them. "Promise."

"That motherfucker," Cynthia declared again, wiping at her face. "Fair. That's your money; you've already paid him in sweat and tears. That sonovabitch."

She looked at her friend, who was gloriously furious. "Your offer is the perfect solution." She was sobbing now. "I'm sure he'll take the money instead. But I don't *want* to sell my share of the bar. I *want* to be a part of it. This is *my* inheritance," she cried. "I don't want to let him take that away from me, too."

She cried with her shame and her anger and her helplessness and she was instantly surrounded in the strong arms of the two women she loved most.

"Ali, you were *never* the bad guy," she said through her tears. "I never...never wanted to tell either of you this because... because I am so-so-so ashamed." Gillian sobbed into her sister's soft black hair. "And I'm so *jealous* of all you have and all you've accomplished. God, I'm so jealous. Which just makes me more ashamed. I am so, so sorry that I've hurt you."

Her sister rubbed her back.

For several long moments, in the arms of these women who kept her safe, she wept for all she'd lost.

She raised her head and wiped her nose with her sleeve. She met her friend's sparkling emerald gaze. "I'm sorry I made you feel convenient. I'm sorry I didn't trust you. I..." She nodded but knew this journey was going to be long. "I'm working on trusting people again." She sniffed hard because she was ready to stop crying. "Even though I wasn't telling you much, I couldn't have gotten through this year without you."

In the last year of therapy, Gillian had acknowledged that she had the kind of focus that allowed her to rise above a town with an intense undertow and stay in a marriage for years with a multitude of warning signs. Her focus gave her blind spots. One of those blind spots allowed her to roll over Cynthia on her way out of Freedom.

"Oh, baby," Cynthia said, sticking out her bottom lip, and Gillian had to look up and blink or she was going to start all over again. "I'm sorry, too."

Alex stepped away to grab a roll of toilet paper out of the supply closet and yelled down for someone to bring up a pitcher of water and Diet Cokes. Their cousin Gina appeared as they were all mopping at their faces, Gillian and Cynthia sitting on chairs while Alex perched on the edge of her desk.

Walking in on their family bawling wasn't an unusual scene.

"What do you want to do now, Juli?" Alex asked. She'd loosened the glue on her eyelashes, so she'd peeled them off and washed her face in the upstairs bathroom. Her brown skin was baby clean. "I love you and that's more important than anything. I'll back your play. But if I keep feeling jerked around, it will break us."

It was a harsh and necessary truth from the sister who never let perception color cold, hard reality. Gillian admired her so much for the way she faced life head-on.

In honor of that, she rested her cold glass on her knee and took a moment to really think about what she wanted, what she could claim now that her truth was known, and what she had no choice but to hand over.

She thought of Nicky's harsh, unsmiling face in the moonlit train station. *I've never missed anyone the way I've missed you.*

Now she couldn't step away from the grant-writing job that she'd never truly wanted to quit. Telling Cynthia and Alex about what had happened with Nicky was one way to ensure last night wouldn't happen again. But the protective impulse she'd had when she'd waved at the lonely heroic boy in the lunchroom and then asked him to play hadn't gone away when she'd given him warding amuletos or clung to his ever-broadening shoulders or almost hit him on the side of an abandoned road. What they'd done, what Nicky had asked for—*one time and then never again*—had been wrong, but she didn't want Cynthia and Alex to punish him for it. She would eventually tell them of her long, complicated sexual entanglement with Nicky Mendoza. She just needed a beat to figure out how.

"I want to stay involved in the bar," she said, meeting her sister's eyes. "I had so many ideas last night." She turned to look at Cynthia. "But I need my kids to be safe, more. And if my happiness is the pound of flesh he insists on to limit his access to them, then I'm going to pay it. Cynthia Madsen, would you like to be part owner of an up-and-coming establishment on Milagro Street?"

Cynthia leaned forward and put her hand over hers on the glass. "I'll just keep it warm for you. We'll work out a plan. You can pay me back."

It was a lovely sentiment from a lovely woman. But it was going to be a long, long time before Gillian could pay back what Cynthia was going to fork over or buy in again when Alex bought Cynthia's share from her to keep it in the family. She squeezed her best friend's hand.

"You can still be involved, Juli," Alex said. "You'll always be one of the Armstead girls."

Her damn sister. Gillian needed another beat and no one said anything for a couple of minutes.

"I'd like to stay part of Loretta's," she finally sniffed. "If you'll have me."

"It's all I've wanted," Alex said solemnly. "What were some of your ideas?"

As midday became late afternoon and Alex yelled down for three roasted pork tortas with French fries, Gillian talked about the inventory system and inquired when they'd be looking into new menus and asked what financial software her sister was using and offered to take that part off her sister's shoulders.

"Oh Jesus fucking Christ yes please and thank you," was her sister's response.

But mainly, she talked about the idea birthed last night and immediately mourned because she thought she'd never get to enact it: creating an event at the end of the summer that tied together the speakeasy launch, the mural unveiling, and—if the Freedom Historical Society could put it together in time—a display of the future Freedom Historical Museum. The event would firmly position both Loretta's and the museum as tent poles for a burgeoning Milagro Street.

"It will display to potential business owners and out-of-town investors here to taste the whisky that there's something growing on the east side," Gillian said. "Something they want to be a part of."

Alex and Cynthia were immediate fans. Gillian took notes at her grandmother's desk as they brainstormed what the event could look like and when she walked out of Loretta's as the light was getting dusky, she held several pages clutched to her heart.

Nicky's Jeep was still parked at the train station.

Consider what powerful magic this is. There is no better way to be bad.

The temptation to cross the street and lock them in again was painful. Only the relief of earning the forgiveness of two of her favorite people kept her focused on walking to her car and racing out of there.

Let's break your curse.

As she sped away, she actually had to huff at the thought. For the first time in as long as she could remember, the day had ended better than it had begun. Better than she could have dreamed. Maybe they'd succeeded.

The thought stopped being humorous when she got home and found a response from a Chicago financial firm in her inbox.

And the theory became terrifyingly possible when she got a text from Nicky later that evening.

CHAPTER 15

I owe it to you to say this in person, but I don't want to assume I can just show up at your door. Not with the way I've behaved.

I was never engaged.

Last night, I did everything in my power to confuse you.

I would rather you hate me for lying to you than blame yourself for helping me "cheat."

If you want me gone, I'll go. If you want me to never speak to you again, I'll do that too. I'll do whatever you want.

I am so sorry.

Nicky was used to nights of lost sleep. Between his tendency to go with a creative impulse no matter what time it struck and the nightmare about his brother that no amount of therapy, meditation, medication, Buddhist retreats, or bruja baths had helped to cure, he'd gotten used to going a few days with only catnaps before he crashed. Still, after one night of staring at the ceiling as he roller-coastered through every peak of tasting her again and every valley of self-disgust, then buzzing through the next night with a high-voltage hum of terror and anticipation, he was amazed how energized he felt driving into Freedom as the first rays of the sun struck his rearview mirror.

Come by the house early tomorrow morning was all she'd texted a harrowing two hours after he'd told her what he'd done.

When he parked in front of Gillian's childhood home, it was the first time he'd ever parked there. They'd been pre-driving kids when he walked her home, and she'd never invited him over when she was inviting him into her body. He strode to Gillian's front porch in the lemony rays of sunlight. Fat sparrows tweeted in the chipped Virgen de Guadalupe birdbath in her grandmother's front yard next door. If this was the last time he was going to get to see her, he was glad it would be in the sunshine.

The wooden front door opened just as his sneaker hit the bottom step of the porch. Through the screen door, he watched her lean over to grab something then turn to use her shoulder to push the screen open.

She was carrying two big mugs of steaming coffee.

He hurried onto the porch to hold the door open for her. "Is one of those for me?"

"No, one's for Joe," she said, raising an eyebrow at him. "He's coming over to kick your butt."

He deserved no less than an early morning ass-kicking.

She looked like she was still in her pajamas: stretchy gray bottoms, a matching strappy tank top, and a black, wide-necked shirt over the tank. Curls dripped around her face while the rest of her hair was gathered into a ball at her nape with a scrunchie. She had on her glasses. He could look right into her deep-brown eyes.

She bobbed the heavy stoneware mug and he took it off her hands, then followed her to the metal rocking love seat that had been on the front porch since they were little. He memorized the just-awake scent of her as they walked: peaches and cream and coffee.

"I had a lot of pretty choice things to say to you when I got your message," she said, tucking herself into the corner of the love seat and putting her bare feet with messily painted bright-blue toenails up on the cushion.

After a second of hesitation, he sat beside her, making the love seat creak noisily.

"You texting me with that mind-blowing piece of information gave me some time to think about it," she said, the mug on her knees. "I came on pretty strong in Cynthia's car."

He knew it; she was going to figure out a way to blame herself for this, too. "Are you worried about consent, Gillian?" he scoffed. "I think I proved the other night, you definitely had my consent."

She looked into her mug. She always clung to her coffee like it was mother's milk. "Then why?"

He took a deep and scalding drink.

"I was hurt when you left," he said as he pushed the seat, rocking them gently. "I would've liked to have been more to you back then. I would've liked to have at least stayed in touch."

Pacing in his room last night until William had thumped the wall with his cane and Nicky had taken his pacing to their ten acres, that was what he'd come up with. *I was hurt when you left.* It encompassed the truth without zeroing down to the ugly reality of it: the depression, the weight loss, his wild-eyed search for anything to make him feel better. William had had to rescue him just like Nicky should've stayed to rescue his brother.

It was a way to maintain his crumbling wall after she'd

blown a hole through it. *I've always been jealous.* Her jealousy—
for him—had demolished any instinct for self-preservation. He
knew his girl liked naughty and he'd made their naughtiness
high octane. Only when the dust settled did he think about
how much it would hurt her.

They sat in silence. The houses across the street were washed
in soft shades of cottony light. The birds in the bath were getting up to some kind of mischief.

"Nicky you…you never said anything," she finally said.

"Neither did you," he said into his mug. "About the jealousy
thing… You always were pretty clear about what you wanted
from me."

He had a lot of time, anger, and resentment invested in her
dismissing him. Had she really wanted that boy with long hair
and empty pockets she said could be with other girls? Or was
she just jealous of the man who so many wanted a piece of?

"Nicky, I'm so sorry—"

He cut her off. "I'm telling you the *why*, Gillian. Whatever
I felt then doesn't excuse me lying to you now." He'd fucked
up and hurt her. He needed to make it right. "I panicked in
that car and I said the stupidest fucking thing I could think of."

He heard her swallow. "Why didn't you tell me later?"

He stared into the blackness in his cup. She was missing the
million-dollar question. *Why did you stay?* William's "illness,"
getting roped into the mural, his dead brother. He was a real
piece of shit.

"You know how we were, hechicera," he said. "It felt like
the only way I could hang out with you without spending all
my time touching you."

He was going for truthful, not seductive.

Her breath shuddered out, as soft as this summer morning.

"It's *my* fault, Gillian, not yours and I just want you to have
faith that there are good men out there and that we're not all
fucking liars and manipulators like I'm proving to you we are."

For a few moments, they sat quietly, nothing between them but the squeak of the rocking metal. Her toes were an inch from his thigh.

Finally, she said, "I don't know how I would've made it without you this summer."

He wanted to get down on the porch and kiss those toes.

"You were the only person I was talking to who I wasn't paying. I don't know if that would've been possible if we'd been…"

Fuck buddies. Lovers. The ways he would've unleashed on her would've left time for nothing else.

"I don't want you to leave."

He exhaled slowly, tried to make it look like he was blowing on his coffee.

"Alex can make a destination out of Loretta's, and if Jeremiah is half as smart as she is, he can make a destination out of the museum."

Nicky eyed the compact, two-story Craftsman house across the street that still shined with newness, although the builder had somehow kept the large, leafy oaks that gave the structure the sense that it had been there for decades. The lot had held a falling-apart shack when they were little; Alex and Jeremiah had made that abandoned lot their home. He'd never known two people more committed to a difficult dream.

"You and the generosity of your mural get them that much closer to what they want," she said. "What…we want."

He was glad she wanted him to stay to complete the mural. Torres Construction was showing up today to build the scaffolding so that next week he, along with help from the community, could outline the huge piece on the wall. He was glad not to have to cancel at the last minute. He didn't need her to want more from him.

"I took your advice," she said. He glanced at her and she met his eyes over her coffee. A curl was about to dip into the cup. "I told Alex and Cynthia everything."

Everything, he wondered. There was no way she'd told them everything.

She shared how she'd bared her soul to her sister and best friend and then they'd come up with a plan: Cynthia would pay Thomas. Gillian would maintain an involvement in Loretta's even though it would no longer be hers.

"It's not ideal," Gillian said. "But it allows me to get the kids out from under his thumb. My attorney is putting together a contract to send him."

"What would be ideal?" he asked.

She huffed. "If I'd never married him. If I'd listened to my own financial advice and was independently wealthy. If I could own his ass."

He focused again on his cup. "I could pitch in if you need more investors."

"Thank you," she said softly. "Truly. Jeremiah offered as well, but he and Alex have been very disciplined about how they incorporate the assets from his trust fund into their lives. I don't want to muddy that water for them. That's where I made my mistake."

Getting more men involved with the bar was not the answer to her problem. She didn't want to be saved, but she especially didn't want to be saved by him.

"Cynthia said something yesterday," she murmured. "She said that I ignored her when she was no longer useful to me." He heard her swallow. "Did you feel used by me, Nicky?"

The question pierced right through him. "Gillian, however I felt thirteen years ago doesn't give me an excuse to—"

"Just tell me."

He dropped his head and stared at his ratty sneakers.

"Well, if that isn't an answer..."

Wild peacocks screamed from where they liked to hang out near the zoo.

Her fist rested on his thigh. "I'm sorry I made you feel unimportant. You've always been important to me. I trust you so much. You showing up here to apologize is one of the reasons why." He felt like he could feel her heartbeat through her fist. "In ten years, Thomas never once owned up to his behavior. You're a good man, Nicky. I forgive you. I hope I can give you a reason to forgive me, too."

He'd never thought about a need to forgive *her*.

Swimming in her peachy smell, soft sunlight, good coffee, and inadvisable relief, he defied all good sense and did what he'd wanted to do since the second she'd opened her door: He touched her. He reached out and covered her foot with his hand. "You need to go to a better nail salon," he said, sliding his palm over the fine skin to her ankle, hearing the hitch in her breath. There was as much blue on her skin as there was on her nails.

"The girl I go to is inexperienced," she said, voice as filmy as sunrays. "But she's cheap. I pay her in Popsicles."

Gillian waved her fingernails in his view and they looked like they'd been colored in with a pink highlighter.

"Quite a find," he said, fingering the knobby bones of her ankle. He could see her loafer tan. She'd been getting a lot of sun this summer and her skin was as golden brown as it'd been all those years ago. He couldn't believe he was touching her again. "Maybe we really did break your curse."

"By cheating on a nonexistent fiancée?" she grumbled. "Funny you mention that—"

The whine of the screen door interrupted whatever she was going to say. Nicky let go of her ankle.

If Gillian had ever brought him over when they'd been screwing around, he bet they would've been caught a lot with his hand in the cookie jar. But it wasn't Mary pushing the door open or Loretta with her shotgun or Tucker who'd always been busy writing or drinking, no matter how much Gillian admired him.

It was Gillian's pedicurist.

"Mama, you're being loud," the little girl complained as she rubbed her eyes so all Nicky could see was a scrunched-up face and long dark-blond hair and a lime-green nightgown with a princess on it. He knew that Gillian's daughter was a good sleeper, a horrible eater, and afraid of nothing but jack-o'-lanterns and boredom.

Seeing a person made within Gillian's body was like getting coldcocked.

"I very much disagree I'm being loud," Gillian said. "Come here." She pulled the girl into her arms and then up onto her lap, snuggling her back against her. The girl dropped her hand and blinked owlishly at Nicky.

Gillian had a daughter with green eyes.

"Did you try to get in bed with me?" Gillian murmured into her hair.

The girl nodded. "You were gone," she pouted. "Who's that?"

"That's my friend Nicky. Nick," she corrected.

"She can call me Nicky," he said.

"This is Naomi." There was so much warmth in her voice, like this was a big deal for her, too. "Naomi, this is my good friend Nicky. I've known him since I was just a few years older than you."

"Oh," Naomi said. She had a wide-bridged nose, like Gillian's had been, and tiny lips that looked painted on and beautiful hair and flyaway eyebrows. She had the imprint of a pillow seam on her round cheek. "Do you like Froot Loops?"

He laughed. It wasn't what he'd expected. "I prefer Cocoa Pebbles."

She wrinkled her nose and he'd seen that expression, on that nose, a thousand times before. "They get all mushy."

"They make the milk taste like chocolate."

"Like poop milk," she replied, concerned for him.

"Naomi," Gillian warned, but then she craned her neck to see who else was coming through the screen door as Naomi sang, "Poop-poop-poop-poop-poop..." and rocked on her mom's lap.

The entire Armstead-Bancroft household was joining them on the porch.

"Nick?" Mary Armstead said wonderingly, her long dark hair trailing down the front of her pink terry-cloth robe, glancing at him and her daughter. A square-chested little boy directing a pissed-off look over Nicky's shoulder held her and her husband's hand. "What're you two doing out here?"

Gillian flashed Nicky a quick look. "We're planning an event. For the museum. There's a lot to do so we thought we'd take advantage of the morning hours. I'm sorry, did we wake you?"

"I was awake," Mary said, her eyes narrowing on Nicky.

He resisted shifting in his seat. He actually was a lousy liar.

Tucker Armstead, in a white T-shirt, jeans, and bare feet, took a look at both women before he cleared his throat. "I tried to distract Ben with *SpongeBob* but he was pretty focused on finding y'all," he said as he leaned over to offer his free hand to Nicky. "Nick, good mornin'. You were about half that size last time I saw you."

Nicky nodded as he shook his hand but didn't say anything.

Their summer together, Nicky had spent as much time distracting Gillian from her worries about her family as he had drawing her attention away from La Llorona. Gillian had thought early-morning walks and constant vigilance could keep her father from descending further into alcoholism. Nicky could have told her what he'd eventually learned—you couldn't will someone away from their addiction—but she'd always been so confident she could get life to line up the way she wanted.

Midway through the summer, Gillian had decided to "surprise" Alex in Chicago with a visit from their father. Alex blamed him for having to move there after some trouble, and she wouldn't let them in the door. They'd come back to Freedom and her father had disappeared for a week.

Gillian had consumed Nicky like air and water that week and he'd made love to her for the first time then relentlessly until she left. He got that Tucker Armstead was working to make amends. He'd still been responsible for making Gillian's life pretty miserable.

She wrapped an arm around the little boy and pulled him close to the love seat. "Baby, I'm sorry," she said. "Were you worried?"

He gave that shrug that meant yes and but didn't take his glare off the yard. Nicky was getting the gist of the kid's message.

"Didn't..." The boy gave a frustrated huff of his sturdy shoulders. With her daughter still in her lap, Gillian leaned over to murmur into his soft brown hair cut into a buzz cut. He tilted his temple against his mom's mouth.

Nicky could just imagine the comfort of those words sinking into his skin.

"Didn't know where the baby was," he said.

Nicky felt an uncomfortable buzz across his shoulders.

Gillian introduced them. Ben's grumpy face settled a little. Although her son still didn't look at him, Nicky knew he was getting weighed and measured.

The buzz became a chain-saw hum. He thought about how the random guys his mom would bring home would either ignore Lucas or tell him to "straighten up." He thought about how badly he'd wanted to knock their fucking blocks off. He thought about how now, if some guy tried to do that to Ben, Nicky was big enough to do it.

"Have either of you checked your email, yet?" Mary asked.

Gillian looked at Nicky. "No."

"Alejandra wants to provide lunch on Monday when the mural volunteers show up," Mary said. "Ask your Granmo and tías to cook and turn it into a community event." She smiled fondly at Gillian. "Whatever you two discussed yesterday got her very excited."

Gillian pressed her lips into Naomi's hair.

"Nick, you should invite William," Mary continued, surprising him. "I haven't seen him this summer."

Tucker chuckled with his arms crossed, brushing down his moustache. "I'd love to hear what he thought of my fourth book. I got very concise reports for the other three."

William liked his solitude and Nicky was comfortable with that idea. It allowed him to avoid admitting that William had a full life and friends in Freedom, a life and friends he may not want to give up moving with Nicky to San Francisco.

"I'll let him know," he said.

Mary and Tucker bribed the kids back inside with the lure of pancakes so Gillian and Nicky could finish up their "talk." As they all left the porch, Naomi was the only one who didn't give him an eyes-on-you glare.

He put his now-cold coffee on the ground, folded his fingers together in his lap, and focused on his Jeep. "Getting introduced to Ben and Naomi was not how I thought this morning was going to go."

"I'm glad you finally got to meet them," she said. "I'm glad they got to meet you."

He'd just met her children on the front porch of the house where he used to play, with her curled up and barefoot next to him. The intimacy of the moment shouldn't have made him want to slide to the wood boards, cradle her ass in his hands, and thank her with his tongue.

Were they going to start needing chaperones like a couple of horny teens? Thirteen years ago, nothing had stopped them touching and tasting and taking once she'd given him the green light.

"Nicky… I'm glad you're not engaged," she said quietly, aware of the ears inside. "I'm glad we didn't hurt anyone."

He squeezed his fingers together as secure as any lock.

"But I'm dealing with a nasty divorce," she continued. "And neither of us plan on being here past the summer."

"No."

Fuck no. His fading memories of Gillian all over town had stung when he'd visited. He couldn't imagine what it would feel like with sparkly new ones.

"So we should stick to friends," she murmured. His resolute, newly divorced, mom-of-two hechicera. "Regardless how it was done, you stopping us in that car was probably a good thing."

He drew his first full breath in thirty-six hours. She would do what he couldn't. She would repair the wall he was tearing down.

"Right?" she asked.

Fuck.

"We shouldn't talk about…curse-breaking anymore?" She was smashing it to pieces. "That's what would be best." She let out a shaky breath and he saw that her hands were held together as tightly as his. "Wouldn't it?"

He shoved to standing and on her front porch, in the morning sun, in plain view of anyone who might be looking, yanked her up onto her feet, pulled her into his arms, and tucked her close against his body.

"Yeah," he said, nuzzling into her neck, soaking up her peaches and cream. "Friends. I'll see you at work."

He let her go and walked to his Jeep without looking back.

CHAPTER 16

When Gillian pulled up to the Freedom train station the following Monday morning to find a line of retirees already waiting in the shade of the station's brick portico, where horse-drawn buggies then cars would drop off and pick up passengers, she was amazed but not surprised.

Because Loretta didn't serve her food at the bar, Freedomites usually had to wait for a coveted invitation to Sunday dinners or the Torres family food stand at Neewollah, Freedom's annual Halloween celebration, to savor her food. But Cynthia's full-page ad in the newspaper, Jeremiah's pitch at the city council meeting, and Alex's flyer around town all mentioned that the Torres family would be serving lunch to the volunteers who showed up on Monday for the two-week effort to trace the Milagro Street mural onto the wall.

Gillian unlocked the train station door and then invited the volunteers to wait for Nicky in the air-conditioning. She retreated to her office.

By the time he arrived twenty minutes later, she had to come back out again. The trickle of volunteers into the station had turned into a steady flow, and Nicky had a hand in his hair as he stared at the benches full of people patiently waiting. She had to bite back a smile. He looked as effortlessly gorgeous as ever in a clinging gray T-shirt, old black jeans, and black Converse. But when he yanked his hand out of his hair, the thick strands stood on end.

"Mornin'," she called cautiously as she walked across the tile toward him.

He turned to look at her with a grimace. "I usually get a few art students from the local college," he said low. "Not..."

He thumbed behind his shoulder. The train station door squealed open as more people walked in.

She had to pinch her lips together at the wild-eyed look on his face. This was not the smooth-talking, easy-smiling, flirtatious man she'd been with for most of the summer. Last week, she gotten proof that his devil-may-care expression could be a facade just like her precise makeup, designer clothes, straightened hair, and nose job had been as she'd swum the shark-infested waters of upper-echelon D.C.

I was hurt when you left. I would have liked to have been something more.

Now he knew that she had been jealous.

A layer had been stripped off them both and now, exposed, they had to figure out how to work in this train station together. Gillian was grateful for the Torres Construction crew that had been here Friday, filling up the space with people and equipment and noise as they'd banged the impressive, three-story scaffolding against the back wall, and she was grateful for the next two weeks of volunteers.

Hopefully, in two weeks, she'd figure out how to deal with the fact that when she saw him maskless, looking so much like that kind, quiet boy she'd spent so much time with, she only wanted him more. In two weeks, she hoped she'd restrained this huge thing growing unchecked and unwanted inside her since she discovered he wasn't engaged. She had no time or space for a thing worse than a crush for Nicky Mendoza. In two weeks, for both of their sakes, she hoped to feel no more than the friendship she'd promised.

Friends helped each other and, right now, she could help him.

She looked at the growing number of volunteers, a cross-section of Freedom's brown, black, and white citizens, mostly fifty years old and up, then asked Nicky three questions: How many people could safely be on the scaffolding at any one time? How long each day did he want to be on premises supervising? What was a reasonable block of time to ask volunteers to work? Co-opting Nicky's standing desk, she quickly developed a volunteer intake form as well as a scheduling spreadsheet. Then she asked volunteers to form a single-file line and began to process them and plug them into the schedule. No one was taking off before the luncheon, when the mural would be displayed for the very first time.

She sent Nicky off to buy more snacks, water, and to make photocopies.

By the time Joe, some other cousins, and the tíos that hung out at Loretta's started trickling in late morning to bring in and set up tables for serving, Nicky was back in command. The art students he'd recruited had all shown up and he was training them in their roles as co-captains. Gillian smiled when she saw the twelve students' chests puff out at the title.

The co-captains would process and schedule the volunteers, assign people to wall spaces, and explain the task. The twenty-five-foot-high, fifty-foot-long wall at the back of the train station was covered in scaffolding and chalk lines that created the horizontal and vertical lines of squares. Each volunteer would receive a printout of their assigned square. When the lights were turned off, the mural would be projected onto the wall and volunteers would trace their portion with thick charcoal pencils and fill in the color codes also printed on their sheets. Co-captains would help the volunteers, fill in the harder-to-reach spots behind the scaffolding bars and boards, and mark squares as "done" when they were completed.

When she saw her family walking in lugging aluminum-covered trays, stands, and Sterno, Gillian handed over the processing duties to Mrs. O'Halloran, her middle-school gifted teacher who she could not bring herself to call Pam.

Little arms wrapped around her thigh and stopped her in her tracks.

"Got you, Mama."

She looked down to see her daughter grinning up at her, her hair hanging down her back, in the same outfit she'd worn for the last two weeks. One of them remembered to throw the rainbow T-shirt and lime-green shorts in the washer every evening after Naomi's bath.

"Hey, baby," she said, smoothing her hand down her hair. Naomi kissed her leg through her linen pants then ran off to join a couple of older cousins playing "the black tiles are lava."

Her attorney had sent the contract to Thomas's attorney over the weekend. There hadn't been a response yet. Cynthia had a check ready to send.

Her children would see their father for a weekend, instead of a week, in August and Gillian would fly with them and stay in a hotel close to Thomas's condo. Her children were her legacy as much as the bar and if she had to sell one to protect the other, so be it.

Gillian looked around for her son in the growing buzz of chatter and laughter in the echo-filled train station.

She couldn't have been more surprised when she saw him standing and talking to William Baldassaro in a quiet corner. William was seated on a train bench with a cane planted between his heavy orthopedic shoes as he listened. Nicky sat beside him, listening as well. Ben was looking off into a corner as he spoke, but at least he wasn't scowling. She'd noted the face he'd made when he'd seen her on the porch with Nicky.

Tucker and Mary stood just behind him, smiling and pleased, as they both held casserole dishes with pot holders.

Gillian went over. She kissed her mom's cheek.

"We stopped to say hello," Mary said, whispering, dark eyes wide, "and William asked if Ben liked ants and Ben started chattering away."

Ben loved his ant-covered T-shirt, but they all knew how rare it was for him to talk to strangers.

She kissed her dad's cheek. "This was my plan," Tucker said, low. "I needed Ben's help mellowing out my biggest critic."

"Go put those dishes down," Gillian said, smiling.

She marveled how her parents, who seemed to spend every waking minute together, walked off side by side already chatting.

On Saturday evening, after she'd plugged the kids into *Sesame Street* in Loretta's narrow front room, she'd sat down her grandmother, Tucker, and Mary to share with them the reality of her marriage and divorce. Tears filled everyone's eyes, but no one seemed surprised. Perhaps she hadn't been hiding her life as cagily as she thought. Her parents had been the world's best caretakers this summer, giving her time and space to come to them, rather than pushing for answers. It was an example of how she wanted to be with her own children when they needed support as adults.

So she needed to figure out why she was still so innately and adamantly against her parents getting back together.

She focused on Ben, who was telling William and Nicky about a recent trip to Cynthia's pool. "And...and...and I went off the slide like this—" He gave a little zoom of his hand that was pretty expressive for him. "And I didn't even get water up my nose."

"Bold *and* courageous," William said, nodding. "Can you swim to the side all by yourself?"

Ben nodded, glancing at William with that half smile he got with people he wanted to like.

"Ben won a blue ribbon for being the best swimmer in his age group," Nicky said quietly. She hadn't realized how much she talked about her children with him.

Her son didn't look at Nicky, but he did start nodding harder. Nicky noticed, and she saw the uptick in his smile.

Gillian fought back the surge of feeling.

She touched Ben's shoulder and when he didn't shy away, a possibility with all the people and noise, she leaned over and hugged him. "Can we go over and say hi to Big Granmo?" she asked.

He nodded again.

She waited for the slow process of William getting to his feet before she leaned in to hug him, too. "William, I'm so glad you made it," she said, meaning it. This man had provided comfort, safety, and respect to a poor traumatized boy and was one of the reasons Nicky had turned out as wonderfully as he did.

He smelled like spearmint gum when she kissed his jowly cheek. "Gillian," he said, looking at her through thick glasses that made his eyes very small. "I don't want to downplay all you've gone and accomplished but, may I say, you sure grew up pretty."

He caught her off guard with the compliment and she laughed. "Yes, you may say it. Let's go say hi to Loretta."

As they made their way over, Ben staying by William's slow-moving side, William asked, "How do you get promoted to *Big* Granmo?"

"You get mean enough to outlive everyone else," Gillian said with a smile. "Just be glad Loretta is still independent in her own house; it's a tradition in our family that the women get enraged and vengeful the instant our autonomy is taken away. We younger women all look forward to when we don't have to be nice to everyone all the time."

Her own Big Granmo, Loretta's mom, María Dolores, had passed away seven years ago, ninety-six and furious since the day they'd moved her out of her own home and into the home of one of her six kids.

Loretta was putting serving spoons in dishes while the tíos waited impatiently with their knives and forks at the head of the serving tables, the crowd queuing up behind them.

"Let the woman breathe," William said, lightly thwacking ankles with his cane as he made his way toward her grandmother.

Tío Martín, Loretta's oldest brother with gorgeous silver hair he Brylcreemed into waves, hissed and stepped back. "Ay, compadre, don't you know a growling stomach is the sincerest form of flattery?"

William ignored him as he leaned over to kiss Loretta's cheek.

"For that, amigo, you get an invitation for Sunday dinner," Loretta said, chuckling. She had on coral lipstick and one of the short-sleeved plaid shirts she wore when she bartended. "Nicky, you too."

Great. All she needed was to see Nicky *more* often.

Gillian watched Eddie, a family friend who was an unofficial tío, observe the interaction between William and Loretta. He was a handsome man, with his close-trimmed black hair and silver-framed glasses. Right now, she felt a pang of empathy for him and his long-held unspoken crush on her grandmother.

Eddie shook Nicky's hand. "Sorry to hear about the end of your engagement," he said quietly.

"We never even got to see her," Martín mourned.

"My daughter's single," Tío Pepe said.

"Does Nick look like a man who needs introductions?" Eddie deadpanned as he crossed his arms over his fit torso.

She hadn't thought about how Nicky's pretend engagement had protected him from not only her attentions, but from the attention of every single woman in town. Now that the word was out that he was no longer taken, she was surprised the train station wasn't mobbed.

She forcibly ripped her mind away from that stomach-churning thought and focused on Ben, who hugged Loretta, then asked to go play with "the baby." She freed him then hugged Loretta herself.

"It's so nice to see you in the thick of things," her grandmother said before she continued arranging food on the table.

Gillian wasn't the hospitality guru that her grandmother and sister were, but she enjoyed using her skills and magic and smarts to fix things and make life easier for others. Holding herself apart from her family had been like holding herself underwater. Now, able to breathe again, she remembered how Dr. Dannon, Gillian's therapist, had gone over the intricate ways an "emotional abuser" isolated their "victim" from the people who loved them. The wise, wise woman knew better than to fill in those labels with the names *Thomas* and *Gillian*.

"I'm sorry I took so long to wade in," she said quietly to her grandmother's salt-and-pepper waves.

Loretta dismissed her words with a puff of air. "You came home to heal," she said, moving a tía's enchiladas behind her large tray of molé-covered chicken drumsticks. "Now you're healing."

Her Granmo had this effortless way of making her feel like a little girl again, the little girl who would lean her head against her Granmo's hip while Loretta brushed her hair until it crackled.

With the power of a longtime bar owner, Loretta raised her voice and invited those who worshipped to join them in grace. Then she asked everyone to observe a moment of silence for the food they were about to enjoy and the people who couldn't be there to enjoy it with them.

As the line began to move, Gillian looked for her children. Her mom was shepherding them through and she motioned for Gillian to stay where she was. Nicky gently reminded William about his diabetes and cholesterol while William expertly cantilevered as much Mexican food as he could on one Styrofoam plate. Nicky wasn't helping Gillian and her unwanted condition. His care for his father figure was making her libido roar back online with a vengeance. The last people she wanted to see in her flushed state as they walked to an available table were her sister and best friend.

"Hey, Nick," Alex said, her hands in the oversized front pocket of her hot-pink canvas overalls. Her eyes sparkled terrifyingly.

"Nick. Hey," Cynthia said. She was dressed in heels and a fitted pantsuit and had the same frenetic look in her eyes.

After waiting for a quiet moment during Sunday dinner, which had been impossible to find when every member of their gigantic family had to hug her and kiss her and comment on how glad they were to *finally* see her, she'd pulled them next door to her parents' deck to tell them about her long history with Nicky, the interludes in the current present, and why he'd faked an engagement. There'd been lots of howling she'd had to hush, a few offers to kick his ass if she wanted, then an endless litany of sex teacher puns.

"How big is his lesson plan?"

"What do you do for extra credit?"

"Does he teach you you're A-B-oh-my-god-I-C-Jesus?"

"That doesn't even make any sense," she'd yelled, laughing so hard she'd nearly peed.

She could have been angrier about the fake engagement but two things mitigated it: the insight from Cynthia that she'd hurt people on her way out of town. And her relief. She was just so glad he wasn't engaged anymore. But she'd set her foot down—hard—on their instant excitement about a possible "something" between her and Nicky. She was just divorced. She had a whole life to figure out and two babies depending on her. He lived in San Francisco. She didn't need them fanning an infatuation Gillian was trying to smother.

Now, Nicky nodded at Alex and Cynthia as Gillian eyed them suspiciously.

"Juli, I forgot to give you this," Alex said, her brown eyes wide.

"I found it," Cynthia added eagerly.

With the premonition of dread showing up too late to be useful, Gillian watched her pain-in-the-patootie middle sister pull rust-colored material from her oversized pocket, pulling and pulling like the most nightmarish of magician tricks as she revealed the long scarf that had slithered unnoticed to the train station floor while Nicky had steered her toward a bench demanding *just one time.*

Alex finally held the wad of it out to her, her eyes devilish.

"We thought you might need it," Cynthia said, voice dripping with fake sincerity. "It gets chilly in the train station."

"You know," Alex said nodding. "When you're *instructing* people about the mural."

"Right, right." Cynthia's head bobbed along ridiculously. "If you're trying to *teach* them about Milagro Street."

With the burn of embarrassment leaking into her hair, Gillian snatched the scarf from her sister's hands. "I can't believe the future of the east side rests on you two juveniles," she whisper-snarled.

They both busted into peals of laughter then staggered off, supporting each other. William huffed then sat at the only remaining chair left with the tíos, officially divorcing himself from the whole foolish incident.

Gillian balanced her plate with one hand while shoving the scarf in her purse with the other, then looked up, mortified, to apologize to Nicky.

The dark, hungry look he gave her could have stripped paint. "You told them," he said.

She didn't know whether to say she was sorry or to invite

him out to her SUV where the tinted windows would allow him to punish her in private.

"I should've mentioned it to you…"

All he did was shift his weight. But, surrounded by talking, laughing people in a light-filled train station with the smell of her grandmother's mole in her nose and the shouts of children running around, he suddenly looked bigger, broader, and one fraying tether from pushing her to the tile.

"You told them," he said again, meeting her eyes, bending his head so his soft voice went no farther than her ear. "You never told them before."

She hoped no one nearby saw her shiver.

No one but him. He gave her a heavy-eyed smile and nudged her and she turned and sat at the first empty seat before she walked into a locker again.

The eyes of her favorite aunt went wide behind her hot-pink glasses as they sat down. "Are you two—?"

"Tía," Gillian cut her off sharply. "It's so nice to see you. How are you?"

Tía Ofelia shuffled her hand through her wavy, chin-length hair as the few other people at the table chuckled. A popular English teacher at the high school, Ofelia had defined chic for Gillian before she even knew the meaning of the word. Now she wore an oversized white shirt and a chunky wooden necklace.

"Alejandra was just telling me about your plan to pair the opening of the speakeasy and the unveiling of the mural in one big party," Ofelia said, armed for eating with a tortilla in one hand and a fork in the other. "It's a wonderful idea."

Ofelia was on the board of the Freedom Historical Society and had been the first person to flag the importance of Milagro Street and Freedom's long-standing Mexican-American community. If Milagro Street rose from the ashes, it would be because of the seed this woman planted.

Her tía knew more about their great-grandmother Rosalinda

Padilla than anyone. She hoped to have a permanent exhibit at the museum focused on her.

"Tía, do you know if Rosalinda worked with Cariña de la Cruz?" she asked.

"On the Bowling Baby case?" Ofelia nodded. "Rosalinda's Sociedad helped to pay for an attorney. Cariña's money was claimed by her husband."

Gillian couldn't believe her tía rolled out those facts like they'd been in the morning's newspaper. "What do you know about it?" she asked.

"That case was a travesty," Ofelia said, swallowing and putting down her tortilla. "People nationwide read about it in their papers like they were watching the *Real Housewives*. A professor at Washburn University wrote an amazing paper on it."

There was modern research on her laundress. "What happened?"

"Her husband, Charles Bowling, was the drunken oldest son of the biggest banker in town," Ofelia said, pushing back her plate and crossing her forearms on the table. "His dad coerced the owner of the Elkhart Hotel to install him as the manager. That's how he met Cariña de la Cruz. She was doing very well for herself running her family's lavandería after her dad died. She was well-regarded and very beautiful. Charles wanted her, and she wanted nothing to do with him."

"Do you have a picture of her?" Nicky asked. His bottom lip shined from the fried chicken leg he'd been eating, and it was a distraction she didn't need.

"I have some newspaper clippings," Ofelia said. "I'll bring them by." She took a drink of her iced tea. The fact that no one got up to get a second plate or dessert spoke to the power of Ofelia's storytelling.

"When she wouldn't give him the time of day," Ofelia said, putting down her red cup, "Charles spread rumors about her 'moral character' to convince the town's wealthy to stop fre-

196 ANGELINA M. LOPEZ

quenting her lavandería. Cariña employed fifteen washerwomen and ten deliverymen. She felt she had no choice but to marry him if she wanted to save her business and their jobs."

Gillian pushed back her plate, no longer able to enjoy her enchilada and fruit salad with lettuce in it. The weight of her outrage was outsized for a century-old story about a woman she'd never met. But it was so unfair.

"Her business and wealth became his when they married," Ofelia continued. "But that couldn't distract Charles's daddy from the color of her skin. Although Latham Bowling was so impatient for a grandson that he pitted Charles and his brother against each other by offering five thousand dollars to whoever produced a child first, he never wanted a grandson as brown as the one Cariña gave him."

Everyone shifted uncomfortably at the table. Each and every one of them had dealt with suspicion about their color or managed it for someone they loved.

"Charles claimed he'd been seduced into the marriage and then bamboozled to go along with a concocted pregnancy. He said he was an unwitting victim of a plan to fool his father. When he found a woman at a shelter for unwed mothers who would claim Cariña's child, most likely with a bribe from Cariña's earnings, he was able to turn the trial and the country's attention on two brown women duking it out each day claiming they were the mother."

"That poor woman," a cousin said. There was no hope of a happy resolution to this story.

"They ruled that Cariña had faked her pregnancy," Ofelia continued quietly. "Charles was granted a divorce and all that Cariña had brought to the marriage as part of his 'restitution.' The woman from the home was given custody of the baby boy. The account of Cariña's reaction in court when the baby was taken away is…is difficult to read."

Gillian blinked back tears and cleared her throat. "Did she ever get her son back?"

Ofelia watched her through her hot-pink glasses and shook her head. "Not as far the researcher could find. The woman from the home and the baby disappeared. As infamous as Cariña was, no one is sure what happened to her, either. One report said she opened a saloon in Colorado. Charles Bowling married a white woman and, a couple years later, jumped in the Viridescent. Hester Bowling kept his name on all their business dealings, but really, she was the one who made the Elkhart Hotel what it was."

Gillian's heart throbbed for Cariña and her lost child. Under the table, Nicky squeezed her knee.

"You guys are the worst," she said, looking at him.

"Yeah," he murmured back. "I'm sorry."

His hold on her leg felt warm and supportive and not remotely sexual.

"Y'all mind if I sit here?"

Gillian turned to see Yesenia, in a T-shirt and shorts, standing there like a ray of sunlight breaking through the clouds. Her black curls once again looked adorable and complemented her wide, dark face.

"Yesenia!" she exclaimed. "I'm so glad you're here." She really was. Yesenia was the beaming hope that women could overcome the abuse of unworthy husbands. She hadn't heard from her since she'd presented her proposal days ago and she'd planned to give her until tomorrow before checking in. She had a couple more ideas that she hoped would sweeten the pot.

Gillian introduced Yesenia to everyone at the table as she sat. Ofelia had enjoyed her baked goods in the teachers' lounge. Nicky asked if she had time to provide four dozen pan dulce for the volunteers every day. When she stammered back a yes and asked what he'd like, he told her to choose.

"Just make them sweet," he said with that smile, and Gillian, Yesenia, and Ofelia took long drinks of their iced tea.

"I'm sorry I haven't gotten back to you," Yesenia said quietly as Nicky and Ofelia chatted. "I wanted to come and see you in person."

Gillian smiled through her disappointment. It wasn't easy to say no to a once-powerful bruja. "Don't worry about it," she said, putting her hand on Yesenia's. "I dumped a lot all at once on you. Perhaps, in the future, we can—"

"I want to do it," Yesenia said.

Gillian clamped her mouth closed in surprise.

"I want to get a loan, like you said, and start investing and… I want to think bigger. I want to be confident. Como tú."

Gillian swallowed her self-deprecating laugh and sincerely said, "Thank you."

"You're right. I work hard, I have special skills, and I deserve it just like those gringos. Señora, por favor, will you help me?"

Gillian couldn't hold back the smile that trembled over her face. "Por supuesto. I'd be honored."

"Do you think you can help mi amiga, tambien? She rents a chair at a salon in Bartlesville, but with real estate prices here in Freedom I told her she could maybe open a salon here. She has a little bit of savings. I told her maybe you can help her."

Gillian felt this burble, like her brain had just been put on a low-lit burner. She knew this feeling. It was the feeling of a good idea about to simmer to the surface.

"Yes," she said. She really wanted to get to her laptop. "I can help her. Is she a good stylist?"

"Very good," Yesenia said. "She does mine."

"Can I get her number? I'll call her."

"Sí, señora. Gracias."

She probably wouldn't be able to get in to see her before her screening interview with the medium-sized Chicago firm for the financial solutions advisor position. The email she'd received from the recruiter had made it sound like it would just be a formality; the firm was extremely interested.

The chance of finally ending her job hunt felt almost too good to be true.

Almost as good as Nicky's hand, still on her leg. As she and Yesenia discussed next steps, his thumb occasionally slid back and forth as he talked to her tía, like it enjoyed the sensation of touching her as much as she enjoyed the touch.

He squeezed her leg and she turned to look at him. "It's time for me to turn off the lights and show off the mural. Are your kids afraid of the dark?"

The windows that ringed the upper level of the train station had been covered for maximum darkness when the projector was on. She wanted to kiss him for his thoughtfulness. "I'll go find them."

"Okay," he said. He ran his thumb over the soft inner flesh of her thigh. "Wish me luck."

"Luck," she said as he let go and stood up. Her leg felt bereft.

She'd always been a tactile person. Coming from her family, you had to be. But simple touches of care had not been part of her marriage. For the first time, she felt a spurt of anger that wasn't self-directed at what those ten years had robbed her of. Maybe touches of care shouldn't be part of their "friendship." But all of Nicky's efforts to be bad and break her curse—his lock-picking and teasing and flirting and touching and kissing and...and kissing—seemed to be working.

She stood up to find her children and thought about leaping and odds of success and the two kids who never let a fantasma or a cadejo scare them away.

CHAPTER 17

The following Friday evening, Nicky kept one eye on the volunteers up on the scaffolding and the other eye on the door. He pulled out his phone, the white light bright in the station that was dark except for the white-blue mural projection.

Gillian was about to be late for her own meeting.

Over the last week, the quiet in the train station had exploded into a hectic, happy roar. The flood of people that'd shown up Monday became a manageable flow of volunteers over the next four days thanks to Gillian and her spreadsheets. Now, a week ahead of schedule, with classic rock blasting through the train station and volunteers chatting up and down the wall, the mural outline was one long evening from being finished. They'd already ordered pizza and Alex was bringing celebratory drinks over later.

Tomorrow, the train station would quiet again as Nicky began the monthlong effort of painting the massive mural.

When he left Freedom at the end of the summer, he'd be leaving behind his largest piece, an ode to the past, present, and future of Milagro Street and its people. There'd been a bit of grumbling on the Freedom Historical Society board that

Nicky's mural didn't focus on Freedom as a whole. However, Joe, Ofelia, and Jeremiah had convinced the group that it was a fair trade since whole decades had gone by when the Chamber of Commerce wouldn't even put Milagro Street on the city map and two historians had written accounts of Freedom's past without acknowledging the Mexican-American community that lived here.

Nicky had made it easier by giving them an option: a free mural that focused on Milagro Street or no mural at all. Freedom's lost history would be showcased.

Nicky took his eye off the door to give a handshake and a goodbye to a high school student who'd stepped up as co-captain to gain her volunteer hours. The girl beamed when Nicky told her to contact him when she needed a letter of recommendation. The co-captains' dependable involvement allowed Nicky to one-eye the process, focus on the fun stuff like bullshitting with volunteers while he got some tracing done, and devote a chunk of his busy week to wandering into Gillian's office so he could be a sounding board and chin-in-his-hand audience as she developed the plan she was about to present to Milagro Street's biggest supporters.

Nicky had been grateful the train station had been chock-full of people whenever he was in her office. Sitting in that grainy, noir, detective-movie lighting with her, her excitement as bright as an oncoming meteor, it was only the audience that had kept him from pressing one hand over her mouth and the other between her legs. She'd always liked the threat of an audience. *Forget what I said,* he'd wanted to beg. *Use me until I'm all used up.*

His "friend" was getting her groove back, and it was burning him alive.

The station door opened as the student walked away.

He had to blink against the sunlight surrounding the person coming in. They were all turning into cave dwellers. But he'd

202 | ANGELINA M. LOPEZ

know the silhouette of her body anywhere. He could trace it in his sleep. Still, he had to look twice. This silhouette had a halo of curls around her head.

When Gillian closed the door and walked toward him, it wasn't only the residual sunspots that left him dazzled.

Gillian had cut her hair. Her curls were now just a little longer than Nicky's hair, hit at her jaw, and—fuck—exposed her neck. In the dim light, it looked like all the highlights had been cut away. Those waves and commas around her head were dark. Were her.

She ran her hand through the curls. "I…uh… I figured I should check Sonia's work." Sonia was Yesenia's hairstylist friend, the new potential business owner in Freedom if Gillian's plan went as she wanted. "I broke the sound barrier driving back from Bartlesville. I think she did a pretty good job."

A pretty good job? He struggled for words other than: *You're gorgeous—I want you—Be mine.* In the dim blue-white glow, her eyes settled on his mouth. He realized he was chewing on his bottom lip. Biting it rather than taking a bite out of her.

"You look great," he finally got out. He gave her a quarter of what he was feeling, hoping it would relieve the pressure. She wore silver hoops in her ears and a floaty short-sleeved summer dress with white flowers on an olive background that showed off her lovely brown legs. "You look happy."

Her wide smile became killer. "I am," she marveled. "I tried an hechizo this morning. Thought I would test if the curse had lifted."

He hadn't tried to pick that lock since the night he'd touched her. "How'd it go?"

"Nothing happened," she said. "But…it felt like something could happen. Like I was on the verge."

Jesus. Fuck. He was the only man who'd reliably gotten her over the edge. He cleared his throat. "You don't need magic for this presentation."

He'd always believed that if Gillian Armstead ever had an inkling of what he felt for her, it would be more disastrous than all the disasters he'd already survived. But for over a week now, she'd had an inkling, and instead of it leaving a crater in him, it'd been nice. It'd been real smiles and soft touches, elegant fingers on his arm to get his attention or a quick hug of thanks, and little asides to all of the history they shared. It helped that she'd always been jealous. Long ago, when she'd said he could be with other girls, that might've hurt her, too.

He was dying to test the boundaries of their friendship but didn't dare. Gillian still planned to leave at the end of the summer and so did he, taking William with him and never coming back. There was comfort in the shackles of friendship. There was comfort in knowing that those shackles were a little tight for her, too.

The big, brown-eyed way she was looking at him now... She'd finally run out of colored contacts during the week and had switched to the far-less-expensive clear ones. The station door opened, letting him off the hook of whatever disastrous thing he was about to say.

Alex, Jeremiah, Cynthia, Joe, and Ofelia entered along with Yesenia Lozano. Gillian's sister, Sissy, had hoped to make it but had called that morning to say she'd be running late. Auditions for her reality cooking show were going well.

The ladies correctly praised and petted Gillian's new cut while she corralled them into the office. Nicky went to turn down the music as Gillian flipped on her office light and got her guests settled in the foldout chairs she'd set up in a semi-circle facing her desk.

When he turned around after checking the coolers to make sure they had enough cold beverages for when the pizza arrived, he saw that Gillian was sitting on the edge of her desk looking at him, holding a copy of her proposal against her knee. She was waiting for him. She didn't need him for this presentation. But still, she waited.

He gave the wad of cash in his pocket to one of the co-captains then entered her office to take a seat in the empty chair instead of at her feet.

"Thanks, everyone, for coming," Gillian said, standing in front of her desk. "Our plan right now is to launch the speakeasy when we unveil the mural. But is there something more we can do with that engaged audience? Something that showcases the potential of Milagro Street and gets that audience invested in helping it grow?" She held up the proposal. "I believe I have an idea that will do just that."

He'd seen her like this before, giving her speech for senior class president, answering the questions from the Neewollah pageant judges. When Gillian's skills and desires aligned, nothing could stop her. As Alex flipped the proposal's cover page, Nicky recognized the way she kept her eyes on her sister. Once every blue moon, he'd gotten the same awed look from his little brother.

"I propose that we position the event as a fundraiser to seed a fund that will grant loans to women and people of color hoping to start businesses here on Milagro Street," Gillian said. "If we receive the grant money, it will be a start to putting businesses back in these buildings. But this fund will benefit people who society doesn't think of as business owners, people who have a great idea but not the resources or support."

Alex's eyes were huge. "That's exactly what Rosalinda did."

"Right," Gillian said, nodding. "And that's the history we highlight: our grandmother, the uncelebrated founder of Milagro Street, sold whisky to raise money for business microloans. We're doing the same a century later. It allows the people who come for the launch to not only enjoy and marvel, but to *do*," she said, her smile wide and eyes bright. "It makes them active participants invested in the future of Milagro Street, which means that they'll come back to Freedom, the museum, Loretta's, and the businesses that benefit from their involvement. That's how we'll pitch it around town. We'll close this end of the street and have live music, local vendors, a kids' fair in the one of the empty lots, an evening ticketed party here in the train station, and a higher-priced premium event at Loretta's."

She pointed at the binder. "I've laid out the financial structure for the fundraiser. Alex and Cynthia, the one downside is that I'm asking Loretta's to absorb the costs and donate the evening's proceeds—"

Cynthia made *pshhh* sound as Alex nodded in agreement. "If the best financial mind I know thinks it's a good idea, then it's a good idea."

When she'd talked about this plan, she'd never once shied away from the fact that Cynthia would be the one making the decisions about Loretta's with Alex. Technically, it still belonged to Gillian; she hadn't heard from her ex or his attorney. The man was drawing out this final effort to bully and antagonize her.

Jeremiah, Nicky, and Joe volunteered to cover Loretta's costs and pitch in as well. With a blinding smile, Gillian pointed out that she already had their suggested donations and tasks outlined on page six. The money she wouldn't accept for herself she'd accept for this project.

Cynthia flipped through the binder. "Gillian, after the party, running this fund is gonna be a shit ton of work." She tucked her auburn hair behind her ear as she looked up at her best friend. "Are you…are you thinkin' about staying?"

He knew Gillian's answer. It was another reason she was so happy.

"No," she said, quick and soft. "I actually have a second interview with a firm in Chicago."

She'd asked him to come down from the scaffolding Tuesday afternoon to give him the news: she'd had a screening interview with a Chicago firm and it had gone amazing. She'd hugged him like she couldn't help it and he'd been able to feel the power seeping back into her.

"Congratulations, girl," Cynthia said, her drawly voice full of sweet melancholy. "Liberty Manufacturing probably couldn't afford you anyway."

Gillian's eyebrows rose with the compliment.

She pointed again at the binder. "Inside, you'll see my five-year plan for the fund. It will start small, we'll hand out just four grants the first year. I can oversee the plan in my spare time until year three when the goal is for the fund to have grown enough to pay for a part-time administrator. A committee, which I would love all of you to be a part of, will choose who gets the grants." As if handing her sister and best friend a salve, she said, "Chicago is close. I promise never to be so far away again."

The distance she was talking about wasn't measured in miles.

Gillian cleared her throat. "Grant winners will get the same entrepreneurial coaching and investment advice that I'm doing now with Yesenia and her hairstylist friend, Sonia." She grinned at Yesenia. "With that in mind, I'd like to propose the first two recipients of the Rosalinda Padilla-Hugh Award."

Alex made a face. "That's what you're calling it?"

"It's up for discussion but it's what I recommend," Gillian said. "She was a Hugh by marriage, we're all descended Hughs, and we might as well try to get them to buy in. Making peace with them is what Rosalinda wanted."

The money Wayland Hugh had made on the east side as a landowner and bootlegger had allowed the large Hugh clan to run roughshod over Freedom for generations. When Nicky had to kick an ass in high school, it usually belonged to a Hugh. But last year the girls had discovered that Wayland's rejected son, Edward, had lost his place in the family because he married Rosalinda. It was their grandmother's last wish that her granddaughters use their strength to heal the east-versus-west-side divide.

Alex rolled her eyes and mumbled something about "peace" and "Hughs" and "hell icing over."

"Anyway," Gillian said over her sister's grumbles. "Yesenia and her friend Sonia would like to be the first new business owners on Milagro Street by occupying the Day Building." She motioned at the beaming woman. "Yesenia plans to open a Mexican bakery and coffee shop on the bottom level. Sonia, who gave me this fabulous haircut, would like to open a hair salon on the second floor."

Joe harrumphed. "*That's* why you were on my ass about inspecting that building," he said. "Yeah, it's the soundest unoccupied building on Milagro Street. I was kinda amazed at the condition it was in."

Gillian nodded. "It's crying out for a fresh start. Inventive, dedicated, hardworking, underrepresented business owners like them are who we want to attract to Milagro Street. Their b-to-c enterprises will encourage loyalty, repeat visits, and foot traffic, which is sorely needed to bring life back to this street."

"Mija, I firmly support you and your goals," Ofelia said. "But are you sure you can't find something to do here? The services for Ben with the Palomino County schools are actually quite robust. This plan is brilliant. I would love to stop one drip of the Kansas brain drain."

"Thank you, tía," Gillian said, smiling.

Yesenia jumped in. "I was just talking to a friend who doesn't know what she should do with her husband's life insurance money."

"You can tell her to give me a call," Gillian said. But she said nothing else about her tía's hopes. He could already see her path out of town. As long as he didn't beg to move to Chicago with her, they could enjoy the rest of the summer and then go their separate ways without injury. It wasn't much to convince himself he believed that.

Gillian sat back on her desk and exhaled. "So that's it. Take the proposal, peruse it, call me if you have any questions, then, next week, maybe we can—"

"Next week?" Alex said with a smirk. "By next week, Cynthia's already gonna have the vendors for the fundraiser lined up, Jeremiah is gonna have a sponsorship from the college, and I'm already gonna have the website built and the event plastered all over social media. Let's do this. I say, 'yes.'"

Agreeing "ayes" came fast around the room. Nicky released his lip from his teeth.

There was a tornado of hugging and laughing and backslapping going on in the office when the pizza arrived so Nicky invited everyone to eat, then doubled the delivery driver's payment and tip to haul ass and bring back more pizza and drinks. Music got turned back up and everyone yelled out ideas for the fundraising event that Gillian wrote down while she sat on the edge of the scaffolding, her shins gleaming in the blue-black light as she swung her feet back and forth, writing with one hand and balancing a piece of veggie pizza in the other. When the pizza was decimated, Gillian's family became Nicky's newest volunteers: they all grabbed a square that needed a few finishing strokes and got to work.

From his spot near the projector, they looked like busy bees in their own honeycomb.

Nicky stayed singularly aware of Gillian. He knew when she retreated to make a phone call in her office. He knew when she was making her way back to him.

"I called to apologize for being late but my kids didn't even notice I was gone," she said with a huff. "You have room for one more?"

"Of course." He'd saved a square for her. It was next to his own. He got her a thick pencil and a printout of her square with the color codes then led her to where they'd be working. It was on the edge of the second level of the scaffolding. Torres Construction had included narrow stairs in between the levels, which were harder to work around but much safer for citizen volunteers unused to clambering around on scaffolding.

Nicky pointed the way but walked behind her. The scaffolding wasn't ideal for anyone in a dress. He didn't allow his eyes to rise above the silky skin at the back of her knees.

Her square included the intricate brickwork at the roofline of one of Milagro Street's buildings and the outermost rays of a sunrise. It only needed a few more strokes and the color codes filled in. Nicky worked close to her, connecting the two squares where the braces blocked the projection.

They were the only quiet spot in the music and chatter and laughter.

"This is the first time I've worked on the mural," she said.

From the corner of his eye, he could see her slim arm moving as she traced the diamond patterns of the brickwork. It felt like she was drawing on his skin. He would know exactly what lines were hers.

"This feels important," she said, checking her sheet to add a paint code. "That's why you drew so many people here this week, even after Granmo's food was gone. You made everyone who walked in that door, regardless of ability, skill, education, or financial status, feel they were an important part of something that mattered."

He ran his tongue along his teeth and didn't stop the movement of his pencil along the gel-smoothed wall. It was darker, right here with the vertical scaffolding blocking much of the light. "I'm glad you got to make your mark on it," he said without looking at her.

She stood close enough for him to feel her warmth. "Me too."

They drew for several minutes in silence and she didn't move away and neither did he and he'd been fortunate to enjoy some wildly filthy sex acts in his life but he was certain he'd never done anything as erotic as drawing next to Gillian Armstead. He thought sketching her created the most combustible happy place feeling. But creating *with* her... He was a little sappy kid and a drowning-in-love young man and a successful adult who knew better and he was in heaven.

She stretched up on tiptoes to complete a pattern over his head.

"Here," he said. "I can..." But rather than stepping out of her way or connecting the lines for her, he put his hand on her hip, on the soft filmy dress, and tugged her in front of him. He dropped his hand off her hip but stretched his arm up near hers to draw. His shadow covered her completely.

Less than an inch separated their bodies. A long, shaky breath escaped her.

"Thank you for everything you did this week," she whispered.

He filled in the couple of lines then just left his hand there. He wanted to curl around her and eat his peach-pie girl up.

He dropped his head near her ear. "I didn't do anything," he murmured into her gorgeous new curls.

She stepped back against him. "Thank you for everything you did." It was like she'd pushed him off the scaffolding. His bones clanged with the impact of her. "I thought I had a good idea but my meter for gauging that is..." Her free hand searched back, touched his hip, and he twined their fingers together. "My meter was on low battery. I needed a power-up. You gave me that."

She pushed her plush little ass back and he realized he was hard. He hadn't meant to be hard. But she fit against him, beneath his nose and in the width of his shoulders and the span of his hips so perfectly. "I'm so glad to be with you this summer." In the music and chatter and laughter, he could hear her whisper as clear as a bell. She gripped his fingers and rubbed her soft, warm, peach-smelling body against him like he was hers to mark. "I'm so glad we still have time left."

He dipped his knees, just a little, not enough to expose her, and let her feel what she did to him. With the slow lunge of hips, he let her know how good he could make it for her.

"Me too, hechicera," he said, his mouth against her temple. "Me too, baby girl." She could be both. His baby to take care of. His girl to have and to hold. His mighty, mighty sorceress to worship.

"Juli?" he heard Alex call. "You still here? We're gonna take off."

He straightened slowly and slid to the right.

"I—" Gillian's voice came out strangled. She coughed to clear it. "I'm all done. I'll walk out with you."

He was tempted to reach out and hold her there, to teach her what can happen when she didn't ask for permission to be dismissed.

"Have a good night," he said softly, staring blindly at the wall.

"You too." He heard her walk to the stairs.

He turned his attention back to his drawing and the remaining volunteers and the music and the chatter and the laughter and he didn't think about how tempted he'd been to break their shackles in a room full of people. He didn't think about how much of this blessed, horrible summer they had left.

And he definitely did not think about how, after tonight, they'd once again be alone in the train station.

CHAPTER 18

Gillian's already busy life was about to get busier. Last week, she'd put together the fund proposal, met with Yesenia and Sonia to draft business plans, mooned over then sexed up her pornographically competent friend, and made substantial headway on the massive grant application.

Next week, she'd add event planning to her roster of duties. Fortunately, "beg for a job" looked like a task that could be crossed off.

But today was Saturday. Today, her only duty, goal, and joy was to spend time with her children.

"Got you, Mama," Ben called, sending her up on her toes as a blast of cold water caught her in the center of her back.

Barefoot in her parents' backyard, she spun on him, aiming the jet from the foam blaster right at his bare, round tummy gone a beautiful deep brown. They'd finally made it to Freedom's public pool. Cynthia had groaned in despair when both children had run into the kiddie pool with its fountains and bubblers, all thoughts of a private pool with a slide forgotten.

Now, Ben sprinted away yelling "No fair!" as Gillian chased him. "You're out!" he demanded.

She chased him between the brick-bordered garden beds. "If I'm out, then who's squirting you with water?"

"Follow the rules!"

"Okay," panted Gillian, taking a few steps to halt before she stooped to hold the neon-colored foam against her knees. Why fight an opportunity to stretch out in the grass and rest?

Cold water spritzed her left butt cheek.

"I got you, too, Mama," Naomi squeaked from behind her.

Why couldn't she lie down and rest? Because she'd taught her kids to fight dirty.

Gillian spun around, roaring, sweeping Naomi up and tickling her lime-green-covered belly as Naomi screamed deliciously.

"Me too, me too," sang Ben, dancing around them in his swim trunks as he shot water into the air that sprinkled back down on them.

"You too?!" Gillian echoed before she plopped Naomi down and roared again, sending the two kids shrieking off in different directions. She clutched her foam blaster and was about to take off after them when she noticed her mother's maroon sedan pulling into the driveway. Crammed into the back seat were paper grocery bags, their handles sticking up like dog ears.

She'd told her mom that she'd do the shopping this week.

"Come on," she called to them, swallowing the irritation in her voice. "Let's help Granmo and Granpo bring in the groceries."

Gillian threw on her white cover-up before following her kids out the gate to the carport.

"I said I'd go to the store," Gillian said as Mary got out on the driver's side and Tucker got out on the passenger. He opened the sedan's back door where the kids were already doing the waiting wiggle. "You guys have got to let me help out more."

Ben tested the bags until he could lug one up, and Tucker handed Naomi a bag of oranges.

"We just needed a few things," Mary said as she walked to the back of the car. Her few things filled the back seat and trunk. "We were out of ice cream."

"Yes," Naomi said, raising her fist over her head as both kids staggered toward the door Tucker was holding open for them.

"At least let me give you some money," Gillian said as she followed her mother inside with an armful of groceries.

Mary thumped her bags down on the countertop. "I don't know what I did with the receipt." She surprised Gillian with a quick hug. "Let us baby you. You deserve it."

Her dad rubbed her back before he followed the kids back to the car.

She'd realized over the last few weeks that she was not the best judge of what she deserved and what she didn't. As she was rebuilding the muscle, it was best to lean on the assessment of people she loved and trusted.

Her parents had put on hold whatever plans they had for themselves in order to take care of Gillian and her children. They'd said, repeatedly and excessively, that they wouldn't have it any other way. She wondered as she continued to watch her dad's careful courtship and her mom's quiet response. Her parents ran errands together, took long walks together, and Mary kept a collection of the little things Tucker picked up for her—a bouquet of clover blooms, a flattened bottle cap from her favorite pop, a piece of quartz—on the windowsill above the sink.

That window through which she could see Loretta's and Alex's homes was a sacred spot for Mary. She'd made a small ofrenda on the sill with a rosary from her dad's funeral and a tiny framed picture of the tía who taught her the arts.

Would Tucker have moved out of Sissy's room under the stairs and into the bedroom of the woman he was still married to if Gillian and her kids weren't present?

She thought of the heat she'd felt on the scaffolding with Nicky yesterday evening, the way it had simmered relentlessly all week and then, at the first opportunity, become hot enough to bubble the gel-prepped wall.

Was that what it was like for her parents?

She realized she was thinking about her *parents* in relation to the sexual tension she felt with Nicky and made the very mature decision to not think about any of it at all.

When all the groceries were inside, Tucker waved them out of the kitchen.

"Go play," he told them. "You'll just mess up my system." His success had allowed for various renovations around the house, but so far, the older kitchen was untouched. Tucker fit the excess of food into the limited cabinet space with a Tetris-like expertise.

Gillian set up the sprinkler in the shade of a big oak tree for her kids to play in, then joined her mom at the bistro table beneath the deck's green-striped awning. Mary had poured her favorite, Chex Mix, into an avocado-green bowl.

Gillian sipped sun tea while a standing fan kicked at the curls of her new messy haircut.

"It's nice to see you relax," Mary said, pushing her perfect wave of black hair off her shoulders while she leaned back in the wicker chair.

Gillian snorted and looked into the bowl to pick out Wheat Chex. "Since I can't do the grocery shopping, laundry, or cleaning, it feels like all I've been doing this summer is relaxing."

"Never in your life," Mary declared. "Mija, you were born with a to-do list and a plan. It was very intimidating to be your mother."

She looked at her mom, who was smiling as she watched her grandchildren. Mary had never said anything like that before.

"You always seemed..." Gillian began.

Not confident. No, Loretta and Alex defined confidence to her. But her mother had always seemed unwaveringly committed to a rosy view, even in defiance of all obvious evidence. "You always seemed very sure of things."

"I had three girls who were strong-willed in three different ways," she chuckled. "If I'd blinked, you three would have eaten me alive."

Perhaps Mary hadn't blinked. But the family dynamic between the five of them—Mary, Tucker, and the three girls—had been unhappy for the second half of Gillian's life. It was hard not to resent her mother for that.

Thomas had his family's banking fortune and his multi-generations of blue blood and an estate with a pompous name on the Maryland coast, but he wasn't the only one with a legacy to preserve. If Gillian was going to embrace a life where the bar and the east side and her hometown played larger roles, she would need to make peace with her parents and the relationship they were working to rebuild.

Why did you let Dad drink? was on the edge of her tongue when her mother asked, "Did you have a nice time last night?"

Gillian focused on finding the most Worcester-y cereal bits and made a noncommittal hum. At her mom's continued silence, Gillian straightened, said, "Stop," and raised the icy glass to her lips.

"¿Qué?" her mother said, oh-so innocently.

Her mother understood Spanish but wasn't comfortable reading or speaking it. Gillian's focus on the language in college made her more fluent than her mom, except when it came to spellwork. Her mother did all of her brujería in Spanish, believing the language channeled the magic better.

"Don't *qué* me," Gillian said. "Turn your inner eye somewhere else. Nicky and I are just friends."

Her mother wasn't psychic, but her ability to read auras and sense energies was doctorate level. Her intuiting skills had been one of the reasons Gillian had been so furious that Mary hadn't headed her father's drinking off at the pass. After last night in the shadows with Nicky, Gillian could just imagine what energies she was giving off.

"The glow suits you, mija," Mary said, the mildest of teases in her voice.

Gillian kept her eyes on her jumping, screaming kids. She couldn't believe what she was about to tell her mother. For all of Mary's talk of the body's humors and the polarity magic of opposing sexual energies, it'd been Tía Ofelia who'd cheerily explained to them where babies came from.

"Nicky had an idea to break my curse," she said quickly.

"¿Y?"

"Y nada," Gillian said. She'd lit a novena candle this morning with a prayer for Thomas to send the signed contract soon so she could resolve the issues of the bar ownership and the kids' visitation. The flame had glowed without a flicker of saintly intervention. "But it feels like the magic is right there." She rubbed the tips of her fingers together. "Like it's one blessed word away from working."

"You are forging new paths, mija. Have you attempted a new opening prayer?"

The question, among brujas, was almost as offensive as asking a left-handed person to write with their right hand or a color-blind person to see the colors they were missing. Gillian had opened every intention with el Padre Nuestro since the first works she'd done on her own when she'd turned eleven. There'd been a tremendous confidence knowing God was on her side.

Her mother wouldn't ask it without good reason. "Who else would I give thanks to?"

"There are many who call to La Virgen de Guadalupe," her mother said with a shrug, as if she wasn't suggesting a blasphemy that could blow Gillian's power away and ensure it never came back. "They leave out El Dios y Jesus entirely."

"La Virgen?" Gillian crinkled her forehead, thinking of the Virgen birdbath in her grandmother's front yard. "She's so…"

"What?"

"Passive. Sweet. Soft." Gillian had wielded the intention of God with her magics. How could she now turn to a lady okay with being stuck in a Midwestern front yard with chipped blue robes covered in bird poop?

She understood why Mary had suggested it. Her mother was the soul of accommodation. She'd forgone her own dreams to become a teacher by working at the bank to support her high school sweetheart-turned-husband in college. She'd enlisted at the bar when Loretta needed help.

She'd dropped everything to take care of Gillian's kids.

Gillian looked into her tanned lap. "I don't think La Virgen is for me."

Mary just chuckled. "Juliana, who wears the pants in the Torres family?"

The women. No one questioned it. Even in the quiet relationship between her parents, it wasn't that her dad had dominated her mother's will. It was that the alcohol had, and her mother hadn't stopped it.

"It's easy to misunderstand the Holy Mother Guadalupe," Mary said. "Yes, she's kinder and more forgiving. But, mija, you know how fierce a mother's love can be. There are many saint cards showing La Virgen beating the devil to a pulp."

Gillian felt an unwanted surge of camaraderie. The reason she'd gotten out of a marriage that would have provided every privilege for her children was for their emotional and mental well-being. She would moderate their exposure to his belittling, his circular arguments, and his foundational belief that he had a right to express his disappointment in his toddlers. Even the weekend-long, four-times-a-year visitations were more than she wanted. But she would beat the negative thoughts he inevitably lent to her children's lives to a bloody pulp.

Mary continued. "All those titles she has, mija—Queen of Heaven, Mother of God, Mother of Angels—she's the facilitator to all the higher powers. She's not the pinnacle of one, she's the gateway to all. She even allows the indigenous people to continue to worship their own gods while appeasing the church."

Gillian knew the story of the Lady of Guadalupe, who appeared to an indigenous man on a Mexican hillside and said she wanted a temple built in her honor. His cloak emblazoned with the miracle of her appearance was still on display in Mexico City. Many believed the Spaniards bastardized her actual name, Coatlaxopeuh. When the indigenous people were being forced to repudiate their own gods or face the wrath of the colonizers, Coatlaxopeuh—who some believed was a version of the Mother Goddess Tonantzin—allowed them to worship their deities right under the Spaniards' suspicious gaze.

Tonantzin Coatlaxopeuh, La Virgen de Guadalupe, protected her children.

"She is a powerful representative of liminal space," Mary said. One of the tenants of their arts was that magic was found in liminal, in-between spaces: doorways, borders, rivers, dawn, dusk, the breath between one season and the next. Where two absolutes met was a line of powerful convergence. "That's why she's a perfect guide for you."

Gillian cocked her head. "What do you mean?"

Mary smiled back like she thought Gillian was joking. "Juliana," she said, her smile fading when she realized she wasn't. "Why do you think your magic has always been so effective?"

Gillian shrugged.

"Because, mijita, you *are* the crossroads." Mary looked exasperated. "You are where everything meets: Mexico and the United States, big city and small town, math and magic, wealth and poverty, the masculine and the feminine, devotion to la familia and admiration for the outside world, the logical and the spiritual. You've felt pulled in two different directions your whole life but you've never needed to struggle to choose one spot over another; you are the doorway. So is La Virgen. You two are made for each other."

And just like that, her mother rocked her world.

She was Mexican-American, a bruja financial planner, from small-town Kansas who'd been big-city successful. After the first part of her life feeling like she couldn't settle into Freedom as effortlessly as her family seemed to, and then another decade and a half of feeling like the East Coast had too many barbs, this was the first time she'd ever considered not having to settle. She *was* a liminal space. And she could find happiness, satisfaction, and power in the in-between. She didn't have to align herself with the rigid, small-minded assessments of Thomas and his ilk, and she didn't have to defy her hard work and education and wide-world view to be able to appreciate her hometown. She didn't have to stand on one side of the road or the other.

She could stand in the crossroads.

Just like Nicky did. All the sparks that had flown each time he'd threatened to break her curse hadn't come just from her and her latent magic; he wasn't just the flint to her steel. Instead, they were two live wires, both powerful beings who were making the most of their in-between existence.

You two are made for each other.

She looked at her mother, really looked at the beautiful, black-haired woman who was a powerful bruja and a compassionate mother and a hardworking hustler who'd supported their family, had even set aside a little to augment Gillian's scholarship, who Gillian had openly disrespected for years.

"Why'd you let Dad start drinking?" she asked.

Mary's face deflated.

This was an old argument, one that they'd had many times before Mary had kicked Tucker out at the end of that fateful summer thirteen years ago and Gillian had stopped speaking to her for a couple of years.

"Juliana," her mother said quietly, looking away. "I never *let* him do anything."

Gillian put her hand over her mom's, over the tiny chip of an engagement ring she'd never taken off. "I'm really trying to understand this time," she said urgently. "Help me understand. With your magic. Didn't you see it coming? Wasn't there any way to intervene?"

She felt that old, throat-clogging frustration that her mother hadn't done more.

She heard the same frustration in her mother's voice. "You think I should've sought out the secret fears and hidden depression of the man I trusted and relied on and was in love with?" Mary's inexhaustible patience was waning. "Found the time between raising three girls and supporting a family of five to keep an eagle eye on my lover?"

It was so weird to be handed this adult perspective of what her mother had faced.

She felt a warm hand squeeze her shoulder.

"Juliana," her father said, his touch sliding away as he pulled up a deck chair to sit next to Mary. Tucker had bright blue eyes and watched her steadily as he put a hand on the back of Mary's chair. "From what I understand from your mother, that's not how y'alls magic works. I needed to want the help. To believe. But all I wanted was a publishing career, and if I couldn't have that, I wanted to feel sorry for myself."

He pulled on the corner of his blond moustache, a gesture as dependable as she'd once believed he was. "You came home that summer trying to fix me and the greatest disservice I've ever done to you is letting you believe you could. That was so unfair to you. The only one who could fix me was me. Your mother is no more responsible for my alcoholism than you're responsible for Thomas being a bad man and a lousy husband."

Her stomach rolled at the thought of that parallel. Her father, her kind, creative, thoughtful, introverted, loving father, was a universe away from Thomas.

She certainly wasn't her mother. "Dad, those are two different—"

"Honey, they're not." He smiled gently. "Just like Thomas, I made sure the women in my life felt responsible for my bad choices."

A startled and mildly pathetic laugh came out of her. Oh, dear Virgen. Had she married her dad?

Both of them, sitting close to each other, were looking at her with so much love. They weren't on opposite sides of this table.

"As hard as you've been on me, mija," Mary said, "it's not a tenth as hard as you've been on yourself. You must forgive yourself. Just because you stand in the crossroads doesn't mean you can control all the traffic."

Forgiveness. She'd thought she'd appropriately blamed Thomas for his narcissism and what it had wrought. But she blamed herself more. Gillian was the oldest daughter of the oldest daughter's oldest daughter, and until she'd gotten married, feeling powerful had been as innate as the brown of her hair and the numbers that unraveled in her brain. Not only did she assume she could fix what was broken, she felt responsible for fixing it.

But just because she was powerful didn't mean she could. Just because she stood in the crossroads did not mean she could control all the traffic. Now it was time to forgive herself.

On that truly astonishing bit of insight, Gillian heard the back door slide open. She swiped the heels of her palms over her eyes.

"Everything okay out here?" Tía Ofelia asked.

She caught her mother's eye and nodded before Mary said, "Yep. C'mon out."

Ofelia patted Gillian's shoulder and took a seat in a spare

chair. "Sorry to bother you, mija," she said. "I wanted to bring by these newspaper clippings I promised you."

Gillian gave her a blank look.

"About Cariña de la Cruz."

Cariña was another woman whose life was hindered by the man she married. So was Yesenia. And... Mary. So many women at the whims of toxic masculinity. Gillian never imagined she would be one of them.

"There's not much more here than what I already shared with you," Ofelia said as she put the manila folder down in front of Gillian on the bistro table. "But I was able to find a picture of Cariña. She was very beautiful."

Gillian opened the folder.

"Oh no." Ofelia started to laugh as she looked out over the yard. "That's a lot of mud."

"My petunias," Mary gasped as Tucker chuckled and said, "I'll get the hose."

"Cariños," Gillian heard her mother call as Ofelia, Tucker, and Mary hustled off the deck. "That dirt stays on the ground."

The squeals and protests faded into the background as Gillian stared at the woman looking up at her from the file folder, goose bumps breaking over her skin in the summer heat.

Cariña de la Cruz was extraordinarily beautiful, even wearing a wide-brimmed black hat, a black dress, pearls, and a somber expression that seemed to be an effort in diminishing her youth and vitality. She looked like a classic Hollywood movie star, with wide-set dark eyes, a peaked nose, and a lush rosebud of a mouth. Seeing her like this, so formal and serene, Gillian might not have recognized her.

But Gillian knew Cariña's face better than her own.

Every time Cariña had appeared to her as La Llorona wailing for the son stolen from her—mi niño, mi corazon, mi vida— Gillian had marveled how a fantasma so terrifying could be so beautiful.

CHAPTER 19

Nicky was nearly dreading the quiet when he opened the door of the train station Monday morning.

This would be the first day of a long stretch of them when he'd be alone in an empty building with a woman he desperately wanted. His desperation was getting more demanding every time she thanked him and acknowledged him and listened to him and asked his opinion. He felt like he was becoming whole right in front of her eyes. He wanted to throw her down on her desk and make up for a lifetime of invisibility.

So he was surprised, relieved, and disappointed when he heard a loud squeak singing off-key from the office. He watched through the office window as Gillian paced, her phone up to her ear.

"Roxanne Medina wants to speak to me now?" Panic was clear in her voice.

As he got closer to her office, he heard another voice loudly shushing.

"No, no, I'm thrilled she wants to contribute to the fund." Gillian spoke above the noise and gripped her new curls. "How did she hear about it so quickly?" Then she closed her eyes and shook her head. "Cynthia Madsen. Of course. No…yes…she's very enthusiastic."

The singing got higher and screechier.

Gillian had to raise her voice. "We're delighted by Mrs. Medina's interest. Unfortunately, right now isn't…"

Nicky leaned on her doorjamb. The singing was coming from her daughter. Naomi was in the same rainbow shirt and green shorts she'd worn at the luncheon, but this time she'd fancied it up with a purple tutu and glittery sneakers. She twirled in dizzying circles as she sang, her long, sun-soaked hair floating out behind her. Standing next to her, Ben had his finger over his pursed lips as he shushed his sister, over and over and over again. His face was growing red with it. He was trying to help.

Nicky waved his hands and Gillian turned to face him, a look of misery on her face.

"Ask them if they can hold on," he said.

Her unquestioning "Can I put you on hold for one moment?" sent him high and made him think low, dirty thoughts.

She pulled the phone away from her ear and pressed the mute button. Naomi stopped singing and twirling. "Mama, I'm bored."

Ben dropped his finger and began to walk along the white tiles of the black-and-white floor. Naomi immediately charged in front and led the way.

Gillian put her hand on her smooth forehead. "I thought I'd give my parents some alone time. But the iPad—" She pointed to the black screen abandoned on the floor. "—it's not coming on and I called Alex, but she's not feeling well and now…" She pointed to the phone and held it out to Nicky with a grimace. "Roxanne Medina wants to contribute to the Rosalinda fund. Her husband wants to send wine for the event."

Gillian Armstead was the most innately sophisticated woman he knew, and yet, for all her hobnobbing, even she found rubbing shoulders with a billionaire and a king a little intimidating.

Billionaire Roxanne Medina, CEO of Medina Now Enterprises, had been born and raised right here in Freedom and was a big reason the town was still breathing. Her husband, the king of a Spanish principality famous for making good wine, was apparently a fan, too. They'd built a place out on the lake and there'd been a rumor that Roxanne Medina was going to bring large-scale manufacturing back to Freedom and save them all.

Even though his fortune relied on them, even though he was becoming one of them, Nicky trusted rich people about as far as he could throw them.

He knew Gillian's panic was over more than the inconvenient timing. She was concerned that she couldn't bring this deal home. She was still getting her legs back underneath her after a decade of her husband kicking them out.

"I can watch them," he said without thinking it through. "We'll go on a walk."

Her lovely mouth opened in surprise. "I—I couldn't ask you to do that. You wanted to get started on the mural."

"I have." Over the weekend, he'd painted the base coat on the top left quadrant.

She shook her head as her children neared the end of their white-tile trail at the far wall. "No, no, it's too much. I can't…"

It occurred to him that her reluctance could be less about the babysitting than the babysitter. He'd hadn't done such a bang-up job with his own responsibility. During that summer, he hadn't been able to hide from her the two times he'd spent the night holding his brother's head over the toilet, the one trip to the ER, and the day his brother was arrested.

"Okay," he said. He put his hands in his pockets and smiled, pushing off the doorjamb. "I understand. I'm here if you need—"

"What do you understand?"

He smiled at her sharp-eyed look. "I haven't spent much time with kids. You don't know if I can—"

"I trust you with my life, Nicky." The lack of fucking-around on her face was like drinking from an icy stream. It was sustenance that ached. "With my life." Her hand went back into her curls and she exhaled big. "If I'm going to be a working mom, I have to accept help. This will not be the only time my workday has hitches and my childcare falls through."

She put down the phone, reached for her big black bag, and pulled water bottles and snack boxes from its depths. She shoved them into Nicky's hands. "I'm not sure how long this call is going to take. Thank you." Then she went to her kids, squatted down to talk to them both in her no-bullshit way, then led them to Nicky. "I love you," she told them, as if *I love you* were words she said all the time. She walked back to her desk and picked up her phone, her back to them. "Okay," she said. "Yes, I can speak to her now."

And just like that, with everything explained and goals aligned and her trusting him when he'd given her every reason not to, he was responsible for the two most valuable things in her life. Nicky threw the water bottles and snacks in the backpack he still had on his shoulder and led her kids out of the train station.

The second they stepped outside, he realized how hot it was on this mid-July morning. The street's black-tar patches already shimmered with heat. They'd stay on this side of Milagro Street in the shade. But where could they go? There wasn't a single car in Loretta's lot.

He looked down at both the kids. Naomi smiled up at him. Ben was staring down the street.

He remembered another burning-hot day when he'd been searching for something, anything, to do and feeling overwhelmed by the responsibility. He was bigger now. He forcibly pushed that day away. He swung around his backpack and wore it over his chest. "Anyone want a piggyback ride?"

Naomi's little hand shot up into the air.

"Okey dokey, one rider." He got down on a knee. "Mount up."

Naomi clambered up on his back and kicked him in the kidney and he held her hands with one of his to keep her from strangling him. He got one hand under her bony rear and was about to stand when he saw Ben's dark brows furrow.

Good boy, he thought. Nicky was totally suspect. "Is it okay if I give Naomi a piggyback ride?"

That furrow softened. "Be careful," the boy said. Ben was built like a fire hydrant. He could take Nicky out at the knees.

"I promise," Nicky swore solemnly, and waited for Ben's nod before he stood. "Okay. Where to?"

Naomi pointed in a direction that thankfully kept them in the shade. "That way!"

They walked and Nicky wanted to gallop but didn't dare with Ben walking beside him, even though he did give Naomi a little extra bounce that had her whooping loudly in his ear. When they reached the end of the block, he stopped and looked both ways, although there was seldom traffic on Milagro Street.

He felt a tap against his hip. When he looked down, Ben was looking straight ahead and holding his hand up to Nicky.

He thought he got it but he wanted to be sure. He'd seen Gillian and her notoriously handsy family ask permission before they touched Ben. "Should I hold your hand while we cross the street?" he asked.

Ben nodded.

He let go of Naomi's hands, kept his forearm under her butt, and took Ben's sweaty hand into his own. Crossing the street with them, holding them like that, it was…it was something. It was something too big to stuff into words.

He loosened his hold when they reached the far sidewalk, but kept hanging on when Ben showed no inclination to let go.

"What's that?" Naomi asked.

Halfway down the block, at the front of an empty lot and in

the shade of a couple of big oak trees, was a free little library Nicky had never noticed before although he'd walked this street multiple times with their mother. It was plain, a little metal box on top of an old pole with *Freedom Public Library* and *Take a Book, Leave a Book* stenciled on the side.

Inside, it was stuffed with a good selection of books including— *yahtzee*—children's picture books.

He held Naomi on his hip so she could see in and together, the three of them picked out a few reads. He spread an old towel from his backpack on the ground for the kids to sit on. He offered to read them a book, and Naomi and Ben quietly strategized over the question for several minutes. It was the most serious he'd ever seen her.

They finally held out a thin chapter book about a little Black girl named Sophie Washington and when Nicky sat down to read it to them, Naomi plopped down on his lap without a howdy-do and Ben leaned against his side. In the eighty-five-degree heat in the shade, Nicky sweated away under a little kid pile as he read about the girl's lemonade stand and her grandmother's secret recipe.

Gillian worried about what her husband had done and would do. But Gillian had done this. She'd made the world a safe place for them, and they were able to trust and love.

His T-shirt was soaked through when the book was finished and he felt his phone buzz in his back pocket. He unstacked the kids and stood, both kids immediately turning their attention to their own piles.

How's it going? the text from their mom said.

He took a picture of them in the shade, looking down at the books in their laps and eating from their snack boxes, and sent it to Gillian.

Good. You?

Still on the call. Good thing I wrote up a proposal with lots of facts and figures I can quote. Weirdly, billionaires don't just hand over money.

It's how they stay billionaires. Don't worry about us. We're good.

Never worried. Not even for a second.

She sent the "thank you" emoticon with the hands clasped together and he sent the kissy face because, goddamn and fuck it, he was feeling pretty kissy face right now.

The kids seemed content and he didn't want to disturb that so he took a few more pictures, planning to integrate them into his mural design, and then he snapped a couple of pics of the free little library. He thought about the tube maze he'd built once with his brother, cardboard tubes connected with electrical tape and strung through the living room and kitchen. He and Lucas had spent the better part of the day putting the maze together and racing their cars through it, amazed and delighted by their success. When their mother woke up to get ready for her night shift, she'd been seriously pissed off about the amount of unused wrapping, towel, and toilet paper wadded around the house. They'd spent the rest of the evening coiling that paper back around its tubes, even missed the Saturday night movie they usually got to watch with the babysitter, but that didn't stop the grins they'd shot at each other.

Lucas's hand had still been badly scarred and it'd been before the series of surgeries that had given him more use out of it. It was a lost happy memory with his brother after the attack when Nicky had forgotten there'd been any.

Nicky thought about getting Ben's and Naomi's help to replace this plain library box with something more colorful. He thought about helping other kids build free little libraries around Freedom, and making all the boxes different shapes and designs that reflected the street and neighborhood. He thought about filling the libraries with books by people of color about people of color, queer folks, kids with disabilities, books that showed the full range of what their community looked like so that kids who didn't feel like they were enough could always find a book that proved that they were.

He thought about Gillian, who always swore she didn't want to be here, putting so much time and effort into improving the east side even though she still planned to leave.

When they started to make their way back to the train station, Ben saw an anthill erupting in a sidewalk crack and Nicky squatted down with him for a solid ten minutes and watched the ants work. He didn't think he'd ever done that before. It was pretty remarkable, watching some scurry away while others dragged back crumbs bigger than they were. Naomi sang to herself again, bored out of her mind, but she put up with it for her brother.

Back at the train station, Gillian was still on her call, but signaled five more minutes when they walked through the door. Nicky waved but wasn't worried. He pulled sheets out of his sketch pad and set the kids up with pencils and markers on the restored benches.

Sitting on the floor between them, with several sketches of possible book boxes already on the page, Nicky was five feet deep into his happy place when he felt a hand stroke his hair.

He looked up into Gillian's deep-brown eyes.

"My parents finished up their walk," she said gently. "They're on their way to pick up the kids now."

He nodded, needing a second, the tug had been so strong. "Yeah, okay." He didn't want them to go. "Cool."

"I found out the most astonishing thing about Cariña this weekend," she said, successfully pulling him the rest of the way out. He stood up next to her. "I wanted to call you and tell you right away but…"

She gave him a soft smile, shrugging, then looked at her children.

He nodded and looked at her children, too. They were already going to be spending a lot of time together. They didn't need to be chatting off-hours, too.

"What you've done here is pretty remarkable," he said. Ben was carefully coloring inside the lines of the garden he'd drawn. Naomi was peeling the wrapper off Nicky's expensive pastel.

"Yes," she said, reaching out and winding her fingers through his. "It means a lot that you think so."

They stared at her children and he held on tight.

She was more than his heart's desire. She was their world. She'd protected them from her husband's toxicity and they'd become these bright, loving, trusting creatures. He would help protect them as well. He had blood on his hands and her acknowledgment, his smashed wall, and their mutual desire didn't erase that. He couldn't offer her forever, not with the pain he'd caused and the debt he owed. And she was too valuable to tease and taunt with moments of ecstasy. He'd loved Gillian from afar for the last decade and he could continue to do so, even when she was in the same room.

When her parents arrived, he let her go.

He was no longer afraid of the silence in the train station. He'd come to church every day and look forward to worship.

CHAPTER 20

Friday evening, Gillian stood with her keys in her hand, counting the number of times they jingled as she spoke to Nicky, who was sitting on his stool. She felt fortunate that, for once this week, she caught him on the ground instead of high up on the scaffolding working on the top third of the mural. When she'd asked him once why he was concentrating all of his energies up there, he'd said, "Drips."

Yes, it made sense that he would cover the yellow, red, orange, and blue drips of the sunrise-to-sunset sky he was painting at the top with other colors as he worked down. Unfortunately, that's what her interactions with Nicky had felt like all week.

Drips.

She jingled her keys as she tried to work up the nerve to ask him to help her this weekend.

"I still can't believe Cariña de la Cruz is La Llorona," he said after she'd weaseled in the topic while asking him about his plans for the weekend, watercooler talk for two coworkers. "I kinda hoped she'd gone off to run a saloon and break some hearts."

Gillian smiled sadly and nodded, looking down at the Keds

she'd found in the back of her closet. "Me too." She'd worn her cutoff jeans shorts and her dad's old button-up, tied at the hips. They were going to start having meetings in Jeremiah's office with community leaders, potential sponsors, and prospective business owners, so today she'd organized the last box of paperwork after whittling down the essential papers to just a few boxes and hauled everything around to make the office presentable again. She'd even dusted and mopped. Nicky was in his paint-smeared pants and a concert tee, a smear of bright yellow across the back of one dark hand.

There was something about being dressed so casually with him that made her want to lean against his side. But there'd been no more touches after her parents picked up the kids, and he'd been so blandly pleasant all week that any physicality between them felt like sexual harassment. He might notify HR.

"I've been thinking about why Cariña focused on me," Gillian said. "I haven't been near the Viridescent since..." She made some meaningless gesture in the air and Nicky nodded, wrapping his fingers around each other. *Since the first day of the summer. In the car. With you.* "It took her a lot of energy to get my attention in the Day Building."

Nicky looked at her, still nodding, dark hair pushed back from his eyes, not smiling, not teasing or flirting. But not Nicky.

"I thought I might go this weekend and ask her what she needs from me."

His brow furrowed as the bones in his face went stiff. "Not by yourself." It wasn't a question.

"No," she said, heart thumping rapidly. "I was wondering if you wanted to go with me."

His lips pressed together like he realized he'd walked into that one. But she never intended the question to be a trap.

The train station door squealed open. "You two still at it?"

Cynthia stuck her head in, her auburn hair falling over her

shoulder. Behind her, the evening sunlight was mellowing out. "It's quittin' time. Come over for happy hour. I already called your mom and she said it's fine."

Gillian laughed. "Are you kidding?"

"Naw," Cynthia said. "I knew you'd worry about the babies." She realized how it sounded and grinned. "Nicky, you want me to call William and ask if you can come over for a playdate?"

He huffed. "No, I'm a big boy."

"Yes. Yes, you are," Cynthia drawled.

"One drink won't kill me." He got off the stool then leaned down to grab his backpack. As he pulled it onto his shoulder, however, he shot Gillian a look like he wasn't sure of that.

As they crossed the street in the buttery evening sunlight to Loretta's, where the outdoor beer garden was already half full, Gillian doubled down on happy chatter with Cynthia and Nicky as she worked to resist feeling responsible for whatever was off between her and her "friend." She hadn't even told him about La Virgen and the new altar she'd set up to worship her because that was a conversation that required intimacy and every conversation since Monday, even the two times they'd eaten lunch together, had been so...pleasant. They chatted every day and Nicky, with his hair out of his face and his hands that he kept to himself and his hardworking body in tempting reach, was interested, attentive, complimentary. He was the perfect cubicle mate, but he wasn't the same man who'd worked to break her curse. Instead, talking to Nicky had felt a little like hanging out with an underling at work or a person asking for an hechizo. He seemed reverent, for lack of a better word.

She hated it. She saw him every day and yet ached with how bad she missed him.

The swinging-into-Friday-night crowd was big inside Loretta's but Joe and Jeremiah were holding a booth and yelled for them the second they crossed under the cowbells. Nicky got as many back slaps as she did hugs and kisses as they made their way through. Word was getting out about what they were trying to do on Milagro Street.

When Nicky slid into the oversized booth, Gillian slid in next to him and Joe sat next to her, making it a tight fit. Nicky stretched his arm over the back of the booth. Cynthia, sitting across the table with Jeremiah beside her, eyed the way Gillian was tucked up close to him and gave her a quick, evil grin as Nicky spoke to Joe over her head.

Gillian warned her off with a scowl but said, "I'm sorry we haven't wrapped up the purchase." It was the rain cloud she wanted to dissipate. "Thomas had some ticky-tack changes to the contract he returned to my lawyer. She's reviewing it then will send it back to him."

Cynthia interlaced their fingers on the table. "Sweetie, I'm not in any rush. I just don't want him jerking you around."

"You and me both," she said, squeezing her friend's hand.

Without a new agreement, the kids were scheduled to go to Thomas in two weeks. She thought that countdown clock had ended, but Thomas was making it feel more like a dramatic pause. She was so tired of being manipulated by him.

Alex broke through her gloomy thoughts when she came to the table wearing a neon-purple sweatshirt dress that hung off one shoulder and showed off her flower tattoos and the top of one glorious boob. She carried a tray of full glasses and a laminated drink menu.

"Ali, are you feeling better?" Gillian asked as Alex handed out the drinks. Gillian was given a slender glass with a raspberry bobbing in it—it was the champagne cocktail Nicky had ordered the night of the speakeasy opening. She was touched by her sister's thoughtfulness.

Alex sat down next to her husband, who wrapped his arm around her and hauled her close, then took a drink of something fizzy and clear with a lemon floating in it.

"Yeah. Yep," Alex said. "I'm on the mend." She slid the laminated drink menu across the table toward Gillian and tapped the back side. "Check this out."

Mocktails and Low-Alcohol Cocktails, it said beneath her skull-and-crossbones-decorated fingernail. Gillian scanned the drinks. A no-alcohol beer and wine option were listed. So was Nicky's champagne cocktail and something made with a cherry shrub and bitters. She laughed when she saw what "Juli's Jugo" had in it.

"Kale and chocolate?" she asked. "How can that taste good?"

Her sister grinned, the balls on her cheeks vibrant. "They're brain food. And, believe it or not, that drink is the biggest seller on that list. The tíos are saying they're not coming anymore if this place becomes a Jamba Juice. It's the only time I've considered selling."

She felt Nicky craning to read over her shoulder, so she raised it up to him as she looked at her sister with gratitude.

"This has always been a place for families," Alex said, a little loud to be heard over the crowd noise she was responsible for creating. "Granmo set the tone that you weren't supposed to drink much when kids were around, but even after eight p.m., people shouldn't feel they have to drink to have fun here. This should be a place that welcomes all adults."

Gillian felt Nicky shift so their bodies were more aligned and she settled against his side as she put the menu down.

"Even if Dad doesn't struggle here, other people might," Alex said, her big heart in her eyes. "I don't want to do that to anybody. Thanks for helping me realize that."

"Ali…" It was happy hour. Gillian didn't want to tear up. "Thank you."

Dahlia stopped by the table to see if they needed anything and Gillian wasn't the only one quickly clearing her throat. She remembered the last time Dahlia had come to a booth to serve her. "Thank you for checking on us," she said, shouting to make sure Dahlia could hear. "You're doing a great job."

Dahlia startled at the burst of noise. "Uh…thank you. Um… you too." She picked up the empty glasses and turned away.

Joe let out a quiet snort. Jeremiah's hand was over his mouth and Cynthia was biting her lip.

Alex was outright chuckling. "You should probably leave the people management to me," she said, her dimples digging in deep.

Gillian didn't even want to look at Nicky. "And you better be entering kale into the inventory system," she said. "That leaf isn't cheap."

Over the next couple of hours, drinks flowed, food filled the table, and people slid in and out of the booth. Gillian didn't move because Nicky didn't ask to move. She thought he was going to, once when his powerful body tensed up next to hers, but when she looked at him, he was focused on something across the bar. Alex, Jeremiah, and Cynthia got up to play darts and Joe switched around to sit across from Nicky as they continued their conversation. A few cousins and high school friends stopped by to catch up with Gillian, and they all expressed sympathy about her divorce, curiosity for what she had planned next, and then filled her in on their own happy, sad, boring, fascinating lives. People had too much on their plates, she now understood, to focus on what the Pride of the East Side was getting up to.

Nicky switched to sparkling water after his cocktail.

Cynthia slid in next to Joe. "Let's go to McGever's pond," she said, emerald eyes sparkling.

Joe laughed. "How much have you had to drink?"

"As much as you," she said. "That's why Alex is driving. She's not drinking because her stomach's off." Cynthia looked at her and Nicky. "We've got a full car but you guys are going to meet us there, right?"

Gillian opened her mouth. "I…" She actually wanted to

go. A night swim at the pond with some of her favorite people sounded amazing. "I could squeeze in with—"

"I can drive," Nicky said. She was nestled so close that she could feel the vibration of his voice against her ribs. "I'll take us."

The seat suddenly felt like it had warmers in it. She licked her lips. "Okay."

"Hot damn," Cynthia said, eyes wide. "I didn't have to twist any arms or anything." She slinked out of the booth and stood, her hands on her hips. Gillian had seen all of that in a bathing suit and it was a sight to behold. They'd all be undressing at the pond. "Alex is gettin' drinks and snacks then we'll get going. We'll meet you there."

"O-okay." Gillian had no choice but to slide out of the booth, too. "See you there."

She walked out of the bar hoping Nicky was behind her, and she didn't look at him as they crossed the street. His Jeep wasn't in front; he must have parked in the station's side lot.

"Are you sure you want to go?" she asked. The night air was the same temperature as her skin. The parking lot lights were bright, but not as bright as the full moon with its mountains and craters. She desperately wanted him to go. "I can always catch a ride with—"

"I'm not ready for the night to be over."

Her insides went warm and liquid. "You and Joe had a lot to discuss," she said, nervously making conversation. "Were you talking about those little free-book boxes that—"

She stopped short in the gravel and gasped.

Nicky cursed low. "I totally forgot I drove it today. I have to run the engine every so often to keep the oil from gumming up."

The car sat under a light pole, far back from the street. It'd been big but beaten up like an aged prizefighter when Gillian had ridden in it, with dents and dull panels and silver duct tape bandaging its seats. Now it gleamed like wet sin, the full moon reflecting in its perfect black finish. If there was any object on the planet that represented immediate, toe-curling sex to her, it was this car.

Thirteen years ago, Nicky had spent the summer teaching her pleasure in it. The first time he'd been inside her, the first time she'd made love, was in this car.

She was afraid it would disappear if she approached it too quickly. "I can't believe William kept it all this time," she breathed. Her awed face looked back from the trim of shining chrome.

"He didn't."

Finally, she looked at him. Even in paint pants and a faded concert T-shirt, Nicky Mendoza shined as diamond bright as the car. "He was gonna sell it," he said, voice down in the gravel. His blue-black hair caught the moonlight as he stared back at her. "I wouldn't let him."

She turned back to the car and stroked her fingers over the warm metal of the handle. She could see Nicky's face in the reflection of the passenger window.

He looked anything but reverent.

When Nicky turned the key in the ignition, the roar of the engine was as familiar as if she'd heard it yesterday. He backed up, pulled out onto the empty street, and drove her into the full-moon darkness of a Kansas summer night.

CHAPTER 21

The first time Nicky saw Gillian Armstead, that first day of fifth grade at his new school, he'd been keeping his eyes down on his free hot lunch of Salisbury steak and vegetable medley, keeping his eyes off the kids who pointed and whispered, while resisting the urge to pull out his school pencil and draw on the shiny surface of the table.

William had retrieved Nicky's backpack from the side of the river. Nicky had stuffed it in the back of his closet, still covered in mud, along with a new backpack with the price tag on it. Whenever Nicky thought of pulling out his sketch pad, and he thought of it a lot, he went to go play with his brother who didn't want to play anymore.

Sitting in the lunchroom, he suddenly felt a yank as hard as the ones he'd been feeling around dark corners. He looked up expecting to see yellow eyes and black fur and dripping fangs, dreading that he'd scream and scramble away when the people around him could see nothing as had happened a couple of times already. He was prepared for life to turn into hell at his new school.

Instead, he saw her.

A Mexican girl his own age, with her brown hair tightly pulled back into a curly ponytail, a clean pink T-shirt, indigo blue jeans, and a rainbow belt, stood in a doorway looking at him. She smiled, a wide, pink-lipped smile that seemed to take up half her face and turned her cheeks into little balls. She had a wide face that came to a peak at her chin. Her face, he realized, was the shape of a heart.

She waved. He didn't need to look over his shoulder; he knew that flat-palmed back-and-forth was for him. It was a "hi" and a welcome and it surrounded him in the buoyancy of his happy place feeling like it was a bubble he'd stepped into. For the very first time since his brother had whispered his name by the river, he lifted away from his guilt and terror.

She turned and ran out to the playground.

Nicky went outside and watched her by the chain-link fence until she came right up to him and demanded he play tag with her and her best friend. After school, he and Lucas waited for her and walked her home.

That night, he pulled out all of his art supplies, carefully cleaned off the mud, and transferred them to the new backpack that William had bought him. He gave her the picture he drew for her the very next day.

The first time he kissed a girl, he wondered what Gillian's lips would feel like.

After the first mind-blowing time he had sex, he thought carefully and long and hard about what had worked and what hadn't, what the next person might like and might not, and what the fantasy Gillian he got to touch in his mind would want from him.

He never allowed himself to think that he might get to put that fantasy to use.

They drove with the windows down, the night wind whipping through her curls, and the moon shining silver over fields of summer-tall corn. He let the classic rock he'd turned up on the radio do the talking and tried to get the rumble of the big American engine to relax his spine. McGever's pond was off Old 85, but thanks to the plethora of fuckable spots on the road, this would be the first time he'd get to see her in it. He was damn glad her fierce sister and protective cousin were meeting them there. He hoped they weren't too far behind.

He'd fucked up by offering to drive.

Being inside the car reminded him of being inside her, plain and simple. For a week, he'd been near her but had kept himself away. All he'd had to do was summon thoughts of Ben and Naomi to remember he was unworthy. But this morning, he'd woken up craving the closeness they'd cultivated this summer. He couldn't touch her, but he could surround himself in the car.

Now she was beside him and they were driving to a spot where they both planned to strip down to their skivvies. As if her slim, naked legs in those frayed jean shorts, the glimpses of skin revealed by her oversized shirt tied low at her belly weren't tempting enough.

She leaned forward and turned down the radio by half. "What were you and Joe talking about?"

He hesitated. He'd gotten more engaged in the conversation than he'd meant to. He had no spare time to launch the idea now and he wasn't planning on staying after the mural was unveiled. But talking about free books and little libraries was a non-sexy distraction from all the things he didn't want to talk about.

He told her about his idea to fund a program that encouraged kids with mentors to build free little libraries in communities with few resources like, for example, Freedom. Joe had thought the industrial studies teacher and her students at the high school would be interested. Gillian suggested promoting the project at her end-of-summer shindig and then Nicky was sharing how the libraries could reflect the neighborhoods—

244 | ANGELINA M. LOPEZ

one could be built in the huge hollow of a hundred-year-old oak where all the mansions were decaying, another one could be created in the vacant emergency phone boxes still standing on Main—and she offered advice on getting grant money from the National Endowment for the Arts then he was telling her about an NEA gala he'd been invited to at the Guggenheim.

By the time they pulled up to the McGever's pond, they were both laughing about a flash-mob of catering staff who'd broken up the gala by ripping off their server uniforms to dance in heavy metal gear to Guns N' Roses. He'd been a guest of the event, but he'd been tapped on the shoulder twice as he walked through the crowd, once to bring more bread and once to clean up a spill. He'd clapped and cheered the dancers and, later, posted bail for those who hadn't escaped security.

"Oh yeah," Gillian said, still chuckling as she rested her head back against the seat and ran her hand through her tangled curls. "People assumed I was the kids' nanny all the time when I was pushing a stroller through Georgetown. I probably took *way* too much pleasure in watching them squirm after I corrected them."

"There's no such thing in taking too much pleasure in that," Nicky said, savoring the image of her holding a child on her hip while she put some snob in their place.

Still grinning, their eyes met. This connection they had based on similar experiences and a shared understanding was alarming and deeply satisfying. They'd both worked hard to rise to their positions, but they'd never be totally free of thoughtless racism. Still, they acknowledged their privilege to control some of that racism that others didn't have.

He turned off the car. The engine's rumble dissipated across the water.

She opened her mouth, pressed her thin lips together, then opened them again. He remembered the smell of her wet in this car.

"It's nice to talk to you," she finally said. "I feel like we haven't talked all week."

He could act like he didn't know what she was talking about, but that's how her husband had twisted her up. At the bar, he'd held her against him without holding her as she told Cynthia that that asshole was still stringing her along. Then he was sure he caught a creeper taking a picture of her with his phone. The guy had hightailed it when he'd seen Nicky's killer stare. Wanting to keep her by his side, tired of other men trying to fuck with what he was supposed to be taking care of, was what had him volunteering for this masochistic trip to the pond.

"It is nice," he said, pushing his door handle and getting out. He stood in the weeds and looked out on the water. The full moon glowed right in the center. Nice. Fuck. So nice.

"I'm getting in." He watched her shove open the door, stroll to the pond, and stop at the edge of the dock that stretched out into the water. She heeled off dirty Keds he swore he recognized. He saw the shirt loosen as she unbuttoned and untied it. He watched her shorts sag. He saw the lovely swell of her ass covered in black satin panties before he remembered to close his fucking eyes.

He heard the soft thump of clothes, the slap of bare feet running across the wooden dock, then a splash and a shriek.

He opened his eyes. The full moon made it bright enough to see her shoving back her newly shortened hair with one hand and beckoning with the other.

"C'mon," she yelled. "The water's fine."

"Your scream that probably woke up Milly and Lina didn't sound like it was fine," he hollered back. He couldn't help but grin. The reason the McGever's pond was such a popular "secret" swimming hole was because of the thorny blackberry bushes that hid it from the road, the underground spring that kept it cool and free of algae even during the hottest months of the year, and the two women who'd bought it from the Mc-

Gevers when Nicky and Gillian were in middle school. The couple had a "don't-ask-don't-tell" policy where their pond was concerned: "Don't do something stupid that lets us know you're down there and we won't sic the dogs on you." If the roar of his engine didn't wake them up, nothing would.

He rounded his car and walked to the end of the dock. She stayed in the center of the pond, treading water and grinning up at him, the moon bright on her face.

He pulled his T-shirt over his head.

He held it away from him as her mouth fell open and her eyes moved like candle wax over his torso. He'd gotten more fit over the summer with the amount of sexual frustration he was taking out on the punching bag hanging in the corner of his studio. Her slow perusal didn't pause at the scars on his shoulder, and it was something to take his shirt off for a woman and not have to explain them.

When he dropped the shirt to the dock, she ducked under the water and swam away, only a ripple and a kick of bare feet letting him know she was real.

He stripped down to his black boxer briefs and dived in in the opposite direction. The water was the cold shower he needed, cool and green and foggy beneath its surface. He swam around, considered sitting cross-legged in the lilies and silt, making friends with diamondbacks and crayfish until he got his head on right.

He finally had to shove up for air. He saw her in profile, waves fluttering out from where she dog-paddled, humming to herself, more content than he'd seen her in a baker's dozen of years. He swam to her half of the pond. Her older cousins had taught him how to swim, just like they'd taught her. He didn't know why that random memory made him want to put his dick inside her.

"You know what?" she asked, almost like she was talking to herself.

"What?"

Other than the night sounds of crickets and frogs, it was quiet. Their voices traveled across the silvery surface of the water like they were speaking in each other's ears.

"We were set up." She spread her arms out on the surface and tilted her head back. He could see the black straps of her bra. "They're not coming."

It was quiet enough to hear that there was no approaching cherry-red VW Beetle, Alex's car.

He swallowed his curse. Of fucking course.

She lifted her head and ran her hand back over her hair. Water made silver trails down her long neck and over her clavicles.

His cock twitched. "We should go," he said.

"Why?" Her slicked-back hair brought out the size of her eyes and the delicacy of her cheekbones. "Are you mad at me?"

Fuck. "No."

The water lapped against her skin. Her silver hoops caught the moonlight. "Then why has it been so..." She waved her hand. "So disconnected between us?" He swore he could feel the water she tread swirl around him like a mermaid's tail.

"I'm trying to take care of you." He turned his back on her and started swimming for the ladder hanging off the dock. He was trying to take care of them.

"Nicky..." she called.

He ducked under and swam harder.

That long-ago summer, his deepest wish had been that she'd want him, acknowledge him, and share what he was to her with her people. Now, her best friend and sister knew enough to scheme to get them naked and alone. But they didn't know about that life-changing fall. They didn't know he couldn't give her what she and her kids needed.

When he came up for air in the shadow of the dock, he was reminded that they had the same swim teachers.

"Nicky," she demanded, her voice at his ear, her cool hand grabbing his slick shoulder, the water churning around them.

"What do you want from me?" he growled, his stuffed-down resentment roaring to the surface. He hooked his arm around her waist and yanked her against him, pressed her wet and sleek against his burning skin as he grabbed onto the dock with his free hand.

"You want to be friends now? Finally?" He'd been trying to be good, to take care of her, and she wanted to be alone with him in the dark. "You didn't wonder about me for thirteen years." Her eyelashes were black spikes of shock. Her hands were against his chest. She wasn't shoving him away. "If you were so jealous, why didn't you ever look me up?"

"I'm sorry I upset you." Her hands curled over the tops of his shoulders. Her thumb smoothed over his scars. "The last thing I want is to upset you."

The last thing he wanted was her sweetness. He flexed his arm and pulled her higher and tighter against him, her body as maneuverable as a fuck doll.

"Why didn't you ever look me up?" he demanded again, fed up of this lifetime of worship. He wanted to take her or forget about her, once and for all.

Her mouth pursed with the hurt of it. She was going to learn.

"It felt like cheating," she said, her bottom lip trembling. "On him and you. I couldn't have thoughts of you showing up in my marriage when I was trying to make it work. The more miserable I was, I didn't want to turn to fantasizing about what you and I had. What we had was too good to be used as some kind of Band-Aid."

She shocked the water and killed him. She hurt him worse than she'd ever hurt him before.

"Why…" He squeezed her against him tight with his one arm because, right now, he wanted to fucking strangle her. "Why didn't you ever say anything? That whole summer…"

Rather than kicking away like she should have done, she wrapped her arms around his shoulders. "I couldn't get stuck here, Nicky," she said, holding him close and asking for his understanding with her bottomless eyes. "I couldn't get stuck where I had no control. I couldn't end up like my mom."

That bright full moon illuminated everything.

He lifted her up to him. He lowered his head, her eyes huge and her mouth sweet and ripe. Her fingers dug into the wet hair at his nape.

She yanked his head back. "Why didn't you ever look *me* up?" she demanded, her breath in his open mouth.

"I was trying to protect you," he said, panting, the tease of her mouth making it harder to think than the pull of her hand.

Her brows knotted up. "What does that even mean?"

Her pussy was resting on his thigh and he was saying shit that got too close to truths he'd avoided all summer.

He yanked his hair out of her hold. "Damn it, girl," he said, as annoyed as he was turned on as his scalp ached. "You've got a big degree, things are finally starting to come together for you, and those two babies are depending on you to keep them safe. You don't need some guy whose only pluses are an active imagination and a grumpy old dad getting his hands all over you and dragging you down. You didn't need it before and you don't need it now."

She cocked her head and he felt like a math problem she was working out. "I'm not..." She narrowed her eyes at him like she was checking her work. "I'm not a saint, Nicky. Is this because I'm a mom?"

"You have to keep them safe. I don't want—"

"And I can," she said fiercely, her fingers gripping into his shoulder meat. "Do you have any idea how powerful the Virgen Mother is? She regularly kicks ass. Do you know how much stress the vagina can take? I've had two seven-pound babies come out of me." He was blown apart and melting. She'd leave him as scum on the surface of the pond. "I *did* underestimate you back then. Who knows what could have happened if I hadn't."

Her fingers were going to leave bruises. "But maybe you've held me in too high of esteem. I looked down on you and you looked up at me and we've both suffered. Now we need to figure out how to meet in the middle. I'm not some golden idol." She searched his face: his cheekbones, his mouth, his scar, then his eyes. She was the singular point on his horizon. "The last thing I want is to be untouchable to you."

No. He had to protect her. He had to keep her safe. He couldn't give them what they needed. He had a debt to pay.

"You sure?" he choked out. "Because if I touch you, I'm gonna take thirteen years of wanting what I couldn't have out on that pussy." He pressed his cock—hard despite the cool water, triumphant despite all he was losing—against her. "You better clear your calendar. Because until you leave, I'm gonna be the bad man that rides your golden cunt until I end your curse."

He expected her to knee him in the dick. He was the one who'd taught her how. He expected her to shove out of his hold and scramble to the ladder and charge to the car. He expected her to call Alex and Cynthia, to tell them to come and get her, and for Jeremiah and Joe to beat his ass then run him out of town. He'd hate to see what the professor could deadlift.

Instead of any of that, his hechicera stared at him for a long moment.

Then she slowly dug her fingers back into his hair as she wound a leg around his waist and used his hip and hair and the dock to raise herself above him. Mesmerized, he helped, hands on her butt as he watched moon-struck water sluice down her body.

"There's powerful magic in the space where two opposites meet, Nicky," she murmured as she looked down at him, her voice filling him. "In the twilight between day and night, in the stillness between blue sky and storm clouds." She paused and licked at her bottom lip and it felt like a component of her hechizo. "In that fierce, tender connection between a mean dick and an eager mommy cunt. Magic roars in liminal, in-between spaces, Nicky."

She rolled her pelvis against his abs with total intention and he felt it in the clench of his teeth, the spasm of his fingers into her ass cheeks. He called her *hechicera* and *gorgeous* and *sweetheart* and *baby girl*, but she'd never called him anything but Nicky.

It was his favorite love spell.

"I want you, Nicky," she said, the power of it racing from her into him. "But not to break my curse or heal my magic or teach me anything. I just…" She bent to kiss him and the happy place feeling flooded him just like her rare cheek pecks had filled him when they were children. "I just want you," she said against his mouth, into his eyes, surrounding him. "For the first time in my life, I want to love you without a reason."

Lovelovelovelovelovelove roared through him like blood and he knew she meant the act, the lovemaking, and he let it be that because if he allowed himself to think anything else, he couldn't have this. He couldn't have her.

And he had to have her because he never thought she'd want him just for him.

He answered with his mouth. He devoured hers, reaching for the ladder, and she wound her legs around his hips as he hauled them both out, planning to carry her to the car and drive her to the farm, but the second his feet hit the dock, so did hers and she was pressing close to keep her mouth on his while sliding her hand over the wet boxer briefs molded to his rigid cock.

"Oh, I missed this so much," she moaned into his panting mouth. Then she tried to drop to her knees.

"Ho, hey," he grunted, grabbing her by her elbows, pulling her upright, stroking down the underside of her sleek arms, over her sensitive pits, down the sides of wet, black bra—beautiful, wet, black-underweared woman, she didn't have any black bras when they were kids. "When I want your mouth on my cock, I'll tell you."

"Nooo," she moaned between little kitten licks into his mouth as he began to drag her off the dock, her hands running over his abs and making them jump. "Don't do…you don't have to do that…just let me…"

But he did have to because his girl liked breaking the rules and what was he if he wasn't her secret sex teacher, the hitchhiker she picked up in a storm, the distraction from La Llorona, or the bad man begging for just one time? How did he please her, how did he make her come, when it was just him that she wanted? Just her Nicky?

How did he take care of this real woman instead of the fantasy he'd concocted?

This real woman's mouth sucked out his soul as they stumbled to the car, as she grabbed his lats, his ass, his biceps, his jaw, hot hands over his desperate shivering skin.

"Baby girl, wait, baby," he groaned, kissing across her palm to get it off him, reaching for sanity as he reached for the driver's door handle.

He remembered her as eager, but this woman was hungry. She was starving.

"Let's…it's a five-minute drive to the farmhouse." He sucked on her middle finger, tasted the spring water and peaches and salt on her, and she shoved the wet satin of her panties against his thigh, making him thump back against the GTO. "I've got a big bed…" He moaned as her tongue joined her finger in his mouth. "A bed above the barn. We can…"

She pulled her finger out with a pop, yanked out the wet band of his briefs, and pet his own spit across the leaking head of his dick.

"Hurry," she whispered with all the force of Amen. "Back seat. Hurry."

His bones melted. He became nothing but what she demanded.

He threw open the back door and collapsed inside. As he crawled backward, she crawled over him, not letting him free of her lips and her tongue and her teeth.

Nicky liked to fuck and he liked to take control and once he figured out how to be clear that he was never looking for a relationship, once he did all he could to prevent hurting anyone, he'd fucked and taken control of a shocking number of people. In all those numbers, he'd never felt like prey. He never felt like a sacrifice, thrown into the back seat with a powerful bruja who had thirteen years of sexual frustration to work out.

With the leather clammy against his back, he tilted back his head and opened up his mouth to let her take it as her hips straddled and rolled against him, as he pinched her nipples, smoothed over her sides, ran his nails down the satin over her ass.

"You're such a good kisser, Nicky," she nearly sobbed into his mouth. "Why're you such a good kisser?"

He grabbed her shoulders and pushed her upright, stared up at her as she stared down at him, wide-eyed and wounded in the full moon's blue light.

"*We* kiss good," he insisted, shaking her a little. She still thought this was him? "Together." She still thought he had some special skill? "You're the best I've *ever* had." His lip curled up as her eyes went even bigger. "Haven't you fucking figured that out yet?"

She made a sound of surprise and fury and excitement. "Oh God," she said, capturing him behind his neck. "Nicky." She pulled him up to her and he kissed her, turning so he was seated back against the leather as she straddled him. He held her close and showed her, once and for all, that the only magic was what they made together and she showed him, although he'd been sketching her his whole life, what he'd never been able to see: He didn't need to be good or bad to please her. He just needed to be him.

He sucked up the column of her throat as he yanked her out of her bra then ripped her, literally ripped the seams, out of her panties, as she showed about the same caution as she pulled his briefs out and off and down, the whole process stupid because neither of them would give up the other's mouth. She shuffled back in and he surrounded her, her tender shoulder blades, her full hips, pulled her close, closing his eyes and pressing his cheek against her chest and just feeling her, her creamy skin, her nakedness, her warmth, her arms wrapped around his neck, up against his solid heat. She was so soft. She smelled so good.

Gillian Armstead was in his arms and he was about to be inside her again and it was all hitting him like a plank.

He stuttered a groan when she rolled her hips to get a bit of him inside her, engulfed his tip with her wet heat. He smacked her ass with the flat of his palm. Her happy sharp yelp let him know she still liked that. "I was having a moment," he snarled.

"You've got all month to have a moment," she panted into his hair. All. Month. "I have an IUD." He turned his head so he could taste her breath in his mouth. "Are we good?"

"Yeah, hechicera," he moaned as she circled him in a little deeper, hugging the head in her. "Yeah, I'm clean for you."

Her mouth pouted with the pleasure as she played with him at her entrance. "Me too," she said. "I tested after—"

She shook her head, her drying curls swaying around her cheeks as she realized who'd entered the car with them, and he grabbed her neck and met her eyes, nodded, *that's right, that cheating asshole isn't here*, but the wet give of her body clenched and he rubbed his thumbs over her nipples and down her hips and offered his mouth up in a kiss and she took it but he could feel her getting dryer and she was only halfway on. He was only halfway in.

She broke off their kiss and leaned her temple against his

forehead, squeezing his shoulders. "I'm sorry," she whispered. "It's been a while and I think my body's forgotten how to..."

Never had he wanted to do violence in service to a woman more.

He nuzzled her ear, licked into the shell, then sucked on that tender spot just below it. "Shhh, don't apologize, baby, my baby, lean back, show me that pretty pussy."

She made a surprised little sound then did what she was told, leaned until her shoulders rested on the back of the seat, her hands behind her on his knees, and wasn't that a perfect picture, her lovely body arched, the pale stretch marks on the inside of her thighs framing his cock, the tip of him brushing her dark, soft bush.

He stared at her and she stared down at him, licking her lips. He committed the view to memory. He was going to paint this.

She moaned when a tear welled out of his slit and flowed down.

Tense and desperate, he lazed back against the seat as he reached for that drip, ran his thumb slowly up his standing dick to gather it up, put on a show and watched her bite into her lip, then reached for her. Her thighs were spread enough for him to enjoy the deep magenta of her and he slid his precum over her hard pearly clit.

"Oh," she moaned, her thumbnails digging into his knee. He rubbed sweet circles with one hand while he stroked his dick with the other, coaxing out more wetness, wiping it up, sharing it with her. She could have everything. She could have all of him.

Her ass was rolling against his thighs as sounds came out of her and the slickness under his thumb became more than him. He put his thumb into his mouth to taste it.

She groaned loud enough to rattle the glass. "Remember..."

He was already nodding as he reached for her clit, and he let go of his cock before they had a replay of their first time.

That first night, when she'd given him her virginity in this car, she'd started to go dry when he was inside her and he'd stuck his thumb in his mouth and she'd gasped, *Oh, that's hot. I love your mouth.* The sound of her voice, the rain of moisture when he rubbed her, and the fact that it had been the first time she'd ever said the word *love* in relation to him had made him draw up and warn, *I'm gonna lose it,* before he'd flooded her.

He had more control now, but not much. He grabbed her arm and yanked her against him, kissed her deep before he growled, "Get it in," and she did, her eyes flaring as she rubbed her wet slit over him, her hips dancing on him before she got him in by degrees, got him in while he ate at her neck and she was wet and ripe and whining, squeezing hot velvet over him as her hips bucked and she thought about no one else. Wanted him to be no one else.

He wrapped an arm around her waist and put his hand between her legs from behind to feel his dick moving in and out of her. "Harder, hechicera," he demanded, kissing her. He pressed his middle finger and she cried out. "My dirty little mommy. You ride that cock hard."

"God," she sobbed into his mouth. "God, Nicky. Just like that."

"If I play with you here, can you come?" he whispered, delicately stroking at the furled muscle. "Or do you want me to play with your clit? If there were two of me, I could fill you in both holes. I could make you ride my lap while I held your knees open and licked your pussy."

"Nicky," she cried out again, grinding down on him and clenching and grasping him to her sweat-sheened body. "Nicky. Yes."

This was him, just him, and he was filthy as fuck and she loved it.

"You come on that cock, sweetheart," he growled, planting his feet and fucking up fast. Just as he was, he could take care of his flesh-and-blood bruja.

"Rigththererighthererightthere," she cried, and he vibrated his thumb over her clit and savored every millimeter of her on his dick and focused on making the woman of his dreams come apart as she took him apart, too.

She was his perfect heaven.

At the end of the summer, she'd become his endless hell. He'd told himself never again, but he already wanted forever. How bad would it be after a month of loving her, when forever was the one thing he could never have?

CHAPTER 22

Gillian was very proud that over the next week they never had sex in the train station.

They never had *intercourse* in the train station.

After an energizing two hours of sleep then a Saturday morning planning meeting for the Milagro Street party in her sister's office, Cynthia crowing the entire time that her pond plan had worked, Gillian had gone to the train station with lunch from Loretta's.

With his hair tied back and a large paintbrush in hand, Nicky had shot that *look* at her from up on the scaffolding, slid down the staggered ladders, stalked toward her, and shoved her up against the entrance door.

He'd licked her insecurities—*Were they really going to do this for the rest of the summer? Was this a good idea?*—right out of her mouth.

She'd gasped for mercy, sore after what they'd done in the car and on the hood and in the pond after a two-year absence of such activity, but then he'd slid to his knees and pulled down her shorts and purred to her "poor little pussy," giving her the sweetest, softest, most indulgent orgasm of her life.

The two pollo adobo lunch specials they enjoyed on a train bench before she kissed him goodbye had gone cold and tasted delicious.

The Milagro Street party was bearing down on them too fast to leave time for a torrid train-station affair. Gillian had completed all the paperwork to establish the Rosalinda fund as a not-for-profit entity and had successfully helped Yesenia secure an SBA-backed loan that would comfortably cover all her start-up costs. She'd finished the first draft of the grant ahead of schedule and was waiting for feedback from Jeremiah, Joe, and Ofelia before she tackled revisions. She'd also sent press releases about the Rosalinda fund to business and finance reporters throughout the region. After a couple of false starts, the release she finally sent highlighted how a small-town Latina was using her pedigreed education and high-profile professional experience to begin a woman-and-minority-focused small-business fund to reenergize a historic street.

She'd gotten calls from every mid-to-large newspaper from Chicago to Dallas. The hiring manager for the firm she was interviewing with had been so thrilled when she'd seen Gillian's name in the *Tribune* that she'd moved up the date of her interview with the executive team. She'd also let her know, in the strictest confidence, that the VP of development from the team had wished her well. They'd gone to school together. Gillian hadn't recognized her married name.

It was a gamble, but Gillian was learning the value of leaping: she'd put down a deposit for a good school in Chicago for Ben and contacted a real estate agent to start looking for a place to rent in a nearby neighborhood.

Early ticket sales for the Milagro Street party were double what they'd hoped for.

Nicky's week had been quieter but just as busy. He'd finished the base coast of the top two-thirds of the mural, completed his design for the Free Little Library up the street, and lined up a few elementary-aged volunteers and a couple high school assistants to help him build it. *Just a test run,* he'd said. Gillian wondered if Ben and Naomi could be involved but didn't feel comfortable asking. The only boundary they'd established for what they were doing was its longevity—just until the end of the summer—but she knew others existed.

She didn't want to jar her contentment. They were both people who loved what they did, loved getting consumed in it, and a couple of her happiest moments over the last week had been sitting in her office while she watched him layer on color with a wide brush, his lovely body moving and bending and reaching. There'd been times when she'd looked up from her spreadsheets and seen him, hands on his hips, staring in and watching her.

They were too busy for shenanigans in the train station (and honestly, too old, they could show *some* restraint), but she'd gone to him four of the last seven nights after she put the kids to bed. Two of those nights, Nicky had taken her up on the invitation she'd made when they were "just friends" and ventured down to the river with her to wait for La Llorona to appear. She hadn't. Although, that Sunday night, when they sanctified their 'til-the-end-of-summer plan with what she did to Nicky in the front seat of his Jeep, he'd panted that La Llorona could've been shrieking in his ear and he wouldn't have heard her. They'd also visited the Day Building. Waiting, they'd traded long, lazy kisses in the lantern glow but never heard Cariña's sorrowful wail.

Gillian felt like she was living in a snow globe, one filled with moon glow and her children's laughter and Nicky's leather-and-paint smell. She was happily floating in this liminal, in-between space, but so much threatened to burst the glass. She couldn't force Thomas to sign the contract and take Cynthia's money, ending her apprehension about the weeklong visit that was still the law of the land until she heard from him. She couldn't make her devotional recitings of the rosary she sent to La Virgen with candle flame and rose-scented incense bear fruit, no matter how much the power crackled just under her skin. She couldn't corral her summer storm of emotions for Nicky into something she could see clearly after the end of August. And she couldn't persuade Cariña out of hiding to ask her what she needed. It now made sense that the sad, beautiful ghost had called to Gillian—she was an ambitious, business-oriented bruja and an hija of the east side.

But she stood in the crossroads with absolutely no control of the traffic.

"Heads up!"

A week and a day after she'd made love to Nicky again, a crack of the bat and the cheers of Freedomites around her had Gillian burying her face against Nicky's chest. He threw protective arms over her, giving her the chance to do what she'd wanted to since he'd joined her, Alex, Jeremiah, and Cynthia at the softball fields. She licked that hard, brown skin in the V of his black T-shirt.

"Quit it," he growled.

"I got it!" she heard her brother-in-law yell excitedly.

She grinned at Nicky before she looked up at Jeremiah. Even though he was standing one bleacher down, the mitt in his hand looked as high as the Liberty torch. The people around him hooted and cheered, no one louder than Alex, as he showed off the softball he'd caught. Jeremiah swore to never threaten the Torres Construction team's win record by playing, but as a partner in the firm working to restore or rebuild the buildings on Milagro Street, he was their biggest booster.

"Jeremiah," Joe yelled from behind the fence, handsome in his catcher's garb, the mask shoved up on his curly hair and displaying his million-watt grin. "You gonna give that back?"

"Oh, sorry," he called, then handed it to his wife, who threw it over the foul ball fence and into Joe's glove. Joe bribed Alex with free handyman labor to keep her from starting a Loretta's team and giving him a run for the trophy.

The softball fields in the middle of Freedom shined brightly under the lights. Children bored by the game tried to catch fireflies near the overgrown berm that separated the fields from where the Viridescent River meandered into town. Thankfully on this warm night, the berm didn't stop the river's breezes that first attracted those long-lost oil millionaires. Teens hung out and flirted by the concession stand where Nicky had bought her a hot dog and a Coke. She'd kissed his cheek and elbowed Alex, who'd made a loud *awwwing* sigh just behind her. The lines between east siders and west siders blurred on these soft summer nights.

Gillian kept a hand on the thigh of Nicky's well-worn jeans as the game resumed and Cynthia, a bleacher below in a Torres Construction T-shirt she'd tied above her belly button, gave her a wink.

"Cici!" Alex shouted. "Holy hell!"

Her middle sister reached down and gave their baby sister, Sissy, a boost up onto the stands then squished her against her mighty chest. "What are you doing here?" Alex asked, rocking Sissy back and forth.

"Had a night off," Sissy gasped in Alex's tight squeeze. "Mom and dad said you two were here." She tilted her head. "Hey, Juli."

Her lovely doe-shaped violet eyes, made even lovelier by the rare eyeliner, mascara, and shadow she was wearing, snapped wider when she saw who was sitting beside Gillian. "And Nick! Hey, Nick."

Those eyes tracked her hand on Nicky's leg. Gillian squeezed it before she stood and smacked her middle sister's shoulder. "Let go, Ali. My turn."

Growing up, it'd been hard to baby her beautiful little sister because *everyone* wanted to baby her. Gillian pulled Sissy into her arms and gave her a tight hug.

She'd texted Sissy after she'd come clean with everyone and let her know that they needed to talk. The family was abuzz; Sissy had made it onto the popular reality cooking show *Yes, Chef.* Because of the NDAs she'd had to sign, there was little more she could share with them until the show aired. Sissy's already busy life as a successful Kansas City sous chef was about to get even busier. Still, she'd found an hour to call, and Gillian had shared everything with her.

Sissy squeezed in to sit next to Gillian.

"Cici, what're you doing here? You look so…?" There was no word she could come up with that didn't sound critical of the way her sister normally presented herself.

Sissy was the heart-shaped face, violet-eyed, lush-mouthed, thick-haired beauty of their family who never wore makeup, put her perfect hair up in a ponytail, and seemed to throw whatever was on hand over her gorgeous figure—usually the oversized scrubs and clogs of a hardworking sous chef. Which was fine. In theory. But Gillian would have felt more at ease with her baby sister's disregard for her looks if she'd seemed happier and more content.

When her sacred arts had been firing, she'd sensed a capitulation in Sissy that she'd hated.

Right now, though, Sissy looked so effortlessly beautiful that Gillian was surprised the game hadn't stopped. Her thick, shoulder-blade-length hair had been cut and styled into beachy waves, her makeup was understated but brought out the tilt in her eyes and the kewpie-doll bow of her mouth, and the high-waisted mustard trousers and tucked-in white T-shirt fashionably brought out her figure-eight shape.

"They want me to start…" Sissy flapped a hand at herself with a grimace. "They said to get ready to show up on social media."

Gillian's eyes narrowed on her. "How do you feel about that?"

Sissy shrugged. "No one made me try out for *Yes, Chef.* I'm ready for a change."

"Like taking over the kitchen of the bar you're a part owner in?" Alex said loudly in front of them, her eyes still on the game.

"Anyway," Sissy said to the shorn back of Alex's head. She leaned forward to look past Gillian, her sable hair cascading off her shoulder. "How are you, Nick?"

He gave her a cautious smile as Sissy's violet eyes moved pointedly back and forth from him to Gillian. "I'm good. How are you, Sissy? It's been a while."

Sissy leaned closer. "It has," she whispered. "Since the time I saw you pulling out from behind the Townes Motel with Gillian in your lap."

"Cici!" Gillian hissed, truly shocked. They used to meet behind the closed-down Townes Motel so Gillian could hide her car there when she took off with him.

Nicky's mouth gaped open before he said, "You're fielding this one," and turned his attention to the game.

Sissy smiled shyly. "What?" As the "nice" one, she didn't get to score a hit like this very often. "Am I seriously the only one who knew?"

"You used to be," Gillian whispered back. She gave a pointed look to Cynthia and Alex, who were both reclined back to catch every word. "Why didn't you ever say anything?"

Sissy tucked a fall of hair behind her ear. "I was fifteen and had no desire to think about you and sex in the same thought," she said. She bumped her shoulder. "You looked happy during a sad time. You look happy now."

Gillian put her hand back on Nicky's leg. "We're having a very nice time this summer."

She now understood how hiding her car and their relationship had hurt him. The waxing moon was the best time to work on projects and the full moon helped bring them to fruition and under the full moon in the McGever's pond—water refreshed the flow of blessings and good energy—Gillian finally understood why she'd hidden from herself even the idea of him for so long. It certainly wasn't disinterest. The pain in her family had affected how she'd treated him back then and the pain in her marriage had made her cordon off her meaningful memories of him. For the weeks they had left ticking down to days, she didn't want to cordon him off or shove him into a role, and she didn't want him to raise her on high. She didn't want to be a muse that she could never live up to. She wanted to be the real woman in his bed as often as they could come together there.

Tonight would be the first time she got to spend the whole night with him. She'd told her parents where she'd be staying in case of an emergency, all of them looking anywhere but at each other, and told her children she'd be sleeping over at Cynthia's. She staunchly forgave herself the white lie.

She was pulled out of her thoughts when she felt Nicky tense under her hand.

"I'll be right back," he said, and he leaped off the side of the bleachers. He stalked behind the stands and disappeared, but if there was any power seeping from her Guadalupe altar, she was feeling it now. Something had happened.

She put her hand on her brother-in-law's shoulder. "Can you come with me?"

Jeremiah's brow furrowed at the urgency in her voice, then those lines went deeper when he noticed the empty seat beside her. "Where's Nick?"

She thought of Nicky's cadejo, that growling black dog he'd said he didn't see anymore. He still avoided all mention of Lucas. Was his brother here?

"Just come with me." She looked at the three women. "You stay here." They heard the big-sister bruja in her voice and, shockingly, complied. She loved, trusted, and relied on them, but their entire family getting up and charging off would have drawn more attention than she wanted.

Jeremiah gave his wife a kiss, scooted around her to jump off the bleachers, then lent a hand to help Gillian down. She went around the back of the stands and stopped. Listened. Felt through the noise and smells and energies. It was like a tug on her sternum. A thread led to a hot, bright point. She pointed to the cars parked in the grass-turned-parking-lot.

"He's back there," she said, and loved her brother-in-law even more for charging forward without a question.

It was quiet and dark on Jeremiah's heels, the cheery roar of the softball games behind them. Past several rows of cars, she heard them.

"She's in public, I have every right to—" The man's voice cut off with a grunt.

"You have no fucking rights," Nicky said, as cold as she'd never heard him.

Jeremiah and Gillian started running.

They turned the corner and saw Nicky behind a broad, red-faced, middle-aged white man in a sweatshirt, holding the man's arm wrenched behind his back while Nicky looked down at something that illuminated his face.

The man yelped for help when he saw them and Nicky looked up, met Gillian's eyes, then hooked the man in front of his shin and toppled him face-first into the grass. He jammed his knee into the man's back, kept hold of his arm, and raised the phone to Gillian.

"He's got pictures and video of you," he said, his lips curling back from his teeth. He shook his head and huffed out a furious breath, then yanked up the sweatshirt, showed a cord taped to the man's body. "He was recording you."

"Get him off of me," the man cried. "I'm a private investigator, he's got no right to—"

He cried out when Nicky, eyes still on Gillian, ground down his knee and twisted the arm farther up. *What do you want?* his clear, angry eyes seemed to ask. *Whatever you want.*

Nicky's status as the boy who'd saved his brother had gotten him harassed and bullied more than once and, from fifth to ninth grade, she'd watched him grow from a boy who'd scrap to protect himself and his brother to a young man who knew how to use his body to stand up for others. When she'd approached him at the bonfire to ask him to be her teacher for the summer, he'd been shirtless because he'd given his T-shirt to a boy whose nose he'd punched. The boy, drunk, had been harassing a guy who stuttered. Nicky had sobered him up.

She could ask him to dislocate the man's shoulder. She could ask him to go to jail for her, get sued for her. She could ask him to malign all of his hard-earned efforts as an artist of color who effected real change by doing something horrible here, something to satisfy her rage at her continued impotence, and it would be all her fault. She'd been so foolish to think Thomas wouldn't follow her here, that hastily signing the divorce papers that left her nothing would satisfy his desire to be omnipotent in her life.

No. No.

She'd done nothing wrong. This wasn't her fault. She couldn't control all the traffic.

"Let him go," she said.

With a final satisfying grind of his knee and a groan from the man, Nicky stood and held the phone out to Gillian.

She grabbed it as she buried herself against his chest.

Jeremiah yanked the man up, but when the man started to thank him, he shook him like a dog toy. "Show me your license."

The man did have a private investigator's license. He did have the right to stalk, spy, and take pictures and video of Gillian with Nicky at the luncheon in the train station and during their happy hour at the bar and here at the softball field.

When he peeled out of the parking lot without his phone, he did it with the understanding that if Nicky and Jeremiah *ever* saw him again, he'd be leaving with much, much less.

CHAPTER 23

Gillian sent an email to her attorney to let her know what Thomas had done. Fortunately, Alex had a friend in Chicago who'd helped them break into the PI's phone and download the images before the man deleted them remotely. She hoped she could use the photos to squeeze some portion of child support out of him. All good-faith bargaining, as if there had ever been any, was over. She would no longer entertain conversations about the bar. She would send her children to him over her cold, dead body. She would counter any efforts to enforce the visitation with evidence of his stalking.

While refusing to put up with more of his bullshit was a fortifying first step, Gillian was realistic that it would take more than that to defeat Thomas Bancroft. Alex had wanted to strategize his demise immediately, using her home as the war room, but it'd been late. They decided to meet up the next afternoon. Her family wanted to help, and she wanted their help.

But she wanted her night with Nicky more.

They'd gotten ready for bed in his loft bedroom quietly, brushing their teeth together in the nicest barn bathroom in Kansas, her wearing a black cotton nightie and him pulling on sleep pants. It'd been sweet, even soothing after the revelations of the night. It was only when they were kissing under his gray sheets, the waning half-moon shining down on them through the skylight, did she realize there was going to be trouble.

She was licking down his torso when he gripped her arms to stop her. "Baby, you've been through a lot. Let me just hold you."

"Why?" she asked as he turned her to her back.

"I want to take care of you," he said, impossibly beautiful with that yearning in his eyes as he hung over her. "After what that asshole tried to do."

His tenderness filled her with rage. "He didn't try, Nicky," she said, pushing him back and hauling up on her elbows. "He did it. He paid someone to spy on me and take pictures of me, and he made me feel powerless *and* responsible." His pained face, his glorious chest, was so beautiful and she'd so much rather be kissing him and riding him than managing his care. "But instead of doing what I've done for the last decade, tomorrow I'm going to get up and lean on you and my family and figure some way to fight back against a man who has all the weapons. Tonight, the last thing I need is for you to make me feel weaponless. Treating me like I'm fragile is not taking care of me." She kicked off the sheet and covers. William could probably hear her down at the house. "He stole my power by being cruel. Don't you steal it by being nice."

Propped up on his elbow, Nicky looked down at her like she was transforming right in front of him, his breath picking up, his eyes narrowing. His eyes traveled over her body in the moonlight: where the nightie was rucked up around her thighs, over her cleavage and her shoulders and the pulse in her neck. He seemed to finally realize what had made her so angry about his *let me just hold you.*

For the first time, they were in a bed together. For the very first time, she was in his bed. The sudden wolfish hunger on his face was why she always thought Little Red Riding Hood was the porniest fairy tale.

"I'm not a good woman, Nicky," she said, rubbing her thighs together. "I liked the threat of you tearing that man apart. I liked you standing by me that way. Let me thank you." She reached for his jaw, ran her hand down it, over the hard marble of his unscarred shoulder, and was so, so grateful that when she pushed, his body moved backward in response. "Let me take care of you." He let her push him to his back as she rose over him. "Let me show you that I can tear *you* apart."

His long low groan shook the rafters as she moved as slow as hot sap over him with her hands and lips and teeth and tongue.

Eons later, she looked up at Nicky, gorgeously naked on his gray sheet, the comforter and his sleep pants shoved to the floor, as he looked down at her in agony.

"Fuck, baby," he groaned, sweat gleaming in the cup of his hip as he drew his thumb over her lips where they were stretched around his penis. "You're fucking gorgeous—" He curled up, love punched, as she dragged her tongue over what was inside her mouth. "Fuck."

Each curse flooded her with power.

She kneeled naked between his strong, almost hairless thighs, but the sheen over his brown skin, his harassed restless movements, the grip of his hand in her hair, and his agonized groans left no doubt who was in control. He hid nothing from her in defense of his masculinity.

With him still in her mouth, she reared up onto her hands to be directly over him. His penis was Goldilocks perfect, just big enough for her to feel the stretch of him inside her, for him to leave her tender if they went more than twice, but not so big that she couldn't get him...

She softened her lips to push her mouth down.

All...

She feathered her tongue as she descended.

The way...

She relaxed her jaw.

...In.

She rested there, breathed through her gag reflex, and felt his penis kick. It might have been years, but there were some lessons you never forgot.

His hand petted over her hair when she knew he wanted to yank. "Hechicera," he breathed. "So good on that cock. My good girl, you make it so, so... Oh God."

Goddess, she thought and it was like he heard, the whine he made, the silky salt he gave her. She wanted to break him free from his bad boy's smile and his caretaker's worry. She wanted him to let go of everything.

When she pulled back up his cock, she made the sucking slide slow and wet and forever.

"Fuckfuckfuckfuck," he chanted like an incantation, like it would keep him from spilling over, so she let him go. She wanted to tease him all night.

She lightly kissed his tip.

"You're driving me crazy," he groaned, grabbing his flesh and squeezing it painfully. "Show me your tongue." He loved this edge as much as she did.

She smiled greedily, looked up at him through lowered eyelashes, and bent her head down—ass up—as she slowly opened her mouth. She played at submission, lolled out her tongue while she swayed her butt in the air.

His "Fuck, yes," through gritted teeth said plainly who was in control. "Just like that."

His body splayed in front of her was moonstruck. His black eyes staring back sparkled. He took hold of his cock and rubbed it against her waiting tongue. Used her to make the tip wetter. Then he traced the head over her lips. He watched, mesmerized, like it was someone else who left that gloss.

"You've been driving me crazy since the second I saw you

tonight." She felt the timbre of his voice in the mattress as he caressed her mouth with his cock. "If you weren't my sweet mommy girl, I'd have dragged you behind the concession stand and fucked you up against it. I'd take you to my favorite restaurant in New York and put you on your knees under the tablecloth. I'd hide you in a mask and eat you out for everyone's enjoyment at this sex club in Paris."

He'd never. She'd never. But the fantasy had her huffing a shaky sob against his wet dick and rolling her hips. She was dripping down her thighs.

She reared up and crawled up him, straddled his thighs. He reached for her.

"Grab the bars, Nicky."

His acclaimed artist hands halted in midair. He clenched them into fists.

She could feel how wet her bush was when she nestled it against his trembling pelvis just above his cock. She wrapped her hands as far as she could around his wrists and, leaning over, pressed them back to the gray metal of his headboard. "Grab. The bars," she ordered into his ear, rubbing her tight nipples against his sweat-soaked chest. He smelled like the expensive leather surely worn by well-paid gigolos. She bit his lobe. "Don't make me tie you down."

He let out a groan that sounded like real pain and he buried his face against his bicep, bringing the four tips of his scar against his chin as he wrapped his fists around the metal. He'd done that the first time he'd come inside her, seconds after he'd warned her he was going to lose it, shoving his face against his arm like the pleasure was more than he could stand.

That generous lover boy had become this incredible nurturing man. She wanted to bathe him in the power he gave her.

With Nicky's fingers clinging white-knuckled to the horizontal bars of his headboard, Gillian straightened, lifted up, and caught his cock in the cradle of her. Rotating her hips, she slowly worked him inside, his breath stuttering as she did it.

The hot, thick slide of him... The sounds of him wanting her...

She snapped open the eyes she'd helplessly closed. She was master here. She straightened her head from where it had lolled on her shoulder and saw him looking greedily at where he disappeared inside her, giving twitches of his mighty hips as his teeth sunk cruelly into his lush bottom lip.

She leaned back. "Want to watch, Nicky?" she moaned throatily, spreading her thighs and rolling her hips, using her thigh muscles to raise herself up and down, letting him see himself sliding in and out of her, gleaming with her.

His lips curled in a grimace. He grunted every time she pulsed down and squeezed. Moonlight caught the sweat in his hair. His fingers were bloodless around the bars.

He was hanging on because she'd told him to.

He was naked in his pleasure and he showed it to her fearlessly. He was letting her tear him apart and drive him crazy and take care of him. He wasn't holding her gently but letting her fuck him mercilessly because she'd said it was what she needed.

Salve Reina, she thought like a sigh. She smelled a wisp of rose-scented incense. She felt the moonlight on her body. She heard the tiniest click, like the work of Nicky's lock-picking tools.

Her love for Nicky flooded through her. She was in love with Nicky. Of course she was. The waning moon was for shedding what one was done with and making way for the new and she was done with feeling responsible for Thomas's abuse. She let her love for Nicky fill her from the well where she'd hidden it.

She loved Nicky. She'd loved him for a very long time.

She didn't want the tears in her eyes because she wasn't done showing him how well she could take care of him but the warm current in her pussy and the infusion of power in her body made him give a savage moan and he gripped the headboard so hard he made the bed creak.

She reached for her clit to make that power roar.

"If you weren't such a good bad man," she groaned, clenching and clenching him as she rubbed, "I'd tie you down and show you off, Nicky." He looked demolished. He looked brand-new and precious. "I'd chain you to a bed, cuff you to a wall." He was helping, lifting his pelvis to dig into her. "I'd make them watch me tease you, please you, adore you, worship you." His breath was bursting hard through his teeth. "Look at you. Look how incredible you are. How perfect. Perfect for me." The pleasure was no longer something she was giving, it was something consuming them both. Her words were fire-licked.

He was flashing in and out of her, yelling as he did it. "I'd force everyone to see what I did to you. I want them to know who you belong to." She spread her thighs wide, arched her cunt down hard, and flashed two fingers over her clit, as real and dirty and magical as she wanted to be.

"I'll make sure they all know you belong to me."

"GillianGillianGillian," he roared, arching up to come in her as she pressed down to come on him. And then she was on her back and he was over her and he was shoving in and in and in as she surrounded him.

Under the light of the moon, they became flesh-and-blood magic, forever fused.

Nicky crawled up to consciousness as Gillian moved out of his arms, out of their bed. Where was she going?

That's when he heard the ringing of her phone where she'd plugged it in on his bedside table.

Muggy with sex and still mostly asleep, he put his hand on her naked back when she sat on the edge of the mattress. "Hello?" she croaked.

He felt the instant stiffening of her spine and came cold-water awake.

"Thomas?" As far as he knew, she hadn't spoken to her ex-husband in weeks. "I have nothing to say to—"

He felt her outbreak of goose bumps.

As she continued to listen, he pulled her down, pulled her against him, cradled her against his body as he covered them in the blankets. He hadn't even considered that she might not want this as she pulled his arm tighter around her.

This close, he could hear what her ex-husband was saying.

"...charges after you assaulted my private investigator—"

"Are you kidding me?" she hissed.

Nicky squeezed her. Rule one was that you never argued with a narcissist. They were rampant in Nicky's world of money and influence.

She moved the phone away from her mouth and let out a long, shaky breath that reached for calm. He rubbed his lips against her shoulder.

She brought the phone back. "You surveilled me and I have the evidence. You'll be hearing from my attorney," she said. She pulled the phone back and her finger searched for the button to end the call. He could see the resolve of her jaw in the faint light.

"Is that the evidence you have?" Thomas said, tinny. He had that flat nothing accent Nicky always heard from D.C.-ers.

Her finger stilled.

"Or do you have evidence that you're an unfit mother who fled the state with my children and then exposed them to a man-whore with a troubled past and a proclivity for violence? My PI made sure to photograph his bruises."

Nicky had taken and given real punches but the resiliency of Gillian's response as she put the phone back to her ear let him know that he'd never been through what she had. "Fled the state?" she asked coolly.

"You took my children out of state without my permission."

"That's not true," she scoffed. "I told you and you agreed."

"Do you have my agreement in writing?"

Gillian's silence was her response.

"There's a reason the Bancrofts put a morality clause in our prenups, Gillian. I won't be humiliated by you playing groupie to a college dropout who spray-paints alleys. I won't have my children endangered."

Her body shook minutely in his arms. He held her tighter. Her voice came out shockingly calm. "What are you saying?"

"Return to D.C. Live up to the terms in the prenup *you* signed. If you don't, I will file for full custody of my children."

She went stock-still, like a current running through her, shocking her. The hair rose on the back of Nicky's neck.

"You don't want that," Thomas said. His voice was reasonable. He believed everything he said was reasonable. "I don't want that. But think about what you've done. You took my children to that horrible little town. Do you know that it's in the second-poorest county in Kansas? In Kansas," he repeated. "You tried to buy me off. You behaved like money would substitute for quality time with my children. Then, that...spray painter. And his brother."

Nicky tensed behind her.

"Only the brother went to prison twice for drug distribution, but honestly Gillian. These kinds of people. Do you believe he's funding that lifestyle with his *art*? How naive are you? One of the times the brother was arrested was while he was living with him. Graffiti doesn't pay for that many rehab stays at Crossroads Antigua. With his brother dead from an overdose, he won't have anyone to hide behind anymore."

She wrapped her fingers around his hand and he realized how tightly he'd been holding her.

Her ex-husband laid out everything Nicky hadn't. Thomas put his own racist spin on it—how unoriginal was it to call a

Mexican a drug dealer? But Gillian was wise enough to suss out the ugly truths Nicky had tried to hide.

She now knew about all the pain Nicky was responsible for.

"It's the simplest concept, Gillian," Thomas said. "You and I had a deal. I asked you to be my wife, forever, and you broke that pact. Then I asked you to live up to a few simple promises you made when you signed the prenup, no one forced you, and you refuse to do that as well. I even attempted to find some fair way to get you what you wanted, you know my money saved your family, and instead of appreciation, you still cast me as the bad guy."

Nicky held her close against the whirlwind of impenetrable arguments although she'd withstood them for ten years and he'd lost the right to protect her.

"You will live up to your promises. You swore that I would be part of your life, forever, and I will be, one way or another. No one breaks a promise they've made to me."

She was impossibly still. Every man in her life had betrayed her.

"I'll be there next Sunday," Thomas said. "Either you all will be flying home with me or just my children will." He hung up on her.

Nicky steeled himself for her to get up from his bed and walk out of his life. She put her phone down and turned in his arms.

"When did Lucas die?" she asked, putting her hand on his face. On the edge of dawn, he could barely see her.

"Almost a year ago." Almost a year since he'd heard the panting snarl of his cadejo, felt its hot breath and hungry drool at his neck. He would have welcomed that terror over the torture of its silence.

Instead of shoving away from him as she should have, she wrapped her arm around his back and buried her face against his neck. "Nicky. I'm sorry he's gone."

"Gillian, I'm so sorry I—"

She put her hand over his mouth. "Not now. Hold me. We need sleep. We have so much to figure out in the morning. Just hold me."

Gillian buried her face against his skin and breathed, just breathed like he was her favorite smell, like breathing him in would help her with her panic and her fear.

He couldn't help her. He'd lied to her. He couldn't take care of her. He couldn't protect her. But he would hold on to her as hard as she would let him for these last dwindling days.

CHAPTER 24

Nicky's Jeep was parked in front when Gillian pulled up to the train station late Friday morning. She flipped down her mirror.

She looked at her hair. Her curls and waves were cooperating thanks to the wonders of the online curly hair tutorials her sister had introduced her to. She looked at her face. Even with the amount of sunblock she slathered on, she was approaching that dark tan of her youth when she was all teeth and whites of her eyes from a distance.

She tapped the nose she'd altered.

There she was. The Pride of the East Side. Divorced from a truly shitty man. With a summa cum laude that she'd run over a few people to get. Mom of two spectacular kids, and hija to people she'd treated like flour she could dust off her hands. Co-owner of the most successful bar in Freedom, Kansas. And the only bruja (she assumed) to be offered a position at the fastest-growing financial firm in Chicago.

Gillian Armstead-Bancroft.

She was no worse or better than all the times she'd checked this mirror concerned about what she projected to her peers, her community, her family, her... Nicky. She was just a little more comfortable with the smudges. She wasn't good or bad, a success or a failure, blessed or cursed, perfect or horribly flawed. She, like everyone, bobbed somewhere in the middle.

She looked straight into her dark-brown eyes. Was she really going to do this? She couldn't control the outcome. The odds of success were low.

Her stomach burbled under the jumpsuit Nicky had peeled off her a month ago. She wore a black blazer over it now. And a bra underneath.

She got out of the car and strode to the train station door.

The days since Thomas's phone call had been busy.

For the first time in known history, Loretta cut Sunday dinner short. She'd rushed everyone out squawking and grumbling by 2 p.m., Sissy had taken the kids over to their parents' house to play, then the rest of the core Torres clan had gathered so they could learn about Thomas's demands, threaten his annihilation, then plan a human shield around Gillian, Ben, and Naomi.

Thomas had no fucking idea what he'd unleashed.

Nicky had stayed quiet but by her side, gripping her hand whenever she'd needed it.

Now, when she pulled open the train station door, he once again gave her what she needed: a stunning distraction from her nerves.

It was astonishing how she could be away from his mural for a few hours then come back and feel true awe when she saw it again. He'd left before her yesterday while she'd completed her hours-long interview with the executive team then spoke to her friend from Brandeis. What she'd learned had made her leave without looking at Nicky's progress.

The base coat was now complete. He would start again at the top and add details, lowlights, and highlights, he'd explained, but it was hard to imagine it being any more glorious. The Kansas sunrise as well as a plains full moon shone like light was actually pouring out of them in that lemony-yellow-gone-to-indigo sky. She couldn't wait to see it finished in a couple of weeks.

Her proposed start day in Chicago was September 1.

On the ground beneath the lowest level of scaffolding, Nicky stood from where he'd been squatting, wiping his hands as he watched her with a naked look of relief that not even the shadows could hide. It was past ten, as late as Gillian had ever come in. In the busyness of her morning phone calls—one from the Chicago firm, one to her attorney—she hadn't had time to consider that he might worry that she wasn't coming in at all.

The relief on his face turned to caution as he stepped out from underneath the scaffolding as she walked toward him. She'd grown used to the caution over the last few days. After ten years of having her emotions disregarded and her hurt dismissed, she even appreciated it. Nicky had a right to be cautious. He'd lied to her by omission all summer long.

She was confused, angry, hurt, all the emotions she'd felt when he told her he'd lied about his engagement. She also grieved for Lucas, that sad, angry little boy who spent so much silent time in her company. She grieved for both of those poor boys and was furious that, for all his talk of taking care of others, Nicky refused to accept care for himself. Keeping her in the dark had forced him to grieve alone. Lucas was less than a year gone. She couldn't imagine the state she'd be in after losing one of her sisters.

But there'd been so much, so many emotions, so many highs and lows about so many things that she'd asked, that Sunday morning when they'd woken up together and he'd tried to apologize, if they could just wait to talk about it. She needed to think. She needed to process. And she needed him.

Now she'd decided what she had to do and she was ready.

When she reached him, she wrapped her arms around his shoulders and kissed him. He kissed her back, sliding his arms around her waist, and his body loosened with relief.

She kissed his lower lip and his upper lip. She kissed his fierce nose. She kissed his high cheekbone. She kissed his ear. "I'm ready to talk now, if you have the time," she murmured into it.

He nodded then rested his forehead against her temple. She felt his thick black lashes against her skin. She smooched the teardrop scar beneath his eye.

She held his hand as she walked into her office then shut the door.

"How did the interview go?" he asked, side-eyeing her as they walked to her desk. He was nervous. That was something he would have covered up with a big smile and bigger flirt at the beginning of this summer. His nerves were fine.

She welcomed the chance to tell him. "Amazing," she said. "My curse is broken."

Those lashes shot wide as he leaned back against the edge of her desk and put his hands on her hips. He was already paint splattered and he smelled like he couldn't go near an open flame. His smell made her high.

"The firm made me an offer this morning." She rested her hands lightly on his muscular forearms. She couldn't control how he would receive this. "I'm going to turn it down."

"What?" The scar puckered beneath Nicky's eye. "Why?"

Her heart thundered in her ears. "I've decided to stay in Freedom."

Nicky let go of her to steeple his fingers behind him. "I don't understand."

She spoke over her rampaging nerves. "The special needs program for the Palomino County schools is pretty well developed," she said. She explained how she'd spoken to the head of the county's program and visited an excellent therapeutic clinic serving autistic children and adults an hour away in Bartlesville. The risk she was taking couldn't be a foolhardy one, not with her children involved.

"Okay…" Nicky said, looking like she'd hit him with a bat. "But what about you?"

She let out a breath of excitement she couldn't contain. After Saturday night, after her night with Nicky, disparate ideas had merged to become a cohesive whole. The solution became so obvious. She'd squeezed researching the concept into every spare second she had this week, and this was the first time she would speak it out loud.

"I'm going to provide financial planning services to women, people of color, and the disadvantaged," she said, feeling the steel invade her spine just announcing it. "I'm going to help people like Yesenia and Sonia and Cariña and…and me. I'm going to provide the guidance and security and information that's remained in the hands of the privileged. I can be that bridge. The Rosalina fund is just the tip of the iceberg—I can provide classes in saving and investing, I can set up at the bar for financial-guidance happy hours, I can work with women at the abuse shelter." She realized she was flailing her hands. She pressed them against her chest. "I can take away money's ability to scare them. I can arm them so no one can use money as a weapon against them."

She'd struck up a conversation with Dahlia as she'd sat at the bar and the awkwardness she'd had as a bar owner slid away as they discussed the bartender's financial goals; Gillian was going to help her save to buy her first home. This was where her whole life, her whole career, had been headed. She hadn't been able to see the beacon in D.C., and she couldn't afford to follow it in a large metropolitan area. But the cost of living was so low in Freedom.

She explained that there were grants to help fund the not-for-profit aspects of what she wanted to do, and she'd already talked to Joe and Jeremiah. "Between the grants, Torres Construction, their personal finances, and advising Jeremiah with his trust, I can cobble together a paycheck while I build my business. I asked them not to mention it to Alex or Cynthia yet, but Cynthia has repeatedly offered me a role at Liberty Manufacturing."

"Why don't you want Alex and Cynthia to know?" he asked. The veins and muscles stood out on his arms as he held himself up on her desk.

"You know how they are." She met his eyes. "And I wanted to tell you first."

A lank of black hair was slipping onto his high forehead. "But your education," he said. "Everything you've accomplished."

He was only echoing back the résumé she'd waved a tedious number of times.

"Honestly, it does make a difference that I can have that Chicago job if I want it," she said. "As a woman whose work at home as a mother and head of household is undervalued, I needed that boost." She pointed behind her as if Nicky could see through the wall. "That bar is my inheritance. What I do with it and for this street and in this town…" She pointed at herself. "That's my legacy. Sowed and cultivated by me, supported and nurtured by the people who love me. I don't want to plant that seed anywhere else."

Nicky held himself like a taut string. She stepped closer but didn't touch him.

"My curse is broken, Nicky," she said and clarified with, "You helped me break it." Regardless of the alarm on his face, she would say it all. "I have my magic back."

It had roared into her like water filling an empty vessel along with her love for Nicky on Saturday night, like feeling coming back to a dead limb. Like that limb, like her love, she'd been cautious with her magic, careful of its delicacy.

In front of her Guadalupe altar, asking nothing and offering deep gratitude to La Virgen with candle and incense and her rosary beads, Gillian had felt an undeniable pull.

"La Virgen helped me discover how I can help Cariña," she told Nicky.

She explained how, as if being guided, she'd spread the borrowed articles about Cariña de la Cruz and the horrible Freedom history book out on her bed. She'd closed her eyes, held her rosary, and rubbed across the bead of the fifth mystery, when twelve-year-old Jesus was discovered in the temple after Mary had searched for him for three days. Gillian felt La Virgen's three-day terror, Cariña's loss, and her own fear for her children and her fight to keep them safe. When once she would have turned one way to ask for aid and intervention, this time she turned another. This time, instead of a bright light, she saw a compassionate woman's dear, brown face.

"¿Donde está el niño?" the woman asked. *Where is the child?*

La Virgen looked very much like her grandmother Rosalinda.

When Gillian opened her eyes again, twenty minutes had passed in a second, her cheeks were wet with tears, a feeling of peace suffused her, and that horrible book was open with her finger against a name.

Greta Hutchinson. Just a name in a list of them. A woman on a committee. There'd been no other mention of Greta Hutchinson in the book. She wouldn't be easy to find.

She said the name to Nicky now and he straightened and surrounded her biceps with his warm, fortifying touch.

"That's incredible," he breathed, eyes as dark and sparkling as the mystery she'd uncovered. "Cariña wants your help finding her child. La Virgen gave you somewhere to look." He squeezed her arms, rubbed them, but again let go. "That's wonderful, sweetheart, but I didn't have anything to do with it."

He truly believed that. He effortlessly discounted everything he'd done for her.

Thirteen years ago, the most cocksure boy she knew hadn't told her he wanted more. In the decade-plus since, while his talent had him lauded and praised, he'd kept his distance. And here, when the instant sight of him had made her hungry for him, he made up an engagement to keep them apart. In the beginning of the summer, she'd thought the distance was for his benefit.

Now she wasn't so sure.

She stepped back to give him space and sat in the chair to give him dominance. "Nicky, you offered up the truth about your engagement when you didn't have to," she said. "I trust you."

He shot her a look of disbelief.

She shrugged. "Sorry. I do." She remembered how cagily he'd avoided lying to her when she'd asked about his brother. *He's not getting into trouble.* "Why didn't you tell me Lucas was gone?"

Still leaning back against her desk, Nicky crossed his arms and looked down to his sneakers. His hair slid forward in front of his eyes. It was the first time he'd shielded himself from her that way in thirteen years.

"I killed him, Gillian."

Wrong, every instinct protested.

She shook her head. "No. Thomas said...drug overdose."

"I killed him," he repeated firmly, not raising his head, not loosening that grip on himself. "I left him and I abandoned him and I was never in time to save him and... I killed him. He's dead because of me."

His words sounded like a chisel etching the certainty into stone.

Wiping the muck of white, male Aryanism from Thomas's story, Gillian had been able to extrapolate that Lucas had been to prison, that Nicky had invited him to live with him, and that Nicky had paid for expensive rehab multiple times. From where she sat, Nicky had been a concerned, involved, self-sacrificing brother.

Nicky was a column of self-hate standing in front of her.

"What happened?" she asked softly.

"After that summer, I fell apart," he said. "I don't blame you. You deserved to leave. But I…" His breath was shaky as it came out of his nose and Gillian held on to the arms of the chair. She'd asked for the truth and now she was getting it. "William found me and cleaned me up and I knew I couldn't stay. Lucas got arrested right before you left."

She remembered that night. Before Nicky had gotten a hysterical phone call from his mother—*Where were you?* Gillian had heard the woman screaming—he'd gone flaccid in her mouth while the rest of him had stiffened on the hood of the car. She'd looked up to see him pale and trembling with his eyes squeezed shut. She'd pushed him down and crawled over him and covered him and kissed him, the most effective *hechizo* she'd learned to make the black dog go away.

"Lucas was sentenced to juvie until he turned eighteen," Nicky continued in that horrible monotone, "so I took the opportunity to run. When he got out, I sent a little money, I came home to help him when I could, but I couldn't come back for good. Not with…"

He made a motion at her.

"I was so damn glad," he said through clenched teeth, "to get away from him when I went up to the middle school." She could see the veins in his forearms. "And I was so damn glad to leave town and leave him behind, and every time he just took off after he moved in with me, I didn't care what was missing or who came by my place, I was just so fucking relieved he was gone."

His head wrenched up. He shook his hair out of his face. His eyes bore down on her to make sure she was seeing him. "My brother is dead and it's my fault."

What she saw was a little boy who'd had too much weight placed on his shoulders and a loving brother who refused to give himself grace. "Okay," she said, surprising him. Those thick lashes fluttered. His chest moved like he'd just finished a race. "Is there anything else you're keeping from me?" she asked.

His brow twisted up. "William didn't need me to stay this summer." He said it like an accusation. "He had heartburn. I used it as an excuse to stay in town. To be close to you. I didn't fall in love with you that summer, Gillian." The monotone he'd used when he'd talked about his brother was being burned away by emotion and the hot sparks in his eyes. "I fell in love with you the second I saw you when I was ten. I've *always* loved you. I *always* will."

She would've been able to glory in it, to make sense of it, to shuffle it into the memories of their years together if uttering the words hadn't made him so sad. Why did it make him so sad?

She stood slowly on weak knees. She'd said what she was about to say to one other man in her life. That hadn't gone well. She was a mathematician, not a poet. But Friday was ruled by Venus and while she'd never cast an hechizo de amor for herself, she hoped she had the incantation right now.

"That's convenient," she said shakily. She put her hands on his crossed, closed-off arms. "I've always loved you, too."

He looked at her like she practiced the dark arts. He looked at her like she'd summoned the black-robed figure of Santa Muerte. "No," he said, moving his arms away from her touch, putting them behind him on her desk. "That's not…"

To believe it, he'd have to rewrite what he'd been telling himself since the fifth grade. She leaned on that logic instead of her instantly hurt feelings.

She put her hands on his chest. "Think about it," she said, forcing him to meet her eyes. "You were the first person I trusted with the truth about my life and I shared it with you minutes after we ran into each other, after I'd done everything in my power to keep it from my parents, my sister, my best friend." Her hands gripped into his T-shirt. "Nicky, you were the first adult I was absolutely myself with—not the good me, not the bad me, just me—in years."

She could feel his resistance beneath her fingers. "When we were kids, you were my closest companion. I actually spent more time with you than I did Cynthia. I got to see you take care of Lucas. I know what a devoted big brother you are."

He looked away.

"You are," she insisted, moving to capture his gaze again without letting him go. She was afraid he'd slip from her office and her life forever.

She could see the pulsing of his jaw. She could see the denial in his infinite eyes. She sent up a desperate prayer.

"Thirteen years ago, you introduced me to pleasure the way a woman could only dream of. But it wasn't because you were practiced or skilled. You were my confidant. You listened. You asked. You cared. And you asked of me, too, both when we were making love and when we weren't. If only I'd absorbed then how important friendship was to love. Just because I didn't understand it and wasn't ready for it doesn't mean I didn't love you."

She hated the way his chin lifted like she was about to punch him every time she said *love*.

"Now you're the most…" She searched for the words that would encompass all she felt for him. "… The most *magnificent* man I've ever known. I've never enjoyed anyone's company the way I enjoy yours. I've never been inspired by anyone the way I'm inspired by you. I've never admired anyone more. I've never…" She was ruining his T-shirt, but she couldn't let go. "I've never felt more essentially myself with anyone.

"I call Cynthia my best friend, but…but it's you. You're my best friend. You're the best friend I've *ever* had. Nicky, I love you."

He was breathing hard, she could feel his breath against her face, and she had to be very, very clear. "Nicky, I'm in love with you. I have been since the first time I saw you, too. *I* waved at you in the lunchroom. *I* asked you to come play with us. You and Lucas waited for me after school, but I'm the one who asked you to walk me home."

She remembered the rightness of leaving the school building and seeing him there, with his too-short jeans and his too-long hair, fidgeting in front of the school gate with his little brother's hand in his. Loving him had been as effortless and comforting as her magic. No wonder she hadn't recognized it.

She got to see the lightning-struck look on his face the instant before he pulled her close and kissed her, and thank La Virgen that he did because Gillian hadn't seen him that terrified since the cadejo growled in his ears. The kiss was long, but his touch was soft. His lick was light, flicking, tasting. The kiss felt like a piece he was creating.

He pressed his forehead to hers. She could feel him, sense him, smell him. Of course she'd found him on that road. She could find him from a million miles away.

"Is that why you're staying?" he murmured in the tiny space between them. "Why you're giving up that job in Chicago?"

She shook her head without separating them. "No. That's for me. That's for them."

"Good." He tipped in and kissed her again. Nuzzled her mouth with the lips she'd praised a million times. Then he was gently pushing her back down into the chair. While she was still muzzy from the kiss and wondering why she was sitting, he straightened and again leaned back on her desk. "I'm going to ask William to move with me to San Francisco. I won't be back after the mural is finished."

"I..." Her very quick, very smart brain went very quiet in her office.

The equation was a complicated one.

She could break it down into its parts.

Each of her fingertips met its mate in her lap.

"You never talk about San Francisco," she said. She kept her eyes on his chest. "I didn't realize you enjoyed it so much."

"It's a place to live."

The faded gray T-shirt was misshapen where she'd tugged it.

"You can live anywhere for your work, right?"

"Yes."

At least his manager would be nearby. She closed her eyes and folded her thumbs into her fists to keep herself from counting.

"Gillian—"

"Are you still angry with me for not acknowledging you?"

"No."

She opened her eyes and looked directly into his gorgeous face. "Is it the kids?"

His breath hitched. "In a way."

She trusted him. He was telling the truth. She let his answer burrow through her pain and made it compute. "Well," she laughed, stunned and without humor. "That's all that matters, then."

"They make me happy, Gillian. Being with them makes me really, really happy." He looked more miserable than she'd ever seen him. "How can I have what I want when my brother never can?"

She'd supplied variables to explain why she loved him, why she wanted them to last longer than a summer.

Nicky was telling her why those variables summed to zero. She needed to check her work. "Do you love me now?"

"More than ever."

He cracked her heart in a way Thomas never could.

She shoved up from the chair and stepped behind it, locked her hands on its back so she didn't reach for him. "But not enough to stay with us. Not enough to give us a chance."

"I have a debt to pay."

"And you'll pay it with me?" Her voice went shrill with anger. "With us? With the family we could have?"

"I can't take care of them." He was hiding nothing from

her. He was telling her the truth as he believed it. "I can't take care of you."

She lifted the chair and cracked it loud on the tile. "I never asked you to." If she'd been Alex, she would have thrown it. "I don't need you tending me like I'm a painting to be admired or a relic to be worshipped. I tried to be an ideal and look where that got me. It kept me married to a narcissist for ten years. The *last* thing I want to be is an ideal."

She swiped furiously at a tear making its way down her face. "Funny, you're the person who helped me get good at being bad."

He put a hand out to her. "Hechicera—"

She stepped back. "Don't." The fact that he wanted to comfort her then leave her just poured salt in the wound. "You know me better than anyone. You provided cover to the nurse's office that time in sixth grade when I got my period in white shorts. You've seen my dad drunk. You literally know the insides of my body. You know the flesh-and-blood me, so if you say you love me, I believe you. I trust you. You've loved me, flaws and all, for most of our lives."

She was crying hard now but it was as much from anger as it was from heartbreak and loss. "And now that you can have me, you turn your back. I would have given myself to you. I would have allowed you to earn the gift of my incredible children. But I can't fight your willingness to sacrifice yourself and what we could have had, and honestly, I don't have the time." She smeared the tears away from her face. "Your flesh-and-blood hechicera is not powerful enough to fight an absent ghost.

"I love you, Nicky." She sobbed it and didn't hide an ounce of her pain. "But I've got a lot of people depending on me that I cannot let down. Please close the door on your way out."

CHAPTER 25

As dawn rose on Sunday morning after two sleepless nights, Nicky finally fell into an exhausted sleep.

He'd kicked the sheets to the end of his twin bed in William's house, and the early breeze coming through his open window was starting to feel like the dank humidity of a too-hot summer day. Morning bird call was becoming the drone of mosquitoes. The black boxer briefs he wore began to feel as heavy as holey jeans his mom wouldn't let him cut and turn into shorts.

Eyes rolling behind his lids, Nicky gripped his pillow, whimpered in his sleep, and slipped into the dream.

He'd thought it was going to be cool and shady down here by the river. Their mom had sent them outside, away from the air conditioner that rattled in the living-room window of their apartment, so she could get some sleep before work. They didn't know any kids since they'd only moved here from Topeka a month ago, and he knew better than to ask if he and Lucas could go to the pool. He'd asked a week ago and hated when he caused that super-sad look on his mom's face when they wanted something she couldn't afford.

He'd shoved an old towel and a bottle of sunscreen (Lucas

was lighter than he was and burned easy) and an empty pop bottle filled with tap water into his backpack. He'd thought, maybe, they could dip their feet in the river that was just a few blocks away. Maybe they could make homemade fishing poles or a shady lean-to under the overhang of the trees or even try to build a raft like they were Huck Finn going on an adventure.

But once they'd crawled down the steep slope through the weeds and brambles to the river's edge, Nick realized this wasn't gonna be any fun.

Lucas had started complaining on the walk over about how hot it was, how he was already thirsty, how Nick hadn't brought any snacks. Lucas was three years younger than Nick's ten years old, but Nick sometimes felt like his little brother was the boss. When they'd slipped down the slope, Nick had grabbed a prickly bush and his palm still stung. He didn't want to put it in the river—all the yards on their walk here were brown, and the river was low and looked sludgy and smelled funny. There wasn't a lick of breeze down here in the ravine, which made the smell and the bugs worse.

The mosquitoes were happy. No matter how many times Nick swatted at them, they came back to buzz around his ears and neck. He licked his dry lips, lips a jerk at his old school called "like a girl's," lips that always got chapped and sometimes bled, and he eyed the last few inches of water in the two-liter plastic bottle by his brother's side.

Lucas was finally happy, too. He'd plopped down on the ground, immediately complained about being bored, then grabbed the water they were supposed to drink and dumped half the bottle into the dirt. Nick had yelled and Lucas had ignored him as he stirred the dirt into mud then started playing in it. Now it was all over his clothes and hair and Nick knew he was going to have to clean him up before they got to go back into the air-conditioning but he didn't know where the hose was in their apartment complex and then he saw his brother pouring more water into his puddle and when Nick yanked the bottle out of his hands, Lucas started yelling and Nick handed it back just to shut him up.

"That's all we got to drink until we go home," he told him, trying to be the "man of the house" like his mom always told him he was. "Don't pour out any more."

He settled a little bit farther up on the bank to try to get away from the smell.

Lucas ignored him as he scooped up a handful of mud and watched it drip in big splats on his shorts.

He'd pulled out his notebook and his dented-up pencil box, trying to find that happy place feeling, but he already felt so tired. He knew once that mud dried, Lucas was gonna bitch and Nick was gonna have to keep him occupied until he piggy-backed him home in a couple of hours. Their mom didn't want to see them before then.

The page empty on his lap, Nick looked away, down to where the brown-green river turned and disappeared, and thought about what would happen if he followed it. What if he didn't say anything to his brother, just zipped up his backpack and started walking? The thought made it feel like mosquitoes had found their way into his belly, even as it allowed him to swallow around a choked-off feeling in his throat. He wanted a drink of water, but he was trying to make it last.

When they'd moved to Freedom, his mom had said it was going to be a fresh start.

He'd liked the sound of those words—*fresh start*—even though they still lived in a crappy apartment and they still didn't know anybody. But he'd believed her, so when the nice lady who lived in 2B and whose fingers were blue from the dye she used at her job gave them a community center catalog and Nick read about the summer art camp, he'd asked if he could go. *Inquire about financial aid,* it said beneath the listing.

He'd pointed that out to his mom, who'd been lying on the cool kitchen tile after work.

"Who's gonna take care of your brother?" she'd asked, without moving her arm from over her eyes.

A high school girl came to sleep at their house when their mom worked nights. But Nick played with Lucas when their mom was resting during the day.

It wasn't Lucas's fault. He was only seven. But sometimes, when Lucas demanded the last of the Cocoa Pebbles even though he'd had more than his fair share of the box, when Nick saw kids his own age riding away on bikes that Nick didn't own and Lucas couldn't ride, when there was an emergency like when Lucas fell out of a tree that Nick told him not to climb and Nick didn't know what to do, Nick hated his little brother.

That black, angry, overwhelming hatred always made Nick feel worse.

He swatted at the mosquitoes, worked to build up enough spit in his mouth to swallow again, and turned to ask his brother if he wanted help making mud pies.

Lucas was dumping the last of the water into his lap.

"What are you doing?" Nick yelled, that choking feeling breaking free in his throat. He shoved his notebook and pencils back into his backpack then ran down the slope, snatching the bottle out of his brother's hands. There was no water left. When he looked at his brother again, it felt like something wild had been let loose in his chest. "I told you we need to drink that!"

But rather than being upset or scared or starting to cry, Lucas just mixed the water puddling between his legs into the muck. "Go get more," he said like it was all a big game. "I'm thirsty."

It was a big game to Lucas. He was only seven and he got to cry when he wanted to and whine when he wanted to and be cuddled when wanted to. It was Nick, man of the house, who had to make sure he was okay.

I'm not my brother's keeper, he'd heard on a TV show once, and he liked to whisper it to himself sometimes when he was scribbling big, black clouds into his notebook. *I'm not my brother's keeper.*

The words bounced around inside his too-tight chest.

He whipped the empty bottle at his brother, heard the satisfying thud of it bouncing off his shoulder.

"Hey!" Lucas shouted, his face squeezing up in that mad look he got right before he told on Nick. "You're a butt!" He grabbed a handful of mud and threw it at Nick.

It splat right into his backpack.

Nick glanced inside to see mud dripping over his notebook full of drawings, on the towel, over his crayons and the special notebook of real drawing paper his art teacher had given him when he'd left his school in Topeka.

Anger felt like an alive thing that wanted to claw out of his chest.

"You're a-a-a son of a bitch!" he screamed back, the worst thing he could think of. He dropped his backpack and fell on top of Lucas, started scooping up handfuls of mud and grinding it into his hair, his face, his T-shirt. Lucas fell back, trying to slap Nick away, but Nick was bigger than him, more powerful, could easily shove away his skinny arms to coat his brother in the mud he'd wasted their water on. He ignored Lucas's yells and sobs, made sounds of his own.

"I told you...just listen to me...you always...hate you, hate you, I hate you..."

The anger that he'd thought was a bottomless pool burned out as quick as rocket fuel. Nick jerked to his knees. He stared down at his little brother, crying and curled into a ball, mud ground into his hair and covering his face, the one clean spot on his cheek showing a long bleeding scratch.

Panic ripped through him. "If you just did what I said!" Nick shouted, his voice breaking.

Lucas cried harder.

"Fine!" Nick yelled, standing and yanking his muddy backpack over one shoulder. "I'm leaving!"

He turned and began scrambling up the steep slope, grabbing the prickly bush again. He needed to get out of here before someone saw him, before his mom found out what he'd done, before he turned around and saw again what he'd done.

He was gonna run away, he decided as he reached the top of the slope and burst out into the burning sunlight. His mom was still asleep and he'd sneak into their apartment and grab some food—he didn't think he'd ever be thirsty again—and he would find his dad and learn to be a trucker and...

A long, low growl filled the ravine behind him. His mind went as blank as a shaken Etch A Sketch. It sounded like the trees were angry. Down below, where his little brother was all alone, Lucas said, "Nick?" his voice soft even though it shook.

He turned around.

On the bank of the river, ten feet from where his brother was pushed up from the mud, staring and petrified, was a gigantic dog. Nick's brain said it was a wolf, just like the one from the *Three Little Pigs*. It looked as long as Nick was tall and even in the thick weeds, Nick could see its ribs in its brown-black fur, its heaving chest, its yellow eyes, its jagged bared teeth.

It growled again and Nick wet himself.

"Run, Lucas," Nick said, not recognizing his own shaky voice. He was supposed to be the man of the house.

Lucas began to cry again, high wheezy sounds as he just lay there, still pushed up on his hands, covered in mud. The animal crouched down on its haunches, its snarl widening to show off its fangs.

"Run, Lucas!"

Nick's scream echoed through the ravine as he ran headlong down the hill toward his brother, his backpack bumping his shoulder. Lucas lunged off the ground a moment before the wolf leaped onto the spot where he'd been lying, its grizzly black body splattering the mud. The animal shook ferociously then chased Lucas, who was scrambling up the slippery slope, panic twisting his muddy, scratched face.

Trying to get to him, Nick felt like he was in one of his nightmares, the one where he couldn't pull his facedown brother out of two inches of water or couldn't find him in a school with endless hallways. Lucas fought the hill, working to keep his balance as he kept one hand stretched out for Nick to save him. The wolf was gaining on him, clawing up the slope, its mouth open and snarling. Getting down the hill felt like running through water, trying to go fast but not slip and send them into teeth and claws.

Nick finally grabbed his brother's mud-slick hand. Their eyes met and Lucas's face lit up. His big brother had him. His brother saved him. His brother was going to keep him safe.

Then his face twisted into a shocked, terrible O before he let out a scream, a horrible, hopeless sound. The wolf had sunk his teeth into Lucas's left hand.

Without thinking, Nick grabbed the metal pencil case out of his open backpack, swung between his brother and the dog, and smacked the animal on its face, holding his brother's arm against his body. Nick could feel the heat of the wolf's snarls, could see the saliva and blood running down its muzzle as he bashed the wolf again and again, trying to get the thing to let loose. The wolf swiped and Nick felt his backpack tumble to the ground.

A lucky swing landed directly on the wolf's nose and with an angry yelp, it released Lucas's hand.

Everything stopped.

Nick whipped around, pushed his brother, and screamed, "Go!" Terrified, he propelled Lucas up the rest of the hill until they gained purchase on level ground. They broke out of the trees onto the narrow access road between the river and the neighborhood. Nick could hear the wolf scrabbling up the last bit of slope.

"Go, go, go," he yelled as they sprinted, Nick staying between his brother and the wolf. In real life, there was a deep ditch and run-down homes on the other side of the road. In his dream, the road was endless and empty and sun-scorched. They were both screaming. Lucas stumbled then righted himself, sobbing and streaming blood. Nick could hear the grunts of the wolf as it raced closer. He got ready for claws to tear open his back.

Then his stomach rolled when Lucas tripped and stumbled to the cracked pavement. Instantly, Nick knew what he had to do.

Nick turned to face the wolf and raised his pencil case over his head. The animal was going to kill him. He knew it the moment he saw the thick chest bunched to leap, the savage teeth as long as Nick's fingers.

Nicky tucked his pencil case into his pocket and turned around, heading for home. Man, he was thirsty. He was going to get a big glass of ice water and he was going to be so quiet, his mom would sleep right through it.

She was gonna be so proud of him.

He ignored his brother's petrified scream.

"Dammit, Nick. Wake up!"

Nicky's eyes startled open as he yelled, the sunlight searing, and scrambled back and away from the claws in his stinging shoulder.

William's hand was outstretched. Full sun made the room too bright and Nicky was up against the headboard in his bedroom in the house, rickety bedside table, chest of drawers, rag rug covering the farmhouse boards.

The sting in his shoulder and under his eye faded. He was lucky he hadn't lost it, the doctors said. He wasn't dripping blood.

The panting Nicky heard was his own. The sweat was real, a clammy paste that stuck his hair to his temples and covered him like humidity. "Oh God," he groaned, pulling up his knees and putting his forehead against them. *I am not going to puke, I am not going to puke.*

After a few minutes of deep, shaky breathing, the mosquito drone quieted and the heat became the chill of air-conditioning against his sweaty skin. He wasn't going to have to bolt for the bathroom like he had so many times before. He felt the mattress shift as William sat back on the edge.

A blessedly cold glass tapped his upraised thigh. "Here," William said. He hadn't even known he'd left.

Nicky grabbed the oversized glass with both hands and gulped down the water. He drank until the cubes smacked his lips. "Thanks," he said, putting the glass against his forehead. "You're getting pretty stealthy with your cane."

"Guess it's no surprise you're dreaming about Lucas," William said.

Nicky lowered a leg. He was naked except for a pair of boxer briefs. He pulled the sheet over his lap and glanced at William, who was glaring at him through his thick glasses. William was ready for his day, hair slicked down and a nice pair of red suspenders on; the light was too bright for it still to be morning.

"Something happened with you and Gillian, didn't it?" William asked pugnaciously. "Now you're making sure to beat yourself up about it."

Both William and Gillian were heartily sick of his shit. "I don't want to talk about it," he said, putting down his empty glass.

William stomped his cane between his knees just like Gillian had banged that chair. "Too bad."

It wasn't the first time William had shaken Nicky awake. The cadejo had disappeared when Lucas died, but Nicky still had the dream to remind him of how he'd let his baby brother down. If he'd watched out for Lucas like he was supposed to, stayed close instead of abandoning him, his brother wouldn't have had to suffer through those five minutes for the rest of his life. Al-Anon counselors and therapists and curanderas and, most often, William had tried to convince him that it was the system and society's disregard for trauma in children that had failed Lucas. Not Nicky.

He hadn't turned his back on his brother the way the nightmare always ended.

He'd stood there with that pencil case raised, prepared to die and hating it, when William had come running with his rifle, saw the dog leap, and took a once-in-a-lifetime shot that knocked it out of the air. William wasn't a good marksman, he'd told the paper and the news stations. Nick, he'd said, with that skinny arm raised in the air, was the real hero.

That's what his mom and the papers and his teachers had called him. "A hero." Kids didn't know what to do with a hero who wasn't in a cape or wearing a fireman's hat, so they treated him like the oddity he was. Everyone ignored him, bullied him, or called him a hero. Everyone except one girl.

He hadn't turned his back on his brother in the last second, but the dream always reminded him of the truth of it: Every time he'd walked away, he'd felt a glorious freedom. He'd abandoned Lucas in that ravine over and over again until the wolf eventually ate his brother alive.

William pulled a handkerchief out of his shirt pocket. "I am so tired of you getting in your own way," he said, wiping at his forehead. "What'd you do?"

"Gillian's going to stay in town," Nicky said, leaning his head back against the headboard. "I told her I was gonna ask you to move with me to San Francisco."

William closed his eyes, shook his head, and breathed ferociously through his nose. "You dumb sonofabitch."

Yep. That was about the shape of things. Nicky went ahead and laid out the spiel he'd practiced a lot but hadn't gotten around to delivering: They'd buy a big house with property in Half Moon Bay. Or in Marin if William didn't like the cold. Nicky would build him a bigger, techier clubhouse.

All he did was make William angrier. The man yanked off his glasses and began to clean them with his handkerchief.

"I found you…" William said, rubbing furiously, "…about to inhale that poison and I dragged you out and I cleaned you up and I wrung you out…" Sunlight caught the glasses and shot into Nicky's eye. "… And I took care of you and you told me it was because of that girl." The bed was jiggling, William was rubbing so hard. "That girl and the smashed heart she left you with." He might rub straight through the glass. "Now she's standing right in front of you, wanting you to grab her…"

William was working himself into a state. Nicky leaned forward and grabbed his thick arm. "You check your sugar this morning?" he asked, looking for the bandage on his fingertip from the lancet prick. When Nicky overslept, he usually woke up to William's *ow!* so he could mock him. "You take your insulin?"

"I'm not hypoglycemic," William snapped, yanking his arm out of Nicky's hold. "I'm cheesed off." He shoved his glasses back on. "You think you can build us a mausoleum where we can be lonely and sad together? You think I'm going to condone that? My family was stolen from me."

The words sounded like they scoured William's throat. They never spoke about his alcoholic son who'd died in a drunk driving accident or the wife who'd left him as a result. Nicky had thought…what? He hardly thought about what William had lost before Nicky had come into his life.

"You can have a family, they're holding their hand out to you but you won't…" William screwed his mouth up. "Son, I love you too much to watch you martyr yourself on the altar of your brother. I don't want that for you. Neither did he."

Lucas had resented every interaction with William. *He likes you, not me,* he'd say.

"You don't know what Lucas wanted," Nicky said, meaning to be cruel. That mausoleum in San Francisco was gonna get real lonely.

"No?" William said, not taking the bait. "How the hell do you think I found you that night?"

Every muscle locked.

He'd been at the bottom of a three-month slide when he'd held that pipe in his hands and stared at the blue-ice pebbles inside of it. He was finally gonna know what all the fuss was about.

In his despair and degradation and shame when William had come barreling into the apartment, doing with his booming voice and sweeping cane and broad shoulders what he couldn't do with physical strength, Nicky had never thought to wonder *how* William had found him. He'd healed, cried, put on a few pounds, packed up, and left town.

Lucas hadn't been there that night.

"Your brother called to tell me where you were," William said.

"No," Nicky said, shaking his head. Lucas had been stuck in juvie, waiting for his trial for possession and intent to distribute. "He couldn't have."

Lucas wasn't there. But Nicky had been with Lucas's friends.

"Well, he did," William said, his voice easing up. "Somehow, he found out what you were up to, he got his hands on a phone, and he called me." His voice was like the far-off hum of grass getting mowed. "He told me where you were. He told me to get you out."

Nicky realized he was still shaking his head. He stopped. "Why haven't you ever told me this before?"

William looked at him for a long moment. Finally, he said, "I wasn't going to let you take what your brother did for you and let you twist it into one more thing to punish yourself with. But you've reached a crossroads, son. You need all the information to figure out which way you're gonna go." Those glasses made his stare engulfing. "Lucas loved you. He wanted you to get out."

His brother had called William. His brother, who'd been so desperate to have Nicky by his side, who could've let Nicky join him in his drug use and addiction—their mom had always warned that their family had a predilection for it, said she'd wash her hands of them if they started—had stopped him. His brother, sober, had shoved him out of the ravine.

Lucas had saved him.

Now Lucas was gone and the cadejo was silent and Gillian, who'd always loved him, was the only one he could turn his back on.

Now that you can have me, you turn your back, she'd said.

"What time is it?" Nicky asked, kicking off the sheet and launching out of bed.

As he grabbed for the paint pants he'd worn since Friday, he caught William's expression. William looked like he was afraid Nicky had finally lost it.

"Uh…just after noon," William said cautiously. "I was looking forward to eating lunch at Loretta's house but with everything going on…"

"Head to the car," Nicky told him, sniffing the pits of the T-shirt Gillian had mangled before pulling it on. "I'll be right behind you."

With his cane, William would need the head start. He'd hate it if Nicky carried him, but Nicky wasn't above doing it. He snapped his fingers. "Let's go."

William continued to stare. "What…"

"Her ex is going to be there," Nicky said, feeling the front pocket of his backpack for his keys and wallet.

He needed to piss, deodorize, and brush his teeth. Thank

God William finally got it, shot up, and double-timed it out the bedroom and down the hall.

Gillian didn't need him to take care of her. That was the last thing she needed, she'd told him. Her family was assembled at the house, including her cousin Zekie, who was a Freedom police officer, and they were more than capable of protecting his girl and her babies. Her curse was broken, she had her magic back, her family was gathered around her, and she didn't need his protection.

He had no more excuses to edge close while keeping himself away.

His whole life he'd punished himself for turning his back on his brother. Whether she needed him or not, he wouldn't turn his back on Gillian now. She may not want him. That's what he'd been afraid of when he never fucking told her. She may hate him after the way he'd behaved. But he was going to be there for her. He'd be there for her when the wolf came sniffing and after, too, if she let him.

There'd be no more straddling the fence about his love for Gillian. No more hiding it. His brother had shoved him and now Nicky needed to decide what he was going to do. All this time, he thought he'd taken his brother's life.

What was he going to do with the life his brother had given him?

CHAPTER 26

When they roared up to park near Loretta Torres's back gate, Nicky had to grip the steering wheel and calm down.

"You good?" William asked as he was getting out with the grocery-store bag of rolls Nicky told him no one was going to eat, not with homemade tortillas as an option. But William refused to come empty-handed.

"Yeah," Nicky said.

He couldn't go tearing into Loretta's backyard like he wanted to, not when he saw who was standing under the carport, behind her hatchback, his little fingers curled into the long gate Loretta had to roll back and forth whenever she wanted to get her car in and out.

Ben was staring out onto the street.

Nicky got out of the GTO, hitched on his backpack, and followed William to the small gate that led into the grass beside the carport. He could hear good-time laughter and kids shouting in the backyard. He nodded to William, who walked through the carport and out into the sunlight, while Nicky took a couple of careful steps then squatted down a yard from Ben in the shade.

"Hey, Ben," he said. "Wha'cha doin'?"

His fingers clenched the metal as his face stayed blank. "Looking for Mama." Even his buzz cut looked stubborn.

Nicky breathed out steadily. His panic wasn't going to help this boy. "She's not here?"

"She's with Daddy," a little voice said behind him. He turned to see Naomi coming from between the car and the shed next to it. In a black dress with smiling white skulls, a gift from her aunt and her newest obsession, according to her mama, Naomi came right up to him where he was squatting and leaned her whole body against him. "Ben won't leave the fence and Granmo and Granpo said he's fine and they're keeping an eye on him but I want him to come play." She stuck out her delicate bottom lip. "Mama's always sad when she's with Daddy."

Nicky rubbed his tongue over his teeth and put his arm around her. "I'm sorry, sweetheart," he said. She tipped her dark-blond head against his.

He wanted to launch off. He wanted to find out where Gillian was and then run to her side. But for once, for maybe the first time in his life, he felt a calling louder than the need to take care of Gillian Armstead. Naomi's baby bones felt precious under his hand.

He scooched them both closer to Ben so her brother wouldn't have to worry about the baby along with all the other stuff he was worrying about.

Naomi was already getting bored. She put her finger in Nicky's hair and started twisting. "Are you looking for Mama, too?" she asked.

"Yes," he said.

Ben spoke with his eyes still focused on the street. "You should draw her," he said. "You're a very good drawer."

Nicky had received both the Bucksbaum Award and the Future Generation Art Prize, his work was in prime public locations throughout the country, and Prince Harrington (one of Hollywood's highest-paid actors and, to Nicky's shock, Jeremiah's estranged brother) had been bugging Virginia all summer about a custom piece. He'd never received a more meaningful compliment than Ben's.

He untangled his arm from Naomi and pulled his backpack in front of him. "I have drawn her," he said, as he unzipped it. He pulled out the sketchbook he'd filled in June. He flipped toward the back, when he and Gillian had been exploring Milagro Street, and held it open for Naomi.

She giggled. "Mama's got a princess bubble hat."

Careful, he turned the book around and held it out for Ben.

For the first time since he'd arrived, Ben's eyes stuttered off the street. Slowly, he turned to look at the drawing. His dark brows jumped and scrunched as he made sense of it.

When Ben's hand slipped from the fence to turn the page, it was the best critical review of Nicky's life.

"Niños, what are you... Nick?"

When Mary Armstead came through the carport shadows five minutes later, her husband right behind her, Nicky was cross-legged on the concrete, slowly flipping through his sketches with both kids canted against him.

She looked as surprised as he felt.

He left them with the sketchbook as he stood.

Mary eyed him. He hadn't showered in a couple of days. He ran his hand through his hair. "How's Gillian?" he said quietly. "They were worried."

"I know," she said. Mary's jawline wasn't as firm as Gillian's and her chin wasn't as sharp, but she still was pretty good at jutting it at him. "What are you doing here?"

From behind her shoulder, Tucker Armstead gave him a sympathetic look.

"I screwed up," Nicky said. There was no reason not to be honest. Gillian had obviously told her what happened, and

Mary was a bruja. "I want to tell her that. I want to support her if she'll take it from me."

Mary's examination of him was slow and thorough. He got an instant assessment from Tucker—the man gave him a thumbs-up behind her back.

Nicky didn't want to get ahead of himself. But he might not mind the novelist as a father-in-law.

Mary finally lowered her chin. "She and Thomas went to that little park by the river to talk. That one off Old 85."

All of his knight-in-shining-armor instincts went on high alert. "By herself?" he whispered. "No one went with her?"

"Cálmete, mijo," Mary said. "She has a plan."

Her small smile showed she wasn't going to share what the plan was.

"That being said…" She knocked her long wave of black hair behind her shoulder. "If we don't get a text from her in thirty minutes, a bunch of us are heading over there. But if someone wanted to just stop by—"

He kissed her cheek. He stooped down, kissed Naomi's head, scritched Ben's hair when the boy leaned into his touch, and told them to take good care of his sketchbook as he grabbed his backpack. Then he was running for the GTO.

Gillian couldn't have been more shocked and yet more certain when the rumbling black car pulled up to where she and Thomas were sitting on a concrete bench at the abandoned attempt at a park between the Viridescent and Old 85. She'd been able to hear the car's engine from a mile away, but she hadn't allowed herself to hope. Now that he was here, getting out and meeting her eyes, checking for consent before he was fully unfurled, *of course* sighed through her.

Of course he was here. Of course he had come.

She got up and stood at the end of the bench, facing Thomas.

Her ex-husband leaped up, too, on his end of his bench. "What's he doing here?" Thomas sneered.

"I asked him to come," she said, resting her hands on top of the concrete.

With the power crackling through her along with her nerves, she had to check within herself to make sure she hadn't summoned him. While she loved him and he'd broken her heart, she'd actually had little time or energy to devote to Nicky Mendoza over the last forty-eight hours. Too many people depended on her. The compartmentalizing she was so adept at had actually served her well for once.

Nicky was here of his own free will.

She kept her chin up, her curls off her face with her pushed-back sunglasses, and her shoulders relaxed in her black Polo dress to hide her tensing as Nicky approached.

She'd appreciated it when he'd grabbed that PI, pulled that rat out of its hole. But that male aggressive energy here would only get in her way. She didn't want him to protect her. She also didn't want him to put hands on her or ask if she was okay. His caretaking instinct, now, would only weaken her. She didn't want him to take care of her.

When Nicky didn't touch her, didn't talk to her, simply slotted in beside her, facing Thomas, and slid his hands into the pockets of the same paint pants he'd worn Friday—he was in the same T-shirt, too—Gillian felt a burst of love for him stronger than she'd ever felt before.

That would be her life if she got to spend it with Nicky, she realized. Just when she thought she'd reached the fullness of her love for him, after a lifetime of loving him, he would surprise her and make her love him more. There would be no bottom. No limit. No end.

The hope of that love thread into the power building inside her.

Gillian crossed her arms as she looked at her ex-husband.

He was fit and handsome with blue eyes and thick blond hair, dressed in powder-green shorts, a striped belt, and a tucked-in, light-blue checked shirt, not at all looking like a man who'd all but threatened to kidnap their children. Thomas Bancroft looked like the living embodiment of what that girl who'd worked so hard to flee Freedom had promised herself. He was fit and handsome and the kind of tall that people commented on. Much taller than Nicky.

Thomas had used that height to yell blame down at her and to tower over his melting-down autistic son.

She breathed in the minerality of the flowing river, the decay of summer-tired weeds returning to the earth, the rose and black pepper she'd anointed herself with, and the new fragrance, leather-and-chemical, that lent a calm to the energy in her fingertips.

She splayed those fingertips toward Thomas now. "These conversations are best with a witness," she said. "I don't want to be accused again of stealing the kids across state lines."

Thomas shook his head as his eyes narrowed with hurt. "I guess that's what I get for believing you wanted to talk out this situation amicably."

It was easy for his deep voice to be so convincingly full of betrayal. He honestly believed he was the person who'd been wronged.

He put a big hand out toward Nicky. "I'm sorry, fella," he said. "I'm just a dad trying to look out for his family. Would *you* want your children around someone with a family history like yours?"

The world was inclined to like a man like Thomas Bancroft, had been taught in movies and advertisements and books about white people that a man like Thomas Bancroft was someone you could rely on. Thomas Bancroft had learned how to use all that to his advantage, how to get people to see the world how he saw it, even how to get them to vote against their own best interests.

Nicky, La Virgen love him, stayed silent.

"Thomas," she said with a river's worth of calm. "Here are my terms: I want reasonable alimony for the decade I stepped away from wage earning in order to perform the duties of managing our home, overseeing the social and charitable events that benefited your career, and raising our children, all tasks which you enjoyed the fruits of but did not perform. I want sustained, reasonable child support until each child is eighteen. I will permit you visitation, four times a year, from Friday morning until Sunday evening. I will fly them to and from wherever you would like the visitation to take place and stay in a nearby hotel. If you would like to earn more visitation privileges, you will need to see a therapist of your choosing for no less than once a week for a year, as well as a specialist who coaches adults on how to parent autistic children. My attorney has included the coach's name in the paperwork."

She held out the bundle of folded documents that she'd pulled out of her purse. She felt Nicky's energy sharpen next to her; he'd slid his hands from his pockets but still rested his thumbs in the fabric, still wanted to project the image of ease.

Thomas's face had grown that shade of red she was accustomed to. The outrage in his jaw usually preceded—for her—a sleepless night as she tried to make sense of his fury and argument. He'd never hit her. He was the kind of man who put the fact that he hadn't in his bonus column.

When he didn't reach for the documents, she put them down on the bench between them.

"And what do I get?" he snapped out. "What about the promises you made me?"

The power flowing through her ran cool and clean. "You get to take the first steps toward a decent relationship with your ex-wife and your children."

"Everything I gave you," Thomas seethed through his perfect teeth. "Everything I saved you from." He put his hand out like he balanced her hometown on top of it. "I came here hoping to fix this. There's no fixing what you've done to us."

She felt Nicky's attention shift to her. She put her hands against her thighs to show him: No finger tapping. No counting.

"Do you deny my terms?" she asked.

Thomas pointed his finger at her as his blond eyebrows snapped up. "I warned you," he said. "I was firm yet fair; I told you ahead of time exactly what would happen." Thomas and his justice. "The children are returning to D.C. with me. My attorney will file for full custody tomorrow. You are not to be trusted. When I'm through with you, you'll only see them during court-supervised visits. The only employment you'll find is at H&R Block. I want my money back and I'm going to drown that bar in lawsuits until I get it. I'm going to…"

The power burst out of her like a shimmer, like a sparkle of glitter Naomi would have loved. The temperature dropped. A cold wind ruffled Thomas's hair forward. He just shoved it back.

"…ruin you," Thomas said, unaware of the silence settling in. Birds stopped singing, frogs stopped croaking, insects went still in the tall grass. Even the river went quiet. "You're going to understand what it means to make a promise to me then break it. I'm going to…"

Thomas didn't feel her magic, but Nicky did. He turned his head to look at her. She turned and stared back. She could see the anger in Nicky's expressive eyes. She could also see the growing nerves in his jaw. He gave her a quick nod.

He would stand by her, no matter what she meted out. He would stay by her side.

He'd helped her break her curse and reclaim what she'd lost. She smiled, while Thomas continued to rant, and told him forever, regardless, no matter what happened, she would continue to love him just as she'd always loved him.

He closed his beautiful eyes like he'd heard her.

She turned back to face Thomas and let her power strengthen and pulse. The smell of black powder to repel enemies and roses to appease La Virgen swirled on the wind that whipped her dress around her thighs.

"... You think you have documents, I have documents, and I'm going to..." Thomas's words faltered as he focused behind where Nicky and Gillian stood shoulder to shoulder. "When I get back to..." His finger curled into his palm. "When..." He narrowed his eyes.

"Who is that?"

The day that was bright blue and sunny five minutes ago was now shrouded in clouds.

Thomas stepped back, puzzled, an expression she wasn't sure she'd ever seen on his face. "Gillian, who...?" Her tall, gym-toned, bully of an ex-husband gave a frightened twitch.

Gillian remembered how scared she'd been the first time she'd heard her. She remembered how he'd made her feel when she'd told him about her.

"What..." Thomas grimaced as his hand clenched into a fist. "Oh God, what...what is she saying?"

Gillian took her hands from her thighs, spread her Keds in the dirt of this place that had made her, and splayed her fingers palm forward. She let her sacred arts, all she was born as and all she'd learned, flow through her and out of her.

"She's saying mi niño, mi corazon, mi vida," Gillian said, echoing La Llorona's mournful words. For the first time, Gillian wasn't afraid. "My child. My heart. My life." The color drained from Thomas's face as Cariña's wail rose. Nicky breathed deeply next to her, steadfast. "Her ex-husband took her child from her, Thomas. He eventually threw himself in this river. I can't claim to know why. I like to think she tormented him to his death."

With his wild eyes glued behind her, Thomas threateningly raised two white-knuckled fists.

Then he shoved them against his head like earmuffs.

"This isn't funny, Gillian!" he shouted over La Llorona's cries. "Is this something you and your family cooked up?"

"You're right, Thomas," she said as the wind made her curls riot. The temperature had dropped twenty degrees, and she felt like steam was rising off her skin with the power running just beneath it. "A man who dangles the welfare of his children solely to torment the woman he married isn't funny at all."

She felt the burn of anger, but no. No. She had to keep control. She'd never wielded her magic like this. She hoped to never have to use it this way again.

"My family is not involved in this," she said. "I asked La Llorona to be here all on my own."

When she walked around the front of the bench, Thomas jolted back. She bent down, swept a finger through a small circle of ash and herbs on the concrete beneath the bench, and stood up with a lit, red novena candle. She returned to her place next to Nicky.

The wind picked up and Thomas grimaced and hunched in against himself, those fists still against his ears.

"I didn't always hide this from you, Thomas," she said, louder, hearing La Llorona's sadness, yes, but also hearing her anger. Her outrage. Her desire to punish. "Anyone else would have noticed the candles left out, the incense in our room. But you never cared to see me clearly."

"Gillian!" Thomas clenched his eyes closed like it would end this nightmare. "Make her stop!"

Gillian tilted her head at her ex-husband, feeling the heat of the candle flame against her face, the gratifying sear of vengeance under her skin. "Do you know how many times I've thought that with you? If I could just make you stop."

The wind swirled around them, trapping Thomas in with her

and Cariña and La Virgen de Guadalupe. They said La Virgen was part Mexica goddess, the most primal of Marys, prepared to go to war and strike blood to avenge her children. Roses rode the wind. Black powder shoved Thomas back.

The smell of leather and paint rose up from the candle's steady flame.

Nicky had come to her. He hadn't stood in front to protect her. Or in back to take care of her. He stood by her side. Nicky trusted her.

"Please..." Thomas finally pleaded, his eyes closed, fists bloodless where they were pressed against his ears. "Please... make her stop."

Please. It was such a rare, gratifying word on Thomas Bancroft's upper-crust lips.

Gillian beckoned back her anger, let it re-twine in her power.

"You will sign that agreement, Thomas," she said, with the solemnity of the final components of her spell. "You will accede to its demands. You will cease trying to interfere in my life or spy on me. Whether you choose to be a decent father or not, that's on you. But if you *ever* threaten my children or my family again, the terror you're feeling now is a tenth of the vengeance I will deliver down on you. ¿Me lo entiendes?"

"Yes, Gillian," he said, shaking his head wildly up and down. "I understand, yes, yes...okay."

She blew out the novena candle. The wails died away.

Thomas cracked his eyes open then visibly startled. Gillian could feel La Llorona's protective presence at her back.

"And just in case you return to D.C. and tell yourself this was all some tamale-induced hallucination..." She pointed at the documents on the bench. "On the last page is a copy of the email you've been sending out to employers I researched on LinkedIn. I've changed my password. You can no longer threaten them with the wrath of the Bancroft family and fortune if they hire me. I have multiple witnesses and a taped phone call verifying that the threats came from you. My inability to get a job was never my fault. It was yours. Just remember: I could haunt you *and* destroy how people see you. That's really what keeps you up at night, isn't it, Thomas?"

She felt Nicky's eyes on her, and she gave him a cheeky side grin. Her friend from Brandeis was disappointed Gillian had turned down the job. But Gillian promised to visit Chicago soon so they could catch up and she could thank her for illuminating what had been obscured.

Thomas stumbled back in his preppy shorts, his eyes going impossibly more terrified. "Oh God, tell her not to come closer. Please make her stop."

"We're done with you," Gillian said dismissively. "I have something to ask her."

"But…" Thomas started to cry. She'd never seen him cry before. "What is that?"

Behind Nicky, Gillian heard a low, long growl. Even with the presence of La Virgen inside her and La Llorona at her back, fear shot like ice through her veins. She turned to look at Nicky, afraid to look behind him.

His eyes had gone endlessly wide. He took in air like he was running.

He reached for her hand and she took it as he closed his eyes.

A lifetime of conditioning taught him to be terrified in this moment. And he was.

The cadejo's snarl had Thomas audibly weeping.

See? he thought hysterically. He'd told all those counselors and psychiatrists this thing was fucking scary.

Gillian's powerful touch grounded him. As jarring as the black dog's appearance was, it was a thread to his brother and what had happened to them right on this river's edge.

He thought he'd lost the chance to ever be visited by the wolf again.

"Cariña, señora, por favor." Gillian's fingers squeezed around his. "¿Qué necesitan?" *What do you both need?* she begged.

Nicky felt the softest sigh against his goose-fleshed skin. It was full of sadness but nothing like her spine-shredding wail.

"Tráeme a mi hijo. Salvarlo." *Bring me my son,* the breeze seemed to answer. *Save him.*

"Yes, yes, we're trying," Gillian said in Spanish, desperate with tears in her voice. "I can't find Greta Hutchinson. How do we find her? How do we find him?"

"Vaya, vaya." *Go, go.* "Salvar al niño." *Save the child.*

His eyes still closed, he could hear Gillian's frustrated sob. "Where, senora?" she cried. "Where do we go?"

"Sigue el alma del cadejo."

Follow the soul of the cadejo.

That's when Nicky felt it. A cool muzzle nudged the back of his hand clinging to Gillian's. She startled, feeling it, too. A scratchy tongue gave a warm lick.

Follow the cadejo's soul.

Every appearance of the cadejo had increased Nicky's terror because so many times after it had shown up, something horrible had happened to Lucas. Sometimes, Nicky was able to save him—pull the bullies off of him, stick his fingers down his brother's throat, yank out of his hands whatever he was contemplating, or getting him to the hospital just in time. And sometimes he wasn't.

But what if the wolf's appearance wasn't just to taunt him about his brother? What if it showed up to warn him?

Lucas was gone. Who could the cadejo want him to save now?

He opened his eyes and looked at his hechicera. "I can't do this alone," he said. The wetness on his face was tears, not blood.

She nodded, crying, too. "My magic, it's a mix of so many peoples and cultures. The name La Virgen de Guadalupe, from the Spanish colonizers, it's a combination of..." Her lip trembled. "Guada, or wada, means river valley and—"

Nicky gripped her hand tight in his, stunned. "And lupe means wolf," he said.

Tears bathed her face as she nodded. "Our love sanctified this area. I knew I would be most powerful here. But I didn't understand... You were necessary, too. I need your power, too."

Gillian. Nicky. La Llorona. El cadejo. Their curses had blessed them. They were an infinite loop of magic.

"I spent a lifetime afraid of it," he said. "I don't know what he wants."

"Ask him," Gillian whispered.

Carefully, closing his eyes again, Nicky pushed their joined hands back so he could smooth over the muzzle and dig his fingers into thick, coarse fur. With Gillian's fingers still gripping his, he scratched behind an ear and heard nothing but calm panting.

What do you want? Who do we save?

"Ow," he said, flinching. The wolf had *bit* him. Although the threat of it had seemed endless, the cadejo had never hurt him before. It actually had been more surprising than painful, even though blood welled. The cadejo had bit the end of his pointer finger as surgically as a bee sting.

The wolf had bitten his finger as precisely as a lancet used to draw blood to check sugar levels.

William.

The big head nudged, hard, at the back of his thigh. *Go.*

It nudged again, this time softer. *Goodbye.*

Tears streamed down his face. *Thank you,* Nicky thought. *I miss you. I love you. Thank you for his life.*

Thank you for my life.

"Nicky..."

He opened his eyes and looked into his love's tear-strewn face. "It's William... William needs us."

"Yes," Gillian said, nodding quickly as she grabbed Nicky's bicep. "We will, Cariña." He could no longer hear the woman's voice. "Gracias. Gracias para tu ayuda."

Nicky felt the spirit and the cadejo dissipate from the riverbank like a hand unclenching. Summer heat barreled in and the birds announced the return of the clear blue sky.

Thomas crumbled to the ground.

Gillian grabbed the documents off the bench as she rushed to him. She stooped down, put the bundle near him, and touched his hair. "May you see the wrong of your torments," she intoned. "May you find your way." She stood. "And don't forget to sign."

She looked at Nicky.

"He's at your Granmo's house," he said.

She nodded.

Then they ran.

EPILOGUE

"He looks so peaceful," Gillian said, leaning her head on Nicky's shoulder.

"Yeah," Nicky said, clearing his throat. "Like he's dreaming. Those are his fancy suspenders. I worked as hard digging them out of the back of his closet as I did on the mural he's missing out on."

"I've seen it!" William barked, keeping his eyes closed with his crossed arms resting on his belly. Loretta and the tíos sitting around the table in this quiet corner of the festive train station chuckled. "I've spent *all day* lookin' at your mural, ya big baby. I'm not asleep; I'm in my mind palace."

Ben, standing between Nicky and William in a button-up white shirt and plaid bow tie his uncle had picked out for him, watched the people dance by to the lively ranchera music from the band. "You were snoring very loud," he observed.

They all swallowed their laughter as William opened his eyes, glared at the adults, then patted her son's back. Without lifting her head from Nicky's shoulder, Gillian quickly grabbed the cup of sparkling cider that Naomi was about to tip into Nicky's lap. With a glittery violet butterfly covering half her face, Naomi smiled excitedly at every person who danced by, hoping to be invited back out onto the floor. The back-and-forth hip-sway and knee-bob couples dance was the first Gillian had ever learned at the many Mexican wedding receptions she'd attended in the basement of the community center. She was so glad some genius (her, it was her) had thought to invite a popular ranchera band out of Topeka to entertain at the Milagro Street party's evening gala.

The daylong Milagro Street party had been a hit, according to breathless reports. She'd spent most of the day away from the crowds enjoying Freedom's future museum, Loretta's, and the outdoor activities on the one cordoned-off block. Instead, she'd showed visitors who'd been led down the street by Cynthia (who wouldn't follow those legs?) the Day Building and another move-in-ready building while explaining the commercial potential of the entire street. She'd have to call the print shop on Monday to double her order of materials to send to interested investors, potential business owners, and possible clients.

But while she'd been absent from the epicenter of the party, her children had relayed every detail as she'd gotten them bathed and into their dress-up clothes. After the mural unveiling that launched the day—Sissy had been smart and had broken tissues out of Loretta's storeroom to distribute to the crowd packing the train station—Nicky and William had volunteered to shepherd the kids around. Gillian learned that Nicky had asked to borrow the face-painting lady's paints then William had begged Tía Sissy for one of her churro funnel cakes but Nicky had taken it away then Ben had loudly explained the magic trick to Naomi when she'd gotten upset about the disappeared bunny but when someone shushed him, William gave the person a "very grumpy face."

As she'd done everything in her power to rinse her daughter's hair without disturbing the glittery butterfly wing, Gillian had let herself feel the bittersweet melancholy of missing out on such a special day in her children's lives. With their access now to their grandparents and tías and tíos and cousins and... and their Nicky and William, this wouldn't be the first special day she'd miss. They now had multiple people to receive love from. It was the best gift she could give her children.

Mary and Tucker came up to the table, breathless and smiling. Her mother's long wave of black hair flowed down the black velvet of her dress. Tucker was in a tan summer suit. It was the first time outside of a funeral Gillian had seen him in a suit. His moustache, she noticed, was ruffled. Her mother's dark eyes sparkled brilliantly.

They'd been kissing, she understood with perfect, punishing intuition.

She kept her head on Nicky's shoulder to avoid drawing her mother's attention.

"Niños, are you ready to go?" Mary asked.

As Ben nodded yes and Naomi violently shook her head no, Gillian was so glad the lease on their little house was signed and they'd be moving in next weekend. It seemed that everyone in her family had a bed, a dresser, or a couch they didn't need. Her mother bemoaned it—*You three can just stay here until you move into the farmhouse,* she'd whispered—but Mary and Tucker, the bruja and the love of her life, needed time and space to figure out where their relationship was taking them next.

Gillian needed to give them that time and space immediately. Every time she hugged her sister, she could feel the light in her growing. Alex and Jeremiah hadn't said anything yet, but in about seven months, Mary and Tucker were going to be busy welcoming another grandchild into the world.

Thinking of her happy, busy, pregnant sister, Gillian closed her eyes for just a second to invoke La Virgen's energy for her. Alex was going to need it: the line to get into the speakeasy had been out the door and down the block when they'd pulled up. Sissy had worried the cooking show wouldn't give her the day off, but when they heard why she wanted time away, they'd sent her with a camera crew to film "color" for her reels. Once their guest-of-honor duties were done here, she and Nicky would head over to Loretta's to lend their love and life force to the seed planted at the corner of Milagro and Penn, a seed planted forty years ago by her grandparents and now bearing so much fruit, regardless of the weeds that tried to ensnare it.

There'd been no word directly from Thomas. His lawyer had sent the signed papers to her lawyer the day after his visit. She'd received the monthly alimony and child support later that same day.

Tucker promised Naomi one more turn around the dance floor while Mary told Ben they could walk around the edge of the party and meet them at the door. Gillian kept her head on her man's shoulder as she watched Naomi spin around and give Nicky a careless smack on his cheek before she launched off, then Ben rubbed his forehead against Nicky's shoulder before he took his grandmother's hand.

Gillian blinked hard but Nicky turned his head and caught her. He smiled and kissed her temple. "How're you doin'?"

"I'm so tired I could cry," she said.

"Me too," he murmured. "We could leave."

He layered the words with intention. Tonight would only be the third night she'd sleep in his bed.

"You know we can't," she whispered back. She pressed her nose to the shoulder of his black blazer and restored herself by breathing in deep, bathing herself not only in his perfect scent but also in the joyous reality that she could wallow in it for the rest of her life. She felt his nose in her soft, floaty curls and knew he was doing the same.

Their wedding wouldn't be for another year. It would take that long to complete the renovations to the farmhouse to provide enough elbow room for all five of them. William, who'd earned every right to his quiet, was soon going to be living with two children. His grumblings about having been indisposed when they'd roped him into that plan would have been more convincing if he hadn't taken himself to his barn workshop the instant he was off bed rest and started working on blueprints. Gillian and Nicky were actually trying to take the development of their family slow, although no one else was. Naomi had climbed onto Nicky's lap between dances like he was sitting in her chair.

While she wanted to introduce Nicky's permanence into her children's lives carefully and thoughtfully, she'd had no qualms about accepting his proposal in the surgery waiting room.

Be mine, he'd said after he'd told her everything, about what Lucas had done and how sorry he was for hurting her and how he wanted to make a light of his life, rather than hiding it away. "I want you to protect me, I want you to take care of me, and I want you to stand by my side for the rest of my life, just like I want to do for you," he'd said, gripping her hand while they curled together on the couch of the lounge. "Be my magic, he-chicera. Be my flesh-and-blood perfect, filthy wife."

Yes, she'd said, in an instant, without a ring, with the smell of hospital disinfectant in her nose, her hair a snarled mess and him in three-day-old clothes. She'd always been his. With assurance from La Virgen that William was going to be okay, it had been a perfect proposal.

Without Cariña and Lucas's intervention, he might have slipped away without anyone noticing.

Her cousin Zekie, who she'd called because she had EMT training, said that William had looked like he'd just fallen asleep in the front room with the game on and others around him chatting and laughing. It was unlikely that Nicky or Gillian would have known he'd had a sudden cardiac arrest even if they'd been by his side. Zekie got his heart pumping again and when he'd been rushed to Freedom's medical center, they'd stabilized him then installed an ICD to keep his heart beating a strong, steady pace for years to come.

"... Years to come," William barked at Loretta as she slid the square of cake Tío Martín sat in front him to her place mat and unapologetically dug her fork in.

"That's right, compadre," she said, beaming, a bead of chocolate frosting on her bright, coral lip. "And now you have me to make sure that comes true."

There were downsides to joining the massive, sprawling, nosy, dictatorial Torres family.

"Not having cake's not gonna make me immortal," he grumbled. "My doctor said my diabetes and cholesterol are genetic issues, not cake ones."

"Does it run in your family?" Gillian asked, handing her grandmother her fork for a bite. Her plate was already wiped clean. Diabetes ran rampant in theirs.

William mournfully watched the fork with its rich, dark chunk exchange hands. "My dad was diagnosed in his forties, but he was adopted so I don't know."

Nicky made a sound next to her. He looked so unbearably handsome with his styled black hair, black blazer, black button-up shirt, and black slacks. When they got home, she was going to peel the bad boy off of him with her teeth.

"Your dad was adopted?" Nicky asked, incredulous. "How come I didn't know that?"

"'Cause you weren't paying attention," William said, unimpressed. He, too, looked quite handsome in his fancy fleur-de-lis suspenders and bolo tie, the few remaining strands of his dark blond hair artfully slicked across his skull. "That's how I got my middle name. My dad was grateful my grandma moved up her wedding date so she could adopt him so he gave me her maiden name."

"Hutch?" Nicky said.

"Hutchinson," William said. "He shortened it. William

Hutchinson Baldassaro would have been quite the mouthful. He shortened it like his own name."

Gillian felt like she and Nicky were at the end of a periscope, zooming away even as they stared at William in astonishment.

The only thing that had marred the last two weeks was her inability to find Cariña de la Cruz's lost son. Not even Tía Ofelia had been able to find a scrap of additional info about Greta Hutchinson. They'd assumed William's health crisis had altered whatever La Llorona was going to tell them. He was far too young to be Carina's child. They'd gone back to the Viridescent, but she'd remained quiet. As William sat hale and hearty and grumbling about cake with them, they weren't going to look a gift horse in the mouth.

But now... "William, was your father Mexican?" she asked, reaching for Nicky's hand.

William's bushy eyebrows jumped at the sudden urgency in her voice. "Not that I know of," he said. "He was told one of his birth parents was Italian."

The tíos chuckled humorlessly. "I've been Italian a time or two," Tío Martín said.

"Yep." Her Tío Pepe nodded. "They could call me Paolo as long as they gave me a job."

Gillian had heard this before from the older generation. There was less stigma about being from Italy than from Mexico. But there might have been another reason William's ethnicity was hidden from him.

She squeezed Nicky's hand. "Greta would have wanted to protect the baby," she said, looking into his dark eyes. "The trial had been so popular."

She thought about what Cariña wanted. She thought about what she wanted for her own children. "Was your dad happy?"

William looked at her mystified, but nodded slowly. "Yes," he said. "He took over his parents' general store in Atchison. Everybody knew him and loved him. He and my mom lived until their nineties; I had to rent out the town hall for his funeral reception. He liked coming to Freedom. I moved here after I lost my family because some of my best memories were fishing on the Viridescent with my dad. Sweetie, why're you crying? Jesus. Nicky? What's goin' on?"

Gillian quickly wiped her face. "What was your father's name?"

"Herz Baldassaro."

"You said it was shortened like yours?"

"Yeah. From Herzchen. It means darling in German."

Gillian put the hand that wasn't hanging tight to Nicky over her mouth to cover her astonished sob. Greta Hutchinson had found and hidden that child, even moved up her wedding date to keep him, but had made sure his mother was honored.

Cariña meant darling, too.

In front of the entire, perplexed table, Nicky surrounded her face in his warm, safe, paint-smelling hands and kissed her. She gripped her hands on his neck and kissed him back. He laughed into her mouth and she tasted his tears and they looked as mad as La Llorona and his cadejo had driven them and as blessedly happy as Cariña and Lucas wanted them to be.

Nicky wrapped his arm around her and pulled her close to his side. "We'll explain everything, William. But how do you feel about ghosts?"

William scoffed. "Livin' in Freedom? I better not mind 'em."

"Good," Nicky said, smiling, a tear hovering in his teardrop scar. "We've got someone we'd like to introduce you to."

As Nicky began to unwind the tale, Gillian again put her head on his shoulder, the shoulder tortured then touched by magic, and looked up at the incredible ode to their hometown. There was Milagro Street, from dawn to full moon, its past displayed in the Mexican-Americans who worked the rails and ran its businesses, its present with Loretta, Alex, Mary, and yes, even Gillian near Loretta's. And its future. Ben, Naomi, and

Yesenia had been thrilled to find themselves in the painting. High in the sky, among the sunbeams, stood Rosalinda, the patron saint of Milagro Street. Next to her was Cariña, her shroud pulled back, showing her beautiful face. And within the clouds, small but very present, was Lucas, strong and healthy, his hand in the scruff of a beautiful black wolf.

His cadejo. Her La Llorona.

Their Freedom. What had once been their curse had now become their blessing.

★ ★ ★ ★ ★

ACKNOWLEDGMENTS

I was a good girl and a good student who believed what the history books told me. That belief meant that, although I attended grade school and high school in Tulsa, Oklahoma, I didn't learn about the Tulsa Race Massacre until my thirties. So when I read about the Hull Baby case in the *History of Montgomery County, By Its Own People*, published in 1903, a book about my home county that begins with the sentence, *The history of Montgomery county reveals this locality as the spot where the Osage Indian made his last stand before the white man's advance in spreading civilization over the plains of Kansas*, I finally knew to be suspicious.

Thank you to Washburn University professor Kelly Erby for her modern-day research on the Hull Baby case, a sensational trial that took place in my hometown and was the basis for Cariña de la Cruz and her lost son. Erby's research allowed me to understand how toxic masculinity has stripped women of their power for a very long time. Carrie Hull never again saw the son she always said was hers and in lieu of a non-publicized reality of Carrie connecting with her son again, I hope I gave her a conclusion that would bring her peace.

Nicky Mendoza is my first Mexican-American hero and an ode to the fact that my life has been blessed with non-toxic men. Thank you Mario, Adam, Danny, Robert, Phillip, Jesus, Frank, Bertram, Michael, Favian, Casey, Roman, and so many other brown heroes who encouraged me to grow strong in this world. Thank you Clay, Mike, Jimmy, Marc, Geff, John, Chris,

Chad, Steve, Hung, Gabriel, Simon, and Peter, always Peter, who continue to show me how good men can be.

And thank you to all the women who've taught me that when we're down, we're certainly not out. Nowhere is that more true than in publishing! Editor Kerri Buckley, publicist Steph Tzogas, and agent Sara Megibow, you ladies know I absolutely couldn't do it without you. Thank you.